PENGUIN CRIME FICTION

# CUT TO THE QUICK

Kate Ross (1956–1998) was the author of four Julian Kestrel mysteries: *Cut to the Quick, A Broken Vessel, Whom the Gods Love,* and *The Devil in Music* (all available from Penguin). *A Broken Vessel* was the winner of the 1994 Gargoyle Award for Best Historical Mystery. *The Devil in Music* was nominated for an Agatha Award for Best Mystery Novel of 1997 and for a Winn Dylis Award, given by the Independent Mystery Booksellers Association to books they most enjoy selling.

# C*U*T

TO THE

# QUICK

## Kate Ross

PENGUIN BOOKS

PENGUIN BOOKS
Published by the Penguin Group
Penguin Books USA Inc., 375 Hudson Street,
New York, New York 10014, U.S.A.
Penguin Books Ltd, 27 Wrights Lane, London W8 5TZ, England
Penguin Books Australia Ltd, Ringwood, Victoria, Australia
Penguin Books Canada Ltd, 10 Alcorn Avenue,
Toronto, Ontario, Canada M4V 3B2
Penguin Books (N.Z.) Ltd, 182–190 Wairau Road,
Auckland 10, New Zealand

Penguin Books Ltd, Registered Offices: Harmondsworth,
Middlesex, England

First published in the United States of America by Viking Penguin,
a division of Penguin Books USA Inc., 1993
Published in Penguin Books 1994

7 9 10 8 6

THE LIBRARY OF CONGRESS
HAS CATALOGUED THE HARDCOVER AS FOLLOWS:
Ross, Kate.
Cut to the quick/by Kate Ross.
p.  cm.
ISBN 0-670-84847-6 (hc.)
ISBN 0 14 02.3394 6 (pbk.)
I. Title.
PS3568.O843494C8  1993
813'.514—dc20    92–50456

Printed in the United States of America
Set in Garamond No. 3
Designed by Virginia Norey

To my father

# CONTENTS

# C*U*T

## TO THE

# QUICK

# *1*
# NO CAUSE FOR CELEBRATION

---

Mark Craddock paced slowly, deliberately, back and forth behind the desk in his study. From time to time he glanced at the marquetry clock on the mantelpiece. The young people were taking their time coming to an understanding, but he would not interrupt them. He had waited more than twenty years for this day. He could afford to wait a little longer.

Craddock's servants called this room the Lion's Den, partly because of the lion's head carved on the back of Craddock's chair, and partly because he himself looked very like a lion, with his thick, tawny hair and flat nose, and the fierce gaze he levelled at people through his small, round, glinting spectacles. The room was proportioned to suit his tall, strapping figure: the ceiling was high, and the mahogany furniture massive. The money and care he had lavished here showed in every detail: the Sèvres inkstands, the portfolios bound with morocco leather, the elegant portrait of Craddock's late wife that hung over the marble fireplace.

Sarah's portrait made Craddock uncomfortable just now. Her eyes seemed grieved, reproachful. Try as he might, he could not avoid her gaze. He had half made up his mind to turn her face to the wall, when a footman came in. "Mr. Fontclair's asked to see you, sir."

Craddock forgot all about the portrait. "Show him in."

And there he was: Hugh Fontclair, Sir Robert's son and heir—
*her* nephew. Craddock surveyed him with satisfaction. The boy had
the Fontclair face, with its high forehead and long jaw, though the
fine dark eyes were his mother's. He certainly had the Fontclair
bearing at the moment—standing tall and straight, eyes proudly
defiant. He stood just inside the door, as though disdaining to come
any closer to Craddock than he must.

"Well?" said Craddock. "How've you sped?"

"I've come to inform you that your daughter has consented to be
my wife. Now, if you have nothing further to discuss with me, sir,
I'll take my leave. Any business to do with settlements and such
things can be handled through our solicitors."

Craddock did not want to let him leave right away. It was such
a pleasure to make him stand there, fuming and longing to be gone.
"Did you tell her anything?"

Hugh's colour rose. "If you mean, did I tell her by what dishonourable means you've brought about this engagement—no, sir,
I didn't. I understood your orders were she wasn't to know." He
added more quietly, "It's not very fair to her, really."

"You let me be the judge what's fair to Maud."

"Would you know, Mr. Craddock?" Hugh burst out. "Would
you care?"

"It never ceases to amaze me how all you Fontclairs talk on about
fairness and honour—as though you knew the first thing about
either!" Craddock leaned forward, his large fists propped on the
desk. "Go back to your father, and your uncle and aunt, and tell
them it's been settled between you and Maud. Tell them it won't
be long before there's a child with both my blood and theirs in his
veins. I hope they *writhe* when they hear it! I'm only sorry I won't
be there to see how they take the news!"

✳

If Hugh had not been in such low spirits, he would have found
it exciting to be in London. His parents rarely came to London,
even during the season. Till recently, Hugh had been content to
live at Bellegarde, pursuing his studies and helping his father run
the estate. But now that he was a grown man—he had been twenty-

one for nearly a fortnight—he was eager to see more of the world. He had been meaning to ask his father to let him go abroad for a year or two. The cafés of Paris, the ruins of Rome, the splendours of the East—he thirsted to experience them all in person, not just in books.

Now everything was changed, of course. If he went on the Grand Tour, it would have to take the form of a wedding trip, which meant it would be no more thrilling or perilous than a picnic in the country. He was simply not ready to marry. Anyone who had ever read a play or a novel knew that the hero's wedding came at the end, not the beginning. He had not had any adventures yet: no pistols at dawn, no midnight clashes with highwaymen. Hang it, no *women*.

He realized that plenty of young married men had their actresses and opera girls. But he could not go that route: his parents' example had spoiled him for the shallow, faithless unions so common among the Quality. Still, his father, Sir Robert, had chosen a wife for himself—he had not been coerced by methods like Craddock's. Hugh told himself he was being unfair to Miss Craddock—none of this was her fault, after all—but he could not help seeing her as a penance, an anticlimax to all his hopes and imaginings. How could marital love take root and flourish under conditions like these?

He was mulling this over gloomily as he drew up his cabriolet outside his parents' town house in Curzon Street. He tossed the reins to his groom and went indoors. Resolutely, he put on a cheerful face. There was little merit in doing your duty, he thought, if you could not at least appear to do it gladly.

Michael, the footman, told him that his parents were in Sir Robert's study. "Is anybody with them?" Hugh asked apprehensively.

"No, sir. Lady Tarleton and Colonel Fontclair are here, but they're in the drawing room."

Lady Tarleton and Colonel Fontclair were Sir Robert's sister and brother. Hugh was not surprised they had called; they must be eager to learn how things had gone between him and Miss Craddock. He was grateful for the chance to talk to his parents alone first. How they had managed to confine Aunt Catherine in the drawing room, he could not imagine. It must have taken all his mother's tact and his father's authority.

He went to the study and told them that Miss Craddock had accepted him. Sir Robert asked a great many questions about her. Did she seem well bred? Had she manners, accomplishments, graces? Was she bookish, and if so, what did she read? Above all, had she any sense of honour? Was she truthful, candid, modest? Hugh was hard put to respond. He had been so nervous and self-conscious, meeting Miss Craddock for the first time and having to offer for her under such embarrassing circumstances, that he had been in no fit state to observe much about her. All the while they talked, he had kept his eyes on a Chinese dragon on the carpet, and now he remembered the dragon's face much better than his future bride's.

Lady Fontclair took his face lightly between her hands. "My dear, did you like her at all?"

"I liked her very well, mother."

"I *must* get to know her before the wedding. Robert, mayn't we invite her to Bellegarde for a few weeks? We could show her the house and the estate, and have her meet the servants and tenants. I want so much to be sure she'll be a good wife to Hugh. We know so little about her."

"I don't think you'll find anything to disapprove of," said Hugh. "But, even if you did, Mother, what could you do? What could any of us do?"

Lady Fontclair smiled ruefully and shook her head.

"You know, it isn't too late to draw back, even now," Sir Robert said suddenly. "If you feel you cannot bring yourself to marry, just to pay for other people's misdeeds, you have only to say so."

"But, sir, I've committed myself to Miss Craddock."

"I understand that. But you've done so under constraint. She would have no right to hold you to your promise."

"I'm afraid I can't agree with you, sir. It was a promise, whatever prompted me to give it. I can't go back on it now. Anyway, I haven't had second thoughts. I'm happy to marry Miss Craddock. I hope I should be willing to do far more than that, to protect our name from disgrace."

Sir Robert said quietly, "When a man of our rank has only one son, it means a great deal to him that his son should grow up to be a man of good character, not merely a man of fashion. I have

Mr. Craddock to thank in one respect: he has tried my son and proved him to be in every way worthy of his name and lineage."

The colour rushed into Hugh's face. "Father, I— I'm nothing more than the man you raised me to be."

Lady Fontclair looked from one to the other, her eyes aglow. But seeing that they were both tongue-tied with emotion, she stepped into the breach. "Then may we invite Miss Craddock to Bellegarde?"

"We can't invite her without her father," Sir Robert pointed out.

"That will be very awkward and unpleasant," she admitted. "But the servants and everyone at Bellegarde will have to get used to him sooner or later."

"My dear, if you wish to invite the Craddocks to Bellegarde, then of course you may."

Hugh smiled. It was not as though there had been any doubt he would agree. When had he ever refused her anything? Yet she always asked his permission before she carried out plans of any importance. It was like a courtly dance they performed: she deferred to his judgement, and he granted her wishes.

"Shall I tell Aunt Catherine and Uncle Geoffrey things went off all right with Miss Craddock?" he offered.

"Oh, my dear," laughed his mother, "you've been through enough! Run along, and leave Catherine and Geoffrey to us."

Hugh obeyed, with a mixture of guilt and relief. He felt sure they would have a row on their hands when Aunt Catherine heard the news. He went downstairs, meaning to get out of the house till the storm was over. But Michael waylaid him in the front hall.

"Excuse me, sir. Mr. Guy is in the library and wants to see you. He asked me not to tell anyone but you that he's here."

"The deuce! What does he want to be so mysterious for?"

"I couldn't say, sir."

Hugh sighed. "All right. I'll see him."

✳

With half a dozen chairs in the library, Guy had chosen to sit on the portable stairs that were used to take books down from high shelves. One of his feet was propped on a step; the other long leg swung freely. Guy was vain about his legs and wore shockingly close-fitting trousers. He was also vain about his wavy chestnut hair, which tumbled about his ears in carefully contrived romantic disarray. He had vibrant brown eyes, a cleft chin, and only a hint of the long Fontclair brow and jaw. His shoulders, chest, and waist were the realization of a tailor's dream.

He sprang up on seeing Hugh. "You've been a devil of a time. I thought you were never coming down."

"What are you hiding here for? Why didn't you let Michael announce you?"

"Because I found out Aunt Catherine was in the house, and I'd rather be pickled in brine than exchange three words with her. I'm still not recovered from the last time I saw her, when we were all at Bellegarde for your coming of age. Another dose so soon would finish me off. I was bent on seeing *you*, though! Tell me—is it true you're going to marry Mark Craddock's daughter?"

"How did you know?"

"The colonel told me." The colonel was Guy's father, Geoffrey Fontclair, the younger brother of Hugh's father. "It *is* true, then?"

"Yes. We became engaged this afternoon."

"In the name of God, why? Mark Craddock's daughter! He used to be—"

"I know what he used to be."

"And Uncle Robert's prepared to swallow it?"

"He's agreed to the marriage, yes."

"Then it's got to be one of two things. Either you've been borrowing on post-obits, and Craddock's holding all your notes of hand, or you've gone and got the girl with child."

"Oh, for God's sake! I've only met her once!"

"Well, it only takes once."

"I didn't meet her *that* way! And I must ask you not to talk about her in that fashion. She's a very respectable girl, and she's the girl I'm going to marry."

"Is she pretty, at least?"

"She's not— ill-looking."

"Oh, my God! As bad as that? Why the devil are you going to marry her, then? It must be money. I had no idea Uncle Robert was hard up."

"He's not—never mind, I can't tell you any more."

"I can't believe Uncle Robert would let you marry the daughter of a cit—any cit, let alone Mark Craddock! What would all our bloody ancestors say? There'll be an earthquake at Bellegarde on your wedding day, with all those knights and war heroes turning over in their graves. When is the wedding, anyway?"

"At the end of June."

"Good God, in only two months? Well, at least I can look forward to borrowing off you, once you've got your hands on La Craddock's fortune. How much is her father forking out?"

"I don't know exactly."

"You've got engaged to a girl whose father is as rich as Croesus, and you don't even know what her dowry is? Hang it, if it isn't her money you're after, what *are* you marrying her for?"

"I'd tell you if I could, but I can't. I'm not allowed. So there's no point in keeping at me like this."

Guy's eyes flashed. "Then I'll find out some other way. I'll lay any odds the colonel knows. Fifty pounds says I get it out of him by noon tomorrow."

But Hugh would not take that bet, although he knew he could have won it. "I'll tell you what it is," Guy said, "being engaged doesn't agree with you. I can understand that; I'm blistered if it would agree with me. I've got an idea. A friend of mine is giving a dinner tonight for a group of fellows, and afterward we're going out gaming. Why don't you come? You haven't got much time left to enjoy yourself as a bachelor."

Hugh felt torn. He knew how Guy and his London friends amused themselves: Pall Mall gaming hells, low dram-shops, discreet "houses" in Covent Garden. He had never sampled those sorts of pleasures himself, and though he was curious about them, he was also apprehensive and a little repelled. He was certainly in no mood for a carouse just now. And yet Guy was right: if he meant to sow any wild oats, this was the time to do it.

Guy threw himself into a chair. His eyes lit on two objects on a table nearby: a satinwood box about a foot long and a large sketch-book. A smile spread over his face. "I'd like to get a look at Cousin Isabelle's nose," he said softly.

"Her *nose?*"

"To see how out of joint it is!" He laughed, jumped up from his chair and walked about. "By God, I'd like to have seen her face when she found out Miss Craddock had cut her out! Or am I in time to see it? Does she know yet you're engaged?"

"She knew I was going to offer for Miss Craddock. But she didn't seem to mind—or, not more than anyone else minded."

"Rot! Didn't mind? She must be fit to tear Miss Craddock to shreds! Of course, being Isabelle, she'll never admit it. She'll just stand about stony-faced, with murder in her heart."

"I've told you a hundred times, Isabelle and I are like brother and sister. She doesn't want to marry me."

"The devil she doesn't! Isabelle and you may have been brought up like brother and sister, but there's a world of difference between a sister and a cousin, and, believe me, Isabelle knows it. Besides, the family's been talking for years about the two of you making a match of it."

"That's mainly been Aunt Catherine's idea. You know how she thinks."

"I know, I know! Nobody's good enough for a Fontclair but another Fontclair."

Hugh nodded. "I do think the parents would have liked me to marry Isabelle. They raised her themselves, and they know she values Bellegarde and our name and traditions as much as I do. But they never pushed us, and I honestly don't think Isabelle cares a straw for me, except as a brother and a friend."

"What about as the future Sir Hugh Fontclair?"

"You wrong her, Guy, you really do. She—"

"Speak of the devil!" Guy whispered.

A young lady stood in the doorway. She was tall and slender, with hair of a light, almost silvery shade of brown. She had the Fontclair face, too long in the forehead and jaw to be reckoned pretty. Her eyes, a light, translucent grey, looked steadily across at her cousins.

"Good afternoon," she said. "I'm sorry to interrupt, but I think I left my sketching box and sketchbook in here."

"Good afternoon, cousin!" said Guy. "We've got some news for you. Hugh's officially engaged."

"Are you?" she asked Hugh, no hint of emotion in her voice.

"Miss Craddock's accepted me, yes," he stammered, wondering how much she had overheard of his conversation with Guy.

"I wish you happy." She held out her hand to him. He clasped it and kissed her cheek.

"Maybe they'll let you be chief bridesmaid," said Guy.

"I should be very honoured." She walked past him and sat down at the table where her sketching things were. Taking a pencil from the satinwood box, she began to touch up a copy she had made of a hunting print on the wall.

Guy followed her. "You know, you ought to cultivate Miss Craddock. She probably knows no end of rich young cits who'd be glad to take a girl without a farthing to her name, as long as that name was Fontclair."

"Thank you, Guy. I shall of course take your advice to heart."

"That's the spirit! Humility, cousin! It's indispensable for poor relations."

"You're very well suited to teach that lesson. I know of no one who better illustrates the effects of a lack of humility."

Guy glared at her. She looked coolly back.

Hugh broke in hastily, "Mother's going to invite Miss Craddock and her father to Bellegarde."

"I shall like to meet her," said Isabelle.

"I wouldn't miss *that* for anything," said Guy.

A woman's voice rang out overhead. The words were not clear, but the strident tone was unmistakable.

"Aunt Catherine's got out of the drawing room," said Hugh.

"Damnation!" cried Guy. "I'm just off. Are you coming tonight or not?"

"Yes!" Hugh decided.

"There's a good fellow! Drive a little way with me now, and I'll tell you where to meet us. Good-bye, cousin!" He kissed his fingers to Isabelle. "We won't bore you with our plans. We mean to enjoy ourselves, which is something you would know nothing about."

He swept Hugh out of the room. "Good-bye," Hugh just managed to say, as the door closed behind them.

Isabelle shut her eyes tightly. "Oh—God!" she whispered, and broke the pencil between her fingers.

# *2*
# WILD OATS

$A$t dinner that evening with Guy and his friends, Hugh felt as though he were living through the whole *Rake's Progress* in a single night. He would never have dreamed men could drink so much and remain on their feet. Of course their host had taken care that they would not have to walk very far: the dining room was well supplied with wine and spirits, and there was a chamberpot in one of the sideboards.

The party consisted of half a dozen young bucks, some of them in the Guards. Guy told them Hugh was going to be married, and at once the dinner turned into a party in honour of his engagement. Hugh did not suppose they drank any more or less for having something to celebrate—they simply made appropriate nuptial toasts, which got increasingly bawdy as the night wore on. Hugh laughed immoderately at their sallies, being himself at that stage of drunkenness when almost anything seems funny.

At last someone shouted that it was time to try their luck at the tables. Hugh was taken aback. He knew they had intended to go out gambling, but it was past midnight, and they were all so thoroughly stitched that he could not imagine them playing any game that required even minimal thought or coordination. But the others were set on going, and Hugh could not miss this chance to find out what a London gaming hell was like. So they all piled into carriages and rattled away toward Pall Mall.

From the street, the gambling house looked demure and unobtrusive, but inside it was sumptuous, with plush scarlet sofas and carpets, striped curtains, and huge crystal chandeliers. Liveried servants offered Hugh yet more claret and champagne, which he knew he should not drink, and which he drank anyway. Something awful was happening to him. He felt borne along by an irresistible tide; whatever the others did, he did, too. That was how he found himself joining the crowd around the hazard table.

Hazard was the most confusing game he had ever played. He was not sure he could have made head or tail of it, even if he had been sober. How did the players keep straight what the main and the chance were from one round to the next, much less what all the other throws meant? And how much was he himself losing? He could not count—could not think at all. Light from a hundred candles dazzled his already hazy vision; talk and laughter roared in his ears. He stared in awful fascination at the white dice bouncing across the green table, the croupier's hands raking in the stakes, the players in their evening coats of dark blue, green, or plum, placing their bets and waiting with held breath for each new cast. Some of them glanced at Hugh, then laughed and whispered to each other, making merry over his blundering and confusion.

A young man in black murmured, close to Hugh's ear, "Would I be far wrong in thinking that you couldn't know less about this game if you'd been born and bred in a nunnery?"

"I *am* getting into deep water," Hugh said faintly.

"Any deeper, and we shall have to drag the river to find you again."

"I'd leave off playing, only I just can't seem to. And— and the truth is, if I let go of the table, I— I'm afraid I'll fall on my face!"

The gentleman in black sighed. "Here. Allow me."

He put an arm around Hugh's shoulders, as though they were having a confidential chat, and drew him away from the table. Hugh was so dizzy that after a few steps he had to cling to the gentleman in black for support. The room spun madly around him, a kaleidoscope of colours and shapes.

He felt himself being lowered into a chair. The room was still spinning; he clasped his head in his hands to make it stop. When he looked up again, the gentleman in black was gone.

He closed his eyes and stayed where he was for an hour or two. He even dozed off, in spite of the noise and lights. When he woke, he found a place to be discreetly sick, then crawled back to his chair, his head aching but reasonably clear.

Guy dropped into a chair beside him. "I thought you'd slunk off home."

"I'm going to, shortly."

"The night's still young, for God's sake."

"Is it? I feel as though it had been going on forever. I wonder how much I lost at that cursed hazard table."

"Oh, it was probably only a flutter. You bolted too soon to get really dished. That reminds me! How did you get so thick with Julian Kestrel?"

"What are you talking about?"

"I saw you walk away from the hazard table with him, arm in arm. Do you know how many fellows would give their eye teeth to be singled out by Kestrel like that? What the devil did you say to make him take notice of you?"

"Was that Julian Kestrel—the gentleman in black?"

"Lord, you *are* green. Of course that was Kestrel. He always wears black in the evening—it's all the crack in the dandy set, and of course Kestrel, being such a howling swell, was one of the first to take it up. You really didn't know who he was?"

"No. I'd never seen him before."

"What did you and he talk about?"

Hugh looked away. "Oh, nothing in particular."

Guy shrugged and staggered off to play *vingt-et-un*. Hugh sat thinking about his rescuer. Julian Kestrel had first appeared in London society a year or two ago, and hardly anything was known about him, though he was said to be related in some dubious way to a landed family in the north. If he had been anything but a dandy, such vagueness about his pedigree would have been fatal, but of course the most spectacular of the dandies were absolved from Society's usual inquisition into breeding and birth.

Hugh had a sinking feeling that he ought to speak to Kestrel before he went home. The man had helped him out of a dangerous scrape, and it would be churlish not to thank him. He shrank from the task: it would be mortifying to face Kestrel again, after making such a cake of himself. And now that he knew who Kestrel was, he did not expect any mercy. The dandies were said to make ruthless sport of young cubs like him.

He circled the tables, keeping a safe distance, and scanned the groups of players. With any luck, Kestrel would be too deep in gaming to be disturbed. No, dash it, there he was in a window recess, talking with a group of bored-looking young sparks. Hugh went up to them and, summoning all his courage, said a bit too loudly, "Mr. Kestrel?"

They all turned toward him, looking him up and down with amused or critical eyes. One man surveyed him through a quizzing glass—a little round magnifying glass strung on a black velvet ribbon. Hugh felt like a horse being offered for sale.

Kestrel smiled faintly and lifted his brows. He had the most daunting eyebrows Hugh had ever seen. "I—" Hugh swallowed hard. "I wonder if I might speak to you for a moment."

Kestrel's smile turned a little wry. But then one of the other dandies snickered, and this seemed, perversely, to decide him. "Will you excuse me?" he said to his companions. Although it was clearly a matter of no great moment to him whether they excused him or not.

He walked a little apart with Hugh. "How may I be of service to you, Mr.—?"

"Fontclair. Hugh Fontclair. How do you do, sir? I— you— you were kind enough to do me a service earlier in the evening."

"Did I?" Kestrel said coolly. "You must forgive me—that was so long ago."

The colour rushed into Hugh's face. "You may not remember it, but I do, sir, most gratefully. I was in difficulties, and a good many people saw it, but no one came to my assistance except you. It may have been nothing to you, but it meant a good deal to me, and I thought it only right to thank you before I went home. Good night, sir." He bowed and started to walk away.

"Mr. Fontclair." Kestrel raised his voice just enough to be heard over the noise around them.

"Yes?"

"You're turning a rather unbecoming shade of green. Can you get home all right, or shall we call a palanquin and have you borne off like a wounded warrior?"

"I came with my cousin, and I don't suppose he's nearly ready to leave. I was thinking I might walk home, at least part of the way, to clear my head."

"Some obliging footpad will clear it for you with a bludgeon, if you go walking round London alone at this hour of the night. There's nothing for it: I shall have to put you in a hackney."

"I couldn't possibly put you to so much trouble."

"My dear fellow, I have enough on my conscience without having to take responsibility for your untimely end. So, if you would be so good—?"

Hugh found it was useless to resist him. They collected Hugh's hat and came to an understanding with some official-looking person about his losses. To his relief, they were not nearly so great as he had feared. He and Kestrel went outside, and Kestrel sent a link-boy to fetch a hackney carriage.

A light rain was falling, and the April night was chill. Exhaustion swept over Hugh. He shrank inside his coat and turned up the collar.

"If you're going to be ill," said Kestrel, not ungently, "you'd best have it over before you get into the hack. Drivers can be devilish unpleasant about those things."

"I *think* I'll be all right. I'm not used to having this much to drink."

"That possibility had occurred to me."

"I'm supposed to be celebrating. I'm getting married in less than two months."

Kestrel looked at him more closely. Hugh stared down at the pavement, prodding it with his toe.

The hackney drove up. Kestrel tossed a coin to the link-boy, who caught it deftly with one hand. Hugh got into the carriage, then let down the side-glass and poked out his head. "Mr. Kestrel, I—"

Julian saw a display of gratitude coming, and ducked it hastily.

"Good night, Mr. Fontclair," he said, and stepped back to let the hackney drive away.

"A bit blue-deviled, that 'un looked," said the link-boy, jerking his head after Hugh's carriage.

"More than a bit, I should say," Julian agreed. Who is he going to marry, he wondered, and why did he make that lugubrious face at the prospect? He's young to be getting married. For God's sake, he's young to be let out without a nurse.

He gave his head a shake, to clear away Hugh Fontclair and his concerns. You ought to have been a parson, he mocked at himself, so you could go about wrapping people's throats in flannel and poking your nose into their affairs. He shrugged, and went back inside the gambling house.

\*

Julian Kestrel lived in a first-floor flat in Clarges Street. The ceilings were high, and the windows large. The walls were painted ivory. The mahogany furniture was handsome but not too plentiful; Julian hated clutter. Here and there were keepsakes he had picked up on his travels: a Venetian glass decanter, a Moorish prayer rug, a marble head of a Roman goddess, an oil painting of the Tuscan hills. Crossed rapiers hung over the mantelpiece; they looked ornamental, but close inspection revealed they had seen a good deal of use. A small bust of Mozart occupied a place of honour by the pianoforte. Under the piano was a canterbury full of well-worn sheets of music.

It was about one o'clock in the afternoon, and Julian was finishing breakfast. He generally stopped for breakfast about halfway through the elaborate process of dressing. At this stage, he was wearing a white shirt with a high embroidered collar, thin-striped grey Cossack trousers, and a dressing gown of bottle-green silk brocade. A coffeepot and a cup and saucer were all that remained of his meal. Every so often his manservant, who was brushing his coat and waistcoat, came over and refilled the cup, first feeling the coffeepot to be sure it was still hot.

Julian was sorting through the morning's post. As usual, it consisted mostly of invitations and bills. He glanced swiftly over the invitations, culling out those he would accept. But one letter gave him pause. He sat back in his chair and read it again, more slowly.

"Dipper," he said, "what would you do if a fellow you'd only met once, and hardly knew from Adam, suddenly wrote and asked you to be best man at his wedding?"

The servant looked up from his work. He was small and lithe, about twenty years old, with a round face and quick-moving, supple fingers. His hair and eyes were the colour of a mud puddle—an almost iridescent brown. "Sounds like a rum go, sir."

"Rather. But everything about this wedding is a little rum. Of course, it's no great novelty for a man of Hugh Fontclair's birth to barter his name for a fortune. But the Fontclairs are an old Norman family, and proud as Lucifer. The *on-dit* is that Sir Robert must be all to pieces, or he'd never allow his heir to marry a tradesman's daughter. And yet there's never been so much as a whisper up to now that the Fontclairs were hard up."

"Maybe it ain't the money Mr. Fontclair fancies, sir."

"Sentimentalist! It certainly isn't the girl. When Fontclair told me he was going to be married, he had much more the air of being in harness than in love." He added thoughtfully, "I don't know much about Miss Craddock. Her father keeps her under close guard; it's said he's afraid of fortune-hunters. There'd be a certain justice in it if she mended some poor devil's fortunes—God knows, her father's been the ruin of enough men. He began as a moneylender, you know, and even among that vampirical lot, he had a reputation for ruthlessness."

"So Mr. Fontclair's asked you to be groomsman at his wedding, sir?"

"Yes, and in the meantime to spend a fortnight at his father's country place in Cambridgeshire. Some sort of family party—the bride and groom, the bride's father, and some of the groom's relations." He frowned. "Why on earth should he want to get on such an intimate footing with me all of a sudden? We've only met once that I know of, at a gaming hell a few weeks ago. He was threatening to make an ass of himself, and I sent him home to bed."

Dipper shot a shrewd glance at him. There had to be more to the story than that. You did not ask a cove to be groomsman at your wedding in return for his chucking you out of a gambling house. But if Mr. Kestrel had done something handsome, there would be no getting him to talk about it.

He fell to polishing the buttons on Julian's coat. "A lot of the swell mob goes to weddings," he reminisced. "If there's a big crowd, and you got the right kind of duds, you can mingle with the guests, and nobody'll ever know you wasn't invited. They're bad places to try and lift any wipes, on account of with all the blubbering that goes on, everybody's always using theirs. Tickers is easy to get, though—nobody's thinking about what time it is. I never had the heart to work a wedding, meself. When people is as happy as that, how can you queer it for 'em by filing their clys? I *ask* you, sir."

"With sensibilities like yours, I often wonder how you ever managed to steal anything at all."

"I picked and chose me marks, sir, when I could afford to. Gentry coves like you, sir, as looked as if they wouldn't miss a few quid here and there."

"You can't judge a man's finances by his clothes. Some of the heaviest swells in London have some of the lightest pocketbooks."

"Oh, yes, I know that *now*, sir."

"Since you came to work for me, you mean," said Julian, amused. He looked ruefully at the pile of bills on the table. "You know, it wouldn't be amiss for us to spend a fortnight out of London, far from gaming tables and importunate tailors. Our finances are becoming a little . . . involved." He glanced at Hugh's letter again, and sighed. "The devil of it is, I shall have to go. It's the only way I shall ever find out why I was invited."

# *3*
# BELLEGARDE

Philippa found it hard to be eleven years old. She knew she should be docile, like her sister Joanna, and do as older people told her without asking for explanations. But that was so difficult, when she felt fully as wise as any adult she knew, except her mother. Her father was a very important man, of course—Sir Robert Fontclair, a baronet, landlord, and magistrate. Yet Philippa, summing up his character judiciously, could not help thinking he did not understand people very well. He had, perhaps, a bit too much honour and not enough common sense.

It might be that he was weighed down by his own authority. Philippa had a poor opinion of authority and did not submit to it very well. When she was forbidden to do something she had set her heart on, she thought the prohibition over carefully, and if she decided it was unfair or unnecessary, she disobeyed it. Which was why, when her governess told her she could not meet Mr. Kestrel until tomorrow, she decided to slip away from the schoolroom and have a peek at him that evening. "We could wait outside his room while he dresses for dinner," she told Joanna. "Everyone else is going to meet him tonight. Why shouldn't we?"

But of course Joanna would have no part of the plan. It would be improper; Mr. Kestrel would think they were nothing but a pair of hoydens. Joanna was thirteen and becoming awfully self-conscious about anything to do with gentlemen—Philippa could not imagine why. But if Joanna would not go with her, she would go alone.

Mr. Kestrel had arrived at Bellegarde just in time for the first dinner bell, which summoned the grown-ups to dress. Joanna and Philippa had dined already, in the schoolroom with Miss Pritchard, their governess. Philippa waited till Joanna and Pritchie were busy working on an embroidery stitch, then stole out of the schoolroom. On gaining the hallway, she raced to Mr. Kestrel's room and stood sentry outside his door.

At last it opened, and a gentleman came out. He was all in black. Philippa feasted her eyes on him—her first real London dandy.

He saw her, and his brows went up. "I don't believe we've been introduced. I'm Julian Kestrel."

"Yes, I know!" she breathed.

"May I ask why you're looking at me as though I were a firework display?"

"You're much better than fireworks. They're all over in a moment, and you're going to stay for a whole fortnight. Besides, fireworks are noisy, and they make too much smoke."

"I'm very quiet," he assured her, "and of course I never smoke in the presence of a lady."

"I'm Philippa Fontclair." She looked at him approvingly, liking him much better than the dull, handsome men Joanna admired. He had a dark, irregular face and hair of a rich brown, like mahogany. His eyes were brown, too, but with a green gleam about them, especially when he smiled, or was looking at you very intently. He was slender and spare and not above medium height, but he had *presence*—the way royalty probably did in the old days, before it was fat and fussy and came from Germany. He looked splendid in his clothes, and yet there was nothing showy or striking about them, except that his linen was so spotless, and everything fit him so well. Being a dandy was not so much what you wore, Philippa decided, but how you wore it.

She thought for a moment, then said brightly, "This is such a big house, I was afraid you might not be able to find the drawing room, so I came to show you the way."

"That was very thoughtful of you."

He doesn't believe me, she thought. He's smart. "Have you been shown around the house yet?"

"No. I've only just arrived."

"Well, the house is very simple, really, if you keep straight in your mind that it's divided into three parts. We're in the middle part now. It's the part I like best. It was built in the time of Queen Elizabeth, and some of the rooms have been kept just as they were in those days. Your room is one of those. The rooms down the hall from yours have been done over in a modern style, and they're quite dull. You might as well live inside a piece of Wedgwood. They're guest rooms, but nobody's using them now. You have this whole corridor to yourself. The panelling is nice, isn't it? It's linenfold."

Julian nodded. "Very handsome." He glanced around, getting his bearings. His room was at the end of a blind corridor. There was a table there, with a basket of flowers on it. Farther down the corridor, on the same side as his room, were two more doors, which must be the redecorated guest rooms Philippa despised.

There was only one door opposite his room. "That's the great chamber," Philippa said. "We can go through it to reach the stairs." She opened the door, and they went in. "This is one of the rooms that's been kept as it was in Elizabethan times. We don't use it very much. It's just to look at."

"It's well worth the looking," said Julian. For the room was resplendent with carved and gilded wood, heraldic designs, and colourful tapestries. The plaster ceiling was a riot of birds and flowers, scrolls and acanthus leaves. Julian, whose tastes usually ran to space, light, and simplicity, was surprised to find himself captivated. It was all so artlessly exuberant. He thought how beautifully it expressed the spirit of an age when continents were being discovered, when Armadas were defeated, and great English poets and dramatists flourished. An age, he thought, when it must have seemed that anything was possible to humankind.

"I've always thought this room ought to have a ghost," Philippa was saying. "It's so old, and nobody uses it anymore—it's just the sort of place to be haunted. Olivier Fontclair would make a good ghost. He's an ancestor of ours who lived in Elizabethan times and was mixed up in the Babington Plot and had to flee the country.

Mama says there aren't any ghosts, really. But, just supposing there were—supposing bad people's souls didn't rest quietly in their graves—wouldn't you think a man who plotted treason against his queen might be condemned to haunt his family house? Especially if he wasn't caught and punished while he was alive."

"If everyone who died with unpunished sins on his conscience came back as a ghost, the living would be crowded out of every home in England."

"You're *cynical*. I thought you would be. Can you sneer?"

"With terrifying effect."

"Oh, do it, please! I want to see it!"

"I'm afraid you're much too young to withstand it. I should be accused of stunting your growth—perhaps even sending you into a decline."

"I wouldn't go into a decline. I'm *robust*. My governess says so. But, come along, I mustn't make you late to dinner."

They went down a monumental staircase, with arcaded banisters and terminal posts topped with gryphons. "Anyway," she went on, "as I was telling you, the house is divided into three parts: the main house, the new wing, and the servants' wing. We're in the main house now. The dining room and the library are on the ground floor. Upstairs there are only guest rooms and the great chamber. Mr. and Miss Craddock's rooms are around the corner from yours. Have you met them?"

"No, not yet."

"I don't like Mr. Craddock. He's gruff and bearish. Miss Craddock is very nice. She often comes to see Joanna and me in the schoolroom. *We* like her."

That emphatic *we* spoke volumes: *We* like her, even if other people don't.

They passed through the vast great hall, with its hammerbeam ceiling and stained-glass windows. "Those doors under the minstrels' gallery open on the screens passage," Philippa said. "You have to cross it to get to the servants' wing. The three parts of the house are all in a row: servants' wing, main house, new wing. We're going to the new wing now."

Julian pictured the façade of the house, which he had seen to advantage when he arrived. Philippa must be taking him to the right-hand wing. which was set farther back from the rest. It was built of the same grey stone, but in a graceful classical design that contrasted starkly with the crenellated walls and mullioned windows of the older part of the house.

Inside, the contrast was just as dramatic. Right-angled corridors gave way to sinuous curves. Intricately carved oak panels were replaced by pastel-painted walls, edged with chaste white mouldings. It was elegant, easeful, and in very good taste—and yet Philippa was right, it did seem a little insipid after what came before.

Philippa gave a little jump. "Oh, how horrid! There's Miss Pritchard, and Hugh and Josie with her. Let's run before they see us!"

"They *have* seen us, I'm afraid."

"Pritchie will give me such a scold for coming to see you!" She folded her hands and cast down her eyes demurely. "Good evening, Miss Pritchard."

The governess was between thirty and forty, painfully thin, with a gaunt, bony little face and shortsighted eyes. She hurried forward to reclaim her charge. "I'm terribly sorry, sir!" she twittered to Julian. "I had no idea where she'd gone!"

"Not at all. It was very obliging of her to show me the way to the drawing room. I expect I should have got lost without her."

Philippa tossed her head and smiled triumphantly at her sister. Joanna pouted charmingly. She was dark-haired, and much the prettier of the two. In a few years, she would be breaking hearts all over the West End.

"See here, Pippa," said Hugh, "you've got nothing to look so smug about. Mr. Kestrel's being very gracious about it, but all the same, you shouldn't have been pestering him."

"I wasn't pestering him. I was being *helpful*. And you're the one who made me want so much to meet him. You said he was the most tremendous beau, absolutely top of the tree!"

Hugh flushed scarlet. Julian's eyes danced, but he had the grace to look away.

"Pippa, you're embarrassing everyone!" Joanna hissed.

"I don't see why—" Philippa was beginning. But Miss Pritchard hastily said good night and bundled her charges away.

"I'm sorry about that," muttered Hugh. "I don't suppose you came to Bellegarde to be teased to death by my little sisters."

"Oh, I don't mind. I rather like making friends with women before they're old enough to be dangerous."

＊

The rest of the company was already assembled in the drawing room. Julian had met Sir Robert and Lady Fontclair when they greeted him upon his arrival. He was slightly acquainted with Colonel Fontclair, Sir Robert's brother, who belonged to one or two of his clubs. Sir Robert's sister, Lady Tarleton, he knew by sight, though they had never been introduced. Mr. Craddock was a stranger to him, as were Maud Craddock and Isabelle Fontclair.

Isabelle must have been a few years older and at least six inches taller than Maud. She had the type of figure Julian most admired in women—statuesque, slender, and effortlessly graceful. Her voice was low-pitched, smooth, and mellow—very pleasing to Julian, who particularly noticed voices. But what struck him most about her was her serenity. Not many people could sit so still, and yet look so natural and relaxed.

Maud suffered by comparison. Her face was pale and pasty, and there were smudges of shadow under her eyes. She had a figure like a Dresden shepherdess's—a tiny waist, with generous curves above and below. Her hair was of a light, streaky shade that was neither blond nor brown. Her nose was small and blunt, with a sprinkling of freckles. She did have striking eyes: large, wide-set, and of a vivid turquoise. But no one had a chance to see them to advantage. She seldom looked up from the floor, and then only long enough to whisper a reply when someone addressed her. Once, though, Julian caught her timidly searching his face. When he looked around at her, she started guiltily and dropped her gaze.

Colonel Fontclair sat by the drawing room fire, his right hand curled round the head of his walking stick. He needed the stick to get about, having been wounded in the leg some dozen years ago, while serving with the Duke of Wellington's army in Spain. Julian had never seen him so subdued as he was tonight. London society knew him as a bon vivant—good-humoured and heedless, with a

fondness for very old wines and very young women  He was handsome, like his son Guy, though his sedentary life and indulgence
in food and wine were beginning to tell on him. His florid complexion and thickening waist disguised his resemblance to Sir Robert,
who was tall, thin, and gaunt, and might serve as a very good model
for Don Quixote in ten or twenty years.

Guy was not dining with them this evening. "You don't mean
to say he's out again!" said Lady Tarleton.

"Well, you know, he has so many friends in the neighbourhood,"
said Lady Fontclair. "And as he's not here very often, naturally he
likes to visit them when he has the chance."

"You know as well as I do, he's not paying civilized calls round
the neighbourhood! He's gone carousing in the village, as usual,
getting up to Heaven knows what mischief and bringing down
ridicule on all of us. How are we to maintain our dignity, when
Guy is forever lowering himself to the level of common artisans and
labouring men? Though I don't know why I should care anymore—
our position is already all but compromised beyond repair!" She
threw a scornful glance at the Craddocks.

"Guy is just high-spirited," said Lady Fontclair. "I'm sure he
doesn't mean any harm. But if you like, I'll ask him to dine at home
tomorrow. Will that content you?"

"Content me! As though anything could content me, as long
as—! Well, I suppose I shall have to make do with it."

Lady Fontclair caught Julian's eye and smiled ruefully, as though
asking his pardon for Lady Tarleton's tantrum and, at the same time,
appealing to his sense of humour. He smiled back, thinking what
a pretty woman she was—dark-haired and dainty, with velvety
brown eyes. Her daughter Joanna looked very like her; Philippa had
the long, thin face of the Fontclairs.

He was seated on her right hand at dinner. Knowing she lived
in the country all year round, he was resigned to conversing mainly
about her children and her garden. He soon found he had not done
her justice. She had a wide variety of interests, the most surprising
of which was medicine. "Dr. MacGregor's been training me for some
time now," she said. "He's our local physician—well, a surgeon,
really, but we give him the title of 'doctor' all the same. I told him

I didn't like the thought of there being a sudden illness or accident at Bellegarde, and no one here at hand who knew what to do about it. I asked him to teach me some simple treatments—how to take out splinters, stanch bleeding, bring down fevers—that sort of thing. He's been so kind. He's given me medical books, and taught me all about bandaging and—well, never mind the rest. It's not especially suitable for dinnertable conversation! Anyway, I've learned to treat my family and servants for small ailments, though of course I consult Dr. MacGregor about anything that might be at all serious. You'll meet him tomorrow; he always dines here on Fridays."

"I shall look forward to that."

"You'll find him very crusty, I'm afraid, but we're all extremely fond of him. Otherwise this is strictly a family party. I hope it won't prove dull for you, coming from London at the height of the season."

"Sometimes the height of the season, like other lofty elevations, is best viewed from a distance."

She dimpled at him. "Mr. Kestrel, you are very charming." Then, suddenly serious, she added, "I'm glad, very glad, to find that I like you. It's so important what friends a man makes at Hugh's age. Young men are so open to impressions—so easily influenced, especially by friends who are a little older and more worldly. I feel sure I can trust you—can't I?—to think of Hugh's good and remember how young he is."

"Lady Fontclair, you have my promise never to mar what you've made of him."

"My dear Mr. Kestrel. And you won't tell him we had this conversation?"

"What conversation is that?" he said blankly.

They smiled at one another.

She turned to Craddock, who was seated on her other hand. Julian marked how her manner changed. She was scrupulously civil, but there was no warmth in her voice. "Are you going to the horse fair tomorrow, Mr. Craddock?"

"I wasn't planning on it, no," he said sharply. "It's been some years since I took a professional interest in horses."

Julian was surprised. Why should the mention of horses touch him on the raw? People said he came of lowly origins; perhaps he had been a horse dealer at one time. If so, had Lady Fontclair been purposely twitting him about it? That did not seem like her. If she meant to hurt a man, surely her attack would be private and direct, not public and insinuating.

Craddock, having made his displeasure felt, put it behind him, and began to talk tersely and sensibly about some local election. Give the man his due: He had courage, and a rough sort of dignity. Lady Tarleton's disdain could not intimidate him, and neither could the too punctilious courtesy of Sir Robert and Lady Fontclair. If he could not always keep his temper, at all events he kept his self-respect, and that was no mean achievement in an enemy camp like Bellegarde. The very servants were hostile to him; when they addressed him, they gave a slight, sarcastic emphasis to the "Mr." before his name, as though they thought it a bitter joke that they should have to treat him with respect.

Julian glanced down the table at Miss Craddock, who was seated next to Sir Robert. How was she bearing up under the veiled hostility around her? He caught her in an unguarded moment, when no one was talking to her. She was lost in her own thoughts, and her face expressed them as candidly as a child's. She was desperately unhappy.

*Damn, damn, damn!* he thought. *I refuse to get mixed up in all this. If she doesn't want to marry Fontclair, it's no business of mine. Why doesn't she just cry off?*

He looked across at Craddock. Was he the force behind the marriage? Because if he was, what chance did a meek eighteen-year-old girl have of standing up against a will like his?

# *4*
## SKIRMISHES
___

After dinner, Julian hoped to get better acquainted with Isabelle Fontclair, but drawing-room company is apt to arrange itself in the most maddening patterns, and he found himself thrown together with Lady Tarleton instead. Her manner toward him was decidedly frosty. She was clearly vexed that he revealed so little about his family background. She dropped questions and insinuations, which he either parried or pretended not to understand. He had no intention of exposing his parents to her scrutiny. He was not ashamed of them, nor (as many of the Quality believed) did he relish making a mystery of his past. He just felt protective of the dead, who could not speak for themselves.

To distract her, he asked her about a painting that hung over the fireplace. It was a portrait of a man in medieval armour. He was clasping his helmet under one arm and holding up his sword, point downward, so that the jewelled hilt looked like a cross. His long brow and jaw plainly marked him as a Fontclair.

Lady Tarleton unbent a little. "That's Sir Roland Fontclair, one of our most distinguished ancestors, and a hero of Agincourt. Of course, the portrait was done much later. My great-grandfather sat for it, wearing assorted pieces of armour from our family collection. But the sword is Sir Roland's own. No one ever used it after his death."

She launched into a history of her family's military exploits. Fontclairs, it seemed, had fought gallantly at Hastings and Crécy, Blenheim and Saratoga. One Fontclair had championed the cause of Charles II so ardently that he was created a baronet upon the king's restoration. Lady Tarleton knew all about them: their horses, their squires, their wounds, their decorations. She did not seem to care any longer to whom she was speaking. Her words spilled out faster and faster, her hands were uplifted, her eyes had a feverish gleam.

A chair scraped. Julian looked around and saw Colonel Fontclair moving toward the door as fast as his limp would allow. Was it Lady Tarleton's stories that had driven him away? She was certainly speaking loudly enough for him to hear every word from his seat nearby. Perhaps her glorification of warfare was exasperating to a man who knew what battle and bloodshed were really like. By all accounts, the Peninsular War had been a grueling campaign—atrocities committed daily, spies lurking everywhere, provisions constantly running short. A man who had been through that four-year ordeal might well find it hard to stomach Lady Tarleton's fairy-tale vision of military life. Especially if he were in a pensive mood to begin with, as Geoffrey seemed to be.

Lady Tarleton was too caught up in her storytelling to pay him any heed. Not so Lady Fontclair: she watched his departure with troubled eyes, and Julian was not surprised when, a little while later, she left the room herself. Going to look for the colonel, was Julian's guess.

He realized too late that he had let his attention stray from Lady Tarleton. When she said, "Would you like to see it?" he had no idea what she was talking about. But he said, "Very much," and left the drawing room with her, prepared to be shown almost anything.

✳

They crossed from the new wing back to the main house—the Elizabethan core of Bellegarde. Candlelight from the hallway sconces gleamed along the gilded wood panelling and threw into relief the cornice mouldings of roses, oak leaves, and clusters of grapes. Lady Tarleton led Julian down a long corridor, past an anachronistic billiard room and a small study, to a door at the end of the hallway. He opened it for her, and they went inside.

The room was full of weapons—swords, pistols, crossbows, maces. Many were cherished antiques, displayed in cabinets or hung on walls, but others were modern guns and knives that must be in everyday use. There was armour, too, for both men and horses, and pennons, powder flasks, and spurs.

Geoffrey Fontclair was sitting at a table in the center of the room. Lady Fontclair stood behind him, her arms around his shoulders. "It's wicked and wrong," she was saying to him gently. "Promise me you will never think of it again."

Geoffrey caught sight of Lady Tarleton and Julian in the doorway. He started violently and clutched at the head of his walking stick. Lady Fontclair looked surprised, too, but seeing his confusion, she mastered her own. She laid her hands on his shoulders for a moment, and Julian could sense her steadying influence flowing to him through her fingers.

She came around the table, smiling. "You've brought Mr. Kestrel to see the gun room—how nice."

"Of course, I hadn't expected to find you and my brother having a private conversation here."

"It's not so very private," said Lady Fontclair. "And we hadn't a great deal more to say, so you mustn't be concerned about interrupting us."

"I'm not in the least concerned!" Lady Tarleton snapped.

The colonel came to his feet with an effort. "Got a bit of a headache," he muttered. "I think I'll get along to bed."

"Of course," said Lady Fontclair. "Shall I say good night to the others for you?"

"That's good of you. Thanks."

She turned to Julian with her merry, sweet smile. "Mr. Kestrel, if you'll excuse me, I've deserted my post in the drawing room for too long. I won't say good night, since I'm sure I'll see you again before we all retire for the evening. Catherine, until later."

Lady Tarleton made a scornful sound through her nostrils. Geoffrey mumbled good night to her, without meeting her eyes. She did not speak to him at all.

The colonel and Lady Fontclair went out, walking arm in arm very gracefully in spite of Geoffrey's lameness. Lady Tarleton gazed after them, her lips twisting into a sneer. "Touching, isn't it," she said, "how fond they are of one another?"

Julian changed the subject hastily. "This is a marvellous collection."

"Yes it is, isn't it? You must forgive me, Mr. Kestrel. That charming little tableau we just witnessed quite made me forget why I brought you here."

What she wanted to show him, it turned out, was the original of the sword in the portrait of Sir Roland Fontclair. With Julian's help, she took it down from the wall. "Isn't it beautiful?" she breathed, turning the jewelled pommel this way and that, to catch the light. "Feel how heavy it is. Sir Roland must have been a very powerful man, to carry such a sword into battle."

She let him hold it, hovering anxiously, like a mother putting her baby into the arms of a stranger. He cut a few swipes in the air, and she seemed a little resentful, as though it offended her that any man but a Fontclair could manage Sir Roland's sword. She took it back and brandished it herself, her hand trembling a little with its weight.

The character of a female warrior suited her, Julian thought. She was tall, like Isabelle, and strong—many women would not have been able to lift the sword at all. He thought she must have been handsome when she was young. Even now, she did not seem old so much as ravaged: her steel-blue eyes were glassy, her cheekbones sharp, her mouth marked off by frown lines. Her hair, instead of fading gradually with age, was dark red, shot with bolts of silver.

She gave him a tour of the gun room, dwelling with particular pride on her ancestors' military decorations. He noticed several that Geoffrey had won for his service under Wellington in Spain, but Lady Tarleton showed no interest in those. Apparently she only cared about heroics of the distant past.

"When I was a girl," she said, "these weapons were displayed all over the house. But after Robert married Cecily, they were all gathered together in one room. She said she didn't want her children growing up surrounded by dangerous objects. Dangerous! Why, when I was their age, I used to play with daggers and dress swords all the time! It made me proud of my family's military tradition. *She* won't even allow her daughters in this room alone. I'm surprised she doesn't go so far as to put a lock on the door."

Julian wondered fleetingly what Lady Tarleton's children would have been like, if she had had any. Little girls running about like Amazons, with quivers on their shoulders and spears in their hands? Well, he was glad she had brought him to see this room. He could easily have whiled away hours here, trying out the grip of different swords or observing how guns had improved over the years, from seventeenth-century muskets to the newest Manton fowling pieces.

By the time they left the gun room, she was in charity with him enough to take his arm. They entered the drawing room—and she froze. She made a small, strangled sound in her throat, and her arm went stiff in his.

The company was grouped around Mark Craddock, who sat on a sofa beside Maud. Isabelle sat at a table across from them, sketching Craddock's face. Hugh stood behind her, watching her pencil dart across the page, while Sir Robert and Lady Fontclair looked on from farther away.

Lady Tarleton rushed at Isabelle. Wrenching her sketchbook out of her hands, she tore off the drawing of Craddock, ripped it to shreds and flung the pieces away. Craddock leapt to his feet and stared at her. The others were too stunned to move.

Isabelle stood up, unhurried and unafraid. "Mr. Craddock has an interesting face, Aunt. He said I might draw it."

"And I say you will do nothing of the kind! You're treating this man as though—as though he were a member of our family, the same as one of us! And he will never be that! He may force his daughter on Hugh, but she'll never really be a Fontclair. And *he'll* never be anything but what he is—a cit, a little trumped-up trades-man, and before that—"

"Don't say it!" Craddock thundered. "Don't say it, I warn you! Another word, and I'll take my daughter and leave this house, and that will be the end of everything. Of *everything!*" he ground out, his face close to hers.

She stared back, breathing hard, giving no ground, but she was silent.

Sir Robert's face settled into a grim, inscrutable mask. Hugh was scarlet to the roots of his hair. Maud Craddock quietly and undramatically dropped her head in her hands.

Isabelle gathered up the pieces of her drawing and tucked them away in her sketchbook. As always, her movements were graceful precise, and confident. Julian thought she made the most ordinary actions look like a ballet.

"Why don't we all go to bed," Lady Fontclair suggested quietly.

She put an arm around Lady Tarleton's shoulders and guided her toward the door. The others followed. Julian went over to Isabelle. "May I?" he said, indicating her sketching box.

"That's kind of you, but it isn't heavy. I carry it all the time."

"All the more reason I should ease the burden, this once."

She shrugged slightly and handed him her sketching box and sketchbook. Trailing a little behind the others, they climbed the spiral staircase that formed the hub of the new wing.

"Would you show me your work some time?" he asked.

"If you like."

"Do you ever paint?"

"No. I find line and shadow more interesting than colour, so I prefer to work in pencil or pen and ink. Perhaps you'd be good enough to sit for me while you're here."

"I can't think of anything I should like more."

She turned a cool, distancing gaze on him. "I sketch most people who visit Bellegarde for any length of time."

"Lest the honour go to my head?"

"Lest you think I mean to flirt with you, Mr. Kestrel. I only want to try my hand at capturing your likeness."

"But I'm not to try my hand at capturing your favour?"

"I should rather you didn't. I mean that seriously." She stopped outside a door. "This is my room."

He gave her back her sketchbook and sketching box, at the same time catching and holding her gaze. "I think it only fair to warn you, I'm becoming rather fascinated."

"If you're in earnest, Mr. Kestrel, then I'm honoured by your attentions, but I appeal to you—don't pursue me. Leave me to myself. If you're merely amusing yourself, then I must tell you, there is nothing I find more tedious than gentlemen who regard me as a challenge. Good night, Mr. Kestrel."

✳

"So you see," Julian said to Dipper later that night, "if there's a rural uprising while we're here, we'll be able to defend ourselves with everything from medieval lances to duelling pistols. I've never seen a household so armed to the teeth. Now I come to think of it, this whole house is reminiscent of a fortress. Look how thick the outer walls are."

He went to the window. It was a bay window, shaped like half an octagon. Some of the small leaded panes were brilliantly stained in crimson, green, and gold. On either side, where the wall was cut away to form the embrasure, were wood panels carved with all manner of animals and objects. Julian had earlier realized that all these carvings were sacred emblems: Mary Magdalen's ointment jar, Anthony's lily, Peter's two crossed keys, Agnes's lamb. Several years in Italy had taught him to know his saints. What their emblems were doing in a bedroom window, he had no idea. Perhaps in Elizabethan days England was more like Italy, where religious and secular decor were gaily intermixed.

The window gave a lovely view of the rear courtyard, which was planted with silver lime trees and bounded on the right side by the new wing, with its fluted columns and delicate balustrades. In the moonlight, the treetops stood out in silhouette against the new wing's pale grey stone. Candlelight gleamed in windows here and there along the upper floor. The window at the far end, where a light shimmered faintly behind white curtains, would be Isabelle's.

Julian left the window abruptly. "This whole place has something of the fortress about it. Nowadays people fill their houses with French windows, so that Nature comes flowing in on all sides, and every room seems to be trying to creep out into the garden. Here I haven't seen any French windows except in the conservatory, and there are hardly any outside doors. A morbid person could start to feel imprisoned in this house."

Dipper stifled a yawn very artfully, but Julian was not deceived. "You'd best go to bed."

"I don't mind sitting up, sir."

"But I mind. You disturb my meditations. I keep wanting to look around suddenly, to see if I can catch you nodding off."

Dipper grinned. "When will you be getting up, sir?"

"Hugh Fontclair's taking me to a horse fair in the morning, so you'd better wake me at some ungodly hour. Seven should be ungodly enough. If I won't get up, bring a spear from that arsenal downstairs and prod me until I do."

"Yes, sir. Good night, sir." Dipper went out.

Julian explored his room more closely. It was a handsome apartment—the Fontclairs were justly proud of it. The walls were panelled from floor to ceiling in highly polished oak slabs, each panel divided lengthwise into three squares, and each square with a lozenge set inside it. Four marble maidens, the Seasons, held up the mantelpiece, while around them swarmed mermaids, satyrs, cupids, and mythical beasts. On the ceiling were vivid stucco reliefs of Elizabethan hunting scenes. The Fontclairs' coat of arms, in painted and gilded wood, appeared at intervals along the cornice and even, to Julian's amusement, on the door of the water closet.

Most of the furnishings were modern, but the massive bed, with its elephantine posts and crimson curtains, could only be Tudor. There were other Elizabethan touches: pewter candlesticks, a linenfold chest, and a portrait of a lady in a ramrod-straight bodice, with a ruff like a white platter round her neck. A pier looking glass hung near the door. The washstand, which had its own small mirror, was mahogany, with a white porcelain basin, a gilt soap dish, and two crystal glasses. There was a white towel draped over a rack at the side, and a gilt ewer on a shelf below.

The early June night was chilly, and the fire did not warm the room very much. None of Rumford's improvements marred the quaint, hopelessly inefficient fireplace. The cold made Julian feel industrious, and he decided to write a letter. He sat down at a small writing table in the window recess. In this little alcove, with the stained glass behind him, he felt like St. Augustine in some Renaissance painting.

He wrote for a while, but there was something disquieting about this night, this place. It was the silence, he realized—that awful silence of a country night that falls so hauntingly on a city-dweller's ears. No carriage wheels on cobblestones, no clattering hoofbeats, no watchmen crying the hour, no revellers carousing in the streets. Of course, this room was bound to be especially quiet. As Philippa had pointed out, it was the only occupied room in this part of the house. Unless, of course, that ancestor who had taken part in the Babington Plot really did haunt the great chamber across the hall. Julian pictured him dancing there in some Elizabethan galliard, surrounded by ghostly companions in platter-shaped ruffs. Perhaps if he listened closely he would hear their minstrels playing—

What he heard was a rap on his own door. The sudden noise, more than the unexpected intrusion, made him start. He took an instant to collect his faculties, and called, "Come in."

# *5*

# THE FAMILY
# ACCORDING TO GUY

The figure who appeared in the doorway, with his long hair, knotted red neckerchief, and boots, might have passed for an Elizabethan privateer, come to join the spectral masque in the great chamber. But it was Guy Fontclair, his face flushed and his gait a little wobbly. Julian did not know Guy very well, but he was not sorry to have someone to pass the time with, even if it meant having to look at the red neckerchief.

"Hello, Kestrel! Survived your first evening here, I see?"

"Did you think I might not?"

"I'm always surprised when anyone gets through dinner at Belle-garde without visible wounds. Mind you, it didn't used to be like that. We weren't always in charity with each other, but it's only since the Craddocks came that we've all been set by the ears. I'll wager there've already been some explosions since you arrived."

"One or two."

"What did I tell you?" Guy pulled a chair close to the fire and began toasting his wet boots. "Every night I'm in two minds about whether to dine here and see how the war goes on or escape to the village to avoid Aunt Catherine. Most of the time blind terror of Aunt Catherine keeps me away—that and all the temptations of the neighbourhood. Some of the local girls can be pretty agreeable,

especially to anyone named Fontclair. Bless those old feudal traditions!"

"Lady Tarleton asked after you this evening."

"The deuce! She only wants me at home so she can claw my head
off whenever she's in the mood. The one she'd really like to blow
up is Mark Craddock, but she can't, because everyone's under orders
to get on with him, or pretend to. It's the damnedest thing, this
marriage! I can't make head or tail of it. If all Uncle Robert wanted
was for Hugh to bring a fat dowry into the family, there are plenty
of other milch cows he could have lit on. Why Mark Craddock's
daughter?"

"What is there about Craddock that puts everyone here in such
a passion?"

"What the devil, you might as well know the truth. It's bound
to come out anyway." He leaned closer. "What do you suppose
Craddock did for a living before he made his fortune in London?"

"Something to do with horses?"

"How did you know that?"

"Just a guess."

"Well, here's something you won't guess so readily. He was a
groom. The man worked in a stable! And which stable do you think
it was? Ours—here at Bellegarde!"

Julian's brows shot up. This was extraordinary. What on earth
could have prompted Hugh to get engaged to the daughter of a
former groom in his family's stables? No wonder Lady Tarleton was
half mad with injured pride. No wonder the rest of the Fontclairs
showed such a distaste for the marriage. And no wonder Guy was
at a loss to fathom what lay behind it.

"That must have been a long time ago," he said at last.

"Before I was born, or just after. Anyway, it was more than twenty
years. He left under a cloud. Uncle Robert gave him the bag—
though they say it was Aunt Catherine who was behind it. I'd give
a monkey to know why. I like to think Craddock tried to ravish her
in a hayloft, but it's hard to believe even he would dare. Though
she used to be good-looking when she was young. You'd never believe
it now. But the colonel swears to it, and he's to be trusted about
female charms."

"It wouldn't surprise me if she'd been very fetching as a girl."

"Well, maybe, if you like that tigerish style. She was one of those wild girls, always tearing round the countryside on horseback and telling people to their faces exactly what she thought of them. Do you know, when she was hardly more than twenty, she went off to the Continent on some female version of the Grand Tour, with nobody to give her countenance but a duenna she could wrap around her little finger. Uncle Robert tried to stop her, but there's never been any holding Aunt Catherine back from what she wanted to do. By God, I can't abide that kind of female! I like women to be docile and come to heel—and if they don't, I make them sorry for it!"

"I wonder you don't keep spaniels instead. Much easier, and less expensive."

Guy stared at him, uncertain how to take this remark.

Julian frowned. "How could Lady Tarleton have gone travelling on the Continent when she was young? Wouldn't that have been in the midst of the wars with France?"

"It was during some truce that went on for a year or so. When the fighting started up again, she came back to England, and soon after that, she married Tarleton. God alone knows why. Except that he came of a family nearly as old as ours, and his rank was on a level with Uncle Robert's. Those are the only things that matter to Aunt Catherine. Of course the match was a disaster. She drove him out of England in the end, with her carping and her fits of temper. He lives on the Continent, and I'm told he's in mortal dread of her coming after him some day. But she doesn't seem to care a fig if she never lays eyes on him again. She'd rather live at Bellegarde and queen it over Aunt Cecily and give her opinion of everything that goes on, whether people want it or not. She ought to have married the kind of man who'd beat her whenever she opened her mouth out of turn. If you ask me, one reason she can't stomach Craddock is that he stands up to her, which is more than poor old Tarleton could ever do."

"Perhaps that's why she wanted him dismissed from Sir Robert's service."

"Could be. But there's no knowing, worse luck. There's hardly anybody left at Bellegarde who was here in those days—only Travis, the butler, and he's as close as a clam. Of course Uncle Robert and Aunt Catherine won't talk. The colonel was away in the army at the time Craddock got the bag, and he says he doesn't know anything about it. I'm not sure I believe him—the fact is, he won't tell me anything anymore. I've been pumping him for weeks about what's behind Hugh's marriage, and will he breathe a word to me? Not a bit of it!"

"Perhaps he doesn't know."

"Oh, he knows, all right! He's been in the thick of this whole business from the beginning. It all started this past April, when Hugh came of age. Of course Uncle Robert put on a bang-up show: a feast for the servants, dancing—the whole feudal rigmarole. Next morning—it was raining, I remember, and I was stumping around with a monstrous headache, and the women were looking sort of peaked and tired out, and we were all moping about in the library, thinking how to keep amused till the rain stopped. And all of a sudden Travis comes in, looking as if he'd just taken a flush-hit on the nob, and says Mark Craddock is here to see Uncle Robert. We were all pretty taken aback—we knew Craddock was plump in the pocket now and had long since shaken the dust of Bellegarde from his feet, and why he should come calling on us was more than we could make out. But, Lord, you should have seen Aunt Catherine! Her legs fairly buckled under her—the colonel had to hold her up. You know, sometimes I think Aunt Catherine's a little mad. But that's by the way.

"Aunt Catherine started blathering about Craddock's impudence in coming here. She said Uncle Robert mustn't see him—said he ought to be thrown out, just as he had been twenty years ago. But Uncle Robert wanted to see what Craddock wanted, so he told Travis to show him in. In comes Craddock, with his steely-eyed look, and that way he has of making any room look too small to hold him. He doesn't waste any time on civilities—just says he's got business with Uncle Robert, Aunt Cecily, Aunt Catherine, and the colonel, and will they see him somewhere alone. Uncle Robert didn't like the sound of that, I could tell, but he agreed, and so all the old people went off together, and Hugh and Isabelle and I were left racking our brains to think what it was all about.

"They were gone a long time—a couple of hours at least—and I was so bored with the whole thing by then that when the rain stopped, I went out riding. I came back in the afternoon, and, by God, you'd think someone had died in the house—it was so still, and everyone looked so solemn. Craddock was gone, Hugh was shut up somewhere with his parents, and the colonel took me aside and said it would be best if I went back to London. Well, I kicked up a dust, naturally. I wanted to know what was in the wind. But I went in the end. It was clear no one was going to tell me a bloody thing, and who wants to stay in a house that's turned into a mausoleum? Besides," he added more quietly, "the colonel was really cut up. I thought for once I'd better do whatever the deuce he wanted."

"And it was on the heels of that that Hugh offered for Miss Craddock?"

"About a fortnight later, I think. She's not much of a bargain, is she? A little mouse of a thing, dull as ditchwater, no life in her at all."

"Perhaps being handed over to an unwilling bridegroom in the teeth of his family's opposition is dragging down her spirits a bit."

"You think there might be something in her after all?"

"My dear fellow, how should I know?" That girl again, he thought. Why does she get under my skin this way? She's probably delighted to marry Fontclair, and only sulking because the mantua-maker is taking too long with her trousseau. And if there's more to it than that—if she's marrying him against her will—what can I do about it? Other than land myself, one way or another, in a devil of a mess.

"Hugh doesn't see anything in her," Guy was saying. "If he were in love, everybody would know about it. He'd be mooning, and making sheep's eyes at Miss Craddock, and fighting duels with anybody who wouldn't swear she was all three Graces in one. Hugh's romantic, poor devil. You should see what he reads. Byron, Walter Scott, all that rubbish. Oh, well, he could be much worse off. He could have ended up shackled to Isabelle."

"Was that on the cards at one time?" Julian became absorbed in smoothing out his shirtcuffs.

"It's been talked about for years—mostly by Aunt Catherine, who's all for breeding Fontclairs with each other. Isabelle is second cousin to Hugh and me. Her parents died without a farthing when she was a child, so Uncle Robert and Aunt Cecily took her in. Uncle Robert's promised her a dowry, by the way, in case you care to have a go at her. I wouldn't set your heart on it, though—Isabelle's thrown cold water on every poor fool who ever dangled after her. It's Hugh she wants. She's mad on the family, just like Aunt Catherine. She's caught it from her like a disease. When Hugh came of age, she probably thought she was going to nick it at last. Then along comes a drab little chit whose father reeks of the stables, and Isabelle's out of the running. By God, she must hate the Craddocks!"

He got up. "Well, my boots have dried out, and I'm going to bed. Alone, unfortunately. Aunt Cecily's maids are devilish strait-laced. Look here, before I go, there's one thing I want to know—though I'm damned if I know why you should tell me. I'm never allowed to get to the bottom of any mystery in this house."

"What mystery could there be that I would know more about than you?"

"The mystery of what the deuce you're doing here. I didn't even know Hugh knew you till I saw the two of you with your heads together at that gaming hell, and now you're going to be groomsman at his wedding."

Julian considered. "I think I'm the chorus."

"The what?"

"Like the chorus in a classical drama. I watch the action and comment on it, without being drawn into it myself."

"Well, I'm blistered if I know why you'd want to be stuck here playing chorus at some daft family drama."

Julian did not know the answer to that himself. "There are worse places to be stuck," he mused, gazing around the room.

"It's not half bad, is it? It used to be my room, you know."

"No, I didn't."

"I stayed at Bellegarde a good deal when I was a boy. My mother died before I was out of leading-strings, and the colonel was always off with his regiment somewhere, so often there was nothing to do with me but quarter me with Uncle Robert. I don't think he liked that above half—thought I was a bad influence on Hugh—but there was nothing he could do about it. Family loyalty—all we Fontclairs are slaves to it, and no one more than Uncle Robert."

He went over to the window, smiling reminiscently. "I used to spend most of my time trying to figure out ways to get out at night on the sly. I got pretty good at climbing out the window and down that tree, but the gardeners saw the broken branches and my footsteps in the ground, and they peached on me to Uncle Robert." He grinned mischievously. "Well, that was a long time ago. Nowadays I can get in and out at night without climbing through windows. I use the back door in the servants' wing. There are dogs loose at night, but they know me, so they don't give me any trouble." He yawned. "Well, I'd better get a few hours' sleep. Are you going to the horse fair in the morning?"

"I think Hugh's planning to take me."

"Good. We can make a party of it—the two of you and the colonel and me. At least it'll keep us away from Bellegarde until luncheon. Mornings are the very devil here these days. Whey-faced ladies are always calling to have a look at Miss Craddock and find out how much her rich papa's spending on her wedding. Poor Hugh!"

✳

"Time to wake up, sir," Dipper ventured.

"What time is it?" came a sepulchral voice from under the bedclothes.

"Seven o'clock, sir."

"Oh, my God." Julian dragged himself out from under the covers. "Don't—" he began, but Dipper was already parting the window curtains. Julian dove under the sheet again to block out the light. "It's appalling," he groaned, "simply appalling, to think that anyone was ever so benighted as to worship the sun. Dipper, if I ever tell you I mean to have a house in the country, immerse me in cold baths and singe me with mustard plasters till my sanity returns."

Dipper was glad to find him in such a tractable mood. When Mr. Kestrel was really out of temper, he did not mock or complain, but went about in a tautly strung silence more disturbing than any show of rage.

At eight o'clock, Julian came down to breakfast impeccably dressed in riding clothes. The meal passed off with an uneasy, "everyone-on-his-best-behaviour" sort of calm. Afterward, Guy, Hugh, Julian, and Colonel Fontclair set off for the horse fair.

"I'm so glad it's turned out such a beautiful day," said Lady Fontclair as they were leaving. "Hugh, what would you say to taking Mr. Kestrel round the estate this afternoon, if you're not too tired after the horse fair?"

"That's a capital idea," Hugh agreed.

"Well, enjoy yourselves, all of you, and don't, I pray you, stand about in the sun without your hats. I'll have hock and seltzer water waiting for you when you come home. Good-bye!"

✳

It was, indeed, a lovely day—the kind of day to win over even a confirmed city-dweller like Julian. The colours of the country dazzled him, after London's myriad shades of grey. Oaks and elms spread their lacy crowns against a sky of vivid cornflower blue. Spotted cows browsed in brilliant green meadows, bounded by roads of a warm, rich brown. Here and there, set back from the road, were cottages of whitewashed brick, with ivy-covered fences and steep thatched roofs.

Julian and Hugh were riding side by side. At one point, Hugh slowed his horse's pace, letting Guy and Geoffrey ride on ahead. "I want to tell you how sorry I am about last night," he said to Julian. "You shouldn't have had to see that fit of temper of Aunt Catherine's. I daresay I oughtn't to have invited you to Bellegarde at all. Things are so awkward right now—anything might happen."

"Is this a delicate way of saying you'd like me to arrange to be called back to London unexpectedly?"

"Oh, no! No, I hope you'll stay. It's very selfish of me, of course. Apart from the fact that it's great fun having you, your being here has a moderating influence on people. You may not think so after last night, but, believe me, things would probably be much worse if you weren't here."

"Is that why you invited me?"

"Yes," Hugh admitted. "I never thought for a moment you'd

really come. I just thought you seemed so—I don't know, detached and sensible and able to keep a clear head about things. And since you're an outsider, people would have to behave in your presence. That sounds an awful thing to say about one's own family, but they're not themselves right now. None of us is. I wish I knew how it was all going to end. This waiting is worse than anything. It's like one of those nightmares where you know something terrible is going to happen, and you don't know what it is, but you know there's nothing you can do to stop it."

# *6*
## OTHER PEOPLE'S
## BUSINESS

The main road to Whitford passed through Alderton, the village nearest to Bellegarde. It boasted a proud old coaching house, the Blue Lion, with a brick lower story painted pink and an overhanging upper floor of timber. The houses had white, blue, or yellow façades, embellished with designs that had been swirled on the plaster while it was still wet. An occasional swinging sign announced a stationer, a greengrocer, a milliner, a blacksmith. The village was very quiet, with women and children, but few men, on the streets. Hugh said the men must have gone to Whitford for the horse fair.

At Whitford, copers had set up shop across the village green, and were loudly extolling the horses they had to sell. The gullible listened eagerly, while more seasoned onlookers cynically shook their heads. Potential buyers walked round and round the horses, inspecting their teeth, their hooves, their coats.

The party from Bellegarde turned their own horses over to a groom and explored the fair on foot. They quickly agreed that there was nothing worth buying, but they strolled about good-naturedly and listened to the horse-chanters ply their trade. Julian, on the alert for their tricks, noted wryly how one horse's knees had been stained to conceal blemishes, and another's gums were burned black with caustic to give an appearance of youth.

After a while Colonel Fontclair went off alone, saying he needed to give his lame leg a rest. Guy, Hugh, and Julian were standing about drinking ale they had bought at a nearby stall, when a reedy voice sounded behind them: "Will you buy a whistle, gentlemen? Some'ut to call your dogs?"

They turned and saw a wizened old man peering at them. He had a face as browned and wrinkled as a raisin, and long, stringy white hair darkened with dirt. He wore stained, baggy trousers and a brown coat buttoned wrong. A cap like a battered flatiron perched on his head. The immense sack he carried was strangely at odds with his drab clothes: it was a patchwork of hundreds of stray bits of cloth, in all manner of colours, patterns, and shapes.

"Hullo, Bliss," said Hugh. "I didn't know you were in the neighbourhood."

"Passing through, as always, sir—passing through. And how is your lady mother?"

"My lady mother is fine," said Hugh, smiling. "If you come to Bellegarde, I'm sure she'll see you don't go away empty-handed."

The person called Bliss grinned, screwing up his eyes into slits. "Oh, I mean to, sir, I mean to. But in the meantime, won't you buy a doll for your young sisters?" He reached into his sack and brought out a rough-cut wooden figure in a calico dress. "Or maybe this one as is so finely turned out"—he jerked his head toward Julian—"might like a comb for his hair or a brush for his coat. And how about you, sir?" His gaze slewed round to Guy. "Perhaps a flute to play to your lady friends?"

"Get along with you, curse your impudence!" Guy said, between laughter and indignation.

Hugh gave Bliss a coin. "Bless you, young sir!" he cried out. Several bystanders looked around, laughing, at which Hugh got very red. Bliss went on, unheeding, "You're a credit to your lady mother, whose al'ays got a kind word and some'ut to give an old man as is struggling to make his way in the world. Not like that Lady Tarleton, who says I ought to be sent to the work'hus. She'll get her comeuppance one of these days!"

"I'd like to see the man who could give it to her," said Guy.

"There's a reckoning in store for everyone, soon or late," the old man said slyly. "*You* ought to keep that in mind, Master Guy."

"Why you confounded old—" Guy was beginning. But Hugh took hold of his arm and drew him away. Julian, following, looked back and saw the old man watching them keenly. His eyes remained fixed on them till the crowd closed in and cut off his view.

"What's the point of arguing with him?" Hugh was saying. "He's only a feeble old man, and queer in his upper story besides."

"I don't believe it for a moment," said Guy. "The fellow's a rogue. He'd slit his own grandmother's throat for tuppence, if he thought he could do it without getting caught."

"That's a curious sack he carries," said Julian.

"Yes it is, isn't it?" said Hugh. "He made it himself. People say it used to be an ordinary sack, but every time it got a hole in it he patched it with bits of material that he cadged off drapers and village women. He's been doing that for so many years that it's nothing but patches now. He's very clever with his hands. He makes all the things he sells—dolls, whistles, pipes, baskets. I think he gets more money begging, though, than he does by peddling the things he makes. Sometimes he does errands and chores for people—he's very spry, though he must be as old as Methusaleh."

"Is Bliss his surname or his Christian name?"

"I don't think anyone really knows. It's the only name we've ever known him by. He's been tramping around our part of the county for as long as I can remember. Every few months he turns up near Bellegarde, and Mother is always kind to him. I think he's really fond of her—but then, of course, Mother brings out the best in everyone. There's no love lost between him and Aunt Catherine, but you'll have gathered that."

＊

At about noon, Hugh assembled the scattered members of his party, and they rode home. Guy was in uproariously high spirits. Colonel Fontclair remained quiet and withdrawn. Julian found it easy to forget he was there at all.

Back at Bellegarde, they went to the drawing room for hock and seltzer water before luncheon. Miss Joanna and Miss Philippa made an appearance, ushered in ceremoniously by their governess, and watched with loving but alert eyes by their mother. They both curtsied demurely to Julian, but Philippa shot him a wary look, probably wondering if he would let on they had met already. She need not have worried; he would not dream of reminding anyone of her breach of etiquette.

She asked him a great many questions about London. Considering that he was such a man about town, she was shocked to discover how many important places he knew nothing about. He had never been once to the pantomime at Astley's, and he could not say for certain he had stood on the spot where Anne Boleyn and Catherine Howard lost their heads. "It was easier for kings to get rid of their wives in those days," she observed. "Thwack! thwack! with an axe, and the king could get married again."

"That must have been frightfully convenient."

"I think history's ever so interesting. I'm writing a history, you know."

"No, I didn't. A history of what?"

"Of my family—all the battles we've been in and the heiresses we've eloped with—that kind of thing. Of course, we don't know much about what our ancestors did before the seventeenth century. There was a terrible fire here during the civil war, and ever so many papers got burnt up."

"That must make it difficult to write a family history."

"No, not really. I just make most of it up. Nobody will know the difference."

Luncheon was announced, and Joanna and Philippa had to return to the schoolroom. After the meal, which was served on the terrace overlooking the formal garden, Lady Fontclair again urged Hugh to take Mr. Kestrel on a tour of the estate. "Should you like that?" Hugh asked Julian. "Or would that be too much riding for one day? The park is quite nice, and we've got some fine model farms. I don't know if you're interested in that sort of thing."

"I try to be interested in very nearly everything. I always think boredom is to some extent the fault of the bored."

Hugh was relieved. He had feared that a fellow like Kestrel, jaded with London life, might not be easy to keep entertained. "I've got to closet myself with the parents for an hour or two, to go over those settlements the lawyers sent. Why don't I come looking for you after that?"

Julian agreed. He was not sorry to get an hour or two to himself. The Fontclairs had a superb pianoforte, and he had been wanting to try it out.

He went to the music room. There was no one there. He opened the piano, laying bare her ivory keys with a little thrill of anticipation. He touched the keys, explored them, finally drew from them the joyous, rippling strains of Mozart's Sonata in C major.

As he struck the final notes, there was a little burst of applause. Looking over his shoulder, he saw Maud Craddock in the doorway. He came to his feet.

She blushed, left off clapping, and hid her hands behind her. "I hope you don't mind my listening. It was very nice."

"I don't mind in the least. I'm flattered you should wish to."

She relaxed ever so slightly. "You're very good, aren't you? I mean, I don't know much about music, but you seem to me as good as the real musicians who play at Papa's parties."

"Thank you." He could not help smiling, but he managed to look gratified rather than amused.

Her gaze shied away from his. She walked past him and began to examine a harp on the other side of the room. "Mr. Fontclair is very fond of music. I— I daresay that's one of the things you and he have in common."

This is rather a coil, he thought. Of course she thinks, since I'm Fontclair's groomsman, he and I must have been Damon and Pythias for years. I can't admit we're barely acquainted without explaining how we came to know each other—which would be amusing, but hardly sporting toward Fontclair.

"We do share an interest in music," he allowed.

She turned toward him suddenly, shaking a little, her face very white. "Mr. Kestrel—may I talk to you? I wouldn't ask, only there isn't anyone else. I— I can't talk to Papa—I've tried, and it's no use. And I can't talk to any of the Fontclairs. They're not my friends—they never wanted me here—I couldn't expect them to. You're Mr. Fontclair's friend—you know him. You understand his family, his world. Will you advise me? Will you help me? I don't know what to do!"

"My dear Miss Craddock." Julian closed the distance between them in a few quick steps. "I don't know how I can be of service to you. But whatever I *can* do, rest assured, I will."

"Thank you," she whispered.

He led her to a sofa, and sat down beside her. She looked around uneasily. "Perhaps we should close the doors, or go out into the garden."

He shook his head. "Closing doors only attracts attention, and in a garden one never knows who may be behind the next cluster of wisteria. From where we are now, we can see clearly into the hall and the rooms on either side of us. No one will be able to get near us without our knowing."

Maud could not help thinking he must have had a good deal of experience arranging tête-à-têtes with ladies. Misgiving swept over her. What was she doing?—meeting alone with a fashionable gentleman, one she hardly knew! Her father said young men of the Quality were all scoundrels, who would compromise a girl as soon as look at her. No matter, she thought desperately, I'll take the risk. Nothing can make things any worse than they are now.

She looked down at her lap, clasping and unclasping her fingers. "I expect you know this marriage between Mr. Fontclair and me— it didn't come about of its own accord. My father arranged it. I don't know how. At first I thought the Fontclairs must owe him money. A lot of people do, and some of them get into quite desperate straits. So I looked through his ledgers once, when he wasn't there. I know I oughtn't to have done that without telling him, but I *had* to know what hold he has over the Fontclairs. But there wasn't any sign that he'd lent them money."

"What other means of— persuasion— might he have used?"

"I think he's holding something terrible over the Fontclairs' heads. He must be—otherwise they'd never have agreed to accept me as Mr. Fontclair's wife." She added in a low voice, "I suppose you know Papa was a servant here, years ago."

"I had heard that, yes."

She looked at him very directly for the first time. "I want you to know, I'm not ashamed of Papa's birth, or mine. Everything Papa has in the world he won for himself, by hard work and discipline and a firm will. I'm proud of him for that. But the Fontclairs couldn't be expected to look at him or me that way. They value different things—birth and rank and having ancestors who came over with William the Conqueror. It's wrong of Papa to try to force himself and me into their world. I told him that. I told him I would much rather marry a self-made man like him than a highborn gentleman who didn't want me. But he wouldn't listen—he still won't. He has his heart set on this marriage. I've never seen him want anything so badly."

"Have you any idea why?"

"I thought at first it was just because the Fontclairs seemed powerful and grand to him when he was a boy. I thought perhaps my marrying Mr. Fontclair was a kind of symbol to him of everything he'd achieved. Now I'm not so sure. Since I've been at Bellegarde, I've begun to think he has some grudge against the Fontclairs, and they against him. Lady Tarleton *hates* him. Of course, that might just be because she's angry about the marriage—but I don't think so. I have a feeling she's hated him for years. And I think he hates all the Fontclairs and wants revenge on them. I'm the revenge, Mr. Kestrel."

Julian hardly knew what to say. "I imagine you've thought carefully about whether you can marry Hugh Fontclair, believing what you do?"

"That's what I wanted to talk to you about. Mr. Fontclair told me when he offered for me that the honour and safety of his family depended on my marrying him. He was very honest about it. He couldn't say he— he loved me. We'd never even met before. He was right to be straightforward and not pay compliments he didn't mean. I asked him what Papa would do to his family if he didn't offer for me, or if I didn't accept. He said he was sorry, but I would have to ask Papa. I'm sure Papa's given orders to the Fontclairs not to tell me. I think, deep down, he must be very ashamed of himself. He's not a bad man, truly, though you may find that hard to believe."

"Judging him by his daughter, I should say he must be the finest fellow alive."

Her mouth dropped open in a little moue of surprise. She smiled shyly. "That was a nice thing to say. Thank you."

It dawned on him, all in a moment, that Miss Craddock was adorable. He could think of far worse penances than having to take her to wife. His eyes must have expressed his appreciation, but all he said was, "You haven't yet told me how I can help you."

"I just need advice. I'm very confused. Is it worse to marry Mr. Fontclair when he doesn't want me, or refuse to marry him and let his family be hurt in some way I don't understand?"

"What about your own happiness? Does that count for so little?"

She blushed again and hung her head, letting her sidecurls veil her face. "I only want to do what's best for *him*."

Ah, he thought, so that's how it is. "Does he have any idea how lucky he really is?"

"What do you mean?"

"I mean, does he know how you feel about him?"

"No. I don't think so. I wish I could say I kept it from him out of pride. I know it's not proper for the girl to let her feelings show, when the man hasn't declared his. But really, it's mainly that I don't want to make a bad situation worse. He'd feel so guilty if he knew. He's kind, Mr. Kestrel. He'd hate to feel he was hurting me.

"I fell in love with him the day he asked me to marry him. He made such a mess of it, you can't think. How could he help it? Imagine proposing to a girl you'd never met before, because her father was threatening to do something bad to your family if you didn't! My heart went out to him. When he said he couldn't tell me what hold Papa had over his family, I said I'd try to find out myself, and I'd do everything I could to convince Papa to give it up. And he said, 'Do you think you can?' with such a look of hope in his eyes! There was nothing he wanted so much as to be spared having to marry me. And all the time I was thinking, If only you really wanted me for your wife, how happy I should be!

"I told him I'd become engaged to him, in order to placate Papa for the time being. But I'm determined to find out how he's threatening the Fontclairs, and to stop him somehow. But what if I fail, Mr. Kestrel? The wedding is only a few weeks away. What if I haven't been able to make Papa see reason by then? If I marry Mr.

Fontclair, he'll be saddled with a wife he never wanted, one he—
he's probably ashamed of. But if I don't marry him, he'll be miserable, too. He pleaded with me to accept him; he said I had the
honour of his family in my hands. So it seems that, whether I marry
him or not, I can only make him unhappy. And that's hard, Mr.
Kestrel—that's very hard!—when his happiness means more to me
than anything in the world!"

There was a long pause. Julian faced facts. He was not going to
be dragged into other people's business. He was going to plunge in
headfirst. "What are we going to do about this tangle?"

"We?" she echoed hopefully.

"I thought I'd apply for the position of knight-errant. References
available upon request."

"You *are* kind."

"Let's just say I'm intrigued—also a little appalled. Miss Craddock, I think you're right: the first thing to do is find out what
hold your father has over the Fontclairs. At least then you'll be able
to gauge how badly he could harm them if the marriage doesn't
come off. And if he really is ashamed to let you know what he's
about, perhaps he'll be driven to drop the whole business, once
you've caught him out."

"That's very sensible, Mr. Kestrel, and I agree with you. But I've
tried to find out, and no one will tell me."

"Then we'll have to find out without being told." He pondered.
"Do you know why your father was dismissed from the Fontclairs'
service?"

"I didn't know he was dismissed. All he told me was that he
worked at Bellegarde for a few years, then went to London. Do you
think that's why he's so bitter against the Fontclairs?"

"I think it might have something to do with it. The little I've
heard suggests he had a falling out with Lady Tarleton."

"Is that important, do you think?"

"Well, there are two possibilities. Either your father acquired
some power over the Fontclairs years ago, when he was in their
service, or it came to him recently. Tell me, did he have any contact
with the Fontclairs after he left Bellegarde? Might they have given
him money, or some other kind of assistance?"

"Oh, no, I don't think so. When he first came to London, he was very poor, and he had to work hard for a long time before he had the money to go into business for himself."

"Then it isn't likely he had any power over the Fontclairs in those days." Probably, Julian reflected, they had not given him another thought after he left Bellegarde. That fit with Guy's account of how bewildered they all were when Craddock turned up again. Or was his return really a surprise to everyone? Lady Tarleton had been so horrified to hear of it, Guy said. Could it be that, for her, it was a long-dreaded event finally coming to pass?

He asked, "Has your father any family or friends left in the neighbourhood—anyone we could talk to about his relationship with the Fontclairs?"

"He hasn't any family except me. And I don't know of any friends he has from the days when he worked at Bellegarde."

"There are always the servants. Servants know everything to the purpose about their employers' lives. That's what comes of living cheek by jowl with people who don't credit you with having ears or intellects."

"Could we question them without their getting suspicious?"

"Not possibly. But my valet could. He's very discreet. He could charm information from them without their having any idea what he was about."

"If you trust him, Mr. Kestrel, I'm prepared to trust him, too. I can't thank you enough for helping me this way. I think Mr. Fontclair is very lucky to have a friend like you."

"I hope you won't make the mistake of thinking I'm doing all this for Hugh Fontclair."

She smiled her shy smile, and the colour mounted in her cheeks.

Hugh appeared in the doorway. "Here you are, Kestrel—"

Miss Craddock got flustered. Kestrel smiled in an owlish sort of way. Hugh had a feeling he was intruding, and broke off in some confusion.

"Are you ready to go?" asked Julian.

"Oh, yes, that's why I came looking for you. Miss Craddock, I'm taking Mr. Kestrel on a tour of the estate. You're welcome to come if you like."

He never failed in his courtesy toward her, she thought—that formal courtesy that made her feel like the merest chance acquaintance. "That's very good of you, Mr. Fontclair, but I'm going on a botany outing with your sisters and Miss Pritchard."

"Oh." Hugh tried to hide his relief. He always felt so awkward around Miss Craddock. He could not imagine what he would have talked to her about for so long. "I hope you enjoy yourself."

"Thank you," she said in a small voice. She turned to Julian, her face brightening. "I've so enjoyed talking with you, Mr. Kestrel."

"The pleasure was all on my side."

"Oh, no."

"The greater part of it, then. Because in London you must meet scores of fellows like me every day of the week. We abound in the West End like ants on an anthill. But you—you're something unique. If nothing else, you've blasted the popular myth that charm can't exist with sincerity."

Hugh coughed. "If you're ready to go now, Mr. Kestrel."

Julian went with him. And not a moment too soon, said a warning voice in his head. You must be mad, flirting with the girl like that under her bridegroom's nose! I don't care if she looked as if she needed it. How many scrapes were you proposing to get into in one fortnight's visit?

He went up to his room to put on his riding boots. They had been splashed with mud at the horse fair, and he had given them to Dipper to be cleaned. Dipper had them ready for him, polished to their usual mirrorlike shine. All part of Dipper's daily routine—nothing out of the ordinary there. Indeed, as Julian said afterward, there was nothing unusual anywhere in his room when he left it. He went downstairs and out to the carriage court, where Hugh and a groom were waiting with the horses.

# *7*
# FOUL PLAY

There's nothing to be concerned about, Hugh kept telling himself. In fact, it's very jolly that Kestrel and Miss Craddock are getting on so well. If he pays her a compliment or two, what harm is there in that? Those sorts of little gallantries don't mean anything; in London, Kestrel probably hands them about like visiting cards. *I* know that—but does Miss Craddock? She's a bit naïve and unworldly. She might take him too seriously. What if she developed a *tendre* for him? Lord, it's really too much to expect of a fellow, that he should have to marry a girl who not only doesn't care a straw for him, but has fallen over head and ears in love with his best man!

But there's no reason to think that will happen. Miss Craddock is a sensible, strong-minded girl—look how hard she's tried to talk her father out of this marriage. I wonder if she'll try even harder now? Well, it would be all to the good if she did. Then we'd be out of this coil, and if she and Kestrel wanted to fall in love, they could, without impugning my honour in any way. I do have to think about my honour, even if my heart isn't engaged.

A brisk ride in fine weather did much to restore Hugh's spirits. He showed Julian the model farms Sir Robert took such pride in. They stopped at a public house in Alderton, where Hugh traded greetings with villagers home from the horse fair. He took Julian round the Fontclairs' park, with its winding lanes, idyllic groves, and pools draped round with willows. Here and there were man-made curiosities: a Chinese footbridge, a topiary castle, a Roman Temple of Mars.

"Is that Colonel Fontclair?" asked Julian, catching sight of a rider some distance away.

"It looks like Uncle Geoffrey," Hugh agreed.

"He seems in a tearing hurry."

"I expect he's just out for exercise. He rides much better than he walks, so he looks to riding to keep himself in form."

The sky was clouding over as they reached the Chase, a tract of dense forest land just north of Bellegarde. The wind rose, and the air felt heavy with unshed rain. Hugh and Julian returned to the house. It was nearly six o'clock—time to dress for dinner, which was at seven.

Julian went upstairs, but Hugh lingered in the great hall, frowning over a crack in one of his boots. He was balancing precariously on one foot, trying to look at the other, when Miss Craddock came down the grand staircase. She ran over to him eagerly.

She looked so pleased to see him, he was taken aback. She had never looked pleased to see him before. She had never seemed to feel anything about him, except regret at the wrong her father was doing him. He was oddly flattered, and a little bit thrilled. "Good afternoon," he said, almost shyly. "I hope you enjoyed your outing."

"Yes, very much, thank you." She looked beyond and around him. "Isn't Mr. Kestrel with you?"

Hugh gaped at her, then said very coolly, "No, he's not, as it happens. I think he went upstairs."

"I *did* want to speak to him!" She bit her lip. "It will just have to wait till after dinner. I'd better go and dress. Thank you, anyway." She smiled distractedly and went back upstairs.

Well, really! thought Hugh. He's certainly gotten far with her in one afternoon! How she can be so brazen?—lurking about for him, waiting to pounce on him as soon as he gets in the door! And I would have expected better of Kestrel. This kind of thing makes one wonder if he can really be a gentleman. She looks different since she met him. She smiles as though she really means it. Dash it, she's sweet and—and unspoiled, and she deserves better than to be trifled with by a worldly fellow like Kestrel. Though she ought to know better than to go all starry-eyed over a man, just because he dresses well and makes pretty speeches. I didn't think she was so shallow.

He went to his room to dress, his thoughts still in a tumult. When he got there, he stared disconsolately at his reflection in the pier glass. He thought he had never looked so countrified, unkempt, and awkward in all his life.

✳

The first strange thing Julian found on reaching his room was that the door was locked. He knocked, but no one answered. He was just thinking he would have to find a servant to let him in, when he saw the key lying on the hall table. Curious. He shrugged and unlocked the door.

He took one step into the room, and stopped. Piled neatly on a shieldback chair were a woman's shawl, bonnet, reticule, and gloves. He stared, then looked swiftly around the room. His eyes came to rest on the bed.

There was a young woman lying there, fully dressed, with the bedclothes pulled up almost to her shoulders. Her red-gold hair was half undone and spread on the pillow. Her head was turned away from him. She appeared to be asleep.

He stood blinking at her for a moment or two. Then he closed the door behind him and went over to the bed.

✳

Sir Robert and Lady Fontclair were in the conservatory. She was sewing, and he was reading aloud:

> "All Nature is but art, unknown to thee;
> All chance, direction, which thou canst not see;
> All discord, harmony not understood—"

Julian appeared in the doorway. Lady Fontclair looked up from her needlework and smiled. "Mr. Kestrel, good evening. We were just talking about you and Hugh—wondering if you'd come back yet, and hoping you wouldn't be caught in the rain."

She glanced out through the glass walls at the dark clouds massing in the sky. Wind whirled through the terrace garden, beating at the flowers and bending back the crowns of trees.

"No, we escaped the storm." In a manner of speaking, he thought grimly. "I'm sorry to intrude, but I need to speak with you, Sir Robert—on a matter of business."

"As you wish. But since we're dining in an hour, and none of us has dressed, do you think it might wait till after dinner?"

"I think it would be better if we spoke now. I'm sorry."

Lady Fontclair's eyes darkened with concern. She was shrewder than her husband, Julian thought. She knew, even from the little he had said, that something was gravely wrong.

Sir Robert rose. Just then a fierce gust of wind flung open the French windows leading to the terrace. "Those windows are always blowing open," said Lady Fontclair. "We really ought to change them so that they open out rather than in."

She would have closed them, but Sir Robert said, "Don't get up, my dear, I'll do it." He bolted the windows to keep them secure, and he and Julian went out.

"Is this strictly a matter of business?" Sir Robert asked. "Because if it is, I suggest we go to my office."

"It might be better if we went to my room. There's—something there I need to show you."

"As you wish." Sir Robert threw him a dubious look.

They went to Julian's room. He had kept the door locked while he was gone; now he opened it and stood aside. Sir Robert walked in. When he saw the girl in the bed, he stopped short, so that Julian nearly ran into him. "What is this?" he exclaimed. "Who is this woman?"

"I don't know. I found her here when I got back from riding."

"I demand to know the meaning of this, Mr. Kestrel. Is the girl ill?"

"The girl is dead."

"Dead! Are you sure?"

"She isn't breathing. She has no pulse. I put my ear to her chest, but I couldn't hear her heart. I held up a mirror to her face, and no mist formed on the glass. After that, I knew there was nothing to be done for her."

It was strange to him how cold and detached his voice sounded. That was not at all how he had felt at the time, searching vainly for signs of life in the girl, unwilling to believe she could really be dead. But then he had seen the washstand—

"She's turning cold," said Sir Robert, who had been feeling for a pulse in her throat.

"Yes, only just. Perhaps she hasn't been dead very long." He added, "I haven't disarranged anything in the room. It's just as it was when I found her. You're a magistrate, I believe?"

Sir Robert's face was very still. Only his eyes were alive, staring down at the girl. It seemed to Julian that he had not heard the question. But at length he answered, without looking up, "Yes."

"Then I shall consider I'm reporting this crime to the proper legal authority."

"What makes you so sure it's a crime? We don't know how the girl died."

"Look." Julian walked round the bed to the washstand. The gilt ewer, which ordinarily stood on a shelf beneath the basin, had been left on the floor. It was nearly empty, but the basin was half full of water. The water was a reddish colour, and the white towel draped over the towel rack was smeared with red-brown stains.

Sir Robert strode to the bed and flung back the bedclothes. The two men braced themselves for a grisly sight—but there was no sign of a wound. They gazed at the girl for a long time in silence.

She was small, slight, and delicately beautiful. Her hair was done up in a knot at the back of her head, but loose strands lay along the pillow, their red-gold colour uncannily bright. Her hands were at her sides, the fingers slack and slightly curled. Her legs lay straight, with the feet turned out. She was very pale. Blue veins showed through her skin, especially on her eyelids. She wore a pale yellow muslin dress, simple and modest, with puffed sleeves and a blue sash. An amber necklace encircled her throat.

"One of her earrings is missing," Julian noticed. The other was still in her ear, a gold teardrop set with an aquamarine. He felt around her head and under the pillow, but the lost earring was not there.

He stepped back. His gaze travelled to the foot of the bed, where the bedclothes were piled. They consisted of a heavy crimson coverlet and a sheet. He looked at the sheet more closely, and all at once he stiffened. On the white linen was a red-brown stain shaped almost like a rose. He drew the sheet up to the girl's neck, and the stain came to rest a little way below her waist.

The two men looked at each other grimly. "We ought to have a doctor," Julian said.

"Dr. MacGregor is coming to dinner tonight." Sir Robert looked at his watch. "It's a quarter after six. He's very likely on his way now. When he arrives, I'll ask him to examine the girl. In the meantime—" He surveyed the room. "Was there anything else out of order when you came in?"

"I haven't looked closely. Once I found she was dead, I only stayed long enough to make a quick search, to see if anyone was hiding here. I looked in the wardrobe and the water closet and behind the curtains, but there was no one here. I did find these, which I assume are hers."

He showed Sir Robert the garments on the shieldback chair by the wall. There was a blue, grey, and yellow India shawl, a straw bonnet with long blue ribbons and a thick veil, a blue reticule of netted silk, and a pair of pale grey gloves.

"They're lying just as I found them," Julian said. He picked up a corner of the shawl. "This has been treated pretty roughly. Look, it's stained with dirt, the fringe is tangled, and there are a good many pulled threads. The gloves are soiled, too. I wonder where she's been today?"

He went back to the bed. It might be useful to make a sort of catalogue of observations—and, useful or not, he found it a soothing way to occupy his mind. "Her dress is dirty, too, and there are grass stains all along the bottom. The hem's been pulled down on the left side, and there's a piece of it torn away."

Sir Robert said abruptly, "When were you last in this room before you discovered the girl?"

That stern, official tone chilled Julian. He realized they were no

longer talking as one gentleman to another. He was being inter-
rogated. "I came here to put on my boots just before your son and
I went riding. I think we left at about half past three."

"Was anyone here with you?"

"My manservant. He helped me put on my boots."

"Did he remain here after you left?"

"I think so, but I don't know how long."

"He will have to be questioned. And when did you return from
riding?"

"A few minutes before six. I came straight up here, and that was
when I found her. Here's a strange thing: When I got here, the
door was locked. The key was just outside, on the hall table. The
last person in the room before me must have locked the door on his
way out. Why? If the girl were dead—"

"Perhaps she wasn't."

"You think someone might have intended to lock her in?"

"I don't know," said Sir Robert. "But locking a door from the
outside serves only to prevent someone *inside* from coming *out*, not
the other way around."

"But if she was alive when whoever locked the door left her here,
then how did she die?"

He bent over the girl, scrutinized her face and hair, and lifted
her eyelids. Her blue eyes were clouded, the pupils unnaturally large.
He looked closely at her hands, laying each one in turn on his palm
and spreading out the small, childish fingers. His gaze scanned her
limbs and lingered on her belly and hips. Despite the ominous smear
on the lower part of the sheet, there were no bloodstains or tears in
her dress to suggest rape.

"With your permission, Sir Robert?"

Sir Robert nodded. Julian carefully rolled the girl onto her side.
The two men gasped, and Julian's fingers tightened involuntarily in
her flesh.

There was a small tear in her dress, midway down her back and
a little to the left. The silk chemise underneath was torn, too, and
the frayed material around the tears was sticky with blood. Julian
delicately put a finger and thumb through the holes and parted the
material. There was a wound in her back, about an inch long and

pointed at either end. The sheet she lay on was soaked with blood where her wound had pressed against it.

He laid her down again gently. "A matter for the doctor, I think."

Sir Robert put a hand to his brow for a moment and closed his eyes. When he took his hand away, his face was reasonably composed. "There's a great deal to be done. Steps must be taken at once to investigate this matter. The household will have to be informed, and the servants questioned. There may well be someone in the house who knows the girl and can explain her presence here. I take it you have no idea who she is."

"No. Not the slightest."

Sir Robert eyed him narrowly for a moment. "I think you had better come with me for the present, Mr. Kestrel. I may need you further."

Julian saw all too clearly that Sir Robert did not trust him. That was hardly surprising: the girl had been found in his room and his bed, after all. Yet it revolted him that he should be suspected of having anything to do with a vicious assault on a woman. For God's sake, keep a cool head, he cautioned himself. Don't give in to the urge to defend yourself, unless and until you've been openly accused.

They went out, and Julian locked the door behind them. He turned to find Sir Robert holding out his hand. "You'd best give me the key."

Julian felt a strange reluctance to give it up. But Sir Robert was a magistrate and the master of the house. He handed over the key, and Sir Robert put it in his waistcoat pocket. "Come," he said. "We'll go to my office."

✳

Sir Robert's office was on the upper floor of the servants' wing. He and Julian passed through the servants' hall on the way. Some of the servants were sitting round the communal table, talking and laughing after their dinner. Dipper was among them, chatting with a pretty maidservant in a mobcap (and doing rather well for himself, it seemed to Julian). Next door, the kitchen staff could be heard preparing dinner for the Fontclairs and their guests.

The servants stood up when Sir Robert and Julian came in. Sir

Robert told a footman to send Travis, the butler, to his office at once. Then he and Julian went out, followed by the servants' curious gazes.

While they waited for Travis, Julian asked, "Do you have to go through the servants' hall to get to your office?"

"Yes. The screens passage into the servants' hall is the only means of access from the main house to the servants' wing. I don't relish constantly passing through the servants' quarters, any more than they probably care for my coming among them unexpectedly. But I don't choose to conduct estate or magisterial business in my family's part of the house. Tenants and villagers come to see me or my clerk at all hours, with all manner of complaints about rents and tithes, or reports of petty crimes. I don't wish to have my family and guests disturbed by such matters."

Travis came in. He was an elderly man with a tonsure of bright white hair. His athletic frame and ramrod-straight stance suggested the retired military man.

Sir Robert issued a series of terse instructions. Travis was to gather all the servants in the servants' hall. Mrs. Cox, the housekeeper, was to keep order there and allow no one to leave without Sir Robert's permission. Anyone who disobeyed would be suspected of complicity in a felony. Rawlinson, Sir Robert's clerk, was to ride to Alderton at once and bring back Stephen Senderby, the parish constable.

Sir Robert gave no explanation for any of these orders, and Travis, though visibly startled, asked for none. Sir Robert eyed him measuringly. "I know you're well able to handle a gun. Take one from the gun room and load it. I want you to search the house as unobtrusively as possible, consistent with thoroughness. Report to me any evidence that an intruder has entered by any door or window. I trust you won't need the gun, but there is a chance you may meet with a stranger who'll give you trouble."

Travis stood straighter than ever. "What sort of intruder am I looking for, sir?"

"I don't know yet. When I've investigated this matter more fully, I shall be in a position to explain what's happened and why I've taken these precautions. For the present, I am counting on you to act discreetly and conscientiously to secure the safety of Bellegarde."

"Yes, sir!"

"One more thing. You'll find the door to Mr. Kestrel's room locked. Don't make any attempt to enter. But look carefully under his window for any sign that someone might have climbed in that way."

Which we know can be done, Julian suddenly remembered, because Guy said he used to get in and out through that window when he was a boy.

After the butler had gone, Sir Robert said, "Travis is the man I most trust, of all the staff. He served under my uncle in the American war, and he's been at Bellegarde for many years."

"This Senderby—what sort of man is he?"

"Honest and dutiful. Not as resolute as perhaps a constable ought to be. I'm afraid the post was thrust upon him somewhat against his will. His usual employment is as a shoemaker and mender of harness. Now, if you'll excuse me, I must tell Lady Fontclair what's happened. I wish I could spare her this news, but I know she wouldn't wish to be spared. She has always been, and always will be, in my confidence in any matter touching the welfare of this house."

"May I be useful somehow?"

"Please be good enough to wait for me here. I won't be long."

Left alone, Julian shook his head, thinking of Senderby. A shoemaker and mender of harness! Was there anything more incongruous and ill-suited for its purpose than the English system of police?

# ∗8∗
# THE DOCTOR
# AND THE DANDY

Dr. MacGregor's gig creaked and swayed as it pulled up in front of Bellegarde. For years now, the wheelwright in Alderton had been angling to build him a new one. But MacGregor had been driving his ramshackle carriage for well over a quarter of a century, and he had no intention of breaking in a new one, when this one had served him so well.

He climbed down from the gig, ignoring the twinge of rheumatism in his joints. Taking out his medical bag, which he carried with him even on social visits, he went to the front door. He had no qualms about leaving the gig in the drive. He knew from long experience that the mare would stay put for the time being without anyone to look after her. She was not much to look at, but she was reliable. This was more or less MacGregor's view of himself as well.

He rang the bell and stood drumming his fingers on the doorjamb till he heard the scrape of the door being unbarred. It opened, and Travis said, "Good evening, sir."

This was MacGregor's first surprise. Ordinarily the front door was opened by a footman. "Good evening, Travis. Anything wrong? You look a little green about the gills."

Travis barred the door again, thrusting the heavy oak beam resolutely into its sockets. MacGregor eyed him sharply. He dined at

Bellegarde nearly every Friday evening, and he could not recall the front door ever being barred at this hour before.

"I'm very well, sir, thank you," said Travis, taking MacGregor's hat. He would have taken his medical bag as well, but some instinct prompted MacGregor to hold on to it. "Would you be so good as to step into Sir Robert's office? He asked me to bring you there directly you arrived. I'll send a boy from the stable to look after your horse and gig."

"His office? Look here, man, what's going on? Something's very wrong here."

"I don't know what's going on, sir. I only know Sir Robert asked me to conduct you to his office, and after that I've other orders of his to carry out."

"So you want me to make haste, is that it? Well, of course I'll do as Sir Robert wishes—but I'll do it with a much better will once someone explains to me what's afoot in this house!"

Travis brought MacGregor through the screens passage into the servants' hall. All the servants were gathered round the large oak table. They looked mightily nervous, MacGregor thought. Mrs. Cox, the housekeeper, sat at the head of the table, prim and stern in a high-necked dress the same iron-grey colour as her hair. As MacGregor and Travis entered, she was glaring, arms akimbo, at a pretty young girl in a mobcap. "Now, Molly Dale," she was saying, "you're to ask no more questions. Sir Robert will tell you in his own good time whatever you need to know."

MacGregor wished the servants good evening. There was a low murmur of response, then a sudden loud wail from Dorcas, the kitchen maid: "Someone's dying, I know it, or the doctor wouldn't be here!"

A nervous start ran through the servants. Mrs. Cox cried sharply, "Don't be silly, Dorcas! Dr. MacGregor's here because he was invited to dinner, the same as he is every Friday."

"I don't know myself what's amiss," said MacGregor. "But whatever it is, we'll soon put it right, you'll see."

They moved on to Sir Robert's office. MacGregor went in, looking eagerly around for Sir Robert. But instead he found a stranger—a young man, very nattily dressed in riding clothes. He stood with one arm resting on the mantelpiece, and one ankle crossed in front of the other. An effective sort of pose—too effective by half. A coxcomb, MacGregor thought.

Travis bowed and withdrew. The coxcomb came forward, extending his hand. "How do you do? I'm Julian Kestrel."

"Duncan MacGregor."

They shook hands. MacGregor expected the coxcomb to offer him a few limp fingers, but Mr. Kestrel's grip was surprisingly firm.

"What's going on here?" MacGregor rapped out. "Where's Sir Robert?"

"He went to speak with Lady Fontclair. I'm expecting him back at any moment."

MacGregor eyed him, taking his measure. Evidently the young man was used to being looked at—a coxcomb would be, MacGregor supposed. He stood at his ease, with lifted brows and a faint, quizzical smile.

"You're Hugh's groomsman, aren't you?"

"I have that honour, yes."

"Maybe you can tell me what's going on in this house. The instant I came through the door, Travis barred it behind me as though we were under siege. Instead of being taken to the drawing room, I find myself hustled into Sir Robert's office. All the servants are in a taking, Sir Robert's nowhere to be seen, and here you are making yourself at home as coolly as you please."

"I'm sorry if I seem unconcerned. I can't see that my kicking up hell's delight would do anyone any good. I'd explain what this is about, but I think Sir Robert wants to tell you himself. He should be back shortly."

"Look here, if somebody's ill, I ought to be with that person, not cooling my heels in here!"

"No one is ill, Doctor. If you must know, someone is dead. No one Sir Robert knows," he added, seeing the quick concern in MacGregor's eyes.

"What have you to do with this?"

"I found her—the body, I mean."

"Are you sure she's dead?"

"Quite sure."

"It sounds like a nasty business."

"It is."

MacGregor paced back and forth, ruffling up the hair at the back of his neck. His hair was thick, black, and spiky, and so was his beard. He looked, thought Julian, like one of the noisier Old Testament prophets. "How did she die?"

"I think Sir Robert means to ask you that."

"I ought to be taken to examine the body at once! What's the point of all this delay?"

"We're waiting for Sir Robert. He has the key to the room where the body is."

"Well, why didn't you say so from the beginning?"

"I can't imagine. I can see I've been extraordinarily remiss."

"See here, young man, there's nothing in this situation to smile about!"

"No, Doctor, nothing whatever. So I'm all the more grateful you made me feel, for a moment, that there was."

"Stuff and nonsense!" said MacGregor, sitting down very hard in a stiff-backed chair.

He was up again a moment later, when Sir Robert came in. "Good evening, Doctor," he said. "I'm glad to see you."

"This fellow's just told me there's been a death in the house."

"Yes, I'm afraid so." Sir Robert sat down at his desk. "Knowing you would be coming this evening, I've made only a cursory examination of the body. I should like you to examine it, if you would."

"Of course, of course. But who's dead, and how did it happen?"

"We don't know who she is. As to how she died, she seems to have been stabbed in the back, but we don't know for sure if that caused her death. I hope you can tell us."

"Do you mean to say a woman's been *murdered?*"

"It appears so," said Sir Robert. "She's a young girl—perhaps eighteen—well dressed. Very pretty," he added after a short pause.

"Where is she? Is she in the house?"

"She's in Mr. Kestrel's room—in his bed, actually."

MacGregor started, blinked, and turned a scandalized gaze on Julian.

Julian lost no time in explaining. "I found her there this evening when I came back from riding. I have no idea who she is, or how she came to be in my room—or my bed." He knit his brows. "She couldn't have been in the bed when she was killed, or not in that position. She was stabbed in the back, and she was lying on her back when I found her, with the bedclothes pulled up to her neck."

"Are you telling me someone killed the girl, and then tucked her into bed as if she were having a nap?"

"I realize it sounds peculiar, but that seems to be what happened, yes."

MacGregor shot him a darkling look, then turned to Sir Robert. "I'd best examine the girl at once."

"If you'll come with me, I'll let you into Mr. Kestrel's room. I've been keeping it locked to ensure that nothing is disturbed. Mr. Kestrel, would you be good enough to accompany us?"

Lest I make a dash for the Continent, Julian thought. "Certainly," he said pleasantly.

MacGregor shook his head, thinking: And I took him for a coxcomb! By God, I hope he's nothing more dangerous!

※

Even though Julian knew what he would find when they got to his room, he still felt a jolt when he saw the dead girl lying in the bed where he had slept last night. The bedclothes were heaped at her feet, as he and Sir Robert had left them. She looked very tiny in the massive Elizabethan bed.

MacGregor gazed at her sadly, then summoned his brisk, professional manner. "I'll work best alone. Give me half an hour or so, and I'll let you know what I've found out."

"Very well." Sir Robert sighed. "I'm afraid it's time I told the family."

"No one knows yet?" said MacGregor.

"Only the three of us and Lady Fontclair."

"How is she taking it?"

"She's distressed, naturally, but she's kept her head, as I knew she would. Of course her first concern was to ensure that Joanna and Philippa were safe. We went to the schoolroom and found them having their tea with Miss Pritchard. Everything was peaceable there—they hadn't seen or heard anything out of the common. We told Miss Pritchard to keep the schoolroom locked, and on no account to leave it or let the children leave it until I give permission. I'm afraid we made her very uneasy. I hope she says and does nothing to upset the children."

"This whole business is bound to upset them," said MacGregor. "But don't be too concerned about that. Children are very hardy—it's easy to dash them down, but they bounce right up again. And your girls are stronger and healthier than most."

"Thank you," Sir Robert said quietly, but with feeling. "You're very kind."

MacGregor shrugged. "I'll just ask Mr. Kestrel a few questions, and then I'll get to work. You say she was under the bedclothes when you found her?"

"Yes," said Julian.

"Both the sheet and the coverlet?"

"Yes."

"Hmm." MacGregor ran his hands over the girl's face and neck. "Was she cold when you found her?"

"Colder than a living person, but not stone cold. I remember thinking she must not have been dead very long."

"You can't go by that. The bedclothes might have kept her warm, at least for a good while. She's cold now. How long has it been since you uncovered her?"

"When was it?" Julian asked Sir Robert. "Half past six?"

"A little earlier, I think."

"And when did you find her?"

"A few minutes before six o'clock."

MacGregor looked at his watch. It was a little after seven. "Was the window closed when you came in? It might have made a difference in how long it took her to cool, if there was a free ventilation of air in the room."

"I remember it was closed, because I looked to see if anyone might have got out that way. In any event, it must have been closed, because it's closed now, and neither Sir Robert nor I closed it, and no one but us has been in here since I found the girl."

"Well, that's sensible enough, I suppose." MacGregor went over to the window. "*Could* anybody have got out this way?"

Julian followed him. "It would be easy enough to climb down that tree to the ground. What would be hard—impossible, in fact—would be to climb out of the window and then bolt it from the inside."

They exchanged puzzled glances. For not only was the window closed, but the bolts were shot into place.

"The murderer couldn't have got out this way anyway," said Julian. "If I'd thought more carefully, I would have realized that. Whoever was last in the room before I came in would have had to leave by the door, in order to lock it from the outside and leave the key on the hall table. Which means the killer most likely went out through the door, but might have come in through either the door or the window."

"What about the girl? You don't think *she* got in by climbing trees?"

"Well, that might have been how she tore her dress at the hem. But I admit it's implausible."

"Well, I'm glad you admit something," grumbled MacGregor. "So we've got a door locked from the outside, and a window locked from the inside. My God, if the killer left the room through the door, he must have walked straight through the house! How could it be that no one saw him?"

Julian turned to Sir Robert. "When I went looking for you after I found the girl, I didn't see any servants in the main house. The place was as quiet as a tomb." He grimaced at the figure of speech. "I beg your pardon. What I mean to say is, it might have been quite easy for the killer to slip out unobserved."

"There often isn't anyone in the main house between half past four and six," said Sir Robert. "That's when the servants have their dinner."

"Is that generally known?" asked Julian.

"I don't know what you mean by 'generally known.' It's known to the members of my household. Mr. Kestrel, can you be implying that someone familiar with the routine of this house killed the girl, feeling confident that he would be able to get out without being seen?"

"The possibility did cross my mind. Needless to say, I wasn't thinking of anyone in particular, and I should be happy to believe that no one at Bellegarde is involved."

"Thank you," Sir Robert said icily. "I have no doubt that my servants are wholly innocent of this crime. Nevertheless, I shall have them questioned, and publicly cleared of suspicion. Will that content you?"

"I never doubted you would do everything justice demands," said Julian. "The question of contenting me doesn't arise."

Sir Robert turned to MacGregor. "Do you think you'll be able to tell us when she died?"

"None too precisely, I'm sorry to say. But I'll do my best."

Julian showed MacGregor the blood in the washbasin and on the towel. MacGregor whistled under his breath. "What a cool customer! Washed his hands afterward, and most likely the weapon, too! By God, if there's any justice on earth, we'll hang the person who did this!"

Sir Robert closed his eyes. After a moment, he opened them and said heavily, "Mr. Kestrel and I will leave you to your work. Will you be good enough to come to my office when you've finished?"

"Yes."

Sir Robert gave him the key to the room, so that he could lock the door behind him when he left. "Now then, Mr. Kestrel, I think before we speak to my family, we should go to my office and see if Senderby's arrived. I want him to begin questioning the servants as soon as possible."

✳

There were two men waiting in Sir Robert's office. Julian recognized one of them as Rawlinson, Sir Robert's clerk. He was about thirty years old and as soberly dressed as a curate, with dark smooth hair and a complexion delicate as a girl's. He was sitting at a table with pen, ink, and paper ready to hand. Beside him was a tall, lanky man in his early forties. He had limp, straw-coloured hair and watery blue eyes. His front teeth protruded a little, giving him the look of a large, ungainly hare. He was leaning forward, his arms resting on his knees, his hat dangling loosely from his hands. He carried a small truncheon, and a pair of handcuffs hung from his belt.

On seeing Sir Robert, he clambered to his feet. "You sent for me, sir?"

"This is Stephen Senderby, the parish constable," Sir Robert said to Julian. "Senderby, this is Mr. Julian Kestrel, who has reported a crime that I wish to have investigated without delay. Rawlinson, you are to attend me this evening and take notes."

Sir Robert gave Senderby a terse but thorough account of the crime. As he listened, Senderby's shoulders drooped, and he twisted his hat between his hands. From time to time he cast his eyes around the room, as though longing for some means of escape. Rawlinson, in contrast, went to work with a will, jotting down the details of the murder as though they were so many rent rates and harvest statistics. But Julian noticed that, as Sir Robert described the girl and told how she had been found in Julian's bed, Rawlinson pressed his lips tightly together, and a blush spread over his fine skin.

Sir Robert ordered Senderby to describe the murdered girl to the servants and ask them if they had ever seen such a person at or near Bellegarde. More particularly, he was to find out if any of them had seen the girl today or knew how she got into the house. "Don't tell them yet that she's been murdered," he said. "Simply relate what I've told you of her physical traits and clothing. If anyone knows anything about her, bring that person to my office. I shall wish to question him or her myself."

Senderby was then to ascertain the whereabouts of each of the servants during the latter part of the afternoon. "Better yet," said Sir Robert, "find out if you can which of the servants was last in Mr. Kestrel's room, and when that person left. Then attempt to discover where each of the servants was between that time and six o'clock. You may wish to take a pencil and paper with you, to note down their answers."

Rawlinson found a pencil and notebook for Senderby, who pocketed them with mournful resignation. "I'll do my best, sir. But, sir—"

"Yes?"

"Well, sir, excuse the liberty, but won't the servants want to know why I'm asking all these questions?"

"Tell them you are acting on my orders—and my orders are that for the present you should ask questions, not answer them." He turned to Julian. "In the meantime, would you be so good as to accompany me to the drawing room, Mr. Kestrel?"

# *9*
# SIR ROBERT
# BREAKS THE NEWS

Lady Tarleton was the last of the Fontclairs and Craddocks to come down to dinner. Mark Craddock watched her closely as she entered the drawing room. She took no notice of him. Maud blushed and looked searchingly from her father to Lady Tarleton and back again.

"Good evening, Catherine," said Lady Fontclair. "I'm afraid dinner's been delayed. Robert is dealing with a tiresome business matter that simply can't wait."

"What sort of business matter?" Lady Tarleton said sharply.

"I believe it's something Mr. Kestrel brought to his attention."

"What business can Robert have with Mr. Kestrel?"

Lady Fontclair hesitated for a moment. "I'm sure if it's anything important, Robert will tell us."

Lady Tarleton stood tapping her fan against her hand. "How long is dinner to be delayed?"

"Not very long, I hope!" Lady Fontclair said, smiling. "I know some of the gentlemen have been out riding, and they must be as hungry as hunters by now."

Sir Robert and Julian joined them soon after. Julian observed them with heightened awareness, in this final moment of calm before they learned of the murder. Lady Fontclair was seated on a sofa beside Maud. Craddock sat as though enthroned, in a high-backed chair.

Hugh and Isabelle were in one of the window recesses, talking about the relative merits of *Lycidas* and *Paradise Lost*. Lady Tarleton stood by the other window, staring out with unseeing eyes. The colonel sat a little apart, his face in shadow. Guy was seated at a tripod table, energetically playing patience.

Everyone looked up when Sir Robert and Julian entered. Lady Fontclair went to Sir Robert and laid her hand on his arm. Craddock's gaze was expectant. Guy's was curious. Catherine's demanded an explanation. No one else seemed more than mildly interested to know what had delayed their dinner.

"I have something to tell you all," said Sir Robert. "I hope you will try not to be alarmed. I assure you, all appropriate steps have been taken to resolve the matter swiftly and safely." His voice began to falter, like a music box running down. "I thought it was time I told you. I'm—afraid—the news may—come as a shock—"

Everyone stared at him. Hugh got up and came quickly to his side.

"What is it, Robert?" stammered Colonel Fontclair.

"A young woman has been found dead in this house. We don't know yet who she is."

There were murmurs, gasps, the rustle of silk dresses, the scraping of chairs.

"What?" shrieked Lady Tarleton.

Guy came to his feet, knocking over the tripod table and scattering playing cards all over the floor. "Dead? Did you say a woman's been found *dead?*"

"Yes," said Sir Robert. "I'm afraid it's true. Dr. MacGregor is examining her to determine when and how she died. But already it appears that she died by violence—that, in fact, she was murdered."

There was absolute stillness.

The first person to move or make a sound was Maud, who ran to her father. Craddock put an arm around her shoulders, and she nestled against him—like a little bird taking shelter, thought Hugh.

"My God, Robert," Geoffrey whispered.

"What are you saying?" cried Catherine, clutching wildly at her hair. "Robert, what's the meaning of this? I demand to know at

once! Do you mean to say there's a strange woman, dead, *murdered*
—here—in our house?"

"Please try to be calm, Catherine. I must remind you that the
children and the servants will look to us to set an example. If we
are not unduly alarmed, they won't be, either."

"How can we not be alarmed? Robert, what are we to do? How
are we to— to—"

"I've commenced an investigation." He described how he had
ordered Travis to search the house, and Senderby to question the
servants.

"Surely you don't suspect any of the servants?" said Lady Fontclair.

"No, my dear, of course not. But that is all the more reason to
have them formally cleared of suspicion at once—to ensure that no
rash and ill-founded accusations are made against them."

"Is there anybody you *do* suspect?" asked Geoffrey.

Sir Robert eyed him narrowly for a moment. "It's too early to
say. I have no information about the criminal, and very little about
the girl. She was perhaps eighteen years old, with reddish hair and
blue eyes. She was wearing a yellow dress—and a shawl, I think—"
He looked to Julian for confirmation.

"A fringed shawl with an India print in blue and yellow. And
she had a bonnet with long blue streamers and a heavy veil. She was
small and slight, and very beautiful."

By the time he finished this speech, all eyes were fixed on him.
"How do *you* know so much about it, Mr. Kestrel?" Lady Tarleton
demanded.

"It was I who found her body."

"Where?" asked Geoffrey.

"In my room."

There was a chorus of sharp, indrawn breaths. For what seemed
to him like the hundredth time, Julian explained that he had found
the girl dead when he got back from riding, and had no idea who
she was.

"How did she die?" Guy asked blankly.

"Dr. MacGregor should be able to tell us for certain," said Sir
Robert. "But it appears she was stabbed in the back."

"Do you mean to act as magistrate in this matter?" asked Craddock abruptly.

"I am a magistrate, and the crime took place in my house. I should have thought it obvious that the matter falls within my authority."

"You're not concerned that people may make charges of partiality?"

"I can assure you, Mr. Craddock, that if I doubted for a moment my ability to act impartially, I would turn this investigation over to another magistrate. I have no such doubts. Should the evidence implicate one of my servants or tenants, I shall commit that person for trial without hesitation. But I think it far more likely that some stranger entered the house—why, I have no idea—and killed the girl, leaving her body in Mr. Kestrel's room. Whether the murderer brought her with him or found her here—again, I don't know. You've all heard her described. Does she sound familiar to any of you?"

No, they said, none of them knew such a person.

Julian's glance lit on Isabelle. She was pale, and her eyes were very grave, but after the first wave of shock she had regained her composure. She was like a quiet pool that may be shaken by ripples, but always subsides back into a beautiful, cool stillness.

Lady Tarleton was haranguing Sir Robert again. "This is a nightmare—an outrage! Why, the murderer could still be here in the house!"

"He's far more likely to have put the greatest possible distance between himself and Bellegarde. But as a precaution I'm having Travis search the house, as I told you before."

"I for one don't intend to stir a step from this room until he's found!" Lady Tarleton walked about, wringing her hands. "How can such a thing happen under our roof? Great heavens, what will people *say?*"

"I hope that by the time this becomes generally known, we'll have discovered who the girl is and arrested her murderer," said Sir Robert. "The sooner the crime is solved, the less likely it is to become a cause célèbre."

"What's going to happen, Robert?" Geoffrey asked hoarsely. "Are we going to have Bow Street Runners nosing about the place?"

"I shall do everything I can to protect our privacy," said Sir Robert coldly. "I can't promise you I shall succeed."

"Is this going to interfere with the wedding in any way?" said Craddock. "Because I tell you here and now, I don't see why it should, and I'll take it in very bad part if it does."

"Of course, Mr. Craddock, you've guessed it!" cried Lady Tarleton. "It's all a plot to interfere with the wedding! We induced some dangerous lunatic to creep into Bellegarde and slaughter a woman in Mr. Kestrel's room—and all to keep your daughter from marrying Hugh! Confess it, Robert! You know that's what we did!"

Lady Fontclair ran to her. "Sit down, my dear. I know it's been a terrible shock. We're fairly reeling with it, all of us. Let me ring for a drink of water for you."

"I've asked the servants to remain in the servants' hall," Sir Robert reminded her.

"I'll get you a drink of water, Aunt," said Hugh.

"Make it a bottle of wine, can't you?" Guy called after him. "Or better still, brandy. Never mind, I'll come with you."

They went out. Isabelle emerged from the window recess and started gathering up the playing cards Guy had left strewn on the floor.

Sir Robert asked everyone to remain in the drawing room until dinner, which the servants would resume preparing as soon as Senderby finished questioning them. "When will *you* dine, Robert?" asked Lady Fontclair.

"Very late, I imagine. Don't worry. I should find it impossible to sit down to dinner, with so many puzzles hanging over my head. Now, if you'll excuse me, I must find out if Senderby or Dr. MacGregor has anything to report. Mr. Kestrel, I'm afraid I must ask you once again to come with me."

On his way out, Julian caught Miss Craddock's eye. Are you all right? his lifted brows asked. She looked white and frightened, but she nodded, and even managed a wavering smile.

*

Senderby was feeling miserably unequal to his task. He had never wanted to be constable of Alderton. He had yielded to the urging of his neighbours, who insisted he had more time for the job than most men in the parish. His shoemaking business was apt to be slow, except in the weeks just after the harvest, when people had money in their pockets. And he was tall and strapping—just the right build for a constable, everyone said. But what did he know about questioning servants and tracking murderers? Till now, he'd had nothing more alarming to deal with than rounding up vagrants for the house of correction, or breaking up fights between farm labourers who'd had a drop too many. Once he had arrested a petty thief, and that was unpleasant enough—but murder! And murder of a woman! And at Bellegarde, right under Sir Robert Fontclair's nose! Oh, Lord, he thought, I wish I was anywhere but here, and anybody but myself tonight!

Now he had to question some forty servants—for that was how many there were, including the indoor and outdoor staff of Bellegarde and the servants who came with guests. Forty of them and only one of him! He could hardly get a word in edgewise, with all their questions and exclamations.

Mrs. Cox, the housekeeper, made some attempt to keep order, but she was too taken up with her own sense of injury to be much use. "If Sir Robert hasn't seen fit to take *me* into his confidence, and I in his service for fifteen years, and always as loyal and discreet as could be wished, then I can't think why any of *you* should have cause to complain at being kept in the dark."

It was a relief to Senderby when Sir Robert and Mr. Kestrel returned from the drawing room. They took him aside, and Sir Robert asked what he had found out so far.

"Please you, sir, nobody seems to know who the girl is, and nobody remembers seeing her today."

"No one knows any young woman who fits her description?"

"Not as how they can recall, sir. A couple of the servants thought they might know her, but when we talked it out, we found they couldn't have been thinking of the same person. That was as far as we got, sir. Except—"

"Except what?" Sir Robert prompted.

"Am I to tell you everything they said?"

"If it pertains to the matter we're investigating, yes."

"Well, sir—one of the grooms said the girl was most likely an acquaintance of Master Guy's."

"What made him think that?"

"It was mostly meant as a joke, sir, because I said the girl was young and good-looking, and—well, sir—Master Guy—"

"Quite so," Sir Robert said drily. He turned to the servants. "Has any of you seen any stranger at or near Bellegarde today?"

They all looked at each other, shrugged, shook their heads.

"Are you certain? This is extremely important."

They gave every appearance of racking their brains, but their answer remained the same.

Sir Robert thought for a moment. "Lady Fontclair had morning callers. Is it possible someone attending them remained behind after they left?"

The servants were positive no one had stayed behind. Asked who else had visited the house today, they said several tradesmen made deliveries to the kitchen, the blacksmith stopped by the stables, and two farmers went to see Rawlinson with a boundary dispute. All these people were well known to the servants. More to the point, they had all been seen to leave Bellegarde by early afternoon.

"Which of you was last in Mr. Kestrel's room?" Sir Robert asked next.

There was a buzz of excitement. Julian found himself the target of some forty curious stares.

At last Dipper stood up. "I think that would've been me, sir."

"And what were you doing there?"

"Tidying up, sir, and getting me master's dinner togs ready to put on when he come home."

"Do you remember what time you left your master's room?"

Dipper wet his lips. Julian knew that gesture of old—Dipper did it when he was nervous or playing for time. "It wasn't quite half past four, sir."

"How do you recall that so precisely?"

"I had a look at the clock, sir, to see how much time I had before dinner."

"And why did you want to know that?"

Dipper looked down, looked up again, swallowed. " 'Coz I wanted to go for a walk, sir. I'd been indoors most of the day."

"The servants dine at half past four. That didn't leave you much time for a walk."

"No, sir. I was late to dinner."

The mobcapped maid, Molly Dale, started to giggle. Sir Robert gave her a look, and she clapped her hands over her mouth.

"So you went for a walk?" Sir Robert pursued.

"Yes, sir."

"Where did you walk?"

"Outside. Round about."

"Round about the house, you mean?"

"Yes, sir."

"Think carefully. Are you quite sure you didn't see a red-haired young woman in a yellow dress, either near your master's room or outside the house?"

"No, sir."

"And you didn't see any stranger going to or from your master's room?"

"*No,* sir. I'd have nabbed any cove what went upon the ding around me master's room."

"Does that mean, you didn't see anyone?"

"No, sir."

"What about while you were out walking? Did you see any stranger going toward the house—or running away from it, perhaps?"

"No, sir," said Dipper, with lowered eyes.

"May I ask a question?" said Julian.

Sir Robert inclined his head.

"When you left my room, were the windows closed?"

"Yes, sir. I closed 'em meself."

"And bolted them?"

"Yes, sir. If you don't bolt 'em, they rattles a bit when it's windy. I noticed it last night."

So much for the theory that anyone climbed in through the window, Julian thought. "What about the key to my room? Do you remember where you last saw it?"

"It would've been in the door, sir."

"It would have been, or it was?"

"I don't rightly remember, sir. It's mostly left in the lock on the inside, and I didn't take it out or do nothing with it."

"You didn't by any chance lock the door on your way out and leave the key on the hall table?"

"Why would I do that, sir?" asked Dipper, wide-eyed.

Julian sighed and shook his head. "I haven't the remotest idea."

# * 10 *
# MEDICAL
# INSIGHTS

"Have you any reason to doubt your servant's word?" Sir Robert asked Julian, as they went upstairs to Sir Robert's office.

"No reason in the world."

"He has no history of lying or dishonesty?"

"He's been with me for two years, and in all that time he's never given me cause to distrust him." *Which is perfectly true, thought Julian, if not perfectly honest. But, for God's sake, whatever Dipper may have done in the past, he's been a model of probity ever since he came to work for me, and he deserves better than to have his past dragged into the light at a time like this. Sir Robert would be bound to think it significant—and I daresay he'd be justified. He doesn't know Dipper as I do, and when a crime's been committed, it's only natural to suspect a seasoned criminal. But picking pockets is a far cry from murder. I should as soon believe I killed the girl myself, in a hallucinatory fit, as that Dipper had anything to do with her death.*

In Sir Robert's office, they found MacGregor pacing the floor. He had finished examining the body, and suggested they all return to Julian's room, so that he could explain his conclusions about the crime on the spot where it took place. Sir Robert ordered Rawlinson to come with them and take notes.

On the way, Sir Robert told MacGregor what little information he had gleaned from the servants. MacGregor was particularly interested in Dipper's statement that he had left Julian's room at nearly half past four. "That's more or less consistent with what I've concluded about the time of death. I don't think she could have been killed much before half past four, or rigor mortis would be more advanced."

"How late might she have been killed?" asked Sir Robert.

"Well, obviously she'd been killed by six, when Kestrel found her, but my guess is she'd been dead for at least twenty or thirty minutes by then. He said she was turning cold when he found her, and that wouldn't have happened right away, especially since most of her body was covered up. So let's say she died between half past four and, oh, twenty minutes to six, at the latest. Rough estimates, but for want of anything better, they'll have to do."

"Senderby is establishing the whereabouts of all the servants between half past four and six o'clock," said Sir Robert. "The sooner they are thoroughly cleared of suspicion, the better."

They went into Julian's room. The girl's shawl, bonnet, and gloves were still piled on the shieldback chair by the wall. The rest of her clothes, down to her undergarments, lay across an armchair. The bedcurtains were closed. Julian wrenched his mind away from thinking of the girl lying naked and cold behind the crimson hangings.

Her reticule was lying empty on a table. Beside it were what must have been its contents: a haircomb, a spool of thread with a needle stuck in it, a handful of coins, and a white lawn handkerchief smeared with dirt. Julian picked up the handkerchief and ran his eyes over it.

"No monogram," said MacGregor. "I looked. The fact is, she hasn't got a blessed thing that would tell us who she is—no monograms, no papers, nothing. All she kept in her reticule are the same sorts of frippery things any woman carries."

Beside the reticule were the girl's amber necklace and the one earring she had been wearing. There was also a silver ornament about an inch wide, shaped like a scallop shell. It had a hole bored in it, through which a blue riband was strung. Julian picked it up. "I don't remember seeing this before."

"She had that hanging round her neck, under her dress," MacGregor said. "I didn't find it till I undressed her."

"Curious," said Julian. "I suppose it must have had some sentimental value. It certainly hasn't any real worth—the silver is paper-thin. It looks like the sort of thing a child might wear. It could well be a childhood keepsake—it's rather the worse for wear, though she's kept it clean and polished."

Sir Robert frowned over the scallop shell, then turned to MacGregor. "Now then, Doctor, please be so good as to tell us what you've learned."

Rawlinson sat down at the desk in the window recess and prepared to take notes. Sir Robert stood with his back very straight and his arm lying along the mantelpiece, as though he were having his portrait done. Julian examined the girl's clothing piece by piece, looking up from time to time when MacGregor said something of particular interest.

MacGregor began, "The girl was stabbed with a sharp, pointed instrument. It struck the aorta at a downward angle—the aorta's the principal blood vessel running down from the heart—and the blow must have killed her almost instantly. The wound is about four inches deep, but the blade could have been somewhat shorter. There's only a single wound track, and no scratches or minor wounds, which means the killer got it right the first time and didn't strike her again."

Julian asked, "Can we assume from that that the murderer knows something about anatomy, or perhaps that he's killed before and knows exactly where to strike?"

"We can assume precious little about anything, I'm sorry to say. It does look as if the killer knew what he was doing, but there's always the chance it was a random blow that just happened to be fatal. One thing's clear: She was struck with a good deal of force. There's bruising round the outside of the wound."

"Does that mean the killer must have been fairly strong?" asked Julian.

"You ask good questions, I'll give you that. I wish I had better answers. I'd like to tell you the killer must have been six foot high and weighed at least fifteen stone, but I can't make those kinds of estimates without knowing more about where the girl was and what she was doing when she died. The amount of force that's delivered by a blow depends in large part on whether the body that's struck is free to move. If the girl were standing in the middle of the room and somebody came up behind her and stabbed her in the back, he'd have needed a good deal of strength to drive the knife in with such a deep, clean thrust. In fact he'd probably have had to grab her round the waist and hold her still in order to kill her that way. On the other hand, if she were up against a wall or lying facedown on the bed or the floor, it wouldn't have taken much strength to drive the knife in. A small man could have done it, or even a woman."

"Is there any indication that she struggled?" asked Sir Robert.

"None that I can find. Mind you, stabbing in the back is the act of a coward. The killer creeps up on his victim and takes him by surprise. This girl was almost certainly killed with a quick, single blow. The killer could have shoved her down on the bed and stabbed her before she had a chance to draw breath for a scream, let alone a struggle. She was such a little thing, she'd have been easy enough to overpower."

There was a silence. Julian asked grimly, "Was she raped?"

"Not a sign of it. No bleeding or tearing—nothing to suggest she'd been interfered with that way."

"There's a stain of blood on the sheet that made me wonder—"

"I know the stain you're talking about, but it doesn't mean what you think. Whatever else was done to her, I'm pretty confident she wasn't raped."

"Might she have been enjoyed with her consent?"

"You mean, was she bedded before she was killed? That's harder to be sure about, but it doesn't look that way to me."

"Was she a virgin?"

"This is a most distasteful line of enquiry, Mr. Kestrel."

"I beg your pardon, Sir Robert. It seems rather important. The girl was very beautiful, and her body was found in a bed. She may have been killed defending her honour. Or she could have been quarrelling with a jealous husband, an unfaithful lover—"

"I must say, your mind runs to extremely sordid possibilities."

"More sordid than this crime?"

Sir Robert was silent.

MacGregor said, "If it's all the same to you, Kestrel, I'd just as soon not give an opinion about whether she was a virgin. I don't think a physical examination's conclusive on that score, and I don't want to speak ill of the girl without just cause."

"She might have been married," Julian pointed out. "Although she wasn't wearing a ring. But she might have lost it, or taken it off. The killer might even have stolen it, and her earring, too, though why he didn't take the rest of her jewelry is anyone's guess." He thought for a moment. "Women who are accustomed to wear a wedding ring often have a mark scored in the third finger of their left hands when it's removed. I didn't think to notice whether the girl's finger had that sort of mark."

"I didn't either," said MacGregor. "I'll have a look, though, presently."

Rawlinson cleared his throat, "Excuse me, Sir Robert. Am I to make notes on the part of the enquiry about whether the young lady was— was—"

"You are to make notes on everything we say that concerns the investigation. That includes Mr. Kestrel's recent enquiries and Dr. MacGregor's responses. You need not record the colloquy between Mr. Kestrel and myself. I'm afraid I'm a trifle overwrought, Mr. Kestrel. I beg your pardon. Naturally, we must consider every possible motive for this crime."

"I took no offence. I beg you won't think of it again."

"The idea that such a repulsive and unspeakable crime was committed under my roof— But I interrupt you, Doctor. Please proceed."

MacGregor nodded. "Now, I can't tell you where in the room the girl was killed, but I know she was moved after she died. Kestrel found her lying on her back under the covers, which she couldn't have been doing when she was stabbed. And why would she have gotten into bed fully dressed? She hadn't even taken off her shoes."

"I'm still trying to fathom what she was doing in my room at all," said Julian.

"Look here," said MacGregor, "are you quite sure you don't know anything about this girl?"

"I am absolutely positive that I've never seen her before. I couldn't know less about her if she'd arrived today from the Antipodes."

MacGregor, to his own annoyance, was beginning to believe him. "All right. Let's get on with it. Here's what I think the murderer did with her body after he killed her. —Hmm. This'll be easier to explain if I show you just what I mean."

He twitched the bedcurtains apart. Julian, Sir Robert, and Rawlinson started, like puppets jerked on a single string. But they were spared the sight of the girl's naked corpse: MacGregor had drawn the bedclothes over her head, and all they could see was the shape of her body lying facedown underneath.

They gathered around MacGregor, who said, "I think that, after he stabbed her, the murderer laid her body on the bed face up, on top of the covers. Here's what makes me think that. A wound like this would tend to bleed inward, most likely into the pericardial sac—which means, by the way, that the murderer probably didn't get much blood splashed on him when he killed her. You'd only be likely to see much external bleeding from this kind of wound if the victim were lying on her back, which would make the blood flow down and out. Now, look closely at the coverlet, there."

At first there did not seem to be anything to see—just the same claret-coloured brocade as the hangings. But closer inspection revealed a darker patch. "Is it blood?" asked Sir Robert.

"As best I can tell, yes."

"May I sit down for a moment?" asked Rawlinson, who was swaying a little.

"Are you all right, man?" asked MacGregor.

"Yes. I'm terribly sorry. Yes." He lowered himself into a chair and clasped his head in his hands.

"Dizzy?" said MacGregor. "It'll pass in a minute or two. The sight of blood takes some people that way. Just sit quiet, and don't take any more notes till you feel more the thing. Do you want a drink of water? There's some left in the ewer."

Rawlinson looked toward the washstand and shuddered. "N—no, thank you. I'm sure I'll be all right in a moment."

Julian was still peering at the spot on the coverlet. "The bloodstain we found on the sheet is in the same place as this stain."

"That's right," said MacGregor. "I think after he stabbed her, the killer laid her down here, on her back. Maybe he wanted to see if she was dead, or he was deciding what to do with the body. At all events, her wound bled into the coverlet, and some blood soaked through to the sheet and made a stain there, too. She lay here face up for—oh, a minute or two, judging by the amount she bled. Then the killer moved her up a little and slipped her under the bedclothes—God alone knows why."

"Can we be sure all the blood is hers?" asked Julian. "The murderer might have been wounded, too."

"You've got a point. There's no telling one person's blood from another's. But if they got into a fight, wouldn't somebody have heard them?"

Julian shook his head. "In this room, at that time of day, they could probably have kicked up the devil of a row without being overheard. The fact is, if a person who knew this house set out to commit a murder here, there could hardly be a better place for it than my room. I was known to be out, your family, Sir Robert, lives principally in the new wing, and the servants were having dinner in the servants' hall. The window looks out on a quiet back courtyard, and it's so obscured by trees that the murderer would hardly have needed to draw the curtains to feel safe from observation."

"You seem determined, Mr. Kestrel, to establish that someone in my employ committed this crime."

"I'm not determined on anything, I promise you. I just find it —curious—that the murderer chose the ideal time and place for the crime."

"Next door to this room are two vacant guest rooms. Assuming for the moment that the murderer knew this house, why didn't he kill the girl in one of those rooms? He would have had the same advantage of being in the quietest part of the house, without the risk of using a room that was occupied by a guest. True, you were out, but you might have returned at any time."

"Those guest rooms are closer to the new wing," said Julian, "and to the corridor where the Craddocks' rooms are. And my coming home would still have been a danger, because I would have been close enough to overhear any disturbance that went on—"

He stopped. A chill ran through him. There was, he thought, one other very good reason to commit the crime here rather than in a vacant guest room: the killer would be able to divert suspicion to Julian, or Dipper.

"If the murderer wanted to kill her in some secluded spot," Sir Robert urged, "he wouldn't have brought her to Bellegarde at all. He would have sought out some lonely part of the Chase, or an abandoned cottage, or some such place."

"You never know who might wander into a forest or an abandoned cottage. But a house like this has a well-defined routine. The more efficient the household—and yours seems very efficient, Sir Robert—the more confidently a criminal could predict when and where he would be likely to escape notice."

Sir Robert said quietly, "This is a nightmare."

"Take a damper, Kestrel," MacGregor advised. "I'm not saying what you've said doesn't make sense, but this isn't the time for it. Let me finish telling you what I've found out from examining the girl."

She might have been as young as sixteen, he said, but twenty was probably nearer the mark. Small and slight though she looked, she was a woman and not a child. There were no distinctive marks or scars on her body that might help to identify her. As best he could tell, she was in good health. She was clean, well groomed, and unaccustomed to rough work. "Oh, and her feet are blistered. It looks as if she walked a dashed sight too far in those flimsy silk shoes she had on."

"And that's all you can tell about her?" said Sir Robert.

"From a medical examination, yes. But it shouldn't be too hard to hunt up someone who knows her. She can't have sprung up out of nowhere—unless you believe in fairies, which I don't. Though if I did, that girl would just about fit my idea of one—so little and delicate she was. Never mind that. The point is, somebody must know her, or at least have seen her—if not at Bellegarde, then in Alderton or somewhere else in the neighbourhood. People here keep a close eye on each other's comings and goings. A girl like that would have been noticed. The women would have been looking at her clothes, and the men—well, you can be sure they'd have noticed her!"

"I think she probably took some pains to keep from being noticed," said Julian.

"What makes you say that?" MacGregor asked.

"Well, she must have had some irregular purpose in coming to Bellegarde. Otherwise, why would she have crept in on the quiet? Of course, I'm assuming she came here of her own free will—but she must have, surely. It boggles the mind to imagine how an unwilling or unconscious young lady could have been dragged into the house without anyone seeing or hearing a mortal thing. At all events, if she were up to some mischief—a robbery, say, or an assignation—she would take care to attract as little notice in the neighbourhood as possible. There's also the veil on her bonnet. Look how thick it is. Women don't wear veils like this for decoration, or even for ordinary modesty, but because they don't want even the barest outline of their faces to be seen."

"She was very finely dressed, for a girl who didn't want to be noticed," MacGregor pointed out.

"That's true. Perhaps it wasn't that she didn't want to be *noticed*, but only that she didn't want to be *recognized*."

"Recognized by whom?" said MacGregor.

"I have no idea. But she does seem to have had at least one enemy."

# *11*
# HARMONY
# NOT UNDERSTOOD

In the drawing room, Sir Robert's family and the Craddocks waited tensely for news of the investigation.

"I've been giving this a great deal of thought," Lady Fontclair was saying. "I feel sure none of our servants had anything to do with that poor girl's death. The murderer must have been a housebreaker, or possibly one of those Radicals who commit acts of violence to stir up unrest in the countryside. But I think a thief is much more likely. We've been very little troubled with anonymous threats or political discontent. I really think Robert is liked and respected in the village and on the estate."

"And you are adored by everyone," put in Hugh, who was seated on an ottoman at her feet.

"And you are a very silly boy." She smiled at him, and her hand passed over his hair in a feather-light caress. "And you interrupt me when I'm trying to tell you all something very serious. Now, I think this man, whoever he is, must have broken into the house somehow and brought the girl with him. Some of these robbers do have female accomplices. I think they call them canaries."

Colonel Fontclair laughed in spite of himself. "How do you know that?"

"I've read it in the newspapers. And I picked up a Newgate novel once. I think it must have been Guy's. You remember, Guy, you used to read them when you were a child."

"And, just think, now I'm landed right in the middle of one." Guy's lips twisted into a smile. He was leaning back in his chair, his fingers curled round the stem of an empty glass. Hugh wondered if he was drunk, and decided he was not. True, his face was flushed, and his eyes were a bit too bright. But Guy tended to get uproarious when he was in his cups, and he was quiet and deliberate now—unusually so.

"If you ask me," said Lady Tarleton, "Mr. Kestrel knows a good deal more about this crime than he's admitting. The girl *was* found in his room. I shouldn't be surprised if she were some—connexion— of his who followed him here from London."

"You don't mean to say you think Kestrel killed her?" Hugh said, shocked.

"Why not? We don't know anything about him, except that he can dance and dress and make himself agreeable at parties. One never does know with these parvenus, what sort of people they really are."

"Now, really, Aunt, that's not fair. Kestrel was out riding with me from half past three until six. We came in together, and I saw him go upstairs, alone. So I know he didn't bring the girl into the house."

"And it was just after six when he came looking for Robert to tell him he'd found the girl's body," added Lady Fontclair. "That wouldn't have left him much time to kill her."

"He wouldn't have needed much time!" retorted Lady Tarleton. "Half a minute would have been enough."

"You don't say so, Aunt!" said Guy. "How do you know?"

"Don't be nasty, Guy," said his father wearily.

"Well, she sounded so positive about it. I just wondered how she knew. I thought maybe she'd been experimenting on her maids, like Cleopatra trying out different poisonous snakes on the slave girls."

"How *dare* you!" cried Lady Tarleton. "Geoffrey, your son is a monster! If anyone in this house is capable of murdering a woman in cold blood, it's he!"

Guy's eyes blazed, and he started up out of his chair.

"No, no, Catherine, how can you say so?" Lady Fontclair hurried to Guy and gently but firmly held him back. "Your aunt was speaking hastily, in anger—which you provoked very deliberately, and it was most unkind of you. We're all shocked and overwrought. You mustn't make things worse. Catherine, won't you sit down for a bit? You've been walking back and forth for nearly an hour, ever since Robert told us the news."

"Thank you, but I'm not tired. Besides, why should you waste your ministrations on me, when the gentlemen appreciate them so?"

"See here, Aunt—" Hugh began indignantly.

"Never mind, my dear," said Lady Fontclair.

"Robert shouldn't keep us all in suspense like this!" Geoffrey burst out. "He must have found out more about this business by now. I'm going to have a word with him." He started to rise.

"Oh, no, my dear, you mustn't." Lady Fontclair flew to him and coaxed him back into his chair. "It's good of you to want to help, but Robert asked us not to leave the drawing room for now. You must stay here and help me look after everyone while he's gone."

Hugh thought: He won't help you, no one is helping you, you're doing it all yourself, as always. He looked closely at her face—at her pale cheeks, and the faint lines crossing her brow and pinching the corners of her eyes. He got up and put an arm around her. "Come back and sit by me."

Something happened that had never happened before. She actually leaned against him for support. It terrified and touched him to feel her slight weight resting against his chest. His mother—everyone's bulwark, everyone's comfort—was seeking strength from *him*.

"Shall I light some candles, Aunt Cecily?" asked Isabelle.

They all murmured eager assent. Daylight had begun to fade without their noticing. The servants were still being questioned downstairs, and no one but Isabelle had thought to perform this simple task in their absence.

She found a tinder box and lit up a silver candelabrum, nursing each flame between her cupped hands until it burned steadily. Hugh watched her with a mixture of admiration and pity, thinking: She'll never need to cling to anyone for support. She has nerves like iron. If she ever did need a shoulder to lean on, she probably couldn't admit it.

He looked from her to Maud, who was sitting quietly by her
father. Her face was downcast, her brows painfully knit. He had
never seen a girl whose good looks depended so much on her mood.
She looked very plain just now, but it was a plainness that tugged
at his heart more than any prettiness he had ever seen.

This is all wrong, he thought suddenly. I'm her bridegroom. At
a time like this, when she's frightened and distressed, she ought to
be with *me*.

The realization swept him to her side. "Miss Craddock, I'm terribly sorry all this has happened."

"I'm sorry, too." But I'm glad you came to speak to me. I wish
you would stay for a while and hold my hand and— Stop it! she
ordered herself. You've promised to set him free. You can't start
making claims on him, just because there's been a murder in the
house, or because you're upset and confused about Papa and Lady
Tarleton.

She fumbled for something to say—anything to distract her from
her own troubles. "You don't think anyone really suspects Mr.
Kestrel, do you? I know he wouldn't be mixed up in a terrible crime
like this."

So that's why she's so worried, thought Hugh. "Pray don't be
concerned, Miss Craddock. I'm sure no one seriously believes Kestrel
had anything to do with the murder."

Now he's irritated and bored, she thought. He tries to be kind,
but he really doesn't like me at all.

Guy asked, "What will happen if the murderer's not found right
away?"

"The usual sorts of things, I suppose," said Lady Fontclair. "The
parish will advertise for information about the criminal, and rewards
will be offered to anyone who helps bring him to justice."

"How big are the rewards likely to be?"

"Are you thinking of turning thief-taker, Guy?" asked his father.

Guy laughed shortly. "You never know. I'm always a few hundred
pounds worse than nothing. I could probably use the money."

Hugh said, "When the Brownlows' hayricks were burned last
year, the parish offered a hundred guineas to anyone who came
forward with information about it."

"Well, you know, the farmers are always especially worried about arson," said Lady Fontclair.

"I should think everyone would be even more worried about murder," said Isabelle quietly.

"This parish hasn't got the time or the skill to carry on a lengthy murder investigation," said Craddock. "If this thing starts getting complicated, Sir Robert will have to send to London for help. And that means Bow Street."

Maud wondered why there was suddenly so much tension in the room. The Bow Street Runners, she knew, were the best—almost the only professional—policemen in England. They were often venal, sometimes unscrupulous, but they must be very good at catching criminals, or their small, select force would not be so much in demand. Maud looked from one person to another and thought: They're not afraid about the murder anymore. They're worried about this terrible secret that everyone knows but me. They don't want an investigation. They don't want policemen asking questions. Something might come out that has nothing to do with the murder—something they've been doing everything in their power to hide.

All at once she drew in her breath. *But how do I know the secret has nothing to do with the murder?*

"Robert would never let London policemen come here, asking questions and interfering in our private affairs!" cried Lady Tarleton.

"They wouldn't need to do that," faltered Geoffrey. "Why should they question us? We don't know anything about the murder. The thing for Bow Street to do is hunt around the neighbourhood for thieves or poachers—those kinds of people."

"Don't fool yourselves into thinking we won't have to answer questions," said Craddock. "If the murder's not solved right away, we'll all be asked where we were this afternoon, and what we were doing, and what we saw or heard."

"Well, *I* didn't see or hear anything to the purpose," declared Lady Tarleton. "I was in my room all afternoon. I never came out till I went down to dinner."

Craddock looked at her through narrowed eyes. She stared defiantly back. "Then I don't expect the police will bother much about you," he said at last.

Maud felt as if she could not breathe. She plucked at her father's sleeve and whispered, "Papa, I need to talk to you—please! Can we go somewhere alone?"

✳

They went through the wide double doors into the music room. It seemed a lifetime, Maud thought, since she and Mr. Kestrel had talked here.

"Well, what's the matter?" Craddock asked.

"Papa, are you—" She swallowed hard. "Do you think you ought to let Lady Tarleton say things that aren't true?"

"What are you talking about?" he said sharply.

"She said she never came out of her room till dinnertime, and I know that isn't so."

"What do you know about where Lady Tarleton was this afternoon?"

"I only know about the end of the afternoon. She wasn't in her room, Papa. She was in yours."

He drew breath as though to shout, then stopped himself. His voice came out in a rasping whisper. "How do you know that?"

"Well, you know I went out this afternoon with Josie and Pippa and Miss Pritchard. Miss Pritchard and I got talking, and I thought how hard she works, and what a dull life she has. And she isn't so very old. It would be nice for her to go on holiday and have a little fun once in a while—"

"Has this got anything to do with what I asked you?"

"Yes, Papa. Because I was thinking that, if Sir Robert and Lady Fontclair didn't mind, I'd invite Miss Pritchard to London for a few days. She could help with the wedding preparations. She so liked hearing about my trousseau, and the wedding breakfast, and everything." She hurried on, seeing his patience was almost gone. "So when we got home, I went to your room to ask you if that would be all right. I was just about to knock on the door, when I heard Lady Tarleton's voice inside. And I was so surprised, I just stood there and couldn't move or do anything at all."

He stared at her, his breath coming quickly. "And then what happened?"

"I did something very wrong. I— I listened for a while. I'm sorry. It was just that the conversation was so strange. It scared me. I— oh, Papa, don't look at me like that!"

"My God, how much did you overhear? What do you know?"

Her throat closed up, and she could not answer.

"Tell me, damn it!" He took a few steps toward her.

"I— I was only there a few minutes! I don't know much at all! And what I did hear, I didn't understand."

"Tell me everything you heard, from the beginning."

Maud repeated it all as best she could. "And then I heard footsteps," she finished, "and I thought Lady Tarleton was coming out, and I ran to my room. I couldn't face her. I felt so shocked and confused."

"Have you told me the truth? Is that really everything you heard?"

"Yes, Papa. I promise."

He looked intently into her eyes. "All right, I believe you. Now listen to me carefully. You're not to tell anyone about Lady Tarleton being in my room, and you're not to repeat a word of what you heard us say. Do you understand?"

"But—but what if somebody asks what *I* was doing this afternoon? You said we might all be questioned by Sir Robert, or the Bow Street Runners."

"Then you'll say you went on an outing with the Misses Fontclair, and when you got home, you went to your room. You don't have to lie—just leave out the part about Lady Tarleton and me. It's got nothing to do with the murder."

"Are you sure?"

"What do you mean, am I sure? Of course I'm sure!"

"But some of what you and Lady Tarleton said sounded so strange. And there's some secret between you and the Fontclairs, and I wondered—"

"Well, stop wondering! What's between me and the Fontclairs is my business, not yours. And I warn you, if you breathe a word about what you overheard Lady Tarleton and me say, you'll do more harm than you can begin to guess. You don't understand what you're meddling in. The Fontclairs won't thank you, and neither will I."

"But if it might help solve the murder—"

"It won't. Don't be a fool, Maud. You're going to be part of this family soon. You don't want to bring it into disgrace."

For Hugh's sake, no, that's the last thing I want, she thought. I wish I knew what to do. If I'd only been able to find Mr. Kestrel before dinner, I could have asked him what he thought that conversation between Papa and Lady Tarleton meant. Now I can't talk to him about it. Because, as long as I don't know what harm I might do by telling anyone, how can I take the risk?

＊

Sir Robert had much the same theory about the murder as Lady Fontclair. "I believe some intruder broke into the house, most likely bent on robbery. He brought the girl with him—they quarrelled —he killed her, and afterward fled from the house. Rawlinson, make a note to have the house searched. I want to know if anything is missing."

"Yes, sir," said Rawlinson, from his seat at the desk in the window recess. He had lit an oil lamp to relieve the dusk, and its ruddy glow illumined the stained glass behind him and conjured up long, wavering shadows on the walls of Julian's room.

"I imagine you'd want to have the house searched in any case," said Julian, "to see if there are traces of the girl or her murderer anywhere besides this room. I suppose we don't even know for certain she was killed in here, do we? She might have been killed somewhere else in the house and brought here afterward."

"I can't see the murderer traipsing about the house with a dead woman in his arms," said MacGregor.

"No," admitted Julian, "neither can I. All the same, it might not be a bad idea to look in the rooms nearby for bloodstains or signs of a struggle."

"Make a note of that, too, Rawlinson," said Sir Robert wearily.

"For that matter, I can't believe this room's yielded up all its secrets." Julian lit a candle at the oil lamp and bent to examine the carpet. "There's dirt on the carpet, and I don't believe it was here when I left to go riding this afternoon. I remember my boots were muddy when I came back from the horse fair, and Dipper made a point of taking them away to be cleaned before I set foot in here." He glanced critically at the feet of the other three men. "It doesn't look as if any of us tracked the dirt in here. Whereas the girl's shoes are very dirty, although she seems to have tried to scrape them clean."

He picked up her shoes. They were made of pale blue silk brocade, torn, frayed, and very soiled. There were green stains on and around the soles. He pointed out jagged lines running through the grime on the bottoms, where she had evidently tried to scrape off the dirt.

"If it was the girl's shoes—and possibly the murderer's—that tracked the dirt in here, it might give us some idea where in the room they went and what they did. The trouble is, there's not enough dirt to make anything like a footprint." He walked about with his candle, peering closely at the carpet. "Most of the dirt seems to be along the side of the bed nearest the door. There's some at the foot of the bed—but not a hint of it anywhere near the washstand, although we know the murderer went there to wash off the blood. I wonder if that means the murderer's shoes were clean? Insofar as there's anything like a trail, it leads this way."

He walked from the door, down the length of the bed, and then to the left. He came to a halt at the wall, straightened up, and stood staring at the wood panelling. "Dr. MacGregor?" he said, without turning around.

The others joined him. By the light of his candle, they could see dark smears along the wall, hardly visible save at close range. The smears varied from perhaps one to two inches long. Three of them formed a horizontal line at eye level, about an inch apart from each other. There were two more smears, somewhat fainter, about a foot below and to the right.

"What do you think that is?" asked Julian, although he was fairly sure he knew already.

MacGregor scraped a little bit off with his thumbnail. "I'd say it's almost certainly blood."

Julian took a few steps back and gazed around him. To the right, the wall turned a right-angle corner and gave way to the window embrasure. To the left was the fireplace. The intervening wall space, where the stains were, was about a yard wide. Just in front stood the shieldback chair where the girl's shawl and bonnet were found.

"Do you suppose this is where she was killed?" asked Julian.

"Could be," said MacGregor. "There are all kinds of possibilities. Maybe she'd just been laying her outdoor things on that chair when the murderer came up behind her and pushed her against the wall and stabbed her."

"Or perhaps she'd decided she wanted to leave and came over here to put her things on again," said Julian. "There's a scratch along the back of the chair that suggests it might have been knocked against the wall in a struggle. Yes, look, there's a scratch on the wall at the same level. And the scratches look freshly made."

Sir Robert frowned. "If the girl were held with her face to the wall and stabbed in the back, how did the blood get on the wall?"

"The murderer could have touched the wall while his fingers were stained with blood," said MacGregor. "That would explain the small separate smudges."

Julian held up his hand to the wall and found that the three smears at eye level were about the right distance apart to have been made by a person's fingers, slightly spread. "I believe you're right," he said. "It looks as though someone had pressed against the wall, so, and smeared the blood downward from left to right. Each of the stains is somewhat darker on the left side. Do we know which hand the murderer used to stab her?"

"His right," said MacGregor.

"So he was right-handed, and more likely to have had blood on his right hand than his left?"

"I'd say so, yes."

"Then most likely he made the smears with a motion of his right hand from left to right." Julian frowned thoughtfully. "You know, there are some problems with this notion that the murderer killed the girl here by the wall. This is the most conspicuous place in the room." He pointed out the window to where the new wing branched off from the main house. "Anyone looking out of a window along that side of the new wing would have a direct line of sight through my window to this very spot. Even with the trees obscuring the view, it would have been risky to kill the girl here."

"Maybe the murderer had the curtains drawn," said MacGregor. "Or, confound it, he might not have been thinking clearly! He might have been in a rage or a panic and not stopped to work out the geometry of who could see what from what angle."

"That's certainly possible," said Julian, so mildly that the doctor was a little ashamed of his belligerence.

"Hm—well—any other objections?" MacGregor asked.

"Something more in the nature of a question. If I were to hold a woman against a wall and stab her in the back—something it's never even remotely occurred to me to do," he added, seeing Sir Robert and MacGregor look at him narrowly, "—but *if* I did, she would most likely slump to the ground, and I should reach out to catch her. Or I might conceivably stand back and let her fall in a heap at my feet—but, either way, I wouldn't have any reason to smear blood on the wall with my hand."

"Dash it," MacGregor exclaimed, "you do know how to make everything three times more complicated. I don't know the answer to that riddle. Maybe the murderer was in shock or lost his balance after he killed her, and had to lean on the wall for support."

"I suppose he could have caught the girl's body with one arm, and propped himself against the wall with his other hand," Julian mused. "Although you wouldn't think he'd put his hand up so high as those top three stains. Of course, he may have been very tall." Julian could not help glancing at Sir Robert, who, like all the Fontclairs, was of a lofty height. "He did move his hand farther down afterward. That would account for the lighter stains below and to the right. He'd rubbed off a good part of the blood on the first three smears by then."

"Gentlemen," said Sir Robert, "don't you think we've strayed from our principal task? Exactly where in the room the girl was killed, and whether the murderer leaned against the wall afterward, don't bring us any closer to discovering who killed the girl, or how he's to be found."

"At this stage, do we really know what might turn out to be important?" said Julian. "We're surrounded by scraps of information that don't appear to make sense. The bloodstains on the wall, the fact that the girl was tucked under the bedclothes after she was killed, the door locked from the outside, the girl's presence in the house to begin with—there must be an explanation for every one of those things, and if we knew it, the murderer's identity might fall into place as a matter of course. It reminds me of the lines of Pope I heard you reading to Lady Fontclair—something about all discord being harmony not understood."

"When Mr. Pope wrote of harmony," Sir Robert said sternly, "he meant the inscrutable pattern of God's work upon the earth."

"Cause and effect are part of that pattern. Every one of these effects must have a cause, and if we could guess the cause—"

"I understand your point, Mr. Kestrel. Thank you. Now I think we should return to the servants' hall and see how Senderby is progressing. Also, Travis must have finished searching the house by now, and he may have found some indication of how the girl and her murderer got in."

"What's to be done with the body?" MacGregor asked.

"The mortician will have to come from Alderton and collect it. If no family or friends of the girl can be found, I shall take responsibility for her funeral myself. But first, I'm afraid I shall have to ask everyone in the house to look at her. I wish I could spare them that ordeal. But since no one appears to recognize her by a spoken description, we have no choice but to ask the household to view her in the flesh."

"We might ask if anyone recognizes this." Julian picked up the silver scallop shell. "If it was a keepsake, something the girl especially prized, it might help to identify her."

"It wouldn't do any harm to take it with us and show it around," said MacGregor.

"Very well." Sir Robert put it in his waistcoat pocket.

As they were leaving, MacGregor said, "Stop a moment. If you don't mind, Sir Robert, I'll answer one of Kestrel's swarm of questions before we go."

He went to the bed and reached under the covers. After feeling about for a moment, he drew out a tiny hand, the flesh blanched almost white. He examined the hand briefly, then laid it under the sheet again. "No sign she ever wore a wedding ring." He closed the bedcurtains, and the four men silently left the room.

Out in the corridor, Julian looked at the floor and frowned.

"What is it now?" said MacGregor.

"There's hardly any dirt tracked out here. But I suppose the carpet in my room would pick up dirt more readily than the bare floor. So much for finding anything in the nature of a trail."

"It could also be that your servant was mistaken when he said he'd left the windows bolted," said Sir Robert. "If the girl and the murderer contrived to come in through the window, that would explain why they tracked dirt in your room rather than out here."

But the murderer would still have had to get out through the house, thought Julian, in order to leave the windows bolted behind him and the door locked from the outside. A fact that Sir Robert is clearly reluctant to face.

They went downstairs. From the dining room, they caught the scent of food and heard the clatter of plate. Julian thought he recognized Lady Fontclair's musical voice, but no one else seemed to be talking very much. Apparently the Fontclairs and Craddocks had little to say—at any rate, in front of the servants.

"I'm glad they've finally been able to dine," said Sir Robert.

Julian flicked open his watch. It was just before nine o'clock— three hours, almost to the minute, since he found the girl's body. He was not sure if time had seemed to pass quickly or slowly since then. This night was like a dream, impossible to measure in hours and minutes. Events moved along inexorably, to some strange, solemn rhythm of their own.

"I need hardly tell you gentlemen how much I appreciate your help," Sir Robert was saying. "Your part in this unpleasant episode should come to an end very shortly, except to the extent you may be called upon to testify at the inquest, or at a trial."

Julian felt a pang of regret. Of course he had no business taking part in a murder investigation. And, God knew, it was no sort of work for a gentleman to go poking about for clues like a Bow Street Runner. Yet he found the hunt intriguing, and would be sorry to give it up. Something deeper was troubling him, too. It was he who had found the girl, in his room, in his bed. He felt *responsible*, somehow. He kept seeing again that little childish hand being drawn out from under the bedclothes—the hand that had not worn a wedding ring, and never would now.

# *12*
# A PROMISING
# SUSPECT

$A$s Sir Robert and his companions were crossing the screens passage into the servants' wing, they met Travis coming in through the front door with a lantern in his hand. His coat and cap were lightly spattered with rain.

"What news?" asked Sir Robert. "Have you searched the house and grounds?"

"Yes, sir. But nary a thing did I find."

"No sign that any stranger broke into the house?"

"No, sir. I looked all over the house, and I made a circuit round the outside, but there was no sign that anybody'd come in on the sly. Some of the windows were closed, and those hadn't been forced. Some were open, but I don't think anybody got in that way. The rain was only just starting, and the ground was soft. There would have been footprints, and the flowers would have been trampled, if anybody d tried to climb in through the windows."

"And that was true of Mr. Kestrel's window, as well as the others?"

"Yes, sir."

"You've done very well," said Sir Robert. But he did not look pleased.

"How many doors give access to the house from outside?" asked Julian.

"Not many, for a house this size," said Sir Robert. "There's the front door." He gestured toward it, down the hallway. "There's the back door in the servants' wing, which leads into a small waiting room for tradesmen and others who come on business. And there are the French windows in the conservatory. They open on the terrace, from which one can descend to the garden and the park."

"If nobody climbed in or out of the windows," said MacGregor, "that means anyone escaping from the house from— let's say, half past four up to this moment now— had to have used one of those three doors."

"No one escaped through the conservatory windows before six o'clock," Sir Robert said. "Lady Fontclair and I were in the conservatory from about four o'clock until six, when I left with Mr. Kestrel. I don't know how long Lady Fontclair remained."

"You bolted the French windows just before we left," said Julian. "Do you remember? The wind had blown them open." He asked Travis, "Did you notice whether they were still bolted?"

"They were, sir."

"Then it's not likely anyone escaped from the house that way after six o'clock, because he would have had to leave the windows unbolted behind him."

"I think that's so, sir."

Julian asked Sir Robert, "Did Lady Fontclair and you leave the conservatory, even for a short time, at any point between four and six o'clock?"

Sir Robert opened his mouth to answer—then paused. "I was gone for perhaps ten minutes," he said slowly. "A quarter of an hour, at most. I'd been reading aloud, and Lady Fontclair had a fancy to hear Pope. I went to the library to get a book of his verses."

"Was Lady Fontclair in the conservatory all the time you were gone?"

"I have no idea, Mr. Kestrel," Sir Robert said coldly. "Naturally it didn't occur to me to ask her."

"So now we're left with the front door and the back door," said MacGregor.

"With respect, sir," Travis said, "I don't think anybody could have got in or out through the front door, either."

"Why is that?" asked Julian.

"Because it was barred, sir, from half past four on. It's kept barred while the servants are at dinner, just as it is at night."

"Do we know for certain that the door was barred on this particular afternoon?" Sir Robert asked.

"I asked Michael, sir." Michael was one of the footmen. "He said he barred the door at half past four, as he always does."

"But he would have unbarred it, surely, when the servants finished dinner," Sir Robert said.

"Yes, sir, he did, about a quarter to six. But he says he sat here by the door after that, so he could open it for people as they came home to dinner. I found him here with Peter"—Peter was another footman—"when I was calling all the staff into the servants' hall on your orders, at about half past six. I think they'd been having a game of dice, though they were too quick for me, and I didn't catch them at it. I sent them into the servants' hall, and then I barred the front door myself. I thought it best, seeing that something was amiss in the house. It's been barred ever since, except just now when I was out in front of the house, and then I had it under my eye the whole time."

"Which means," said Julian, "that from half past four on, the front door was either barred or attended by a footman."

"Yes, sir."

"So that no one can have got out that way, either, without our knowing about it."

"That's right, sir. Because he'd have had to leave the door unbarred after him." Travis glanced uneasily at Sir Robert. It seemed that Mr. Kestrel's questions were anything but welcome to him. Travis set his jaw tightly and compressed his lips. Julian knew he would get nothing more out of him without a struggle.

No matter, he thought—what he's already told us is disturbing enough. If the murderer was a robber who broke in with the girl, he must have got out again after he killed her. It seems he can't have used the front door, the conservatory doors, or any of the windows. That leaves only the back door, and to get from my room to the back door, he would have had to pass through the servants' hall. Could he possibly have done that without being seen? Because if he couldn't, there won't be any other means he could have used to escape from the house. And at that point, we shall have to conclude that there was no mysterious stranger—that the murderer is one of the servants, or one of us.

Sir Robert sent Travis to fetch Senderby from the servants' hall. When the constable arrived, Sir Robert asked him what he had learned of the servants' whereabouts and activities between half past four and six. Senderby's notes took some time to sort out—writing and spelling were not his strong suit—but the gist of them was that each of the staff could give a reliable account of where he had been and what he had been doing during the crucial time. Rawlinson, Mrs. Cox, and Travis had been dining in their private room. The rest of the servants had been at dinner in the servants' hall, except a couple of stablelads who had been looking after the horses. Everyone had at least one person who could vouch for his or her whereabouts between half past four and six.

Sir Robert was looking more grim every moment, and Julian thought he knew why. With the servants cleared of complicity in the murder, and the chances of an unknown intruder becoming more and more remote, it was as though a web of accusation were being woven round Sir Robert's own family. Every new piece of information he gathered was one more silken thread.

But there was a complication. Julian felt a most unpleasant jolt on hearing Senderby say, "So the only one of the servants who was off alone for more than a minute or two is Mr. Kestrel's man, who went for a walk outdoors just before half past four."

"Yes, I remember," said Sir Robert. "When does he say he returned?"

Senderby floundered through his notes. "He didn't recall, sir, but the maid, Molly Dale, she knew. Said he gave her a start by popping into the servants' hall, suddenlike, and she gave him a bit of a scold for being late to dinner. She looked at the clock, to see just how late he was, and it was ten minutes to five."

"So he was out walking alone for twenty minutes," said Sir Robert thoughtfully.

Julian felt a prickle of warning up and down his spine. Confound Dipper! he thought. A Cockney born and bred, a child of the London streets, and this one afternoon he must needs have a craving for fresh air and flowers! But what can they make of that? They have no grounds to suspect him. It's true he was the last person in my room before the body was found, but he had every right and reason to be there at that hour.

They went into the servants' hall. Most of them were still gathered around the long table. Sir Robert began by showing them the silver scallop shell and asking if they had seen it before. They passed it from hand to hand, looking at it curiously, but no one knew anything about it.

Sir Robert next asked if any stranger could have passed from the main house through the servants' hall to the back door at any time after half past four. The servants were positive on this point. The servants' hall had been full of people all that time. No stranger could have come through there without being seen.

"I wish to pose some questions to Michael," Sir Robert said.

All eyes turned to a tall blond footman, with a round face and fair, freckled skin. He stood up nervously. "Yes, sir."

Michael confirmed that he had kept the front door barred from half past four until a quarter to six. "I unbarred it about twenty minutes past five," he recalled, "just long enough to let in Mr. Craddock. He'd been out riding, and he rang while we was at dinner. Then I looked at the hall clock and, seeing as it was early yet, I barred the door again."

At a quarter to six, Miss Pritchard, Miss Craddock, and the Misses Fontclair came home from their outing. Michael unbarred the front door to let them in. "Then Peter and me, we sat by the door together—talking," he finished hastily.

"Playing at dice, more likely," muttered Travis.

Michael coloured. "Well, anyway, sir, about six o'clock I let in Master Hugh and Mr. Kestrel, and after that Colonel Fontclair. And then Mr. Travis came and told us we was wanted in the servants' hall, and he barred the door again."

MacGregor was shaking his head. He can see it, too, thought Julian—the web that's tightening round the Fontclairs. Round Craddock, too: he returned to Bellegarde early enough to have killed the girl, though Miss Craddock didn't—not that I could have suspected her in any case. But it's devilish hard to imagine any of the others committing this crime, either. Why should they have done it? And why in my room? And why— oh, a thousand other questions. But I don't think Sir Robert has any choice now but to find out what his family and Mark Craddock were doing between half past four and twenty minutes to six this afternoon.

"When did Colonel Fontclair come home?" Sir Robert asked Michael.

"I don't rightly remember, sir. I s'pose he was gone about an hour, all told."

"How do you know when he left?"

"He come in here, sir, while we was at dinner, wanting to know if there was anybody in the stable who could saddle his horse. And somebody said there was, and he went out all in a taking."

"What makes you say that he was in a taking?" asked Sir Robert sharply.

"Well, he— he looked flustered, sir," Michael faltered. "He was in a hurry and didn't stop to say good evening or ask after people's health, like he usually does. And when we told him there was a couple of lads out in the stable who could saddle his horse, he went out like the devil was after— I mean, like he was in a hurry to be gone."

There were nods from the other servants.

Sir Robert had grown very pale. He stood motionless, save for the quick rise and fall of his chest. Somehow he kept his voice quite level. "You understand, all of you, that we need to obtain information on even the most trivial points. Does any of you remember precisely when Colonel Fontclair left to go riding?"

The servants consulted with each other and agreed that it was after five o'clock—perhaps five or ten minutes after. It was certainly no earlier than five.

Sir Robert was white and still as a statue.

Into this painful silence came a high, clear voice. It was Molly Dale, the pretty mobcapped maidservant. "What I don't understand, Mr. Dipper, is how you got back in the house?"

Dipper stared, wet his lips, and did not answer.

"What do you mean by that question?" asked Sir Robert.

"Well, seeing that the front door was barred, sir, all the time we was at dinner, I just wondered how Mr. Dipper got back in from his walk outside." She gazed at Dipper, perplexed, her head tipped to one side like a bird's.

Mrs. Cox shook a finger at her. "Haven't you been told often enough not to meddle in matters that are none of your concern?"

"Thank you, Mrs. Cox," said Sir Robert, "but I wish to hear what Molly has to say. What makes you think Mr. Dipper didn't come in through the back door?"

Dipper was staring at the table before him, as though memorizing every crack in the wood. Molly caught her lower lip between her teeth, and her eyes grew wide with distress.

"I am waiting for an answer, Molly," said Sir Robert.

"I— I don't know what to answer, sir! Am I getting Mr. Dipper in trouble somehow?"

"Listen to me very carefully, Molly. When you speak to me now, you are not merely addressing the master of this house, but a magistrate engaged in the enforcement of His Majesty's laws. You are bound to answer truthfully and completely any question I put to you."

"Y— yes, sir."

"Now I ask you again: How do you know that Mr. Dipper didn't enter the house through the back door in the servants' wing?"

"Well, because I saw him, sir. I was over at the cabinet, there." She pointed to a large walnut cabinet next to the door leading into the screens passage. "I'd got up from the table to get a cloth, because Peter knocked over his ale and it spilled all over the floor underneath my chair, and all at once Mr. Dipper popped in through that door and said he was sorry to be so late to dinner. And he gave me a fright, because I didn't hear him come in, and I jumped up in the air and said, 'Lord, Mr. Dipper, you should be ashamed of yourself, to scare a girl so.' And then I teased him a bit for being late to dinner. So I know he came in from the main house. And that's all I can remember, sir, honestly it is."

"You've done very well. Thank you." The blood was flowing back into Sir Robert's cheeks, and his voice rang out clear and strong.

"Dipper, you've presented us with a problem. You say you went out for a walk shortly before half past four. Molly says you came in to dinner from the main house some twenty minutes later. I should like you to explain how you got back into the main house from outside. We know you cannot have used the front door, which was barred, or the conservatory windows, since Lady Fontclair and I would have seen you."

Dipper rose, and dragged up his eyes to meet Sir Robert's. "I didn't go out for a walk, sir."

The other servants stared at him, holding their breath.

"Then where did you go when you left Mr. Kestrel's room this afternoon?"

Dipper threw one remorseful look at his master, then burst out, "I went downstairs to the room where all the guns and knives is kept!"

The servants stared, gasped, whispered, nudged each other.

"Take him to my office for questioning," Sir Robert ordered Senderby briskly. "Rawlinson, you will take down his statement. Mr. Kestrel, you may be present if you wish, seeing that he's your servant."

Senderby edged nervously toward Dipper. In height and build he all but dwarfed the lithe little valet; it was like watching a lion creep up fearfully on a mouse. But how could Senderby be sure what Dipper might be capable of? He had never had to deal with a murderer before.

But Dipper went with him meekly. Sir Robert said he would follow as soon as he had had a word with Travis and Mrs. Cox.

MacGregor wondered what he ought to do now. He could stay here and help quell the commotion among the servants. He could join the Fontclairs and Craddocks for whatever was left of dinner. Or he could go along to Sir Robert's office and hear what Kestrel's man had to say for himself. As he stood debating, he felt a hand clasp his arm. He turned and confronted a pair of wild, earnest eyes he hardly recognized as Kestrel's. "He didn't do it," the young man whispered. "He cannot have done it! I *know* him."

MacGregor reminded himself that he had never trusted Julian Kestrel. He had less cause to trust him than ever, now that his servant had been proved a liar, and might turn out a murderer besides. But MacGregor's trust in people sprang from instinct, not reason, and his instincts about Kestrel were muddled just now. All he knew for certain was that he could not look into those eyes and tell the fellow to go about his business.

He said, "If he's innocent, Sir Robert will tumble to it quickly enough."

"Why should he, when he has every reason to find him guilty?"

"See here, Sir Robert's an honest man and a magistrate! You can't think for a moment he'd charge a man with murder unless he had just cause?"

"I don't know what 'just cause' means. I only know that if Dipper is cleared of suspicion, Sir Robert will have no choice but to look for the murderer among his own family. How in the name of heaven can he hope to be objective? Think what a convenient culprit Dipper would make—a Londoner, an outsider, a servant, but not one of the Fontclairs' own. Sir Robert has only to bind him over for trial and close the investigation, with no more enquiry into who else might have committed the crime!"

"I've known Sir Robert for years—as many years as you've been alive, most likely—and I tell you, he's as honourable a man as ever drew breath. He'll give your servant a chance to explain himself, and if there's not enough evidence to hold him, he'll set him free and go on with the investigation, no matter what the cost to his family. That's the kind of man he is."

"I hope to God you're right."

MacGregor watched him walk distractedly about, and suddenly grinned. "I'm glad to see you can get yourself into a pother about something. I'd begun to think you were nothing more than a fashion plate out of some London magazine."

Sir Robert called, "Are you coming, Mr. Kestrel?"

"Are *you* coming?" Julian asked MacGregor.

"I suppose I might as well," MacGregor grumbled. "In the mood you're in now, there's no telling what crack-brained thing you might say, if I'm not there to tug on the reins."

"Oh, I won't lose my head. I can't afford to. I've got to keep my wits about me, and my temper in check, or I'll be no use to Dipper at all." His face relaxed into a smile. "You'd hardly credit that in London I'm renowned for my sangfroid."

"I'm not sure I don't like you better without it. But you're right—if ever you needed a cool head, you need it now."

# * 13 *
# NO ONE'S
# FRIEND

<hr>

Two oil lamps were burning in Sir Robert's office, one on his desk, and the other on the writing table in the corner where Rawlinson was taking notes. Sir Robert sat at his desk and looked across at Dipper, who stood in the centre of the room. Julian placed his chair strategically beside them, where he could watch them both. MacGregor paced the room, his shadow flitting in his wake. Outdoors, the wind was blowing fiercely, driving pellets of rain against the windowpanes.

Sir Robert said to Dipper, "I have a duty to advise you at the outset that you are not required to answer my questions. I cannot compel you to give information against yourself. I strongly suggest, however, that, if you have information that may excuse or explain your conduct, you present it now. Otherwise, I shall be forced to draw highly damaging inferences against you. Do you understand?"

"I think so, sir."

"What is your full name?"

"Thomas Stokes, sir."

Sir Robert looked up sharply. "I thought you were called Dipper."

"Dipper's a nickname, sir."

"Did you know Dipper wasn't his real name?" Sir Robert asked Julian.

The nickname, as Julian well knew, had been given to Dipper

on account of his dexterity at dipping his hand into other people's pockets. "He told me his real name when I engaged him. But he said he was accustomed to be called Dipper, and as I thought it suited him, I've kept it up." He added, very deliberately, "I haven't the remotest idea what it means."

Dipper's jaw dropped, and he started to shake his head in protest. Julian's eyes shot him a warning: Don't be an ass. I've lied for you, and I'm going to go on lying. If you try to stop me now, you'll only dish us both.

"What *does* it mean?" Sir Robert asked Dipper.

"I dunno, sir. Me father give it to me when I was a kid."

"How old are you now?"

"I'm twenty, sir."

"How long have you been in Mr. Kestrel's employ?"

"I think it's been about two years, sir."

Sir Robert turned to Julian. "You engaged him as your valet when he was only eighteen? Had he any previous experience?"

"Not a whit. He was a complete *tabula rasa*. I was able to train him exactly as I liked."

"What were you doing before Mr. Kestrel engaged you?"

"I didn't have no reg'lar work, sir."

"How did you support yourself?"

"Not very well, sir."

"Have you any family?"

"No, sir. That is, me parents is dead, and I dunno what's got me brother and sister."

"How did you come to be employed by Mr. Kestrel?"

Dipper hung fire for a moment or two. "I found his ticker—his watch, sir. I give it back to him."

MacGregor thought: Of all the deuced funny ways to go about engaging a manservant! Especially for a fellow who cares as much about his clothes as Kestrel seems to. Dash it, the man gets more puzzling every minute.

"Let's proceed to the events of this afternoon," said Sir Robert. "Do you still claim you were in Mr. Kestrel's room until shortly before half past four?"

"Yes, sir."

"Were you alone there all that time?"

"Yes, sir."

"I have asked you this already, but as you lied to us before, I'm obliged to repeat my earlier questions. I hope you mean to answer truthfully this time?"

"Yes, sir. But, sir, I didn't wrinkle about nothing except going for a walk outside."

"I shall get to that presently. Did you at any time today see a young woman with reddish hair and blue eyes, wearing a yellow dress?"

"No, sir."

"Are you acquainted with anyone who fits that description?"

"Not so as I can recall, sir."

"Have you ever been in trouble with the law in the past, Stokes?"

Dipper wet his lips. "No, sir."

"When I asked you earlier what you did on leaving your master's room, why did you say you went for a walk outside?"

"I didn't take it, sir!" Dipper burst out.

"Take what?"

"I dunno, sir. Whatever it is that's been pinched. I didn't take it, I swear!"

"Nothing has been stolen that we know of. Someone has been murdered."

"My Gawd!" Dipper looked at Julian. "Do they think I done it, sir?"

"You've confused matters a bit by telling us you went out for a constitutional at a time when you were actually in a room full of possible murder weapons."

"Oh, sir, I didn't—I wouldn't—you got to believe me, I wouldn't do nothing like that!"

"Why did you tell us you went outside when you were really in the gun room?" asked Julian quietly.

"I was afraid, sir. I knew I hadn't any business in there, but I wanted to see it. You was telling me about it last night, sir, remember?—how there was all kinds of barking-irons there, and maps, and flags, and bits of metal as knights used to put on their horses. I got a hankering to see it meself, and when I found I had a little time before dinner, I piked downstairs and had a peery. And it was the lummiest place, sir—I never seen nothing like it. I was so took up with looking at everything, I forgot about dinner, till I snilched the clock and saw how late it was, and I broomed it to the servants' hall."

"See here, lad," said MacGregor, "this won't do at all. If you weren't up to any mischief in the gun room, why didn't you own up you were there? You couldn't have thought you'd get into any serious trouble, just for going in and having a look round."

"It wasn't so much that, sir. I took fright when I saw we was being questioned by a nabsman—a constable, I mean. I thought something must've got lifted, and I didn't want to get mixed up in it. I thought if I said I was in the gun room, everybody'd be down upon me about why I was there, and it just seemed safest to say I was out of the house. I didn't know about the front door being barred, and that. I just didn't think at all." He looked at Julian. "I'm sorry, sir."

Sir Robert said, "I think it only fair to warn you, Stokes, you're in a very grave position. When questioned by a magistrate, you told a lie, and apparently you would have persisted in it, if Molly hadn't spoken. I have no way of knowing what else you may have said that is not the truth. You admit to being the last person in Mr. Kestrel's room before the body was found there. And you admit that, at about the time when the victim must have been stabbed to death, you went secretly to a room where knives are kept ready to hand."

"The body was found in me master's room, sir?"

"Yes."

"Well, sir, if there's one thing I'd never do, it's clip some cove's wick and leave him laid out stiff in me master's room! And get me master in trouble like that? Not likely, sir!"

"The victim was not a man," said Sir Robert. "It was the young lady I described to you earlier."

"What—you mean the mort with the red hair and the yellow dress? Who is she, sir?"

"We haven't identified her yet. I will, however, give *you* another chance to do so, if you can."

"I'd like to help you, sir, but *I* dunno who she is."

"Very well. Senderby, see if he's carrying a weapon, or any property that might have been stolen."

Dipper stood up. Julian wished he would not look quite so much as though he were used to being searched. Senderly felt inside his coat and turned out his pockets. All he found was a handful of coins, a penknife, a handkerchief, a small clothesbrush, a needle and thread, a paper of pins, and some sugar candy.

"What room in the house have you been given?" Sir Robert asked Dipper.

"I'm sharing with the footmen, sir, Michael and Peter."

Sir Robert ordered Senderby to search Dipper's room. For the time being, Dipper was to be kept locked in Rawlinson's office which was down the hall from Sir Robert's.

"Is that really necessary?" asked Julian.

"He's implicated in a felony," said Sir Robert. "He must be kept under lock and key until I determine whether there's sufficient cause for an arrest. Rawlinson, be good enough to show Senderby where your office is. Then tell Travis to look in the gun room and find out if any knives are missing or show signs of recent use."

Rawlinson and Senderby went out, with Dipper between them. Dipper threw Julian a last remorseful look. Julian winked at him. Dipper broke into a grin, and winked back.

"Well, Mr. Kestrel," said Sir Robert, "have you anything to say in your servant's defence?"

"I don't defend his lack of candour. He ought to have told the truth. But I don't see his lying as proof that he killed anyone. He only lied to divert attention from himself, because he was panicked at the very idea of being questioned by a constable. To people of Dipper's class in London, a constable can seem a very formidable beast. A costermonger or a crossing-sweeper doesn't readily think of the law as his friend."

"Nor should he," said Sir Robert. "The law is impartial. It is no one's friend, and everyone's."

"Well, be that as it may, there's a tendency among Dipper's sort of people to keep out of the clutches of the law, either for good or ill."

"What do you know about his life before you engaged him? He seems to use many of the cant expressions of thieves."

"I believe that's not uncommon in the East End. For that matter, it's not uncommon among young bloods in the best families. In that respect, Dipper may be getting above his station."

"What do you think, Dr. MacGregor?"

"I think a good part of what the boy said may be moonshine, but there's one thing I believed. When he swore he'd never have gotten his master in trouble by leaving a body in his room, that seemed to come straight from the heart."

"Has he ever shown signs of nervous instability or a violent temper?" Sir Robert asked Julian.

"Pardon me, Sir Robert, I don't mean to laugh, but when I recollect we're talking about Dipper——! Sir Robert, he has the softest heart in Christendom. He can't even kill spiders. He gathers them up and ushers them out the window as though they were royalty. Perhaps he has it in him to commit a murder—perhaps we all do, under some set of circumstances or other—but in Dipper's case it would not—could not—be this particular murder. To kill a young woman in cold blood, and then tuck her into bed and go blithely off to dinner as though nothing had happened—no, Sir Robert, I'd stake my life on it: He isn't capable of that."

"Can I ask you a frank question, Kestrel?"

"I've never known you to hesitate in the past, Doctor, and I shouldn't wish you to."

"Here it is, then. Your man seems very loyal to you, and if you've really done as much for him as he says, he's got reason to be."

"What I've done for him is to pay him very inadequately to wait on me hand and foot at any hour of the day or night."

"Rubbish! I can read between the lines of what he said. He was living hand-to-mouth in London, and you took it into your head to engage him as your manservant, even though he talks as if he came out of a flash house, and he can't have known the first thing about getting up shirt frills, or whatever he does for you. Oh, yes, I'd say I've got it about right, or you wouldn't be looking out of the window instead of at me. He's loyal to you, and he's right to be. But my question is, how far would he go to do you a service? Has he got it in him to put a person out of the way, if he thought you needed it badly enough?"

"I don't know. I know he's devilish efficient and clever, and if he did decide to commit a murder for my sake, I'd like to think he'd make a neater job of it than this. But I find it very hard to believe he could stab a woman in the back for any reason. Besides, how could he do me any good by killing a woman I've never met and don't know from Eve?"

"We've got to identify that girl," said Sir Robert. "The whole investigation hinges on that. Only when we know who she is will we know who might have had a reason to kill her."

Julian drew breath and plunged. "Are you going to finish questioning everyone in the house?"

"I thought I *had* finished, Mr. Kestrel."

"You haven't accounted for the whereabouts of some of your family and Mr. Craddock at the time of the murder."

"Do you mean to say you wish me to treat my family and guests as though they were under suspicion?"

"I am one of your guests, Sir Robert, and I've been under suspicion ever since the murder was discovered. Believe me, it hasn't been a pleasant experience. I can understand your reluctance to put your family through it. But how can the murder be thoroughly and fairly investigated, unless everyone in the house, however seemingly above suspicion, is questioned about what he or she was doing when the girl was killed?"

"You cannot mean you would have even my wife—my sister—questioned about this crime!"

"The law is impartial," said Julian quietly. "It is no one's friend, and everyone's."

Sir Robert drew a long breath. "So be it, Mr. Kestrel. If you'll come with me, gentlemen, we will ask each of my family and Mr. Craddock where they were and what they were doing between half past four and twenty minutes to six."

# * 14 *
# A TICKLISH TASK
# FOR A MAGISTRATE

---

Before going to the drawing room to question his family, Sir Robert finally told the servants about the murder. By this time, they were so worn out with speculation that the news came as more of a relief than anything else. On hearing that Mr. Kestrel's valet was being held for further questioning, they assured each other they had always known Dipper was a bad lot. He had a wicked look about him; anyone could see it. "Only think of it," said Dorcas to Molly Dale, "he sat by you all evening, and you not knowing he had blood on his hands!" But Molly was crying bitterly and did not answer.

Travis was back from inspecting the gun room, and reported to Sir Robert that no knives were missing or showed signs of recent use. Julian was relieved, since any suggestion that the murder weapon came from the gun room would make things worse for Dipper. Unfortunately, the lack of such evidence did not establish anything much in Dipper's favour. Proving innocence, Julian realized, is apt to be much more difficult than proving guilt.

Sir Robert told Travis to have the girl's body brought downstairs to a small study, where the servants could file in one by one and look at her. Travis and Mrs. Cox were to supervise the viewing, and report to Sir Robert if anyone recognized the girl. Julian's room would be kept locked until tomorrow, when a more thorough search could be conducted by the morning light.

Julian was, of course, obliged to move into another room. He asked Sir Robert if he might have the vacant guest room next door to his old room. Sir Robert agreed.

"What in blazes are you up to now?" MacGregor wanted to know.

"I wish I'd progressed so far as to be up to something. I just have a presentiment about that part of the house. I think that, if we understood the 'where' of this crime, we might understand the 'who' and the 'why' as well."

✳

"Do you mean to say you expect *us* to make a statement about what we were doing at the time of the murder? And that man is going to write it down?"

Lady Tarleton pointed an elegantly gloved finger at Rawlinson. He ducked his head and pretended to be busy with his notes.

"I am taking statements from everyone who was at or near Belle-garde at the time the girl was killed," said Sir Robert. "In the case of all of you, of course, I look upon this as a formality. But if I refrained from questioning any of you, out of respect for your birth or position or character, my forbearance might appear to have far different, more dishonourable motives. Surely you wouldn't wish to have it said that I feared to ask my own relations the same questions I put to the servants about where they went and what they did this afternoon?"

"But there's no reason we should be demeaned in this way," argued Lady Tarleton, "when it's perfectly obvious who killed the girl. That creature Mr. Kestrel brought among us must have done it. Other-wise, why did he go to the gun room, and why did he lie about it afterward?"

"I grant you, a number of suspicious circumstances seem to point to Mr. Kestrel's servant. But until we have more positive proof, the investigation must continue. However distasteful the task, I must ask each of you to account for your whereabouts between half past four and twenty minutes to six this afternoon. I put it to you plainly:

Unless you have the goodness to answer my questions, I shall have no choice but to turn over the conduct of this enquiry to some other magistrate, whose impartiality is not open to doubt."

None of the Fontclairs wanted that—Julian could tell by the troubled silence that followed Sir Robert's words. Were they afraid an outsider might stumble on the secret that Craddock was holding over their heads? Or did they have an even more sinister reason to shrink from a full and fair investigation of the murder?

Hugh stood up. "If you'll permit me, sir, I should like to be the first to make a statement."

His mother smiled warmly at him. Sir Robert's smile was more restrained, but his eyes shone with pride and approval. "Please proceed."

"Well, there's not much to say, really. Mr. Kestrel and I went riding at—oh, it must have been about half past three. I showed him the park and the model farms. We didn't come back to the house until about five or ten minutes to six. Should I go any further?"

"Why don't we cover the period up to six o'clock, when Mr. Kestrel discovered the murder? First tell me: Were you and Mr. Kestrel together all the time you were out riding?"

"Yes. Yes, I'm sure we were."

"Did you see any strangers, or anything out of the common, anywhere near Bellegarde?"

"No, sir."

"And what happened when you returned?"

"Michael let us in, and we went into the great hall. Then we said something civil to each other about having enjoyed ourselves riding—that sort of thing—and Mr. Kestrel went upstairs. I stayed in the hall, and after a bit Miss Craddock came down and asked—" Oh, the deuce! he thought. I don't want to say she was asking after Kestrel. It will sound awfully funny, and it might put her in an awkward spot, what with the murder happening in Kestrel's room. "She asked if we'd had a good ride," he finished lamely.

Maud gaped at him. Why had he hidden the fact that she was looking for Mr. Kestrel? Did he think her forward for seeking out Mr. Kestrel that way? If he did, he was really being very unfair!

What other friend did she have at Bellegarde? *He* had certainly never taken her into his confidence, or asked to be taken into hers.

She realized Sir Robert was speaking to her. "Miss Craddock, would you be good enough to continue?"

She stood up shakily, conscious of her father's hard, intent gaze on her. She felt as though she were standing in a hot, bright light. In a voice so low that Sir Robert had to ask her several times to speak up, she described her outing with Miss Pritchard and the girls. "We came home at about a quarter to six. And I— I went to my room to dress for dinner."

"How did you happen to come downstairs again some ten or fifteen minutes later, when my son spoke with you?"

"I— I thought I'd left my parasol in the great hall. I hadn't. It was a silly mistake. I had it in my room the whole time."

Maud thought: Now I've lied to satisfy Papa, and I've lied so as not to contradict Hugh. And why I should do such a wrong thing for either of their sakes is more than I can say.

Hugh thought: Look how readily she took me up when I gave her a chance to conceal she was looking for Kestrel. If there were nothing hole-in-corner about her feelings for him, wouldn't she come right out and admit she asked me where he was?

Julian thought: Damnation. This is exasperating. Each of these infernal innocents is holding something back, and there's no telling whether it has anything to do with the murder, or whether it's merely some romantic muddle of their own.

"Shall I speak next?" said Lady Fontclair. She smiled at Sir Robert, her wide dark eyes looking confidently into his. "All through the period we're talking of, I was in the conservatory. I was tending to the plants, and sewing, and listening to you read aloud. I didn't see any strangers, or anything unusual."

"At one point," Sir Robert prompted, "I left the room."

Her eyes strayed for the first time. "Yes. Yes, that's true. I think you went to the library to get a book—Pope's verses. A few minutes later, Isabelle came in from the terrace. That was at twenty minutes past five—I remember, because she asked what time it was. You came back some five or ten minutes after that. You can't have been gone above a quarter of an hour, all told."

"Thank you, my dear. Isabelle, will you continue?"

Isabelle came gracefully to her feet. "I went out to my favourite seat in the rose arbour this afternoon. I don't remember precisely when I left, but it was closer to three o'clock than four. I brought my sketchbook and sketching box, so that I could design a pattern for Miss Craddock's wedding slippers. I'm to embroider them for her, as a wedding gift. When I finished, I thought it must be nearly time to dress for dinner, so I came in through the conservatory windows. Aunt Cecily was there. I asked what time it was, and she said it was twenty minutes past five. I said thank you and went upstairs.

"When I got upstairs, I thought I would go and look for Miss Craddock, so I could show her my design and see if she approved of it. I went to her room and knocked on the door, but she wasn't there. So I went to my own room and worked for a while on some other sketches. Then I rang for my maid and dressed for dinner."

Julian said, "Miss Fontclair, if you walked from the first floor of the new wing to Miss Craddock's room in the main house, you must have had to cross the corridor that leads to my room."

"I didn't cross it, precisely. I went down it a little way and then turned left into the corridor where Miss Craddock's room is."

Julian mentally retraced her steps. His room was at the end of a corridor. She would have come down that corridor from the opposite end, and at the point when she turned left, his room would have been only a few doors ahead. Was it too much to hope that she might have seen or heard something before she made that turn? Of course, by the time she came home at twenty minutes past five, the murderer might long since have killed the girl and fled from that part of the house. But, still—

Sir Robert apparently had the same thought. "You may well have passed close to Mr. Kestrel's room at or near the time of the murder. I don't wish to distress you with that idea, but merely to impress on you that your observations of that part of the house could be of the greatest importance."

Isabelle took time to think. "I'm afraid I didn't make any observations. I was there a very short time, and my only concern was to speak to Miss Craddock. Once I knew she wasn't in her room, I went directly to mine. I didn't stop to look about me. Everything seemed just as usual."

"And you heard nothing out of the ordinary?"

"No, Uncle Robert, I didn't."

"If you should remember something later—any detail, however small, that seemed strange or out of place to you—will you let me know?"

"Yes."

"Geoffrey?" Sir Robert turned to his brother.

"Afraid I don't have much of anything to say. Bit of a bore, after Isabelle. I went riding till after six, and then I dressed for dinner. That's about all."

Sir Robert continued to gaze at him expectantly.

"Well," said the colonel, beginning to fidget, "what more do you want to know?"

"The servants say you didn't leave to go riding until after five o'clock. In order to obtain a complete statement, I must ask you where you were between half past four and five."

"For God's sake, Robert! Have we got to the point where you're questioning the servants about me behind my back?"

"I questioned the servants about everyone's comings and goings this afternoon. Now, if you would be so good as to complete your statement—?"

"I was in my room! Are you satisfied? First I wasn't doing much of anything, then I put on my riding boots. Then I went out."

"Did your manservant help you with your boots?"

"My God, do you need a witness? He was dining. I didn't bother to ring for him. I can put on a pair of boots myself!" He threw himself back in his chair. "I'm afraid I don't remember which foot I started with. Sorry."

Sir Robert stood very still. It took Julian a moment to realize he was trying to command his voice. At last he got out, "Some of the servants thought you seemed disturbed about something when you left to go riding."

"I wasn't disturbed about leaving a dead woman in Kestrel's room."

"I didn't suppose you were. I'm merely attempting to make a thorough enquiry."

"Well, I don't have anything else to say."

"Very well. Catherine, may I trouble you to continue?"

"Oh, by all means. As long as everyone else is being put through this senseless humiliation, I mustn't be behindhand in bearing my share. It's some comfort that I can be very brief. I never left my rooms—my bedchamber and boudoir—from shortly after luncheon until I came down to dinner. My maid came to help me dress sometime after six. Otherwise, I was alone."

"May I ask what you were doing all that time?"

"I consider it an insult you should ask, but of course I am bound to answer. I was sewing—working on my embroidery. Is there anything else you wish to know?"

"That will suffice. Thank you. Guy?"

"Between about half past three and half past five, I was asleep. Then I woke up, rang for my man, and dressed for dinner. I came downstairs sometime between six and half past."

"You were asleep in your room?"

"Yes, sir. I was fagged out this afternoon. I'd been out a good part of last night, and then I got up early this morning to go to the horse fair. I didn't have anything else to do, so I slept for a couple of hours. The col—my father would remember that. I saw him just before I went up to my room."

Geoffrey nodded. "I asked Guy if he wanted to play a rubber of piquet, and he said he was sleepy and was just on his way upstairs to have a nap."

"When was that?" asked Sir Robert.

"I don't remember exactly," said Geoffrey.

"It was just before I went up to my room," said Guy. "Half past three."

"And where did this conversation take place?"

"I found Guy in the library," said Geoffrey. "He left, and I stayed."

"Did the two of you see one another again before dinnertime?"

"We couldn't very well have," said Geoffrey.

"I told you, Uncle, I was asleep," said Guy.

"Mr. Craddock, you appear to be the only person who has not yet given a statement. If you would be so kind—?"

"I took my horse out for exercise this afternoon. When I got back it was still a good while before dinner—I'd say, between half past four and a quarter to five. I handed over my horse to my groom and went for a walk. I came in at twenty minutes past five. I know, because I looked at my watch. I went upstairs to my room and dressed. That's how and about it."

"Were you alone all the time you were walking?"

"Yes."

"Where did you walk?"

"In the Chase. There's a little clearing there I had a mind to see again."

Lady Tarleton spun around to look at him, eyes blazing. He did not glance her way. Sir Robert was facing away from her and did not notice her reaction. "Did you see anyone in the Chase?" he asked Craddock.

"No."

"Michael says he let you in at the front door at about twenty minutes past five."

"That's right."

"Did you see anyone on your way to your room?"

"No. And no one saw me, that I know of. My man came up to help me dress, but that wasn't till after six. So I don't have what the lawyers call an alibi. But then, which of us does?"

# * 15 *
# LADY TARLETON
# AT BAY

"If you must talk in terms of alibis," Sir Robert said coldly, "allow me to point out that Lady Fontclair was with me throughout the period in question, apart from a very brief interval when I was in the library. And my son, Mr. Kestrel, and Miss Craddock are absolved from suspicion, if Dr. MacGregor is correct that the girl was killed no later than twenty minutes to six. We know from their statements, as confirmed by Michael, that none of them returned to the house until after that time."

"If I understand Dr. MacGregor correctly," said Lady Tarleton, "the only reason he thinks the girl was dead by twenty minutes to six is that Mr. Kestrel says she was cold when he found her. And we have only Mr. Kestrel's word for that."

"I also touched the girl and found her cold, only a matter of minutes after Mr. Kestrel discovered her," Sir Robert pointed out.

"And I had other factors in mind besides the coldness of the body when I gave an opinion about the time of death," said MacGregor. "Based on the onset of rigor and the loss of blood, I'd have said she was most likely killed between half past four and half past five."

Lady Tarleton tossed her head. "As long as we're all answering questions, I should like to ask Mr. Kestrel if by any chance he chose to rid himself of some—creature—he'd formed a connexion with, by having his servant kill her in our house, so as to throw suspicion on us."

"I hope you'll be reluctant to believe that of me, Lady Tarleton —just as I'm reluctant to believe that any of you could have killed the girl in my room, so as to throw suspicion on *me.*"

"None of you is under suspicion," said Sir Robert. "I cannot counsel you strongly enough not to make a difficult situation worse by accusing one another."

"Robert, you're growing hoarse," said Lady Fontclair. "And you've had nothing to eat, and it's nearly midnight. Why don't you and Dr. MacGregor and Mr. Kestrel have dinner? We've all finished making our statements. Surely there's nothing more you can do about the murder tonight."

"I'm afraid there are a few tasks left to perform." He gave her a brief, strained smile. "One of those tasks is to ask each of you to look at this and tell me if you recognize it."

He reached into a pocket of his waistcoat, and held out his hand. The silver scallop shell glinted in the candlelight.

"What is it?" asked Hugh.

"It's an ornament that the young lady was wearing around her neck."

"How revolting!" Lady Tarleton backed away. "Surely you don't expect us to touch that thing!"

"All I ask is that you look at it long enough to tell me whether you've seen it before."

Lady Fontclair held out her hand to him. "May I?" she asked gently.

He gave her the scallop shell, still strung on its blue ribbon. She looked at it closely and earnestly, then shook her head and offered it to Hugh. Sad and a little awed, he ran his eyes slowly over first one side and then the other. He passed it to Isabelle with a look of apology, as though he would have liked to spare her this ordeal. But Isabelle took it with a steady hand and looked it over as though she were being asked for an artist's opinion of its quality.

It seemed settled that the scallop shell would travel in a circle around the room. Colonel Fontclair came next. As Isabelle brought it to him, he shrank back a little in his chair, staring at the gleam of silver between her fingers. He reached out slowly and took the scallop shell, looked at it, then handed it to his son. Guy gave it the briefest possible glance and practically thrust it into the face of the next person, who happened to be Maud. She gazed at it in puzzlement, then passed it to her father.

Craddock gave it his narrow, flinty-eyed stare. Then he brought it to Lady Tarleton. He seemed to loom up on her as he approached, making her tall, proud figure look amazingly slight and vulnerable. "Do you want me to hold it for you, or will you take it?"

She held out her hand imperiously. He gave her the scallop shell. She turned it crisply from one side to the other. "It means nothing to me. Here, Robert. Take it back."

Sir Robert stared at her outstretched hand. Lady Fontclair and Julian, standing on either side of him, stared too.

A red stain was spreading over her white glove, fanning out from the side of her forefinger nearest the thumb. When she saw it, she flung the scallop shell on a table and jerked her hand away.

"My dear, you're hurt!" exclaimed Lady Fontclair.

"It's a trifle. I thought it would have stopped bleeding long since. I wrapped it in a piece of linen, and it seemed to do very well."

MacGregor came forward. "Let me see it."

She pressed both hands to her breast, the left clutched around the right. "It's nothing, I tell you!"

"I'll be the judge of that. Give it here, madam, if you please."

She made a sound between a sigh and a snort, and thrust out her right hand. MacGregor carefully removed her long glove and unwound the thin strips of linen she had wrapped around her finger. "Nothing serious, but a very ugly cut. How did you do it?"

"I cut myself on my embroidery scissors. It was when I was working in my room this afternoon. I don't know why it should start bleeding again after all this time."

"It started bleeding again because it didn't have a proper dressing. You ought to have gone to Lady Fontclair. She knows how to look after this kind of thing."

He dabbed the blood away with his handkerchief. Julian, stealing a glance over his shoulder, saw that the gash extended from the base of her forefinger to the middle joint. He tried to remember if she was right-handed. Yes: he pictured her brandishing Sir Roland Fontclair's sword in the gun room last night. She had used her right hand, he was sure.

He said, "I don't quite understand how you cut your finger, Lady Tarleton."

"And *I* don't understand why that should be any concern of yours!"

"I beg your pardon. I was just trying to picture how a right-handed person could cut the lower part of her right forefinger with a scissors. If you'd been cutting with the scissors, your forefinger would have been inside one of the holes, not near the blades."

"The effrontery of this is beyond all bearing! How *dare* you question me like this? Next you'll be saying I cut myself while killing that wretched girl! Anything to cover your servant's guilt, I suppose! And *you!*" She raked the men in her family with her gaze. "You can all stand by and see this nobody—this social hanger-on, with his trumpery airs and graces—publicly cast doubt on my honour and question my word! If you were any of you worthy of our name, you'd demand satisfaction on my behalf! *He* would have done as much!" She flung up a yearning gaze to the portrait of Sir Roland Fontclair.

There was a shocked silence. The Fontclair men looked at each other, tense and uncertain. Julian wondered if Dipper had thought to pack his duelling pistols.

"See here," said MacGregor, "nobody's giving anybody that kind of satisfaction! I don't mean to take the reins of this business away from Sir Robert, but duelling's a barbarous, heathen custom, and I'm sure Sir Robert, being a magistrate, would agree with me it's no way to settle a quarrel between honest Englishmen. The fact is, there's nothing amiss in Kestrel's asking how you cut your hand, Lady Tarleton. This is a murder investigation. If there's any misunderstanding about what people were doing this afternoon, we've got to clear it up. Anyway, I need to know just how you cut your hand, if I'm to treat it properly. So you might as well tell us and have it over."

Sir Robert let out a long breath. Hugh and Guy dropped back

into their chairs. Julian made a small flourish with his hand, as though taking off an imaginary hat to MacGregor. MacGregor tried, halfheartedly, to glare at him in return.

"If everyone is against me," said Lady Tarleton, "if I must be cross-questioned like a common felon, then of course I have no choice but to submit. I have nothing to conceal. Though I'm afraid what I have to say will hardly justify the trouble you've taken to find it out. I dropped my scissors on the floor while I was working with it. It broke. I picked it up too hastily and cut my hand. It's as simple as that."

It's anything but simple, thought Julian. How could you pick up a broken scissors from the floor, however carelessly, so as to cut your finger all the way from the knuckle to the middle joint? Oh, no, Lady Tarleton, that won't do at all.

✳

The servants had viewed the murdered girl's body. Sir Robert found them in a fever of excitement, their horror mixed with fascination and a sense of their own importance. Here they were at the centre of a crime that might become as famous as the Ratcliffe murders! Most of them were full of pity for the girl, while a few said she was probably no better than she should be, but no one had the slightest idea who she was.

Sir Robert had no choice but to return to the drawing room and ask the Fontclairs and Craddocks to look at the girl. They were joined by a quaking Miss Pritchard, who had put Joanna and Philippa to bed with their doors securely locked. It was agreed that Sir Robert and Lady Fontclair would break the news of the murder to them early next morning, to make sure they did not hear of it first from gossip among the servants.

Meanwhile, Julian took MacGregor aside. "I want to thank you for putting a damper on what might have blown up into a very ugly quarrel between me and the Fontclairs. An affair of honour would have been deuced inconvenient just now."

"It wouldn't have come to that. Sir Robert's a sensible man, at bottom. He'd never have allowed what you young bucks are so wrongheaded as to call an affair of honour. All I did was give him time to think, and let his conscience get the better of his family pride. That's the Fontclairs' besetting sin—they've all got at least a dash of it. Lady Tarleton's the worst—she thinks she can ride roughshod over everything and everybody, just because she's a Fontclair. The colonel's too indolent, and that good-for-nothing son of his is too selfish, to give much thought to the family name. But make no mistake: If it were really threatened, they'd defend it quick enough, and they might be much more dangerous than Lady Tarleton, because she's got scruples of a sort, and they don't. Sir Robert's different—he really tries to do right and not put his honour above England's law, or God's. But it's a struggle for him—he's head of the family, and the proudest of the lot of them. You don't know what it costs him to hear you out with patience, when you put it to him that one of his family might have had something to do with the murder."

"What about Miss Fontclair? Is she as fanatically proud as the others?"

"Isabelle? She's a puzzle. But if I had to take a guess, I'd say she sets as much store by the family name as Lady Tarleton. What she's got that Lady Tarleton lacks is self-control. She's disciplined, like Sir Robert. Whether she's got his moral sense is something else again."

✳

The dead girl lay face up on a divan in a small study. A quilt was wrapped around her up to her neck. In silence, the Fontclairs and Craddocks filed past her. Each of them held a candle to her face—looked at her—passed the candle to the next person—and withdrew into the shadows.

Julian stood unobtrusively near the head of the divan, so he could watch their faces as they looked at the girl. He hoped against hope he might learn something from their reactions. For it seemed more and more likely that one of them had killed her. Lady Tarleton, Craddock, Colonel Fontclair, Guy, Isabelle—none of them had a complete alibi for the time of death, and their statements ranged from dubious to unbelievable. Even Sir Robert and Lady Fontclair had each been alone for a quarter of an hour between half past four and six—long enough to have stabbed the girl in Julian's room and returned to the conservatory.

He found it hard to observe this ritual with the calm, alert detachment he needed. It was all very well to conclude, as a matter of logic, that one of these people must have killed her. It was quite another thing to see them filing slowly past her, and to picture each of them driving a knife into her living flesh. But he must not let his feelings cloud his judgement. Compassion was all very well, horror was only natural, but neither would do the girl any good now. The only thing of value left to give her was justice. And that was another reason—as if Dipper's predicament were not enough! —why he must do everything in his power to solve the murder.

No one admitted to recognizing the girl. They got through the viewing fairly well—all except Guy, who stuffed his handkerchief in his mouth and ran out of the room. That might have meant something, or nothing, and the same could be said of all the suspects' reactions. Craddock's grimness, Lady Tarleton's revulsion, the colonel's dread—they could all be symptoms of guilt, or merely the natural responses of innocent people at the sight of a murder victim. Not that Julian would have described any of those three as innocent. They might not be guilty of murder, but they were each hiding something, he felt sure.

And speaking of hiding something, he would have to find out what Hugh and Miss Craddock lied about when Sir Robert was questioning them. Now that they had seen the dead girl in the flesh, they might be more willing to reveal anything they knew that could throw light on her murder. Maud was especially moved; there were tears spilling down her cheeks. To Julian's surprise, she avoided both Hugh and her father, although Hugh offered her his handkerchief, and Craddock tried to put his arm around her. The only person she would accept comfort from was Lady Fontclair. But she took a moment to seek out Julian and whisper, "I just wanted to tell you, I'm sorry people are saying you had something to do with all this. *I* know you didn't." Julian could only be grateful he need not count Miss Craddock among the suspects.

Isabelle looked more shaken than Julian had ever seen her. After the viewing, she sat in a corner of the study, her hands clenched, fighting for self-command. He went up to her and said gently, "You don't have to stay here any longer. They'll be coming soon to take the body away."

She drew a long breath and rose. He offered her his arm, but she shook her head. "No, thank you. I can manage."

They walked out together. After a while she said, "Do you suspect Aunt Catherine?"

"I don't know what to think. I wish she'd told the truth about how she cut her hand."

"Are you so confident you know when a person is telling the truth?"

"No, but sometimes it's fairly obvious when someone is—mis-remembering."

"I wonder you didn't notice when your servant—misremembered—about going for a walk outside."

"The people you trust are at a great advantage in lying to you. You don't expect it. Which is why it's just as well not to trust too many people."

"I suppose there's no danger you might trust any of us."

"Can I afford to?"

She gave him one of her cool, direct gazes. "I wouldn't, if I were in your place."

# *16*
# PLAN OF
# CAMPAIGN

It was after one o'clock in the morning when Sir Robert, MacGregor, and Julian finally sat down to dinner. Most of the household was in bed, although a few servants remained to wait at table. Rawlinson and Senderby had ridden to Alderton to arrange for the village mortician to come to Bellegarde and collect the girl's body. Sir Robert thought it best to send it quietly to Alderton tonight, before news of the murder created a sensation in the village.

Rawlinson and Senderby also had instructions to bring back two men from the village, a carpenter and a stationer. They would be sworn in as special constables, charged with assisting Senderby in the murder investigation. It gave Senderby some satisfaction to think of waking up his neighbours in the middle of the night and pressing them into service as his deputies. All of Alderton had been so eager to force him into the office of constable! Now he would see how some of *them* liked pestering people with questions and searching people's rooms, with Sir Robert Fontclair looking over their shoulders at every turn.

What remained to be decided was the fate of Dipper. Senderby's search of his room and belongings had turned up nothing of interest. He had been locked in Rawlinson's office for several hours; he could not be kept there all night. Sir Robert announced his decision to MacGregor and Julian after they had dined, and the servants had

left them alone. "I intend to commit him to gaol—not the county
gaol, but merely the lockup in Alderton. I don't propose to charge
him with the murder yet. I have too little evidence, particularly
about the victim's identity, to feel justified in binding him over for
trial. But I have it in my power to hold him for three days, at the
end of which time I shall consider releasing him, if no further
evidence against him has come to light."

"Will you let me stand surety for him instead?" asked Julian.
"Only name an amount of money, and I'll put it up."

"I'm afraid that, where the crime is so serious, there can be no
security short of confining the accused in gaol."

"If he were to bolt, it would look like an admission of guilt. And
he couldn't get very far without being caught and brought back."

"You force me to be blunt, Mr. Kestrel. I cannot permit you to
stand surety for Stokes, because I am not completely satisfied you
had nothing to do with the crime yourself."

"I see," said Julian softly. "In that case, Sir Robert, I have another
request. I should like to take part in your investigation of the
murder."

"What exactly do you wish to do?"

"I wish to be kept apprised of whatever you discover, and to make
enquiries myself."

"Do you doubt my ability to handle this investigation?"

"No, not at all. I just want to assist you. I've often been told it's
every Englishman's duty to enforce the law. That's why we supposedly have no need of police, and why any man can be called up
on the order of a magistrate to help keep the peace."

"I haven't called upon you to help me, Mr. Kestrel."

"I have volunteered, Sir Robert. I think it's not merely my duty,
but my right. My servant stands accused of the murder, and although
I don't believe for a moment you'll find any more evidence against
him than you have now, I believe that juries, faced with especially
atrocious murders, like to find someone guilty. I don't relish the
notion of Dipper's being hanged for want of any more plausible
suspect turning up. Besides, it's been hinted, and more than hinted,
that I had a hand in the murder myself. My honour is implicated.
With respect, I think you cannot refuse me."

"I admit, there is something in what you say. Very well. You may take part in the investigation and make enquiries yourself, provided you can do so with discretion and without giving offence."

"Thank you, Sir Robert."

"Don't think I'm unaware that your primary aim will be to determine whether one of my family is guilty. That you or anyone else could think such a thing pains and affronts me more than I can say. But I recognize that the possibility must be explored, and I should rather have you explore it, informally and quietly, than invite London policemen into my house to question my family and guests. If, a week hence, we haven't come near to solving this crime, then I shall have no choice but to appeal to the Bow Street Runners. But I hope and trust that, with God's help, we shall get to the heart of this matter ourselves."

He rose and excused himself, saying he must find out if Rawlinson and Senderby had returned with the special constables. After he was gone, Julian said to MacGregor, "He could spare himself a good deal of anguish by turning over this investigation to another magistrate."

"This is his ship, and he's the captain. He won't give up command unless and until there's clear evidence one of his family had something to do with the murder."

"And he's invited me to ferret out that evidence, if I can. What a devil of a task. I wish I could believe the murderer was a housebreaker, or some disgruntled labourer bent on terrorizing the landed gentry. But the evidence just doesn't point that way."

He reviewed with MacGregor the problem of access to and from the house—above all, the impossibility that any stranger could have escaped without either being seen or leaving a door unfastened behind him. "That's a poser," MacGregor admitted. "But as to how the murderer got *in*—he could have come in with the girl. We know she sneaked in somehow, late this afternoon. If one could do it, why not two?"

"You're assuming she got in shortly before she was killed. And we don't know that, do we? She could have been here for hours, even days."

"And nobody happened to notice her?"

"This is a very large house. She could have hidden in some unused room—or someone could have hidden her."

"Confound it, Kestrel, this is a respectable English house—not something out of *The Mysteries of Udolpho*!"

"I don't know. I'm beginning to feel distinctly like a character in one of Mrs. Radcliffe's novels. All right: Let's suppose the girl got in within the last four-and-twenty hours. How might she have done that without being seen? Travis is positive no one climbed through any of the windows. That leaves us with the front door, the back door, and the French doors in the conservatory. Any one of them might have been left unlocked and unattended long enough for the girl to slip in. But how could she have known that? She'd be taking an immense risk, entering through one of those doors and hoping no one would be there to see her."

"But, man, she got in somehow!"

"Oh, unquestionably. But I think she had the cooperation of someone in the house—someone who watched for her and let her in when the coast was clear. That would have been easier at night than in the daytime— No, perhaps I'm wrong. Guy told me dogs guard the house at night. She couldn't have come near without their raising an outcry."

"Not if somebody they knew was with her," MacGregor pointed out reluctantly.

"True." Julian looked thoughtful. "Guy came in last night at one or two in the morning. I know because he stopped by my room. He was bosky, but still fairly lucid. He said he uses the back door to get in and out at odd hours."

"You think he might have brought the girl in with him?"

"He complained of not having any female company last night. That might, of course, have been a blind."

"I wouldn't put anything past him. Bringing a girl into the house for the worst of reasons, right under Sir Robert's nose—he'd be more than capable of that!"

"But what is the worst of reasons? Dalliance—or murder?"

"I was referring to what you call dalliance, and I call fornication. But, murder—he might be capable of that as well."

"But why? And why in my room?"

"To throw suspicion off himself, maybe. Let's say he keeps the girl in his room all night, and she's still there with him the following afternoon, when he says he was taking a nap. She makes him angry somehow, or she threatens to—to—I know!—to go to Sir Robert and Lady Fontclair and tell them he's been keeping her there."

"I can't see him resorting to murder just to avoid a dust-up with his uncle."

"I don't know. It's in his interest to stay on Sir Robert's good side. He's always up to his ears in debt, and Sir Robert's been known to help him out. But, never mind, let's just say he decides to get rid of the girl for some reason or other. He finds some excuse to take her to your room between half past four and half past five, knowing there won't be anybody in that part of the house at that hour. He's gotten a knife from somewhere, and he kills her. He tucks her into bed—God knows why, unless it's just his vicious sense of humour. And when her body's found, he pretends to know nothing about her."

"It's not a bad theory. God knows, that tale he told about an afternoon nap always seemed a little thin. And it does sound like the sort of thing that would amuse him, to leave a corpse in my bed and see what I would do. But there are legions of questions. If he brought the girl in with him last night, why did he stop by my room and talk to me, as though he had nothing better to do? And what did he do with her in the morning, while he was at the horse fair? Then there's his reaction on hearing about the murder. He seemed as horrified as any of us. He may be an extremely good actor, but—" Julian shrugged and shook his head.

"Maybe what horrified him was guilt, or the fear of being found out."

"Maybe. Though it's hard to believe the same person who cold-bloodedly tucked the girl's corpse in my bed would feel much remorse about it afterward."

"This thing gets more confusing and complicated the more we talk about it. I don't know how you lured me into speculating about Guy in the first place. I've known the Fontclairs for some thirty years, and I'd as soon not believe any of them committed this crime.

I tell you frankly, I'd much rather your servant were guilty than anyone related to Sir Robert and Lady Fontclair."

"I understand that. What I find remarkable is that you can still be objective. You could easily have made up your mind that Dipper was the murderer, and blinked away any evidence against the Fontclairs."

"Believe me, that's what I'd like to do. But the truth is, I just don't think your man is a murderer. There's something about him —his face, his way of talking, his—I don't know, sweetness, though it seems a funny word to use about a young man."

"I know exactly what you mean. I had the same feeling about Dipper when I first met him—and in those days he was as dirty and unprepossessing an object as ever crawled out of the East End. He has a gift for outshining his circumstances. No matter what trouble or squalor he's steeped in, it seems as though his being there were all a mistake that would be cleared up presently. He's been with me for two years, and in that time he's proved his worth to me a hundred times over. Put simply, Dipper is as close to an angel as anyone I've ever known."

MacGregor looked at him thoughtfully. "You're a puzzle, Julian Kestrel."

"I thought we were talking about Dipper."

"We were. But when you talk about him, or about the murder, I get some sense of what you're really like. When you talk about yourself, what you say is all fustian. If I'd met you over dinner, and there hadn't been a murder or any kind of upset in the house, I'd think the same as I did when I first laid eyes on you—that you were a coxcomb, vain and light-minded and too clever for your own good, or anybody else's."

"And now?" asked Julian, almost shyly.

"Now I'm not so sure." MacGregor grinned. "If I ever make up my mind about you, I'll let you know. Meantime: How are you going to go about this investigation of yours?"

"I'm going to try to clear up some small mysteries, in the hope of shedding light on the large one. I want to ask Mr. Craddock why his mention of a clearing in the forest should so upset Lady Tarleton.

I want to have a talk with Miss Fontclair, because I find it hard to believe her artist's eye could be as unobservant as she says it was when she passed near my room this afternoon. And I should like to ask Guy—oh, a number of things. What I'd most like to know is how Lady Tarleton really cut her hand, but I'm damned if I know how to get at that subject without putting her on the high ropes.

"I'd also like to find out how the girl got her clothes so dirty and wore out her shoes. I think tomorrow I'll take a walk round the grounds and see if I can find any trace of her. Somewhere there's a bit of yellow muslin she tore off the hem of her skirt. The chances of its turning up aren't great—but, still, one never knows."

"She could have torn her skirt weeks ago."

"I doubt it. I think she took great care with her appearance. She was very fetching, and a good deal of money had gone into her clothes. Besides, she had a needle and thread in her reticule. She could have mended her hem in half a crack—women can do that sort of thing blindfold. But if she tore the dress not long before she died, she wouldn't have had any chance to mend it."

"I don't wish to insult you, Kestrel, but I'm beginning to think you'd have made a very good lawyer."

"I couldn't have abided the wig. I never see a barrister tricked out for court without thinking he looks as if a wire-haired terrier had settled on his head."

MacGregor gave a grunt of laughter, and rose. "Well, I wish you luck in this bloodhound game you're playing. I expect I'll see you at the inquest, if not before."

"Actually, I was hoping to call on you tomorrow."

"What for?"

"Well, to have another argument, anyway. I've been finding them very bracing. Seriously, I want to talk to you about the murder, and the investigation, and the Fontclairs in general."

"See here, you're not dragging me into taking sides against the Fontclairs!"

"I don't want you to take sides. Your objectivity is what I value most. Everyone here has something to hide or someone to protect. This house was thick with intrigue even before I arrived: the Fontclairs have a secret of some sort, and Craddock knows it, and he's

using it to force a marriage between his daughter and Hugh. I don't
know if the secret has anything to do with the murder—I shouldn't
be surprised if it did. But I know my chances of solving the murder
may hinge on my learning all I can about the Fontclairs—their
history, their character, their connexions. You've known them for
a long time, and you seem to understand them remarkably well.
Your help would be invaluable to me."

"Give me one good reason why I should throw in my lot with
you, against my longtime neighbours and friends!"

"They don't need you," said Julian simply, "and I do."

MacGregor glowered at him. "You can come at the end of the
day. I'll have finished seeing patients by then, unless some emergency
crops up. Mind you, this doesn't mean I've made up my mind to
trust you. In fact, it's mostly to keep you under my eye, because
there's no telling what mischief you might get up to on your own."

"Thank you, Doctor. I'll try not to wreak too much havoc in the
meantime."

"Havoc, fiddlesticks! And don't look so pleased with yourself!"

✳

Rawlinson and Senderby had returned with the special constables.
Sir Robert gave them their orders. They were to find out if the
murdered girl was known, or had been seen, on the Bellegarde estate
or in any of the nearby villages. In particular, they must ask after
her at all the local inns and posting houses. Finally, they were to
determine whether any strangers had been seen in the neighbourhood
during the past few days. Senderby was to have handbills printed,
describing the girl and requesting information about her or her
murderer. Sir Robert himself would offer a hundred pounds to anyone, other than an accomplice to the crime, who helped bring about
a conviction.

The mortician arrived. While he and Sir Robert were discussing
funeral arrangements, Julian was permitted to speak to Dipper. He
went with Senderby to Rawlinson's office, where Dipper was still
confined. On the way, he asked, "Does he know he's being committed to gaol?"

"I've told him, sir. He took it pretty well."

"What sort of place is this lockup of yours?"

"Not so bad of its kind, sir. A bit dark, on account of the windows being small and high up. A bit musty, maybe. A bit cold, but that don't matter so much at this time of year."

Julian, who had heard what pestholes some village gaols were, presumed the worst. He stopped Senderby in the corridor. "Here. See that he's comfortably housed and well fed, and has a fire if he needs one. And you needn't mention to him that we had this conversation."

"This is a lot of money, sir—I wouldn't know what to do with it all."

"Do what you like with it. Feed him on champagne and lobster salad, and yourself as well, for all I care. Just see that he's not in want. I shall visit him tomorrow, and if I find he's been neglected or ill-treated, I shall make myself very unpleasant to whomever is responsible. Do you understand?"

"Yes, sir."

They went on to Rawlinson's office—a cramped little burrow of a place. An oak writing desk took up most of the space, while all around it were shelves of ancient books and stacks of parchment. Dipper had fallen asleep at the desk. When Julian and Senderby came in, he lifted his head and blinked. His face lit up. "Sir!"

Julian felt he was being hailed as a rescuer, and had done nothing whatever to deserve it. He said sharply to Senderby, "That will be all."

"Sir Robert didn't say I was to leave the two of you alone."

"Did he say you were to remain with us?"

"Well—no, he didn't say that, neither."

"Then you may go. If you're afraid I might help Dipper escape, you can lock us both in."

Senderby backed toward the door, away from those challenging eyes. "That's all right, sir, I— I don't need to do that."

He slipped out of the room. Julian glanced out after him, to make sure there were no eavesdroppers lurking. The moment he closed the door, Dipper burst out:

"I can't tell you how sorry I am, sir, giving Sir Robert the dead heave like that. It's all on account of, when you're on the cross, like

I was before I knew you, sir, you never tells the truth to a beak—not if he was to ask you if the sun is out, or if London Bridge is in London. It's a long time since I was in the ring, but it all come back to me, suddenlike, when Sir Robert started asking me questions. I thought something'd been pinched from your room, and maybe you'd told Sir Robert I used to have light fingers, and he'd think I done it—and what was worse, maybe *you'd* think I done it. And if you ever thought I could steal from you, sir—why, sir, I'd lie down and die. So I said I was outdoors, clean away from the house, up until I come in to dinner. I didn't know they could prove I was wrinkling. And now they think I croaked that mort as was found in your room, and that won't do you no good, sir."

"It does seem likely to dampen people's enthusiasm for inviting me to country house parties. There's only one way to clear both our names: I've got to find out who really killed the girl."

"How will you do that, sir?"

"By being generally inquisitive. By snapping at heels and listening at keyholes and skulking behind arrases. But depend upon it, I *will* do it. You'll barely have got used to that lockup where they mean to put you before I'll have you out again. Even if the murderer's not found right away, Sir Robert can't keep you in gaol for more than three days without charging you, and since he won't find any more proof against you than he has now, he'll have to let you go."

"I'd like that, sir. But being in the stone jug's not so bad. I been there lots of times in town, and now I'll get to see what it's like in daisyville. It'll be a education, like."

"That, as my esteemed friend Dr. MacGregor would say, is moonshine. And it's very impertinent of you to comfort me when I'm trying to comfort you."

"I'm sorry, sir. Sir?"

"Yes?"

"Do you forgive me, sir? For trying it on with Sir Robert, I mean."

"I'll forgive you anything, if only it will stop you looking like a woebegone lamb. Do you think that, next time a magistrate asks you a question, you can remember you're now a law-abiding subject, and have nothing to lie about?"

"I will, sir—I wish my eyes may drop out if I don't!"

"What worries me is that, if this crime isn't solved within a week, Sir Robert plans to send to London for help. The last thing we need is to have some Bow Street Runner recognize you for a notorious thief."

"I dunno if I ever got to be no-tor-yus," said Dipper modestly. "But a lot of robin redbreasts'd know who I was if they clapped eyes on me."

"Then we've got to get to the bottom of this crime as soon as possible, before your redbreasted friends start flocking to Alderton." He pictured the Bow Street officers—stout, pugnacious men, their thumbs thrust into the armholes of their red waistcoats. "Are you sure you remember nothing out of the ordinary—no matter how small or insignificant—in or around my room before you left it this afternoon?"

"I've thought and thought, sir. I didn't see or hear nothing."

Senderby poked his head in. "Sir Robert says I'm to take Mr. Stokes away now."

Dipper turned to Julian. "Your togs is all in order, sir. Michael's got the polish for your boots. Good-bye and good hunting, sir."

"Good-bye. Never doubt for a moment, we'll catch our fox."

✳

There was nothing more to be done that night. Julian retired to bed in the guest room next door to his old room. He recalled what Philippa had said about the renovated guest rooms on this corridor: "You might as well live inside a piece of Wedgwood." That certainly described this room, with its pastel-painted walls and delicate mouldings of ribbons and rosettes.

It was nearly three in the morning by the time he got to bed. At last I've got leisure to think this whole thing out from beginning to end, he thought. And at once he fell asleep.

# *17*
## KNIVES AND
## OTHER MATTERS

---

Julian dreamed he heard a woman screaming, and woke to find that the screaming was real. It came from the direction of the servants' wing. Starting up from his bed, he pulled on trousers, a shirt, and his dressing gown. He rushed across the hallway, through the great chamber and down the grand staircase. On the lower flight of stairs, he stopped. His eyes met Guy Fontclair's.

Guy was coming through the great hall from the direction of the screens passage. He wore riding clothes and carried a rain-drenched greatcoat with a short cape attached. His boots were mud-stained, and his wavy hair stuck to his brow in curlicues. The smell of wet wool hung thickly about him.

He got rattled on seeing Julian. "I might have known you'd be stalking round the house at this hour, like Hamlet's ghost, or Macbeth's, or whoever's ghost it was."

"I heard a woman scream."

"That was Dorcas—stupid little jade! You'd think she'd never seen a man with a cape over his head before."

"It was you who made her scream, then."

"Don't say that as though I crept up behind her with a knife! All that happened was, I came in through the back door and ran into Dorcas in the servants' hall. I had my cape flung over my head to keep the rain off, so she couldn't see who I was. She started shrieking fit to bring the house down. I had to shake her before I could get her to leave off. And of course the servants came pouring in from all sides and gaped at us as though we were a Punch and Judy show. Damn their eyes!"

"You can't blame them for being in a nervous state."

"Well, they had no call to jump down my throat like that. I come in the back door at this hour all the time."

"They probably weren't expecting you to be out on a night like last night."

"I go out in all kinds of weather, damn you! I'm not somebody's grandmother!"

"Neither am I, but I'd have needed a devil of a good reason to be out in a storm like that."

"I had a good reason. I wanted to get out of this house. I couldn't sleep, thinking about all of us traipsing past that girl's body with a candle, looking at her."

"You seemed to be much affected."

"I was sick, if that's what you mean. I don't like looking at dead people. Not that I've seen all that many, in case you were thinking I go around leaving them in other people's beds."

He came over and sat down wearily on the stairs. Julian sat down beside him. "That's one reason I've never gone into the army," he added, "though I think the colonel would have liked me to sport his regimental colours, and family tradition says there's got to be at least one Fontclair in uniform every generation. It's not that I'm a coward! I like a good fight as much as anyone. But death is different."

Can this be a performance? Julian thought. It sounds absolutely sincere. And yet, isn't it exactly what a murderer would say, to excuse his squeamishness on being confronted with the body of his victim?

He said, "A woman's death is certainly different. I found it painful, too, seeing how young and frail she was, and how beautiful."

Guy got up abruptly and walked a few steps away. "It's a damned rotten business," he muttered.

"The murderer has to be found."

"I know that! Everybody knows that."

"Sir Robert's agreed to let me take part in the investigation. My man is in gaol and may be charged with the crime—I have a large stake in finding out who really killed the girl. Will you answer a question?"

"What is it?"

"You told me the room where the girl was killed used to be yours."

"What the deuce is there in that?"

"I thought you might have some idea why the girl and the murderer might have gone there. Could they have been looking for something?"

"I'm damned if I know. It's too bloody early for riddles. I'm all to pieces, and I'm going to bed."

"I just have one more question. I wish I could think of a more subtle way to put this—but are you in the habit of carrying a knife?"

"No, I'm not! I have a pocket knife, but I didn't bring it with me to Bellegarde. I can prove that if I have to."

Julian stood up. "Thank you for answering my questions. If you think of anything strange or remarkable about the room, will you let me know?"

"Why do you keep harping on the room?"

"Because I think it's important, in some way we don't understand." He yawned. "What a dreary time of day this is. The blackest night is brighter than a rain-soaked dawn in England."

He went back to his room. The house was very still. Apparently none of the Fontclairs and Craddocks had been roused by Dorcas's screaming. That was not surprising: Julian's room was closer to the servants' wing than any of theirs. His old room was closer still: as best he could visualize, it must abut Rawlinson's office on the upper floor of the servants' wing. He wished he had a plan of the house, so that he could study exactly how the rooms were arranged. Perhaps Rawlinson could find one for him.

He went back to bed, though without much hope of being able to sleep any longer. But exhaustion came to his aid: when next he opened his eyes, it was nine o'clock.

*

Miss Craddock came down to breakfast with the others, but found she could not eat. As soon as good manners permitted, she left the table and went into the library. Julian followed her. Hugh, seeing them disappear one after the other, felt as though someone had given his collar a nasty twist. Confound the man! he thought. Why did I ever invite him?

"Oh!" said Maud. "Mr. Kestrel."

"Am I disturbing you?"

"No."

"I was concerned, seeing you at breakfast. I thought you looked distressed. I think you still do."

"Well of course, I'm troubled about the murder. Everyone is."

"No one more than I. But, all the same, I managed to sleep a little last night." His gaze lingered on the shadows under her eyes. He might as well have reached out and traced them with his fingers.

"I *am* worried," she faltered. "But—I can't tell you why. I wish I could!"

"Yesterday you seemed to trust me. You enlisted me in your service—cavalier extraordinary."

"Yesterday there hadn't been a murder, and all sorts of things hadn't happened."

"Miss Craddock, if you know something—anything—that might throw light on the murder, I can't urge you strongly enough to tell it. A man I believe with all my heart to be innocent is under suspicion. A guilty man may go free."

She clasped her hands and walked about distractedly. "I wouldn't for the world keep anything back that might prove your servant's innocence, or help catch the real murderer. But, you see, this may not have anything to do with the murder. And it isn't my secret. If it were, I wouldn't think twice about telling you. I trust you, Mr. Kestrel—indeed I do."

"Will you think very carefully about whether you ought to keep this back? In an investigation like this, the most obscure, unlikely things could have an importance we can't begin to guess."

She shook her head. "Once you tell a thing, it's told forever. You can't take it back. If I made a mistake—"

"Every kind of concealment is dangerous now. My servant is in gaol because he kept something back, thinking it could hurt him to tell it. And in the end it was his hiding the truth, far more than the truth itself, that spoke against him."

"I just don't know. I have to think. I *will* think." She nodded firmly. "I promise."

\*

By midmorning, the sky had cleared, and the house was full of sunshine. Sir Robert ordered Travis and one of the special constables to comb Julian's old room, the corridor, and the rooms nearby for evidence that might have been missed last night. Julian watched the search for a while, but finding it a methodical business, unlikely to produce any revelations, he went to speak to Rawlinson in his cubbyhole of an office.

Rawlinson was looking haggard. He was one of those people, Julian thought, who crave the safety of familiar tasks and a comfortable routine. The murder had introduced a foreign element into his world, and he was restive, bewildered, and a little resentful.

"What can I do for you, Mr. Kestrel?"

"Would you be good enough to lend me the notes you took on the enquiries last night?"

"Those are official papers. I don't think they ought to leave my hands."

"Could we compromise and say they won't leave your office? I can look at them here."

"Well—I suppose that would be all right. Sir Robert says you're to take part in the investigation."

"Exactly. Thank you. There is one other thing. I would be very grateful if you could find me a plan of the house—the more detailed, the better."

"I think there were plans drawn up when the new wing was built. I'll see if I can find them."

"Thank you."

Julian sat down at Rawlinson's desk, and Rawlinson gave him his notes on the investigation. "There's pen and paper there," he said, "if you'd like to make any notes of your own." He coughed. "Would you mind if I left you? I have all kinds of business to attend to. This murder is taking up a really shocking amount of time."

"Not at all," said Julian readily. The room was too cramped for two people, anyway. Rawlinson must have the constitution of a mole, to be able to work in here.

Rawlinson went out. Julian took out his penknife to sharpen a pen, then looked at it thoughtfully. The blade on an ordinary penknife was, of course, too short to have stabbed the girl to death. But what a devil of a lot of knives we use in everyday life, he thought. There must have been scores of them at Bellegarde last night that the murderer could have used. Knives in the kitchen, knives in the stable for cutting twine and physicking the horses, pruning knives in the conservatory, hunting-knives in the gun room. The men may carry pocket knives—though Guy says, with a good deal of unnecessary vehemence, that he didn't bring his to Bellegarde. The women most likely have scissors—we know Lady Tarleton does—and those scissors women use for fancywork have infernally thin, sharp blades. Then, of course, Dr. MacGregor's been teaching Lady Fontclair medical treatments, which means she may have a knife for removing splinters or lancing boils. And an artist needs something to sharpen her pencils, though she probably uses a penknife, like this one.

He gave up that line of enquiry for now. Dipping his pen in ink, he wrote at the top of a sheet of paper: "Day of the Murder: Chronology." Then he wrote for some minutes, using Rawlinson's notes to confirm his memory:

| | |
|---|---|
| *Morning* | *Hugh, Guy, Colonel Fontclair, and I were at horse fair* |
| | *Lady Fontclair had morning callers* |
| | *Whereabouts of Sir Robert, Miss Fontclair, Lady Tarleton, and Mr. and Miss Craddock unknown* |
| *1.00* | *Luncheon* |

| | |
|---|---|
| *About 2.30* | *Miss Craddock and I talked in music room* |
| | *Sir Robert, Lady Fontclair, and Hugh reviewed legal papers* |
| | *Lady Tarleton in her room sewing all afternoon* |
| | *Whereabouts of Miss Fontclair, Guy, Colonel Fontclair, and Mr. Craddock unknown* |
| *About 3.00* | *Miss Fontclair went to work on embroidery design in rose arbour* |
| | *Mr. Craddock went riding: time of his departure unknown* |
| *About 3.30* | *Hugh and I went riding* |
| | *Dipper brought my boots to my room and remained there after I left* |
| | *Miss Craddock went on botany expedition with Miss Pritchard and the Misses Fontclair* |
| | *Colonel Fontclair found Guy in library* |
| | *Guy went up to his room and took a nap* |
| | *Colonel Fontclair at some point went to his own room* |
| *About 4.00* | *Sir Robert and Lady Fontclair went to sit in conservatory* |
| *About 4.25* | *Dipper left my room and went to look at gun room* |
| *About 4.30* | *Michael barred the front door* |
| | *Servants had their dinner* |
| *Between 4.30 and 4.45* | *Mr. Craddock walked to clearing in forest* |
| *About 4.50* | *Dipper came to dinner in servants' hall* |
| *Shortly after 5.00* | *Colonel Fontclair came down from his own room to servants' hall in an agitated state and asked if there was anyone in stable who could saddle his horse, then left through back door and went riding* |
| *Between 5.15 and 5.30* | *Sir Robert went to library to look for book of Pope's verses; Lady Fontclair remained in conservatory* |

| | |
|---|---|
| *About* 5.20 | *Miss Fontclair came in from garden through conservatory windows, asked Lady Fontclair what time it was, went up stairs in new wing and crossed to main house to look for Miss Craddock, went down corridor leading to my room then turned toward Miss Craddock's, finding Miss Craddock not there she went to her own room* |
| | *Mr. Craddock rang at front door, Michael let him in and barred door again, Mr. Craddock went up grand staircase to his room and remained alone there till six o'clock* |
| *About* 5.30 | *Sir Robert returned to conservatory* |
| | *Guy woke up and rang for his manservant* |
| *About* 5.45 | *Miss Craddock returned from botany expedition, went to her room* |
| *About* 5.55 | *Hugh and I returned from riding, I went up to my room and found body* |
| | *Miss Craddock came downstairs, spoke with Hugh in great hall, went back to her room* |

All very neat and orderly, he thought, but limited in its usefulness. For his chronology assumed that all the Fontclairs and Craddocks told the truth about their movements yesterday, when in fact he felt sure that some, or even most, of them had been lying. Still, there was something to be said for making himself familiar with their stories, so that he would be quick to notice any discrepancies.

He gave some thought to the condition of the suspects' clothes. All the Fontclairs and Craddocks except Sir Robert had dressed for dinner yesterday evening. That meant that, if one of them killed the girl, he or she had an opportunity to change clothes after the murder, and perhaps to clean any bloodstains off his or her garments. The girl's clothes had been dirty, but that did not mean the murderer's were. Indeed, the fact that no dirt had been tracked near the washstand suggested that the murderer's shoes, at least, were clean. And if any of the suspects' clothes were soiled, there might be perfectly innocuous explanations. Geoffrey and Craddock had been out riding before dinner. Isabelle had been sitting outside. Guy had changed back into his riding clothes and gone out in a violent rainstorm.

All in all, Julian did not think a search of people's clothes would be very illuminating—which was just as well, since Sir Robert probably would not allow it. If someone's clothes did have a story to tell, it would most likely come out anyway. Each suspect's wardrobe was cared for by a maid or valet, who would notice if any garment was stained or torn, or mysteriously went missing. Surely any servant who had such information would tell it for one reason or other—moral duty or fear, the desire for importance or the lure of an official reward. Unless, of course, loyalty to the Fontclairs triumphed over all other considerations. Loyalty—that was the bane of the investigation. There was simply no knowing who might not lie to protect someone else from prosecution, or the family honour from disgrace.

✳

It might have been loyalty that made the Fontclairs' servants so chary of talking to Julian when Sir Robert was not by. Either that, or they believed he had committed the murder, or connived with Dipper to commit it.

The simplest question was enough to put Michael, the footman, on his guard. "Do you know where Miss Fontclair is?" Julian asked him.

"No, sir."

"Do you know if she's in the house?"

"No, sir."

"No, you don't know, or no, she isn't in the house?"

"She went out, sir."

"We begin to make progress. Have you any idea where she went?"

"No, sir."

"Did she ride or drive, or was she on foot?"

"On foot, sir."

"I gather she often sits in a spot called the rose arbour."

"I wouldn't know, sir. My duties don't take me into the garden."

"Where in the garden is the rose arbour?"

"I couldn't say, sir. My duties don't—"

"—take you into the garden. So you said. You might as well tell me, Michael. I'll just keep asking till someone does."

The boy looked down from his tall height with a harassed, rebellious face. At last he sighed and gave it up. "You go out through the conservatory windows, sir, and down the terrace stairs. You keep going down the main path, till you reach the wilderness garden. The rose arbour is there."

"Thank you very much."

Walking stick in hand, Julian descended the terrace stairs and followed the central garden path. It led between orderly beds of flowers, through topiary arches, and past small fountains where tritons sported with water nymphs. But beyond a tall border of hedges, Nature shook off the restraints of pruning and mowing. Rhododendrons grew in charming confusion, apple trees offered their little wild fruits to the birds, magnolia blossoms fluttered against austere birches, poppies splashed colour over the ground. Julian shaded his eyes and looked about him, trying to catch the sight or the scent of roses.

In the end, he found the arbour quite by chance. It appeared suddenly round a corner of his path: an archway of delicate latticework, with a marble bench inside. Roses, pink and red and white, climbed the sides of the arch, dangled from the top, and nestled in the gaps of the wrought-iron trellising.

Isabelle sat among the roses, her dove-grey gown dappled with sunlight, her open sketchbook in her lap. Her bonnet lay on the ground nearby. She must have heard him coming, for she was looking toward him expectantly. It would be no small feat, he thought, to take Isabelle Fontclair by surprise.

"Good morning," he said. "I came here hoping to find you."

"You have questions for me, I suppose."

"I did. But seeing you here, with the sun on your hair and the roses clustering round you, I've all but forgotten what they are."

"Must you begin again, Mr. Kestrel?"

"I'm sorry. I know you asked me to leave off. But when you sit in the most idyllic spot in the garden, wearing a halo of sunshine in place of a hat, how can you expect me to keep my head? A poet would be driven to frenzy in this place—any man with blood in his veins would be hard-pressed not to throw himself at your feet. I think on the whole my behaviour's been a marvel of restraint."

"I think you have it in your power to restrain it further. Would you please hand me my bonnet? I only take it off in order to work."

"If you really had an artist's soul, you wouldn't do such violence to the landscape as to cover your hair and cast the shadow of a hat brim across your face."

"This is my favourite place, Mr. Kestrel. Please don't be so unkind as to drive me away from it."

"God forbid I should be unkind to you. I'd be kindness itself, if you would let me."

"Do you mean to give me my bonnet, or must I get it myself?"

He brought it to her. She put it on. The wide brim curved over her brow, giving her rather long face a heart shape. "Thank you."

His eyes fell on her drawing. "Is that the design for Miss Craddock's slippers?"

"Yes. I showed it to her this morning. She seemed to approve of it. Would you like to look at it?" She offered him the sketchbook. "It's to be white silk thread on white satin."

It was a pattern of star-shaped flowers—myrtle, he supposed. They looked wonderfully natural, yet were arranged with symmetry and grace. How like her, he thought, to lavish such care and virtuosity on a detail of Maud's wedding clothes that would hardly be noticed. He suddenly remembered Guy's conviction that Isabelle had wanted to marry Hugh herself. If that were true, how must she feel, crafting a wedding gift for her successful rival?

"I have to start on them as soon as possible," she said, "or they won't be finished in time for the wedding. Unless you think the wedding will be put off, on account of the murder?"

"I couldn't say. It's possible."

She would have taken back the sketchbook, but he asked, "May I look at your other drawings?"

She nodded. He would have liked to sit next to her on the bench, but she did not make room for him, so he stood beside her. He flipped to the beginning of the sketchbook and leafed through it. Her work was very fine. A sense of sun and shadow pervaded her landscapes, without any need for colour. Architectural details of

Bellegarde were drawn with skill and understanding. She captured people, especially her family, with a light, deft touch. One sketch that Julian particularly admired showed the Fontclairs in their drawing room: Sir Robert reading, Lady Fontclair smiling at the colonel across a card table, Lady Tarleton sewing with a look of grim concentration on her face. Hugh was daydreaming, Joanna was looking at fashion plates, and Philippa was building a house of cards. It was as though Isabelle had wanted to portray each person doing something typical of him or her. Elsewhere she had made studies of their faces, showing how the family features varied in each: austere in Sir Robert, stark and dramatic in Lady Tarleton, jaunty and a little weak in the colonel, open and earnest in Hugh. She had exposed, with truth but not without compassion, the contrast between Joanna's conventional prettiness and Philippa's thin, plain, lively face.

He opened his mouth to ask a question—then thought better of it. He praised her work, and they talked about her training and technique. "But you didn't come here to talk to me about art," she said at last. "If you want to question me about the murder, I'd just as soon have it over."

"Of course. Miss Fontclair, you're an artist, and your work shows you have an eye for nuances—for details most of us would miss. It intrigues me that you passed so close to my room at about twenty minutes past five. Of course, the murder might have taken place as much as fifty minutes earlier. It could also have happened within about a quarter of an hour afterward, though in that case the girl and the murderer might well have been in my room by the time you passed by."

"Aren't you overlooking the possibility that *I* am the murderer?"

He was taken aback. "I suppose I am. Are you?"

"No. But I can't think of any reason you should believe me."

"You really are the most remarkable woman."

"Again, Mr. Kestrel?"

"I wasn't flirting with you—not just then, anyway. I'm impressed, that's all."

"Thank you. What exactly is your question?"

"Are you sure you can't remember seeing or hearing anything out of the common, from the time you came in through the conservatory windows till you reached your own room?"

"I've been thinking about it ever since last night, but I still can't remember anything to the purpose. I do think, if there'd been anything out of place, I would have noticed. I *am* observant, and I know the house well. As to hearing anything—I wasn't really paying attention. If there was some noise in your room, I didn't notice. I don't think there could have been raised voices or a struggle. I would have heard that."

"I have one more question. I'm afraid it's unpleasant."

"Your questions do tend to be. What is it?"

"How do you sharpen your pencils?"

Her eyes widened. "You *are* being thorough, aren't you?"

"Well, it would be a great help to identify the murder weapon. I don't have much hope on that score. If I were the murderer, I should probably have thrown it down a well or buried it under a loose paving stone, or some such thing. Still, I've been trying to find out if any knife's gone missing."

"My knife hasn't gone missing. I have it here."

She opened her sketching box. Her pencils and India rubbers were neatly arrayed inside. In a slot of its own was a knife with a mother-of-pearl handle. She gave it to Julian.

"You use this to sharpen your pencils?" He drew the knife out of its black velvet sheath. The blade was three or four inches long.

"It's not very practical," she admitted. "A penknife would be easier and safer to use. Aunt Catherine is always warning me I'll cut myself with that one. But you see, that knife belonged to my father. It's one of the few things I have of his. Most of his possessions were sold when he died. He was deeply in debt."

"Who were your parents?"

"My father was Simon Fontclair. His father and Uncle Robert's father were brothers, so of course Uncle Robert isn't really my uncle, but my first cousin once removed. My parents died of influenza when I was three, and Uncle Robert and Aunt Cecily took me in. It was very good of them. My father didn't leave me a farthing. He had all manner of schemes to make his fortune—a half-finished invention, a plantation in Barbados—but they always came out bluely. He was a weak man," she finished succinctly, "but he was a Fontclair."

Julian gave her back the knife. "Did you ever leave your sketching box unattended between half past four and six o'clock yesterday?"

"No. I had it with me when I came out here to work on my design for Miss Craddock's slippers, and when I came in, I brought it with me. So no one could have used my knife to kill the girl. Except me, of course."

He asked frankly, "Miss Fontclair, if you had seen or heard anything that might implicate one of your family in the murder, would you admit it?"

Isabelle met his gaze steadily. "No, Mr. Kestrel, I would not."

# ✳ 18 ✳
# DICK FELTON'S
# EVIDENCE

On returning to the house, Julian was summoned to Sir Robert's office. Sir Robert told him that the search in and around the room where the body was found had turned up nothing of interest—nothing stolen, no sign of a struggle, and no indication of how the girl or the murderer got in. The search was being extended to the rest of the house.

"Have you heard from Senderby yet?" asked Julian.

"No, but he should be coming shortly to report on his enquiries in the neighbourhood." He added, "The vicar and his wife called a little while ago. They said the news is all over Alderton, and of course it's causing a tremendous stir. God grant we'll be able to solve the crime quickly, and put an end to the panic and the morbid curiosity it's excited."

I believe he means that prayer sincerely, Julian thought. He really can't credit that any of his family could be guilty.

Sir Robert handed Julian some large sheets of parchment. "Raw-linson told me you'd asked to see a plan of the house. These are the designs for the new wing, which was built in my father's time. The architects also made these sketches of the main house and the servants' wing, though those parts of the house weren't touched during the renovation."

Julian spread out the three ground-floor plans on a table: the servants' wing, the main house adjacent to it, and the new wing branching off the rear corner of the main house. He laid out the first-floor plans in the same pattern. The house looked odd and unfamiliar, seen from this bird's eye view. Vast, imposing rooms like the great hall and the great chamber were reduced to small square blocks, while a cubby-hole like Rawlinson's office looked far larger than it really was.

He said, "I can't conceive of anyone approaching the front door secretly. There's nothing but open space around it—the carriage court, the drive and the front lawn. The route through the garden to the conservatory windows provides more cover, but the best way to enter the house in secret would be from the back, through the silver lime grove or the kitchen garden." He pointed to the small room where the back door was. "I believe you told me this is used as a waiting room."

"Yes. For tradesmen and other people who have business in the servants' wing."

"It seems to be just beneath Rawlinson's office, which is next to my old room. So near and yet so far."

Sir Robert nodded. "Anyone standing at the back door could look up at your room, but in order to get inside it, he would either have to scale the wall and climb in through the window, or come in through the back door and go through the servants' hall, across the screens passage, through the great hall, and up the grand staircase."

"Scaling the wall is an interesting thought. It's not likely anyone climbed the tree outside the window, since the ground wasn't disturbed at all. But underneath the window, a few feet away from the wall, is a paved walk, which wouldn't show footprints or marks made by a ladder. Though it's hard to imagine anyone being so bold as to set up a ladder in broad daylight, even with all the servants at dinner and the family dispersed about the house and grounds. Besides, if there was a ladder, what became of it? The murderer can't have used it to get out again, because the window was left bolted from the inside."

Look at it how you will, he thought, the same conclusion always results. The murderer must be a member of this household—someone who could let the girl in on the sly, take her to my room and kill her, and then go about his business as though nothing had happened. He would have to be an acrobat, or a magician, to get into the house, kill the girl, and disappear without a trace.

✳

"Mr. Kestrel!"

"Yes, Lady Tarleton?"

"I want to speak to you. Come into the library."

When they got there, she turned to face him, her head high, her blue eyes flashing. "My brother tells me you mean to go on playing the policeman, intruding on our privacy and asking us insulting, outrageous questions. I don't know in what den of ill breeding you may have been brought up, but civilized people, when staying as guests in other people's houses, do not accuse their hosts of telling lies and committing monstrous crimes."

"I haven't accused anyone. I've simply been asking questions. Some of the answers I've received make matters even less clear than before. Which means I'm obliged to ask more questions—at the risk, I know, of making myself a very unwelcome guest."

"You've done rather more than ask questions, Mr. Kestrel! Last night you as good as accused me of telling blatant untruths."

"I was puzzled by some things you said. That isn't quite the same as branding you a perjuror."

"A perjuror! How dare you!"

"Lady Tarleton, I beg your pardon if I've offended you. Believe me, if my servant's life, and my own honour, weren't at stake, I would gladly take your word sooner than ride roughshod over your feelings."

"You flatter yourself, Mr. Kestrel. I assure you, my feelings aren't at the mercy of any such impertinent upstart as you. I don't know why you must needs meddle in the investigation, anyway. Why can't you leave it to Senderby and the special constables? What do you suppose we appoint them for, if not to do the sort of necessary but distasteful work that a *gentleman* would never dream of stooping to?"

"If I saw someone drowning or about to be trampled by horses, I wouldn't ask myself whether it's a gentleman's task to jump into the river or spring to the horses' heads."

"Oh, I see! We are to hail you as a hero, then."

"I didn't mean that!" he said, stung. He checked himself, got a grip on his temper, and smiled. *A touch, Lady Tarleton*, he admitted—*but the bout is far from over. So, on guard!*

As he turned back to her, his gaze lit on the chatelaine at her waist. He remembered she had worn it yesterday, too, before she changed for dinner. It had five slender chains, each with a ring at the end to hold some household item: a purse, a thimble case, a pincushion, a dainty notebook.

"What are you staring at?" she demanded.

"I was noticing that one of your chains is empty. Is that where you used to keep your embroidery scissors?"

"Again about my scissors! Is it a crime, Mr. Kestrel—is it a moral outrage—to drop an embroidery scissors and cut one's finger picking it up?"

"One of us seems outraged, Lady Tarleton, but it isn't I."

"I suppose you expect me to show you the broken scissors. Shall I go and fetch it and prove I've been telling the truth?"

"That would be extremely kind of you. Thank you."

She gaped at him. She had been speaking sarcastically, never dreaming he would have the effrontery to send her on such an errand. Yet she would not go back on the offer, once given. *She has scruples of a sort*, MacGregor had said of her, and it was true.

"Very well, Mr. Kestrel! I can't tell you how contemptible I find you—demanding physical proof of a lady's truthfulness! But if I must lay the scissors in your hands to make you believe me, so be it. Wait for me here." She swept out.

While she was gone, he strolled about the library, spinning the two great globes, one terrestrial, one celestial, and running his eyes over the books. They were shelved in regimental order, according to author and subject. The volume of Pope's verses was back in its place among Pope's other works. He wondered how Sir Robert could have taken a quarter of an hour to find it yesterday.

"Here you are, Mr. Kestrel." Lady Tarleton flung the scissors down on one of the long, polished tables. "If there are any other demeaning errands you'd like me to run, please don't hesitate to ask."

"Thank you." He picked up the scissors. It was badly damaged. The two pieces had come apart, and the thinner, sharper blade was dented and scratched. There were traces of a dark stain on it that looked like blood. Lady Tarleton's blood, most likely—but, as MacGregor had said, there was no way to tell. This wicked little blade could certainly have been used to kill the girl. But stabbing a person, however viciously, would not have etched these scratches in the metal. On the other hand, neither would merely dropping the scissors on the floor.

"You're still suspicious, aren't you?" she said. "You mean to go on prying and persecuting us all—when the real, the obvious killer is already in gaol! And I for one will see him hanged with the greatest satisfaction!"

"I don't think so, Lady Tarleton. Because before that happens, I swear I will take this house apart stone by stone and wring the heart of every person in it, till I find out who really killed the girl."

Her hands went to her throat. "What— what are you going to do next?"

"Among other things, I'm going to question Mr. Craddock. I'd like to know more about that clearing in the forest he went to have a look at yesterday."

She trembled. Her fists clenched and unclenched. "There are some things at Bellegarde you mustn't meddle with."

"That may be so. But there are other things I *must* meddle with, and the devil of it is, I don't know which are which."

"You'll cause more harm than you can begin to guess! But you don't care, do you?" She laughed bitterly. "A kestrel is a kind of falcon, isn't it? Mr. Kestrel, you were very aptly named for a bird of prey!"

✻

Luncheon was served before Julian had a chance to talk to Craddock. Halfway through the meal, a servant brought word that Senderby had arrived. Sir Robert and Julian hastily excused themselves and went to Sir Robert's office.

Senderby had two people with him. One was a boy of seventeen or eighteen, with a ruddy face, unruly brown hair, and a snub nose. He wore a short coat, grubby trousers, and boots. The other was a middle-aged woman in a faded brown calico dress, the sleeves pushed up above her scrawny elbows. Her greying hair was scraped back from her face and covered with a limp straw bonnet.

"You know Mrs. Warren, sir," Senderby said to Sir Robert, "and Dick Felton from the Blue Lion. They're the only ones I can find that had any talk with the girl afore she died."

Mrs. Warren plucked at her apron. She looked as if she expected to be charged with the murder at any moment. Felton seemed to be enjoying himself. He stood rocking back on his heels and looking around him with shrewd, interested eyes.

Sir Robert said to them, "You have been brought here to give information regarding the young woman who was found dead in this house yesterday evening. My clerk"—he gestured toward Rawlinson—"will take down your statements and ask you to sign them. I urge you to be as thorough, accurate, and, of course, truthful as possible. This is a very serious crime, but with the help of conscientious witnesses like yourselves, I feel certain we will soon bring the murderer to justice." He sat down at his desk. "Felton, please come forward. Preliminarily, your name is Richard Felton, and you are an ostler at the Blue Lion posting house in Alderton. Is that correct?"

"Yes, sir." The boy stepped forward eagerly. At a nudge from Senderby, he took his hands out of his pockets.

"When did you first see the young woman in question?"

"The day afore yesterday. She drove up to the Lion in a yellow bounder."

"That is to say, a hired chaise and pair?"

"Yes, sir. She hired it in Hammersley. I reco'nized the postboy and the horses."

"Hammersley is a village some ten miles south of Alderton," Sir Robert told Julian.

"Yes, I remember. I changed horses there on my way up from London."

"Did the girl come from London?" Sir Robert asked.

"I dunno where she started, sir. All I know is, Hammersley's the last place she changed horses."

"Had you ever seen her before?"

"I didn't see her then, sir—not properly. She had a veil over her face. But I've been showed her body, and it's the same young lady. No doubt in my mind about that."

"Had she any baggage?"

"She had that bag, there." He pointed to a blue worsted travelling bag with wooden handles, on a table behind him.

"Have you looked through it yet?" Julian asked Senderby.

"Yes, sir. I made a list of what's in it." He fumbled in his pockets till he found a paper, from which he read haltingly, "One blue dress, one handkerchief, one hairbrush, one looking glass, one nightdress, one cap, one—er—change of ladies' linen, one string of wood beads with a cross attached."

"A rosary?" asked Julian, surprised.

"I think that's what it is, sir. I never seen one before."

"A lot of foreigners mumble over beads," said Felton. "They don't know no better."

"Was the girl a foreigner?" asked Sir Robert.

"Yes, sir."

"How do you know?"

"By the way she talked, sir."

"You mean, she spoke with an accent?" said Julian.

"That's the ticket, sir."

"What kind of accent?"

"A *foreign* accent," said Felton impatiently.

"I mean, from what country?"

"I don't know that, sir."

"Does anyone know?" Sir Robert asked Senderby.

"No, sir," said the constable heavily. "She never gave her name to anybody or said much about herself."

"Was there a name on anything you found in her bag?" asked Julian.

"No, sir."

"What about papers, keys, merchant's labels on her clothes?"

"No, sir."

Sir Robert and Julian exchanged baffled glances.

Julian tried out a little French, Italian, and German on Felton, but it was no use: he could not match any accent with the murdered girl's. Sir Robert bade him go on with his story.

"I helped her out of the chaise and got her bag out of the boot. She tipped me handsome, and I stayed around her for a bit, hoping to earn a little more off her somehow. Besides, I was curious about her. She was a stranger and a foreigner, and dressed like a swell. Pretty, too. I couldn't make out her face too well, but she had as trim a figure as you'd ever wish to see."

"The gentlemen don't need to hear that," chided Senderby.

"Sir Robert said to be truthful and thorough," the boy retorted. "Anyway, I asked her if she was going to the inn, and could I carry her bag. But she held tight to it and looked around her, furtivelike. Said she'd rather stay some place quiet, not so public as the Lion. Asked me if I knew any place like that nearby. I told her about Mrs. Warren—how she's got a room in her cottage that she lets to lodgers. I warned her it was a plain kind of place, not suited to the likes of her—begging your pardon, Mrs. W. But she said she didn't care, so long as it was respectable. She made such a point of that, I began to think she must be a lady and not"—he winked—"a ladybird, if you know what I mean.

"The end of it was, she thought she'd like to stay there and asked if it was far. I said, 'It's just a spit and a stride, miss. I'd be glad to take you there.' But she jibbed at that—started backing away and said oh no thank you, she wouldn't bother me to go with her, and would I just give her directions where it was. So I did. She tipped me again—plump in the pocket, she must have been—took her bag and walked off. I'd have liked to follow her and see what she was about, but just then the *Paragon* drove up, and I had to see to the horses and the passengers and all. So that was the last I saw of her—alive," he finished darkly.

"What time of day was it?" Julian asked.

"If the *Paragon* was on time, which I think it was, the young lady must have arrived a bit before seven."

"If she left the village on foot, other people must have seen her," said Sir Robert.

"Most of the village was indoors," said Senderby. "Either that or they were watching the *Paragon*. Nobody's got eyes for anything else when the stagecoach is coming in. Still, a few people saw her walk away from the main village street toward the south footpath, that leads to Mrs. Warren's cottage. After that, nobody saw her but Mrs. Warren—till she was found dead here."

# *19*
## MRS. WARREN'S
## EVIDENCE

It was Mrs. Warren's turn to make her statement. She got through the preliminaries well enough. Her name was Deborah Warren, she lived alone in a cottage half a mile west of Alderton, her husband had died some years ago, and she supported herself by growing vegetables and doing fine sewing for weddings and christenings. Her cottage, which she rented from Sir Robert, had a spare room she let to the occasional woman lodger.

"And, oh, sir, I hadn't had a lodger in weeks, and I did need the money so, or I'd never have taken her in! Right from the start I feared she was no better nor she should be, what with her being a foreigner, and travelling all alone like that. Pretty, too, and dressed in them fine clothes—and no ring on her finger! But she looked well able to pay for her room and board, and I just couldn't bring myself to turn her away. And she never did pay!" Mrs. Warren's voice rose to a wail. "It's a punishment on me, that I let a wicked girl under my roof! God forgive me for speaking ill of the dead, but she must have had something wrong about her, or she wouldn't have got herself killed like that!"

"How much did she owe you?" said Sir Robert.

Mrs. Warren, who was dabbing her eyes with her apron, looked up and blinked at him hopefully. "I reckoned it out at two shillings ninepence, sir."

"I shall take responsibility for the debt. Rawlinson, be good enough to pay Mrs. Warren before she leaves."

"Oh, God bless you, sir, thank you!" She blew her nose. "In all fairness to the young lady, I can't rightly say she never meant to pay, for she went out yesterday morning leaving her bag with all her things in it behind her, like she meant to come back, only— only—" Her voice trailed away.

"When did you first meet her?" Sir Robert asked.

"She knocked on my door about half past seven the night afore last. She gave no name, and I didn't ask for one. She didn't seem to want to say much about herself, and I didn't like to ask, because, as I told you, sir, I wasn't easy in my mind about letting her stay, and I didn't want to know no more about her than I had to. I just called her 'miss.' I showed her the room, and she said she'd take it. She didn't make any fuss about the cost." Mrs. Warren furrowed her brow. "I don't know what else to tell you. I asked her if she'd be wanting her meals, and she said yes."

"Did she tell you why she had come to Alderton?" asked Sir Robert.

"No, sir."

"Did you ask her how long she meant to stay?" asked Julian.

"Why, yes, sir, now you mention it, I did, and she said—she said— It's hard to remember rightly! I feel struck all of a heap by what's happened. I never was in trouble with the law before in all my days."

"You're not in trouble with the law," Julian assured her. "You're helping the law unravel a very knotty problem, and we're all grateful."

She looked at him timidly. "I'm sure I want to do my duty, sir. It's just that it's hard. It's—it's been a hard day."

We're going about this all wrong, Julian thought. How can she be anything but dazed and fearful—here in her landlord's house, with Rawlinson taking down her every word, and all the law's majesty brought to bear on her lone self? We ought to have called on her at her cottage, where she'd feel more relaxed and in command of things. I think I'll do exactly that myself, later on, and see if she finds it any easier to answer questions.

Mrs. Warren was still trying to remember how long the girl said she meant to stay. "I think she said as how she didn't know. We left it that she'd spend the night, and let me know next day if she needed the room any longer."

"What did she do for the rest of the evening?" asked Sir Robert.

"She come down to the kitchen and had her supper—just picked at it, really. Then she went back to her room. She didn't come out again till morning."

"How do you know that?"

"My room's just across the hall from hers, and I sleep very light, sir. I'd have known if she left her room during the night."

"What happened next morning?"

"She came down and had her breakfast—about seven, I think. Then she put on her big shawl and her bonnet with the veil, and went out. And— and that was the last I saw of her."

"Did she say where she was going, or when she'd be back?"

"No, sir."

"Which way did she walk?"

"Down the footpath toward the village. I lost sight of her after she rounded the curve."

"But she never got to Alderton," said Senderby. "Leastways, I can't find nobody that saw her there. The fact is, nobody saw her at all, from the time she left Mrs. Warren's till her body turned up here."

"Where else besides the village does this footpath lead?" Julian asked him.

"A branch of it leads to the main road west out of Alderton, toward Whitford. If she was on that road, we'll find somebody that saw her. The horse fair was that morning; there was a lot of traffic going to Whitford."

"You must keep making enquiries," said Sir Robert. He added, after a pause, "The same road leads southeast through Alderton to Bellegarde."

Mrs. Warren nodded. "So I told her, sir."

Everyone spun around to look at her. "How did you come to tell her that?" said Sir Robert.

"She— she asked, sir," gulped Mrs. Warren.

"She asked you where Bellegarde was?"

"Yes, sir."

"Why didn't you tell us this before?"

"I forgot it, sir!" Her face crinkled up, and she pressed her handkerchief to her mouth.

Julian asked gently, "How did she happen to mention Bellegarde?"

"I was showing her her room, and she looked out the window and said, in her funny speech, 'Please can you tell me where is the house called Bellegarde?' I said it was a mile or two southeast. And I asked her, 'What would you be wanting at Bellegarde, miss?' And she seemed to take fright, and said she didn't want nothing there, she'd just heard it was a beautiful house, and she might like to see it. But I must confess to you, sir, I— I had a feeling that wasn't true. I thought she'd made it up on the spur of the moment, like. Oh, deary me, I should have shown her the door after that, I know! It's bound to lead to no good, having somebody sleep under your roof that you can't trust not to tell you a story."

"Did she tell you anything more about why she came to Alderton, or why she was interested in Bellegarde?" There was an edge of desperation in Sir Robert's voice.

"No, sir."

"Think very carefully." Sir Robert leaned toward her over his desk. "Did the girl make any other mention of Bellegarde, or anyone at Bellegarde, during the time she stayed at your house?"

"I don't think so, sir. No— no, I'm pretty sure she didn't."

"Have you told us all the conversation between you and the girl, both the evening she arrived and the following morning?"

"Well, yes, I think so, sir—but it's hard to remember, as I said."

Julian was thinking: Assuming someone at Bellegarde killed the girl, did that person know in advance she was coming to Alderton? Or did she just turn up at Bellegarde and give the murderer a nasty surprise? He asked Mrs. Warren, "Did any messages come for the girl while she was staying with you?"

"Not that I know of, sir."

"Did anyone try to speak with her?"

Mrs. Warren shook her head.

"Did any strangers come by your house, either the day she arrived or the day she left?"

"No, sir. And I keep a close watch for strangers. Living alone as I do, and my cottage being a bit out of the way, I'm always afeard of thieves."

Sir Robert thanked Felton and Mrs. Warren, and Rawlinson showed them out. The boy went reluctantly, Mrs. Warren with palpable relief. Sir Robert got up and walked around his desk, frowning. "This investigation is in every way irregular. As a rule, the victim's family or friends would take the lead in bringing her murderer to justice. But since we still know next to nothing about who the girl was, I shall have to continue to take sole responsibility for the investigation."

He turned to Senderby. "You must redouble your efforts to find people who saw or spoke with her. And question my servants again. We know now that the girl had a foreign accent: that may strike a chord in someone's memory."

"We also know she changed horses at Hammersley, on the London road," said Julian. "If she started her journey in London, she would have had to change horses at least twice before that. Postboys and ostlers might remember her. She may even have spoken with an innkeeper or fellow traveller. Or she might have been seen at a toll gate."

Sir Robert nodded. "One of the special constables must trace her journey back to wherever it began. He must go to each posting house and turnpike gate she passed through and glean whatever evidence he can about her identity, the purpose of her journey, and any person who was seen in her company. At the very least, once we know where she came from, we can make enquiries about her there."

Julian was not hopeful that she had dropped clues about herself on her journey. She had clearly wished to keep her movements and identity a secret. She had not told her name to anyone in Alderton, she had spent the night in a retired cottage, and next day she had left Mrs. Warren's in the early morning, only to appear out of nowhere at Bellegarde in the late afternoon. Still, her appearance had been striking enough to attract attention. Someone, somewhere, might have observed something useful about her. Of course, if she had begun her journey in London, it would be the devil's own work to trace her there. They would have to circulate advertisements, offer rewards. And the Bow Street police would be almost certain to take over the investigation.

He put those concerns aside for the present. His next task was to go to Alderton and see how Dipper was getting on. He decided not to call on Mrs. Warren till tomorrow; she needed time to recover from today's interrogation. Instead, he would pay his promised call on Dr. MacGregor. He felt the need to have a good long talk about the Fontclairs.

✳

Julian decided that, instead of riding to Alderton by the main road, he would walk there through the Chase—the tract of thick woodland to the north and northwest. That was the route he suspected the murdered girl had taken to reach Bellegarde. If she had come by the main road, she would have had to pass through the center of Alderton, where someone would surely have seen her. Of course, she might also have skirted the south side of the village and approached Bellegarde through the park. From there she could easily have passed through the formal garden to the terrace and entered the house through the conservatory windows. But the forest provided more cover and seclusion, which would likely have appealed to someone as secretive as the girl.

He wondered how she had known the way, whichever route she took. She had asked Mrs. Warren where Bellegarde was, as though she did not know the neighbourhood at all. Perhaps the murderer had met her and shown her the way, or she had asked someone for directions. But if the latter were true, who—and where—was that someone?

It took him nearly an hour to get to Alderton through the Chase, but he was moving slowly, taking time to explore as he went along. Fortunately the weather continued fair, so he could use the sun to find his way through the maze of meandering paths. There were broken branches and trampled leaves to suggest someone had recently passed this way, but last night's rain had washed away any footprints.

From time to time the trees parted to form a clearing, curtained off from the rest of the forest. One of these clearings might well be the one that Craddock visited yesterday.

He emerged from the Chase beside a stream that ran parallel to the main road. There was a footbridge, close to an old abandoned building that must have been a mill. He crossed the bridge and walked about a quarter of a mile to the main road. There he doubled back southeast, and soon reached Alderton.

From then on, curious spectators dogged his steps. People came out of their houses or paused in their work to gape at him from a safe distance—in case, he supposed, he should suddenly become violent or deranged. For of course the whole village knew by now that the mysterious girl had been found in his bed, and that his servant was in gaol under suspicion of her murder. Ignoring the watchers as best he could, he went to Senderby's cobbler's shop and told him he wished to visit Dipper.

Dipper had the lockup all to himself, which was just as well, since it was barely ten feet wide. It was shaped like a beehive, with a little domed roof and a padlocked door. The only light came from two small slits set high in the brick walls. There was a pallet bed on one side and a makeshift privy on the other. The smell of the place was foul. "You hadn't ought to come in here, sir," Dipper told Julian.

"No human being ought to come in here. But if you can spend a night and a day here, I daresay I can stomach it for a few minutes."

"It ain't so bad, sir. I've dossed in much worse cribs nor this. I had a glimmer last night,"—he pointed to the remains of a small fire—"and the grub's first-rate." He added, "I think you ought to take it out of me wages, sir."

"Take what out of your wages?" asked Julian coldly.

"Whatever you forked out to keep me in quod. I'm no gowk, sir—I been in and out of the jug since I was a kid, and I know you don't live so high as this unless somebody's flapped the dimmock. And what I say is, you ought to take it out of me wages, on account of I wouldn't be in here if I hadn't tried to gammon Sir Robert."

"It's immaterial to me how you found your way into this paradise. I don't want you coming out of it ill, and of no use to me whatever.

And that means I have to ensure you live like something other than a gutter rat."

"That don't mean I shouldn't have to pay for it, sir."

"I refuse to have this argument with you. It's ridiculous and undignified, and I won't hear any more about it."

Dipper gave it up. "How's the hunt going, sir?"

Julian told him what had been learned so far about the murdered girl. "And she spoke with a foreign accent," he finished. "But, of course, that may have been assumed. If she used a veil to disguise her face, why not an accent to disguise her voice?"

"That's an old dodge, sir," Dipper agreed.

Senderby joined them, saying he had to lock up the gaol so that he could return to the investigation. Julian said to Dipper, "I'll look in on you again tomorrow."

"I wish you wouldn't, sir. I'll be airing out your clothes for days."

"I expect that girl Molly would be happy to help you. Since you left, she's been looking so peaked, she could probably do with some airing out herself."

He came out of the lockup, blinking at the change from darkness to daylight. A small crowd was on the watch for him. He flicked off his tall silk hat and made them a bow. They scattered in some confusion. He smiled wryly, turned to Senderby, and asked how to get to Dr. MacGregor's.

# *20*
# CATALOGUE
# OF SUSPECTS

"Well, let's have it," said MacGregor, plumping down in a homely easy chair. "Which of the Fontclairs have you decided is a cold-blooded murderer?"

He and Julian were seated in his back parlour. It was a bachelor's snuggery, small and cosy, with furniture worn enough to be lounged in or knocked about with impunity. Julian leaned back in a wing chair, stretching out his legs. "I haven't decided. I'm very open and unbiased in my suspicions at this stage. The fact is, I think a case can be made against any of the Fontclairs except Hugh."

"Do you realize what you're saying? You're saying that a member of a highly respected old family—a family that's spawned military heroes, members of Parliament, leaders of county society—is a murderer. And not even a killer in an honest fight, but a treacherous, cowardly murderer, a stabber in the back and a liar! I've known the Fontclairs some thirty years. Sir Robert is one of the fairest, most conscientious landlords you'll ever see. And Lady Fontclair is beloved all over the parish. There's not a soul in Alderton she doesn't know by name, and if someone's in trouble, there she'll be, with a kind word and an open purse. The others—well, they have their faults, but I won't believe one of them's a murderer—not till I've seen proof so plain there's no gainsaying it."

"I wish I had it to show you. But the little we've discovered so far raises more questions than it resolves." He told MacGregor what Felton and Mrs. Warren had had to say.

"It sounds as though we've got precious little to show for all this investigating. And even so, you're convinced one of the Fontclairs is guilty."

"Or Mr. Craddock."

"Well, make your case against each of them. I'll hear it"

"In a very belligerent spirit, prepared to pounce like an angry Scots terrier on every flaw in my reasoning."

"If you don't want an honest opinion, you can keep your reasoning to yourself!"

"I do want it. That's why I came."

"Well, get on with it, then," MacGregor grumbled.

"I suppose it doesn't matter where I begin. I'll take Lady Tarleton first—an honour I doubt she'd appreciate if she were here. She has no one who can vouch for her whereabouts between half past four and six o'clock yesterday. She has a severe cut on her hand, which she explains by saying she dropped her embroidery scissors, it broke, and she cut her hand picking it up. I've seen the scissors: it's thoroughly battered, and I don't believe it could have got into that condition by being dropped from anything short of a precipice."

"Are you suggesting she really cut her hand while stabbing the girl to death?"

"I'm only saying it's possible. You did say you thought the murderer could have been a woman. And you said there was no way to tell if all the blood on the bedding and the washbasin was the girl's."

"Have you got a theory about why Lady Tarleton would have lost her mind and attacked a young female with a scissors?"

"Motive is my Achilles heel. Without knowing who the girl was or anything about her, how can I know why anyone would have wanted her dead? Lady Tarleton has the devil's own temper, and she's been cutting up savage about Hugh's marriage to Miss Craddock ever since I got to Bellegarde. I can see her resorting to violence to prevent it—but how would the girl's death accomplish that? The most it could do would be to delay it for a time. I can't see Sir Robert mounting a wedding celebration for his heir, with the spectre of an unsolved murder hovering over his house and the village."

"It's true that Lady Tarleton's as angry as a hornet about Hugh's marriage. But with her family pride, that's only to be expected. Craddock was a groom at Bellegarde, you know, years ago. That's bound to rankle with all of them."

"Guy told me it was Lady Tarleton who brought about Craddock's dismissal. Have you any idea why? You've lived in Alderton long enough to have been here in Craddock's day."

"I remember hearing he'd been turned off, but nobody told me the reason, and I didn't ask. The Fontclairs do more or less as they like at Bellegarde, and well beyond it, too. They're a power to be reckoned with, Kestrel. There aren't many people, high or low, who'd dare accuse any of them of murder. You'll see that at the inquest. Mark my words, the coroner will handle them with kid gloves. You won't hear *him* pressing Lady Tarleton to explain how she cut her hand."

"So much for justice," said Julian ironically.

MacGregor could not blame him for feeling that way. No one could say with truth that English justice wore a blindfold. If Kestrel ever came to the point of accusing one of the Fontclairs, he would have to prove his case beyond all possible doubt. Anything short of certainty, and the barrier of privilege that enclosed the Fontclairs would protect them from retribution, though suspicion and scandal might cling to their name for generations to come.

Julian broke the silence. "Do you know anything about Lady Tarleton's husband? I understand he lives abroad."

"He does, and has for a long time. She doesn't seem to be eating her heart out missing him. She's got plenty of money and the run of his house in Suffolk—though she never goes there. If you ask me, she's always thought of herself as a Fontclair first and Sir Bertrand's wife second—or third or fourth, more likely. After he left, and even before, she spent most of her time at Bellegarde, only going down to London for the season. Thinks she knows how to run the place better than Lady Fontclair. Always telling her what to do—and Lady Fontclair, being the good soul she is, at least makes a pretence of listening."

"Did they quarrel—Lady Tarleton and Sir Bertrand?"

"They were always quarrelling. She used to ridicule him in front of people, making him out to be weak and craven. Which he was, there's no denying it, or he wouldn't have let her ride herd over him that way. She was extravagant, too. He was plump in the pocket, Tarleton was, but she made quite a hole in his purse, and he could never make out what the money went for. I wouldn't put it past her to have spent it just to spite him. But there's a streak of intemperance with money in the Fontclair family. You can see it in Guy. Isabelle's father was like that, too."

"His name was Simon?"

"That's right. First cousin to Sir Robert, and as unlike him as day is to night. Simon never could cut his coat according to the cloth. He was always trying to live like the fellows he knew who had ten times his income. He married a woman with no more sense than he had, and they hatched a grand scheme to make their fortune running a plantation in Barbados. But they made a hash of it. They came back poor as rats, with a baby daughter in tow. Lord knows how they managed after that. They lived in London, so I didn't see much of them. I expect they borrowed from Sir Robert. Though I'm sorry to say, I wouldn't have put it past Simon to dabble in something—er—"

"Not altogether on the square?"

"It's possible. They were none too scrupulous, Simon and Mrs. Simon. I'd as soon not speak ill of the dead, but it's just as well for Isabelle she came to live with Sir Robert and Lady Fontclair."

"I wonder if there's anything in all this that might shed light on the murder."

"It's ancient history, most of it. I don't see what it could have to do with a crime that happened yesterday."

"Some crimes have their roots in events that happened decades, even centuries, ago. In Italy, where I lived for some time, quarrels often outlive the quarrellers, and are passed on to the next generation like so much family silver. Never mind, we'll go back to my case against the Fontclairs. We've talked about Guy already. He has no alibi for any of the period in question. My old room used to be his when he was a boy, and he was accustomed to getting in and out of it on the sly—although he used the window, which the murderer most likely didn't. He was sick at the sight of the girl's body. And I don't know if this means anything, but he went out last night in a violent rainstorm, and got into a funk when he was caught coming in at dawn. Again, no motive, though it's tempting to speculate about a lover's quarrel or a frustrated seduction. Though I don't know why we should confine those sorts of suspicions to Guy. Colonel Fontclair is known to have a taste for game pullets—that is, for very young girls."

"Colonel Fontclair is an officer of the first water, a hero of the Peninsular War."

"In other words, he's had a great success in the profession of killing."

"Killing a woman in cold blood is completely different from killing a man in battle!"

"I understand that. But the fact remains that a man who's fought a long and gruesome war must be inured to taking human life in a way that the rest of us wouldn't be. Colonel Fontclair's been moody and pensive ever since I arrived at Bellegarde. He has no alibi for the period from half past four to five, when he went out riding. And the servants who saw him leave say he looked as if the devil were after him."

"He's lame," MacGregor pointed out.

"He can walk. And he could easily overpower a small, slender girl. You know, we wondered how the killer made those smears of blood on the wall. A lame man would be particularly likely to lean against the wall for support."

MacGregor got up and paced about, running his hands through his hair. "You'll have me believing *anything* before you're through. See here, there are a thousand ways that blood might have been smeared on the wall."

"There's something else. The evening before last, after dinner, Lady Tarleton brought me to see the gun room. We found the colonel and Lady Fontclair there. She had her arms around his shoulders. She was saying, 'It's wicked and wrong. Promise me you will never think of it again.' "

MacGregor stared. "But— but that could mean all manner of

things! You can't think he told her he was contemplating murder!"

"I don't know what he told her."

"It might have been anything," MacGregor urged. "They've always got their heads together, those two. They're great friends— have been for years. He wanted to marry her once."

"Did he?"

"Now don't go looking at me as if I'd dug you up a buried treasure! It's no great matter. The colonel met her and paid court to her before Sir Robert did. He was a dashing young officer in those days, and broke a good many hearts. I don't know if he ever got to the point of making her an offer. Sir Robert came along and fell over head and ears in love with her, and won her for himself. The colonel married Guy's mother, who died before Guy was breeched. That's all there is to it."

Julian wondered. He pictured the colonel and Lady Fontclair leaving the gun room arm in arm. Lady Tarleton's insinuating voice rang in his ears: *Touching, isn't it, how fond they are of one another?*

"Look here," said MacGregor, "when you said you could make a case against all the Fontclairs except Hugh, you can't have meant to include Lady Fontclair among your suspects?"

"Yes, I did. But we'll pass over her if you'd rather."

"No, let's hear what you've got to say. I'd just as soon know the worst."

"You know, I like her, too."

"You don't like anybody, and you don't trust anybody!"

"I can't afford— No, what's the use?" He rose. "Would you rather I put an end to this discussion, and this visit?"

"Look here, did anybody ask you to leave?"

"Not in so many words."

"Then sit down and behave yourself! You ought to know better than to take to heart what I say when I'm in a temper."

Julian smiled, and sat down again. "The case against Lady Fontclair. It's not a strong one. If Sir Robert is telling the truth, he left her alone for only about a quarter of an hour during the period between half past four and six. She wasn't entirely alone even for that short time: Miss Fontclair passed through the conservatory and

spoke with her. There might just have been time for Lady Fontclair
to let the girl in through the conservatory windows, bring her to
my room, and kill her. But even assuming she *could* do it, it's devilish
hard to imagine that she *would*."

"Then why not rule her out?"

"Well, there are some disturbing facts. Lady Fontclair says you've
taught her a good deal about medicine—treating injuries, removing
splinters, that sort of thing. That means she has some knowledge
of anatomy, and probably isn't as squeamish as most of us would
be about cutting into human flesh. And she must know the house
and its routine better than anyone. It was most likely she who decided
which room I would have. And she repeatedly urged Hugh to take
me out for a long ride late yesterday afternoon."

"Clearing the way for her to kill the girl in your room while you
were out? Kestrel, I know her, the same as you know your servant.
She wouldn't do a thing like that. I could imagine her firing a gun
or raising a knife against—oh, say, a housebreaker who threatened
her children. But, if nothing else, she'd never plan a murder at
Bellegarde, and take the risk that anyone in her family, or even any
of her servants, would take the blame for it."

"This might not have been a planned crime. But I admit, what
you're saying rings very true."

"What about Sir Robert? Is he on your list of suspects?"

"Yes, but I grant you, the odds are Lombard Street to ninepence
he had nothing to do with the murder. He has an alibi for most of
the period in question—assuming he and Lady Fontclair aren't lying
to shield each other. And, given his sense of right and justice, it's
devilish hard to imagine him committing a crime like this. What
isn't so hard to imagine is that he thinks or fears one of his family
is guilty. The question is, does he have a particular one in mind?
And how far would he go to protect that person?"

"I don't like to think of the dilemma he'd face if he thought the
murderer was one of his own family."

"It may be worse than that, you know."

"How could it possibly be worse?"

"It may not be only one of them. Two or more of them may have
planned and carried out the murder together."

MacGregor clutched at his hair. "See here, Kestrel, isn't it just possible this is all the work of some aggrieved labourer attacking the local squire? It happens, you know, though it hasn't happened around Alderton for Lord knows how many years."

"I don't know much about those sorts of rural conflicts, but wouldn't there have been a threatening note left behind—a demand for redress?"

"Well, probably." MacGregor heaved a sigh and resumed his pacing.

"Finally, there's Miss Fontclair. There's a good deal of circumstantial evidence against her. She admits to having passed close to my old room at about twenty minutes past five. She had her sketching box with her, which contains a small but very sharp knife that she uses to sharpen her pencils. She's been very frank about all this. That may mean she has nothing to hide—it may also mean she's trying to disarm us with a semblance of candour. Actually, there's a third possibility: she may be trying to draw suspicion away from someone else."

"Who?"

"I don't know." The most obvious person, he thought, would be Lady Fontclair, whom Isabelle said she had met in the conservatory when she came in through the French windows. But suppose Isabelle had been lying? Suppose Lady Fontclair had not been in the conservatory while Sir Robert was gone? Suppose that, instead of seeing her there, Isabelle had seen her a little while later, outside Julian's room?

He went on, "Of course, as a suspect Miss Fontclair presents a number of problems. She was outdoors for the most of the time in which the girl could have been killed. She might have brought the girl in with her through the conservatory windows—but in that case, we have to posit some sort of conspiracy between her and Lady Fontclair, who says she came in alone. She might have let the girl in through the front door, but Michael was letting Mr. Craddock in that way at about that time. They might all have missed one another, but it seems farfetched. And there's still the enigma of motive. Why the deuce would any of these people want the girl dead?

"Now for Mr. Craddock. He says he went for a walk in the Chase after his ride. He may have met the girl there—either by chance or by design—and arranged for her to join him at the house. He returns to Bellegarde and rings to be let in. Michael opens the door, then goes back to the servants' hall, and Craddock goes up to his room. His window looks out on the front court, and he watches from there till he sees the girl coming, then he steals down the stairs and lets her in through the front door. He brings her to my room, remembering that I've gone out, and knowing there won't be anyone else in that part of the house at that hour. But, again—"

"I know," said MacGregor gloomily. "No motive."

"Precisely. One thing I mean to find out is why he went for that walk in the Chase, and why Lady Tarleton was so upset about it. I'd give a monkey to know more about the history between those two."

"That finishes your list of suspects. But when all's said and done, whether you like it or not, your servant is still a pretty strong contender."

"I know. The devil take Dipper—why did he have to tell that lie?"

"Let's hope it's the only lie he told."

"It is, I promise you. Though I wonder—"

"Every time you say 'I wonder,' I know there's trouble brewing. What is it now?"

"Is it possible I'm involved in the murder in some way I don't understand? It happened in my room. And I've thought from the beginning it was odd I was invited in the first place. Hugh and I hardly know each other."

"Then why did he ask you to be his best man?"

"He says he expected fireworks between his family and the Craddocks and thought I'd be a moderating influence. The truth is, he mistook me for a knight out of Walter Scott, because I once fished him out of a scrape in a gaming hell. That's one of the hazards of cutting a figure in London. I don't mind fellows copying the cut of my coat or the way I turn a phrase, but I hate like the devil being hero-worshipped."

"It's a big responsibility, having to live up to some young cub's admiration. Much easier to fob people off with dandified airs and a fine suit of clothes. Give 'em something to dazzle their eyes, and maybe they won't try to find out what's underneath it all." He relented a little, seeing the young man's startled face. "Touched you on the raw, have I? I can't help it—I have to say what I think. The fact is, I can't stand waste, and it seems to me you're squandering some fine gifts, leading the life you do. Why, with your intellects, you could be a barrister, a scholar—a doctor, when it comes to that. Wouldn't that be a better use of a mind like yours than thinking up new ways to tie a neckcloth or polish a pair of boots?"

"Possibly. But you see, I have no education. My father was a gentleman, but he married an actress, and his family cut him off with a shilling. I have no money to speak of, and no connexions. In our England, bless her heart, there's no profession for a man like me. If I didn't dress extremely well, I'd be invisible."

He rose. It was time he returned to Bellegarde; he would be late to dinner as it was. He went out to the front hall to retrieve his hat and stick, MacGregor following. Just as he was leaving, MacGregor caught his arm.

"Kestrel!"

"What is it?"

"Don't you feel like Daniel setting off for the lions' den, going back there? If you really think one of the Fontclairs is a murderer, how can you sit down to dinner with them, sleep under their roof?"

"I don't see that I have any choice. The investigation is centred at Bellegarde, and I want to be in the thick of it. Besides, I want to keep a close eye on the Fontclairs. Sooner or later the murderer's mask will slip, even if by only an inch. I mean to be there when it does."

"Do you think whoever was brute enough to stab that slip of a girl in the back would think twice about doing you a mischief, if he thinks you're on the brink of finding him out?"

"In that case, I may be safer at Bellegarde than anywhere else. Another crime in the Fontclairs' own house would focus suspicion firmly and irrevocably on them."

"For God's sake, man! Do you want to be the next person found in somebody's bed with a knife wound?"

It dawned on Julian that MacGregor was really concerned about him. He was touched. "My dear fellow, don't worry."

"I'm not worried," grumbled MacGregor. "I just think you might be even more trouble dead than you are alive."

# *21*
# TRINKETS
# LOST AND FOUND

Next morning, the Bellegarde household went to church in Alderton. Some of the family, particularly the colonel and Lady Tarleton, did not want to appear in public so soon after the murder, but Sir Robert insisted. The Fontclairs must present a serene and confident face to the world, he said, both as a matter of pride and to allay worry in the village. Sunday services would be an excellent opportunity for them all to appear in public, and show they had nothing to fear or be ashamed of.

As they entered the church, a wave of whispers rose. Heads turned; parents hastily admonished their children not to point. Every eye followed the Fontclairs and their guests as they took their places in the family pew. The vicar was hard-pressed to get and keep the attention of his flock.

He seemed unsure how openly he ought to refer to the murder. As he bade the congregation pray for the dead girl's soul, he stole an uneasy glance at the Fontclairs, as though he feared to offend them by drawing attention to the scandal hanging over their house. No doubt he felt the need to keep in Sir Robert's good graces; it was most likely Sir Robert who had given him the living of Alderton. Yet if he really understood his patron, he would realize that no one would be more concerned than he that the dead girl have the benefit of everyone's prayers. He himself would pray for her all the more fervently if he knew, or suspected, that one of his own family had killed her.

Julian, who attended church very rarely, and mainly for the music, was surprised to find the service such a comfort. The old, sonorous words had tremendous power to soothe and inspire. At a time like this, faced with a difficult task and a fearful responsibility, he was grateful to lay aside his own will and feel strengthened and sustained by something outside himself.

Some of his party were finding it hard to concentrate on the service, with the villagers gawking at them and murmuring behind their hands. Lady Tarleton seethed with frustration, for all her efforts to seem haughtily unconcerned. The colonel looked shamed and self-conscious. Guy was so restless he could barely keep his seat.

Maud's eyes were closed, her fingers tightly clasped and her head bent over them. Was she asking for guidance about whether to reveal the information she was holding back? Julian suddenly knew beyond all doubt that she would tell it. She was too honest, too scrupulous, to keep it a secret much longer. Maud Craddock was a daughter-in-law after Sir Robert's own heart, if only he knew it.

✳

After a luncheon of cold meats, jellies, and blancmange, at which Lady Tarleton was particularly ill-tempered, Julian went to visit Mrs. Warren. He had seen her in church that morning, and she seemed in a little better spirits than yesterday. After services, she had been beset by a crowd of villagers peppering her with questions about her mysterious lodger. Julian, seeing her trying vainly to fend them off, went and stood close by. While they turned to gaze at him with their usual fascination, Mrs. Warren scurried away.

He set off for Alderton on horseback, skirting the south side of the park. For the murdered girl, this would certainly have been an easier route to Bellegarde than the Chase. The rough going there would have slowed her, and she could all too easily have gotten lost among the twisting paths. Her dirty, worn shoes and ripped skirt did suggest she had picked her way through woodland. On the other hand, those green stains round the hem of her skirt would most likely have come from walking through tall grass, not the under-growth of a forest.

Mrs. Warren lived in a small, square cottage of whitewashed brick, with a blue door and blue paint round the windows. The paint was peeling, the thatched roof was sparse in places, but the vegetable garden beside the house was lovingly tended. Round the house and garden ran a white picket fence.

As Julian tethered his horse and approached the door, Mrs. Warren peeked out from between the curtains of a ground-floor window. She looked more apprehensive than pleased to see him. But she unbolted the door and let him in, nervously tucking stray wisps of hair under her cap. "I'd have left the door open on such a fine day, but with a murderer loose in the neighbourhood, I'm afeard to. Will they catch him soon, do you think, sir?"

"I'm sure they will. The more they know about the victim, the easier it will be—which is why I've come to try your patience yet again with questions about her, on the chance you've remembered something more since yesterday."

"I'm sure I'd be quick to tell it, if I had. Lawk-a-daisy me, I wish I was better at keeping things straight in my mind."

"I think you remember things very vividly, once your mind is jogged to focus on them. I have an idea. Why don't I knock at the door, just as the girl did, and you let me in and act out for me everything that happened the night she arrived?"

"You mean like play-acting, sir?"

"Well, you needn't be another Mrs. Siddons. Just take me wher-ever you took her, and try if you can recall what the two of you talked about, and what you did."

She eyed him uncertainly, then nodded. "I'll try it, sir."

He went out again and knocked. Mrs. Warren, on the other side of the door, said, "I heard her knock, sir, and I called out, 'Who's there?' And I heard a voice—high, like a little girl's, with a funny accent—saying as how she'd heard I had a room to let. I opened the door then, just a crack,"—Mrs. Warren suited the action to the words—"and looked at her. And then it was just as I told Sir Robert: I didn't like the look of her, so young and all alone and dressed so fine—but I needed the money so, I thought I'd at least let her in and see what she had to say for herself."

She opened the door all the way, and Julian came in.

"I took her into the kitchen first." She opened a door on the right side of the central hallway. There was a door on the left side, too, and a stairway at the end of the hall. Probably there were only four rooms all told: two on the ground floor, and two above.

The kitchen was shabby but clean, with a big cooking pot suspended over the hearth, a broad deal table, and a walnut cabinet to hold the crockery. Utensils, scarred by years of scouring, hung along the walls, and a rocking chair with a big shawl draped across it stood by the fireplace.

Mrs. Warren described how she had told the girl what lodging and meals would cost, and taken her upstairs to show her the room. She took Julian upstairs now. "That's my room, sir," she said, pointing to a door on one side of the hallway. "This was hers."

She opened a door opposite. The room was small and neat, with a bed, a table and chair, and an old chest to hold the lodger's belongings. There were bright calico curtains at the windows, and a ballad, the kind sold at country fairs, pinned up on the wall.

Julian examined the room. It was spotless. There was no sign that anyone had slept here only a few days ago. Mrs. Warren was too good a housewife—she had swept and scrubbed away any clue the girl might have left behind. He felt defeated. What was he doing here? Why should he pester Mrs. Warren and waste his own time, when there was nothing new to learn?

Mrs. Warren repeated her account of how she had shown the girl the room, and the girl had looked out the window and asked where Bellegarde was. "Then she started unpacking of her things, and I went down to get the supper ready. We didn't talk at supper, and afterward she went upstairs and got ready for bed—" She broke off. "Now, there you are, sir. That's what comes of letting myself get so rattled as I've been. I'd forgot all about that until now."

"About what, Mrs. Warren?" He kept his voice calm and steady. T̲ ̲ ̲was no time to alarm her with a show of eagerness.

̲ ̲ ̲en she put on her nightdress, she found she'd lost that gin-
̲ ̲ ̲she wore around her neck. Shaped like a scallop shell, it

was, and made of silver. My, wasn't she in a pother when she found it missing! She come running downstairs in her nightdress, saying as how she'd lost the most precious thing she had, and she had to find it straightaway. I asked her if it was worth a good deal, for it did cross my mind, sir, I might be accused of stealing it, and me not even knowing she had such a thing. She wore it underneath her dress, you see, so I hadn't seen it afore. She said it hadn't any value except to her. It was give to her by somebody she loved, who had to leave her when she was small."

"Did she say who that person was?"

"No, sir. I thought at first it was some love token, and said as much, but she got up on her high horse at that, and said as how her love wasn't the kind to be ashamed of. How it was pure and dutiful. The love of a daughter. That was what she said."

"She used those words—'a daughter'?"

"Yes, sir. So it might've been a gift from her father or mother, but she didn't say clearly. She was half distracted, running about and wringing of her hands, and gabbling in her foreign tongue. And all the while she was looking everywhere for her trinket. It was all I could do to stop her running outdoors to see if she'd lost it there, which would have been daft at that time of night. I said, 'Be patient, we'll search the house from top to bottom, and happen we'll find it.' Which we did quite soon, sir, under her bed. The ribbon had broke, and the trinket must have fallen off and bounced under there without her knowing."

"Did she say anything at all about the person who gave it to her?"

"No, sir. I don't even know if it was a man or a woman. But there was one more thing, now I think of it. She said she couldn't bear to lose her trinket now, when they was going to meet again so soon—she and whoever give it to her."

"To meet again," he repeated slowly.

"Yes, sir. But she didn't say where or how, and I didn't want to know. It all sounded hugger-mugger to me."

"What happened after you found the scallop shell?"

"She kissed it, and held it against her heart. Whoever give it to her must have been all in all to her. She had gewgaws much finer, but I never saw her take on so about any of them."

"That reminds me: One of her earrings was missing when her body was found. Have you come across it anywhere?"

"Why, sir, if I had, don't you think I'd have turned it over to the law? I wouldn't keep what isn't mine, sir!"

"I never thought you would," he said hastily. "But considering what a strain you've been under, a thing like that could easily have slipped your mind for a while."

"I didn't find no earbob, sir. What a one she was for losing things, to be sure!"

The girl had hung the scallop shell round her neck again, Mrs. Warren said, using a ribbon from her bonnet. She sewed the broken ribbon on her bonnet in its place. "Very skillful with her needle, she was. I never saw a hat trimmed quicker or prettier."

She had nothing more to tell him. Before he left, she shyly offered him a drink of her homemade cowslip wine. He accepted, although he did not think he would like it, and was right. He thanked her with real gratitude for all her help, and rode away.

His mind teemed with speculations. A silver scallop shell, given to the girl by someone for whom she felt a daughter's devotion. Someone she had not seen in years, but expected soon to meet again. At Bellegarde? If so, had she been killed to prevent her making contact with that person? Or had she met her death at the hands of whomever it was she loved?

✳

Julian rode to the village to visit Dipper, and to find out if Senderby had anything new to report. Alderton was quiet, seeing it was Sunday, but there were people, especially young couples, strolling up and down the main street. Julian's presence created the usual stir. He was so accustomed to being stared at from a safe distance that it startled him when someone walked right up to him and spoke. "Mr. Kestrel, sir!"

"Mr. Felton. Good afternoon."

"It's Dick, sir. How's the investigation going? Have you found out who did for the girl yet? 'Did for' is criminal talk for 'killed.' I read it in a book about a Bow Street Runner. Are they coming, sir, the Runners? I'd give anything to see one in the flesh!"

"The investigation is going tolerably well, we don't know yet who committed the murder, 'did for' has a certain vigour but I'm rather partial to 'hushed' or 'croaked,' and as far as I know Sir Robert has no plans to call on the Bow Street Runners."

Felton gazed at him, round-eyed and respectful. "You *are* a downy one, sir."

"Thank you. You haven't remembered anything more about the murdered girl, by any chance?"

"No, sir." Felton kicked a pebble moodily. "I hoped I would, so I could go back to squire's house and see how the investigation was going—maybe even help out someways. Just wait till I'm older, and I've got a bit of money put away! I'll be off to London then, and join the Runners myself. That's a life for a man, that is—not looking after other folks' horses all day and half the night." He glared at the Blue Lion across the way.

"Aren't you too busy at your work to help in the investigation?"

"Why?—have you got something for me to do, sir? Because I've got a brother who's a labourer and out of work, and he could take my place at the Lion for a few days, if I was needed to do important police work."

"I don't know yet if you'll be needed. If I gave you a task to perform on the quiet, could I trust you not to blow the gab by chaffing to your friends?" Sometimes Dipper's vocabulary had its uses.

"I'd be as silent as the grave, sir! I wouldn't say one word, not if murderous cutthroats was to threaten to roast me alive, I wouldn't!"

"I don't imagine it will come to that. But I'm glad to know I can count on you if I need help—unofficially."

Felton assured him that he could count on him a hundred times over. By this time, he had made up his mind about Mr. Kestrel. He was a Bow Street Runner himself, decked out in an extraordinarily convincing disguise as a gentleman.

❋

Senderby had news. He had found someone who saw the girl on the day she died, after she left Mrs. Warren's. "His name's Fred

Morley, and he's the son of one of Sir Robert's tenants, who works
a farm south of Bellegarde. Fred was on his way to the horse fair
early Friday morning. He took the main road to Whitford, and had
just passed through Alderton when he saw her."

"What was she doing?"

"She was standing in the road, sir, talking to Bliss. He's an old
pedlar and beggar—a little bit daft, but clever with his hands. He
comes through here every so often. Most likely it was the horse fair
brought him this time."

"Yes. I saw him there." He remembered the wizened old man,
with his shabby clothes and colourful patchwork sack.

"Oh, so you know who he is. Well, Fred says he saw Bliss talking
to the girl and pointing down the road. He thought at first Bliss
was pointing at him, but as he got closer it looked more like he
was giving the girl directions."

"If he was pointing toward Morley, he must have been pointing
east—toward Bellegarde."

"That's right, sir."

"Did he hear anything they said?"

"No, sir. When he got close to them, the girl saw him and took
fright. Leastways, she hurried away from the road, and Bliss stood
looking from her to Fred, like he wasn't sure what to do next."

"What happened then?"

"That was all Fred could tell me. He did wonder who the girl
was, out all alone dressed in such fine clothes, and talking to the
likes of Bliss. But he was in a hurry to get to the horse fair, and he
was afeard that if he stopped, Bliss would beg from him or try to
sell him something he didn't want. So he rode on past the girl and
Bliss, and that was all he saw of them."

"I suppose the next step is to question Bliss."

"Easier said nor done, sir. No one's seen him since Friday morning,
when he was hawking his wares at the horse fair. He was probably
on his way there when the girl asked him for directions. I don't
s'pose there'll be much he can tell us about her, which is just as
well, because it may take a bit of doing to find him. If he left these
parts on Friday after the horse fair, there's no knowing where he's
got to now."

"Does he have a route he usually follows?"

"He goes wherever there's fairs or weddings, or any kind of do where folks are likely to be openhanded with their money. I'm just on my way to report to Sir Robert, and with his leave I'll start an enquiry after Bliss. I expect he'll turn up fast enough if he hears there's a reward for information about the girl. There's not much he won't do if there's money in it, and no great risk to be run."

"Does he have any usual haunts in the neighbourhood where you could look for him?"

"We'd know if he was anywhere near Alderton, sir. He don't make any secret of his presence. Contrariways, he's always begging off folks or pestering them to buy his wares. I'll look in at the old mill, though, after I've seen Sir Robert. That's where Bliss mostly sleeps when he's in the neighbourhood."

"The old mill—that's by the stream, northwest of Alderton?" Julian recalled seeing it yesterday when he emerged from the Chase.

"That's right, sir. We haven't used it since the new mill was built, and it's fallen into a sorry state. The parish keeps meaning to pull it down, but somehow we haven't got round to it, and in the meantime gipsies and such like use it now and again."

"Has anyone been staying there lately?"

"Not so far as I know. Unless Bliss slept there the night before the horse fair."

It occurred to Julian that, while Senderby was making his report to Sir Robert, he could go to the old mill himself and have a look around. He supposed he ought to tell Senderby what he intended, but he did not. If he learned anything of interest, he could always let Sir Robert know about it afterward.

The truth was, he was repenting of his promise to share his discoveries with Sir Robert. He did not feel he could trust any of the Fontclairs, and his instincts were to play a lone hand whenever possible. If that meant practising a secrecy inconsistent with his honour, so be it.

✳

Before he left Alderton, Julian looked in on Dipper, who was now sharing his cramped, unwholesome quarters with a sheep-

stealer. They appeared to be getting on famously. Dipper regarded
the sheep-stealer with great respect and curiosity. He himself had
never stolen anything larger than a pocketbook, much less alive.

Leaving his horse at the Blue Lion, Julian set out on foot for the
old mill. It was going to rain. The air felt thick and sluggish, and
a dead white haze was slowly but surely blotting out the sun. If
he'd had any sense, he thought, he would have changed out of the
clothes he had worn to church. A coat moulded to his figure like a
glove, a high shirt collar, and a starched neckcloth were not the best
attire for tramping about on a rainy day, exploring abandoned
buildings.

He crossed the main road and made his way to the stream that
ran parallel to it. Here the grass grew in lush profusion, springing
up in clumps like shocks of hair. He found the footbridge he had
crossed yesterday. On the other side of the stream was the old mill,
its weatherboarding decrepit, its sack-hoists serving now as perches
for fat pigeons.

Inside, the mill was cool and musty. The windows did not let in
much light, but cracks in the weatherboarding and roof helped relieve
the dimness. As his eyes adjusted, he made out an expanse of bare
floor and, off to one side, a partly enclosed area where the wheels
and machinery were. The floor was coated with grime. Some of the
boards were loose, with damp earth oozing through the gaps. The
walls were dirty, too, and strewn with spiders' webs. A throaty,
monotonous murmur above his head told him the upper story had
been taken over by the pigeons.

He was careful where he walked, because he did not want to
disturb the pattern of grime on the floor. It was full of footprints.
Most were too blurred for him to make out their shape, but he
thought there were at least two pairs of feet, one much larger than
the other.

Several floorboards had been pulled up and laid aside. On the
exposed earth was a circle of stones, enclosing a pile of ashes and
blackened bits of wood. Julian took off his gloves and felt the ashes;
they were cold. The fire had probably been built within the past
few days, but there was no telling exactly when. Someone had slept
by it, too, leaving a long smudge in the dirt on the floor.

He continued exploring. Along one wall, he found a great many footprints leading nowhere, overlaid on one another so that he could not make out their size or shape. It looked as if someone had been pacing up and down along the wall, probably for some time.

At one end, this trail of footprints gave way to one large smear. Here, perhaps, the pacer sat down—with his or her back against the wall, most likely, since there was a smudge there, too. It was a godsend that the place was so filthy: positions and movements showed as clearly as they would in newly fallen snow. But what could he deduce from all this? Only that someone, probably Bliss, had slept here during the past few days, and that at least one other person had been here as well.

Then he saw it—the gleam of metal through a gap between the floor and the wall. He pried a floorboard loose and thrust his hand underneath. His fingers closed round a small, cold object. It was a gold teardrop earring, set with an aquamarine.

So the murdered girl had been here. It was most likely she who had paced this trail and sat against this wall. He recalled that the seat of her dress and the back of her shawl had been stained with dirt. He took out his quizzing glass and closely examined the place where she must have sat. His search was rewarded: caught in a splinter of wood in the wall was one long red-gold hair.

He removed the hair carefully, wrapped both it and the earring in his handkerchief, and put the handkerchief away in his pocket. Before he left the mill, he considered going up to have a look at the first floor. But the stairs were half rotted away, and the cobwebs draped across them showed that no one had used them for a long time. He decided with relief that he could leave the pigeons undisturbed.

He came out of the mill, shading his eyes against the sunlight. Why had the girl come here? he wondered. Was this where she was going when she left Mrs. Warren's in the morning? He did not think so. When Bliss was seen giving her directions, he had been pointing east toward Alderton and Bellegarde, not north toward the stream and the mill.

The stretch of road where Fred Morley had seen her with Bliss was very near here. Morley had said she hurried away from the road when she saw him coming; she might have found the mill and taken refuge there. The luxuriant grass by the stream could have made the green stains round the hem of her skirt. And the mill was very near the Chase, through which she could have walked to Bellegarde. But if she were so eager to get to Bellegarde, why did she go into the mill, pace the floor, sit huddled against the wall? Was she waiting for something—the right time, a message, a companion?

Perhaps she had not found the mill herself. Bliss might have shown her the way. Morley had not known whether Bliss remained with her after he passed by. Of course, Bliss had been at the horse fair later that morning, but he could have brought the girl to the mill first. If so, it might have been he who showed her how to reach Bellegarde through the Chase. Everyone said he would do anything for money, and the girl evidently had the means to pay him well.

That could explain why he had not been seen in Alderton since the horse fair. He might have known, or suspected, that the girl was up to no good, and thought it prudent to disappear before anyone found out he had helped her. He might be all the more anxious to hide his connexion with her if he knew she had been murdered. Or would he have come forward with information, in order to collect the reward?

It was all speculation. Only one thing was clear. Bliss must be found, and soon.

# *22*
# JULIAN TESTS
# A THEORY

On his way back to Bellegarde, Julian debated whether to tell Sir Robert about his discoveries at the old mill. If he were caught concealing evidence, he would be excluded from the investigation —perhaps even suspected of complicity in the crime. Yet he was still in two minds as he went upstairs to his room to dress for dinner.

A sharp-nosed girl was hovering in wait for him at the top of the stairs. "Please you, sir, I'm Miss Craddock's maid. My young lady told me to watch for you to come back, and ask if you'd be good enough to meet her in the music room."

Julian thanked her and went back downstairs. He could tell by her sly smile that she thought there was a hole-in-corner love affair brewing between him and Miss Craddock. Hugh had all too clearly jumped to the same conclusion. That was awkward, but perhaps not such a bad thing for Miss Craddock. A romantic like Hugh would not be disposed to fall in love with a girl who was thrust on him unsought and unwanted. He would expect to woo his beloved, fight for her, struggle against obstacles to win her. And there was no denying a rival made a very good obstacle.

He found Miss Craddock walking about the music room, twisting and untwisting her fingers. "I hope you didn't mind my asking Alice to watch for you. I thought you'd be willing to meet me here, when you knew what I had to say."

"I should be willing to meet you anywhere, even if you had nothing to say at all."

"You're so kind to me, and I've tried your patience so sorely!—keeping a secret from you that might possibly have something to do with the murder. I told you I'd think hard what I ought to do, and I have thought. I've made up my mind. I'm going to tell you everything."

A maddening scruple forced him to say, "You know, my involvement in the investigation is—unofficial. Strictly speaking, you ought to make your statement to Sir Robert."

"I thought of that. But you see, what I have to say is about his sister—where she was at the time of the murder. And they're so loyal to each other, all the Fontclairs. I think Sir Robert means to do right, but I don't see how he can be impartial. I'm sorry to say this about Hugh's father, but I just don't trust him. I'd rather talk to you."

"Talk to me, then."

They sat together on the sofa. She confessed, "I left something out of the statement I made to Sir Robert about what I did on the afternoon of the murder. It's true I went on a botany outing with Miss Pritchard and Josie and Pippa. But what I didn't say is that when I came back, at about a quarter to six, I went to Papa's room. I wanted to ask him if I could invite Miss Pritchard to London for a holiday. I was just about to knock on his door when I heard voices inside. Mr. Kestrel, Lady Tarleton was in there with him. She wasn't telling the truth when she said she was in her room all afternoon."

"Do you know what she was doing there?"

"She was quarrelling with Papa. I'm afraid I listened at the door. I didn't mean to, but I was so startled to hear her voice. She was saying, 'I've regretted that, scourged myself for that, for more than twenty years.' "

Their eyes met, full of foreboding.

"Did he say anything in reply?"

"They both said something, but I was so flustered, I didn't hear it distinctly. I was just going to move away from the door, when suddenly Papa shouted at her. It was terrible! He said there was no truth in her—just a monstrous, swollen pride that devoured everything in its path. He said her reputation was everything to her: there was nothing she wouldn't sacrifice for it, and they both knew it. And then he said, 'Do you know what you are, the whole lot of you Fontclairs? You're like one of those fruits that looks ripe and shining on the outside, while the inside is rotten and stinking. I only wish the rest of the world could have seen what I saw when I came in and found you—'

"But I don't know where he found her, because she cried out, 'That's enough!' She warned him to keep his voice down. She said she couldn't bear any more. Then she said, 'If you say anything to anyone about this—! You may think I've been making empty threats, but you little know—you can't begin to understand—how much I hate you. You think I won't dare to betray you. Well, we'll see, Mr. Craddock! We'll see!' "

Maud came out of her trance of memory with a gasp and pressed her hand to her mouth. Julian took her other hand and held it in both of his. "Did they say anything else?"

"I don't know. I heard her coming toward the door, and I ran away. I shut myself in my room. My head was whirling. All I could think was that Papa must know something shameful about Lady Tarleton—whatever it is she's been regretting for more than twenty years. Perhaps that's the secret he's been holding over the Fontclairs' heads. But why was he so angry and upset with her? And what was she threatening to betray *him* about?

"All I could think of was to talk to you. You know the world better than I do. You might understand what that conversation meant. I came looking for you when you got home, but you'd already gone up to dress. Then after the murder, when I told Papa what I'd overheard, he said I mustn't tell anyone. He said I'd get the Fontclairs into terrible trouble if I did. I felt so bewildered! I didn't want to hurt the Fontclairs, or expose Papa for a liar. And I was afraid— just a little—that his quarrel with Lady Tarleton did have something to do with the murder, even though he said it didn't. Oh, not that I think for a moment— Mr. Kestrel, Papa wouldn't kill anyone! At least, he might kill a man who attacked him, but not a young girl. She can't have been much older than I am."

"I understand." But he was thinking of all the debtors Craddock had driven into prison—all the rivals in business he had destroyed. Would a man like that stop at cold-blooded murder?

"In the end I had to tell you," she finished. "I kept thinking about what you said—that there was no knowing what might be important to the investigation. I thought, suppose some innocent man were *hanged* for want of information I knew that could have saved him? I'd never forgive myself."

"You've done the right thing. I promise you, I'll hold what you've told me in the strictest confidence, and reveal it only to the extent I must. But I may have to confront Lady Tarleton with it, in order to get the truth from her about where she went and what she did on the afternoon of the murder."

"What if she won't tell you?"

"She will, in the end. Because I shall give her no peace under heaven until she does."

✳

While he dressed for dinner, Julian thought over all he had found out today, from his visit to Mrs. Warren to his conversation with Maud. He felt as though he were sorting swiftly through the contents of a desk, taking papers out of first one drawer and then another, comparing, rearranging, looking for patterns and inconsistencies. He recalled with sharpened interest the family history Guy had recounted to him on the night before the murder. And a theory took shape in his mind that, amazingly, fit all the facts.

It might not be true, but it gave him something to work with—a tool, or a weapon. Of course, even to hint his suspicions to Lady Tarleton would be like putting fire to powder. But if he had to set off an explosion to get the truth from her, he would.

He had no chance to speak to her alone till after dinner, when the gentlemen joined the ladies in the drawing room. She had withdrawn into a window recess, and he followed her there.

He kept his voice low but did not whisper; whispering only attracted attention. "Lady Tarleton, I have something very important to speak to you about. Will you come with me to another room— the library, perhaps?"

"Of all the effrontery! No, I will not come with you, Mr. Kestrel!

Do you think I'm a lackey, to go hither and yon at your pleasure?"

"I thought you might rather talk in private. But if you prefer, I'll tell you here and now what I have to say."

"I don't want to know what you have to say!" she hissed.

"I'm afraid you have no choice. I want to know what you were doing in Mr. Craddock's room on the afternoon of the murder. And, by God, I will have an answer."

She gasped. Her hands found their way to her throat.

"The library?" he repeated.

She closed her eyes and nodded jerkily. He took up a small candelabrum, and they went out.

The library was dark and silent. Julian set his candles on a table and turned to face Lady Tarleton. She lifted her chin and demanded, "What makes you think I was in that man's room?"

"I know you were."

"If Mr. Craddock told you that, he was lying. And Robert will take my word against his, you'll see."

"It wasn't Mr. Craddock who told me. It was someone who overheard your conversation with him."

"*No!*" She flung herself at him, all but tore the lapels off his coat. "Who overheard us? What have you found out?"

"Only that you were in Mr. Craddock's room, and the two of you quarrelled. I don't know what it was about—I was hoping you could explain—"

She hung on him, staring into his face with wild, dilated eyes. "Then you don't know—you haven't found out—"

He gently loosed her hands from his lapels and guided her to a chair. "May I get you some water—or wine, perhaps?"

"I don't want anything. Except an explanation! Why are you putting me through this horror? What do you want from me?"

"The same thing I want from everyone in the house: a true account of your movements on the afternoon of the murder. You said you never left your room. I know now that you did. I should like to know when you left it, whether you went anywhere besides Mr. Craddock's room, how long you were in his room, and why you went there."

"Why I went there is nothing to you!"

"If it has any bearing on the murder—"

"It hasn't!"

"I can't know that for certain till you tell me."

She threw back her head. "Find out if you can, Mr. Kestrel! I shall tell you nothing. I was in Mr. Craddock's room—very well. Why don't you ask your mysterious informant what I was doing there? I don't believe your informant knows anything, and I don't believe you do, either. Do your worst! Tell Robert—tell everyone! You won't get a word out of me. But when all this is over—when your brute of a servant's been convicted and hanged—then I shall do plenty of talking! I shall make it known all over London how you tried to fasten his guilt on one of us. And that will be the end of you, Mr. Kestrel! You'll be driven out of good society—even servants will cut you dead!"

He had no one to blame but himself, he thought. Because she was a woman, and so distraught, he had been too soft with her— reasoned when he should have insisted. She had the whip hand now, and he would have to wrest it back. He fanned his anger, beating down his chivalrous instincts.

"If you won't tell me what I need to know," he said, "I shall have to draw my own conclusions. And when I take this up with Sir Robert, I shall tell him what those conclusions are."

"What do you mean? What conclusions?"

"This investigation is like putting together a Chinese puzzle. You have an assortment of odd facts, and you try to arrange them in a pattern. That's what I've done. It may be all wrong from beginning to end, but it's the only pattern I can find. A young lady, a foreigner, turned up in Alderton three days ago. She must have been about twenty years old. Her hair was reddish, and her eyes were blue."

He had been walking about as he spoke, but now he stopped and fixed his gaze on her. Her red hair was straggling down from its chignon. Her blue eyes stared into his.

"The night she arrived in Alderton, she asked Mrs. Warren where Bellegarde was. And she told Mrs. Warren she would soon be meeting again someone she was devoted to—someone who had to leave her when she was very young. It was that person who gave her the silver scallop shell she wore around her neck—the trinket you were so reluctant to touch.

"Suppose for the sake of argument that the person she looked forward to seeing again was at Bellegarde. And suppose that person was—her mother."

Lady Tarleton was rigid. A muscle near her mouth twitched. Her hands clenched into fists.

"Now some family history. Mr. Craddock was a groom at Bellegarde some twenty years ago. You were a fierce and venturesome rider. If Craddock was the groom you took on your rides, you could have been alone with him for long periods of time, far from Bellegarde.

"At some point you demanded that Sir Robert dismiss him. No one seems to know why. Craddock is still in a passion of rage against you, and you return his hatred with interest. But you feel something more, too—guilt, and bitter regret. You said to him, 'I have scourged myself for that for more than twenty years.'

"One other significant fact. As a girl, you made a trip to the Continent against your family's wishes. You took advantage of a lull in the wars with France, which must have been the Peace of Amiens. That was in 1802—some two-and-twenty years ago."

"What—what are you implying?"

"Did you leave a daughter behind you in France, Lady Tarleton?"

She shot up from her chair and struck him in the face.

He barely blinked. "I take it you prefer not to answer."

"How dare you! How *dare* you! No! It isn't true! That wretched girl was not my daughter! How could you think such a thing?" She staggered away from him, shaking violently. "You've stumbled on a piece—a very small piece!—of the truth. Mr. Craddock, in his unparalleled effrontery, once sought to put his hands on me. We were riding together in the Chase, and I'd dismounted in a small clearing—yes, Mr. Kestrel, the clearing he was taunting me with the other night! He tried to take liberties—he, a servant I'd trusted to ride with me alone, to whom I'd shown all manner of favour, far beyond his deserts! I escaped from his repulsive advances and rode home and told Robert what he had done. Robert very properly discharged him at once. For the sake of my reputation, we said nothing in public about the reasons for his dismissal. To have it known that a creature like Craddock had so much as lifted a hand to touch me would have soiled me forever. A mere groom! The refuse of a stable! And I a Fontclair!

"Of course Mr. Craddock has never forgiven us. He was so puffed up with pride, he couldn't see how great a distance there was between him and me. He actually thought I might return his feelings! You ought to have seen him—swaggering, boastful, proud—thinking that because servant girls fell into his arms, Catherine Fontclair might do the same! I soon disabused him of that notion! But he's hated me and my brother all these years, and now fate's given him a chance to take revenge. He means to marry his mouse of a daughter to Hugh—to mingle his blood with ours. There's nothing I wouldn't do to stop him—nothing! That's why I went to his room. Nothing else could have brought me to set foot there, and take the chance I might have to confront him alone. I knew he was out riding, and I hoped to be gone before he returned, but I wasn't so lucky. He came back and found me."

"What did you hope to gain by going to his room?"

"I've got to tell you, haven't I? If I don't, you'll just keep digging, probing, ransacking us for guilty secrets— No! I won't let you humiliate me any longer! You thought I'd given myself to a groom and borne him a child. Perhaps you even thought I murdered that child to keep my shame a secret. Well, you were wrong! It isn't I who've brought our family to the brink of disgrace and put us in Craddock's power. Geoffrey—Geoffrey is the criminal in our midst! And not just a murderer, Mr. Kestrel. Murderers are only hanged. Traitors are drawn and quartered, and their property taken by the Crown. That's what would happen to Geoffrey if we didn't conspire with Craddock to hide his guilt. And but for the dishonour it would bring on our name, I could see it happen and not even shed a tear!"

# *23*
# NEMESIS

"Colonel Fontclair committed treason?" Julian said dazedly.

"It was during the Peninsular campaign." Lady Tarleton sat down and smoothed out her skirts, suddenly purposeful and calm. "Of course you know he served under Wellington in Portugal and Spain. He was decorated many times for bravery in the field. Until a few months ago, we were all proud of his achievements. We thought he was a worthy successor to the military heroes who've borne our name.

"What we didn't know was that he'd been ensnared by a Bonapartist spy—a creature named Gabrielle Deschamps. He met her after the siege of Badajoz. She was hiding in a church—of all places!—and he took her under his protection. A pity there was no one to protect him from her! By the time the army moved on, Geoffrey fancied himself in love with her. He saw her whenever and wherever he could. And he wrote her letters, some half a dozen of them. I don't know what they said; none of us has seen them. But they passed information to her—information she sold to the French army! He gave aid and comfort to the enemy in time of war, Mr. Kestrel! Just to keep some harlot's favours! Was there ever anything so contemptible? I can hardly believe he could be my brother, and a Fontclair!

"He thought his treachery would never be discovered. He lost track of the woman after he was invalided out, and for a dozen years he heard no more of her. But there's such a thing as retribution, Mr. Kestrel, and God saw fit to visit it on all of us, as well as on him who earned it. This past April, just after Hugh's coming of age, Craddock came to Bellegarde and demanded to speak with Geoffrey, Robert, and me. He'd got hold of Geoffrey's letters and threatened to make them public, unless Robert agreed to a marriage between Hugh and Craddock's daughter.

"A pretty revenge, was it not? I had scorned him years ago; now he would marry his daughter to my nephew—make her mother to the next generation of Fontclairs. And imagine how he relished holding over our heads how Geoffrey'd disgraced us all! We'd always been so proud of our ancestors' military glories, and now to fall so low! It amazes me Geoffrey still lives. If he had a vestige of honour left, he would put an end to himself rather than bear the remorse and humiliation. But he held on to his worthless life—more than that, he begged Robert to accede to Craddock's demands, to save him from disgrace and prosecution. Of course Robert agreed—not for Geoffrey's sake, I trust, but to protect our family honour and pass on a spotless name to our descendants."

Julian recalled how, on his first evening at Bellegarde, Geoffrey had bolted from the drawing room on hearing Lady Tarleton talk of their ancestors' military exploits. No wonder. Her every word had been a reproach, pointing up the contrast between their past glories and his own looming disgrace. "But how did Colonel Fontclair's letters end up in Craddock's hands?"

"By a circumstance some would call coincidence, but I call Nemesis. One of Mr. Craddock's loathsome business interests is a string of pawnshops he owns in the City. He was visiting one of them when he found a woman's jewelry casket, of black and gold japan work. Whoever pawned it hadn't redeemed it, and the man who manages the shop for Craddock had put it out for sale. Craddock had a fancy to give it to his daughter. While examining it, he discovered it had a false bottom. He looked underneath it—and there he found the letters. At all events, that's the story he told us."

"Did the jewelry box belong to this woman Gabrielle Deschamps?"

"I have no idea. Geoffrey says he doesn't remember her having such a box, but why we should believe anything Geoffrey says is more than I can conceive."

"Who pawned the box?"

"We don't know."

"But don't you want to find out? If it was Mademoiselle Deschamps who pawned it, she may be in England. Colonel Fontclair could buy Mr. Craddock's silence, only to face a new threat of blackmail from her."

"We thought of that. We're not fools, Mr. Kestrel. We asked Craddock who pawned the box, but he said the pawnbroker didn't know. The stupid fellow remembered nothing about the transaction at all."

"But pawnbrokers are required by law to keep the name and address of everyone who pawns goods with them."

"Well, this pawnbroker had lost the name and address of whoever pawned the box. Or so Craddock said. We couldn't very well go and question the man ourselves. We didn't dare let it be known we had any interest in the box or the person who pawned it. I shouldn't think it was the Deschamps woman. Why would she have pawned it with the letters inside? They were valuable—she could have sold them to Geoffrey for a high price. Most likely she's dead, or the box was stolen from her. It must have fallen into the hands of someone who either didn't know the letters were there or didn't think them of any importance. But when Craddock read them, he realized what they could be worth, and how he could use them against us.

"Now do you understand why I went to his room while he was out? I was looking for those miserable letters. I hoped against hope he might have brought them with him to Bellegarde. I waited in my room till nearly five o'clock, when I was sure all the servants would be at dinner, then I crept into his room and searched it. Repulsive though it was to touch his clothes, his shaving things, his bed linen—I searched everywhere. If I could only get those letters away from him, his hold over us would be broken. We could throw him out of Bellegarde as we did years ago, and his daughter with him.

"Now I'll tell you about my embroidery scissors—it's fascinated you for so long. There was a strongbox on the floor of Craddock's room. I tried to open it, but it was locked. I was convinced the letters were in it, and it maddened me that I couldn't get at them. I tried to drag it away with me, but it was too heavy. Then I tried to pick the lock, using one of the blades of my embroidery scissors, but that didn't work. Finally I jabbed at the lid with the scissors, trying to prise it open. That's how I cut my finger. And just at that moment Craddock came in! Only conceive of my humiliation! To be caught in his room like that, searching his things!"

Her story rang true, thought Julian. The scratches on the scissors could well have been made by poking the blades inside a lock or under the rim of a strongbox. And it was easy to imagine her making such a frenzied attack on the strongbox that she cut her finger. He saw why she had lied: not only would it have galled her to admit Craddock caught her searching his room, but she would have had to explain what she was looking for, and the story of Colonel Fontclair's letters would have had to come out. Craddock had supported her lies in order to keep his hold on the Fontclairs—for a blackmailer's power vanishes once the secret he knows is made public. Craddock and the Fontclairs had different motives, but their goal was the same: to keep Geoffrey's misconduct hidden at all costs.

"Craddock came in from riding at twenty minutes past five," he said, "and, according to my informant, you were still in his room half an hour later. Were you quarrelling all that time?"

"Who is this informant of yours?"

"I should rather keep—him or her—out of this."

"Some skulking servant, no doubt. If I ever find out who it was, I shall have the wretch dismissed without a character. Listening at keyholes!"

"Lady Tarleton," he said quietly, "what is it you've been regretting for more than twenty years?"

She looked at him sharply, warily. After a moment she said, "I've always wished I'd had Craddock punished for trying to take liberties with me. But Robert and I were anxious to protect my reputation. Of course I was blameless, but there might have been a scandal all the same. Malicious people might have said I'd encouraged Craddock somehow. So Robert gave him a reference and wages in lieu of notice in exchange for his promise not to make known why he was turned out of Bellegarde. But afterward I was sorry we'd been so lenient with him. He—he practically tried to assault me. We ought to have had him arrested. That's what I've regretted all these years."

Julian frowned over this but made no comment. "In your quarrel with Craddock, you threatened to betray him about something, if he revealed something about you. What was all that about?"

"I didn't want him to tell my family he'd caught me searching his room. I was mortified enough without their knowing. I said— I threatened to make public that he was blackmailing us with Geoffrey's letters. He didn't believe I would do it. He knew I didn't want Geoffrey's disgrace to come out." Her eyes narrowed. "What else did your spy hear us say?"

"Mr. Craddock said you would sacrifice anything for the sake of your reputation. And he said he wished the rest of the world could have seen what he saw when he came in and found you—where?"

"In his room, trying to open his strongbox," she said impatiently. "Where did you think he meant? In *your* room, murdering that girl?"

That was the crux of the problem, he thought ruefully. What, if anything, did all this have to do with the murder? Well, at least he knew at long last how Craddock had bent the Fontclairs to his will. And since it was only natural to suspect a link between blackmail and murder, both Geoffrey Fontclair and Mark Craddock had a good deal of explaining to do.

✳

On returning to the drawing room, Julian asked to speak with Sir Robert in private. They retired to the small study at the back of the main house where, two nights ago, the household had filed by to look at the murdered girl. Julian wondered if anyone would ever care to sit on that sofa again.

"Senderby was here this afternoon," said Sir Robert. "He told me Morley's story about seeing Bliss with the murdered girl. He said you already knew about that."

"Yes. Has Bliss been found yet?"

"No. One of the special constables is making enquiries. It shouldn't be difficult to find him. He's too old and hasn't the means to travel quickly, and he stops often along the way to beg and hawk his wares. But I shouldn't think he'd have much to contribute to the investigation. It seems he spoke with the girl only briefly, to give her directions on the road."

Julian thought of the girl's earring and the strand of her hair, which he had wrapped in paper and buried in a container of tooth-powder in his dressing-case. Those clues certainly suggested that there had been more than a casual connexion between the girl and Bliss. But he could not bring himself to tell Sir Robert about his investigation at the old mill.

"It wasn't Morley's story I wanted to speak to you about," he said. "I'm sorry to bring up a subject that must be extremely painful to you, but Lady Tarleton's told me about Colonel Fontclair's letters." He repeated her account of Craddock's blackmail scheme, and of her attempt to break open his strongbox.

Sir Robert heard him out with surprising calm. "It's something of a relief that you know," he said quietly. "We've been finding it harder and harder to keep Geoffrey's secret from you. I sometimes wonder if we were visited with this murder as a punishment for hiding his guilt. Just when we most wish to escape notice, the investigation's shone a beacon on us, lighting up our every move-ment, thought, and feeling. It's making a mockery of our secrecy, and Craddock's threats. Mr. Kestrel, my brother is a criminal, and I am a magistrate. My concealment of his crime is indefensible. If you choose to reveal it, you'll be acting as a British subject should, and I—I shall be the first to commend you for it!"

Julian thought: What must it cost a man like this to lie for his brother, to give in to the blackmail of a former servant, to suppress information that might be needed to apprehend a murderer? No doubt he's acting in part out of a desire to save his brother's skin, but what really drives him is honour—the need to protect the name he cherishes. He has his ancestors to think of, and his descendants. Their claims on him are stronger even than his sense of justice.

He said, "The only crime that concerns me is the murder here two days ago. If Colonel Fontclair's letters have nothing to do with that, then I count them no business of mine."

"Do you think the murder and this matter of the letters are linked?"

"Very possibly. Have you asked your brother and Mr. Craddock whether the girl might be connected somehow to Gabrielle Deschamps, or the letters?"

"I haven't asked them specifically, no. I'm afraid I've tended to shun the very idea."

"I understand. But I think we ought to ask them now."

"And you are quite right, of course." Sir Robert pulled the bell-rope, and sent a servant to ask Colonel Fontclair to join them. "Mr. Kestrel, I don't believe my brother had anything to do with that girl's death. For all his prowess in battle, he isn't cruel or brutal by nature. His sins are sins of irresponsibility and weakness. About Mr. Craddock, I can't be certain. But I promise you this: If it transpires that the murder is linked in any way to my brother's misconduct, nothing on earth will prevail upon me to keep it hidden any longer. I've already cheated justice by conspiring to suppress the letters. Further than that, I cannot go."

✳

"I wish I could explain to you what she was like!" Geoffrey waved his hands helplessly. "She could make a man do anything. It was like—like being bewitched. She could torment a fellow until he went out of his senses. You could never be sure of her. Even when she was in my arms, she always seemed somewhere far away. Laughing at me, maybe. Thinking of someone else.

"It was partly that campaign. It wore down the hardiest of us. It went on for years, one skirmish after another, and one day we'd have the advantage, and the next day the French would. The heat was stifling, the terrain was rough, supplies were hard to come by. The Spanish were like wild animals, and our troops not much better. I was bored and restless. But in the end, it was that woman. I've never known another who could do to me what she did.

"I never told her anything important. It wasn't as though I sold my own men, gave them up to the French! Little things, that's all I told her! Things the French probably knew about anyway. I didn't see her for long stretches at a time, and when I wasn't with her, I worried about her being with other men. I was crazed with jealousy. I had an idea she'd be faithful to me if I kept her supplied with information. I didn't tell her anything of consequence, you've got to believe me! But those letters—I have a feeling they'd look pretty bad if they came to light now."

Sir Robert's gaunt, patrician features were pinched with distaste. He had obviously heard all this before. "Neither Mr. Kestrel nor I is interested in your explanations. What we wish to know is whether your letters might have any bearing on the murder."

"I don't see how they could."

"You can't think of any reason to connect the girl with Mademoiselle Deschamps?" said Julian.

"What reason could there be?"

"The girl was foreign. She could have been a relation, or a servant."

"I wouldn't know about that," Geoffrey muttered.

"When did you last hear from her? Mademoiselle Deschamps, I mean."

"I lost track of her after the French were driven back over the Pyrenees. I was wounded and sent back to England at about that time. Gabrielle might have been killed—a lot of the French in Spain were. But she might have escaped to France. I never heard anything more about her. I'd all but managed to forget her, till Craddock turned up and said he had my letters."

"Didn't you ever wonder what became of them?" asked Julian.

"I tried not to think about it. It would be like Gabrielle to keep them. She'd never let anything slip through her fingers that might be turned into money. But how the letters got in that jewelry box, I'm damned if I know."

Julian considered. "If Gabrielle died, who would be likely to inherit her possessions?"

"I don't know."

"Did she ever mention any family?"

"No." He shifted in his chair, and looked miserably at Sir Robert. "What's going to happen now?"

"Mr. Kestrel and I will continue to search for a link between the murder and this matter of your letters. You must understand that, if there is such a link, I can't shield you any longer. The whole story will have to come out."

"What if there isn't a link?" Geoffrey's hollow eyes shifted from Sir Robert to Julian.

"I assure you, Colonel, I have no interest in revealing anything I've learned about your family that isn't related to the murder."

Geoffrey rose heavily. "If you're finished with me, I'll go now."

"I have a few more questions," said Julian. "On Thursday evening, Lady Tarleton and I found you in the gun room with Lady Fontclair. She was saying to you, 'It's wicked and wrong. Promise you will never think of it again.' What did she mean?"

Geoffrey's ruddy colour deepened. "I was thinking I might just load one of the guns and—and settle my accounts. Cecily made me promise not to. She said I'd show more courage by facing up to things. And she said my death wouldn't stop Craddock from using my letters against the family." He paused, then asked hoarsely, "Anything else?"

"I was wondering if you're in the habit of carrying a knife."

"I have a pocket knife," stammered Geoffrey, eyes dilating.

"Did you have it with you on the day of the murder?"

"I— I don't remember."

Sir Robert moved away, as though he really could not bear to look at Geoffrey any longer. "If you're satisfied, Mr. Kestrel, I think we can allow my brother to go."

Geoffrey started toward the door, then turned and said piteously, "Have you got to tell Guy about my letters, and everything?"

"We've been keeping it from Guy," Sir Robert explained to Julian. "Geoffrey didn't want him to know, and I saw nothing to be gained by burdening him with the knowledge."

"Does Hugh know?"

"We had to tell him. It wouldn't have been right to ask him to accede to Craddock's demands without telling him what was at stake."

"And Miss Fontclair?"

"She hasn't been told. She takes such pride in our name and lineage that I wanted to spare her knowledge of this dishonour."

Geoffrey turned his face away, and hobbled slowly out of the room. Sir Robert looked after him stonily, then rang for the footman and told him he wished to speak with Mr. Craddock.

# *24*
# MANOEUVRES

"So she's told you about the letters, has she?" said Craddock to Julian. "I don't know what she expected to gain by it. Maybe she thought by putting me in a bad light she could implicate me in the murder. But she'll pay a high price, if this business of the letters is made public. The Fontclairs can call off the marriage, but that'll be small comfort to them, compared with the ruin of Colonel Fontclair. I didn't realize she hated me so much she'd sacrifice her own brother to spite me."

Julian said, "That seems no more strange than that you should sacrifice your own daughter to spite her."

"What do you mean by that?" Craddock said sharply.

"I mean that, whatever wrongs the Fontclairs may have done you, Miss Craddock is innocent, and I think she deserves better than to be used by her own father as an instrument of revenge."

"Don't meddle in matters that aren't your concern, boy! I won't stand for it. I know what your game is: you want to scuttle the marriage between my daughter and Hugh Fontclair, so you can get Maud and her hundred thousand pounds for yourself. You've been making up to her ever since you got here—don't think I haven't seen it. Well, you'd better know one thing at the outset, and I'll tell Maud the same: she'll never see a ha'penny of my money if she marries any man but Hugh Fontclair."

"My dear sir, I have no designs on either your ducats or your daughter. But I have a very high regard for Miss Craddock, and I won't stand by and see her delivered up to an unwilling bridegroom, with a taint of blackmail on her that will poison her relations with him and his family for the rest of her life."

"I didn't force her to accept him! She made that choice."

"She was choosing in the dark. She didn't know what was at stake—how much harm she might do the Fontclairs if she refused."

"There was no reason she had to know that! All she had to know was that I'd found a fine husband for her—good family, good character, money of his own. It was a good, solid match—no father could have arranged a better! How I arranged it was a matter of business that didn't concern her."

"In your place," said Julian, "I should have been ashamed to tell her, too."

"By God, sir, you go too far!"

He raised a fist. Julian tensed himself to parry the blow. But Sir Robert got between them. "Mr. Craddock, you force me to remind you, it's within my power to arrest you for an assault committed in my presence. As for you, Mr. Kestrel, be so good as to remember I sent for Mr. Craddock, not so that you could quarrel with him, but to allow you to question him about a possible link between the murder and my brother's letters."

Craddock threw Julian a hard, wary look. "What do you want to know?"

Under questioning, he recounted how he had come upon the letters by chance, while making a visit of inspection to one of the pawnshops he owned. "It was in March, about three months ago. The jewelry box caught my eye. I thought Maud might like it. Vorpe—Silas Vorpe, who runs that shop for me—said he had put it out for sale about a month before, because he'd had it a year, and the owner hadn't redeemed it or paid the interest."

Craddock had inspected the box and discovered the secret compartment containing the letters. "I read them, and a nice mixture of whining love letters and military information they were. It fairly made me sick. My first thought was to turn them over to the government and the newspapers. But it just so happened I'd recently read in the society papers about a celebration in the offing for Hugh Fontclair's coming of age. I got to thinking. I saw there was a better use for the letters. You know the rest."

"Didn't you want to know who'd pawned the jewelry box?" asked Julian.

"Of course. I asked Vorpe, but he couldn't say."

"Doesn't he have to keep a record of the name and address of everyone who pawns goods with him?"

"He couldn't find the record of this transaction. The man's as dull-witted as they come. I keep him in my employ because he's meek and does as he's told, and I don't think he cheats me—or no more than most of my underlings do."

Julian was skeptical. "If he'd lost the record, how did he know a year had gone by since the jewelry box was pawned, and it was time to put it out for sale?"

"He attaches a duplicate ticket to each item that's left in pawn, showing what was paid for it, and when it's due to be redeemed. I told him he keeps too many different bits of paper about him. This isn't the first time he's lost a record. I said if it happens again, he'll get the bag."

"Did he remember anything about the person who pawned the box?"

"No. I told you, the man's got more guts than brains. But in fairness to him, he has customers in and out all day, every day. He couldn't be expected to remember one who came in more than a year before."

"Does he know about the letters?"

"Not so far as I know. I didn't tell him."

"Have you any idea at all who pawned the box?"

"No. But whoever it was must not have known the letters were there, or didn't think they were worth keeping."

"Yes," mused Julian, "that's what Lady Tarleton said, too."

"I'd still like to know why she told you about the letters."

Julian said, because he was curious to see how Craddock would react, "I think she wanted to stop me asking questions about what happened between you and her twenty years ago."

"You poke your nose into everything, don't you? What happened between me and Lady Tarleton is none of your business!"

"I agree there's no reason to rake up that matter again," said Sir Robert. "It was thoroughly enquired into at the time—"

Craddock laughed shortly.

"I gave you a fair hearing," Sir Robert insisted, "and you had nothing to say in your own defence."

"I wouldn't answer your sister's accusations, because I knew there was no chance you'd take my word against hers."

"Are you saying that my sister was lying?"

"Yes. She was lying."

"You never tried to force your attentions on her?"

"She was lying," Craddock said stonily.

"I won't deign to answer such an accusation."

"Of course not. I know I'm not gentleman enough to quarrel with a Fontclair on equal terms."

"It ill becomes us to quarrel at all, now that we're so soon to be linked by marriage. We owe one another at least an appearance of loyalty and respect."

"If all you're asking for is an appearance, I think I can manage that." He turned to Julian. "What do you mean to do, now you know about Colonel Fontclair's treason?"

"I mean to find out if it has any bearing on the murder. If it hasn't, it's no affair of mine."

"I suppose you'll tell Maud about the letters?"

"Not unless I have to. I thought you might rather tell her yourself."

Craddock eyed him grimly. "All right. I'll tell her. But don't think she'll come round me—make me change my mind. As long as I have the letters, I'll hold the Fontclairs to their bargain. And it'll be the worse for them if they don't keep it!"

He went out. Sir Robert sighed. "We'd better go to bed. We have the inquest in the morning."

"Just a moment." Julian told him about his visit to Mrs. Warren, and the information he had gleaned from her. It would probably come out in her testimony at the inquest tomorrow, and he would as soon not be had on the carpet for keeping it back.

He still said nothing about his finds at the old mill. On his way up to bed, he remembered Dick Felton, and his eagerness to help in the investigation. The boy was observant; he might well have a talent for that kind of work. At any rate, Julian meant to find out. He had just the job for an aspiring Bow Street Runner.

✳

Sir Robert's image appeared in Lady Fontclair's dressing-table mirror. She turned and smiled at him. He came forward from the doorway and sat beside her, in the chair that was always kept there for him. Her maid edged discreetly out of the room.

He had come to tell her about Kestrel's discovery of Geoffrey's secret, and about the latest finds in the investigation. He had also come to watch her take down her hair, which always gave him a solemn, secret thrill. While he talked, she took out the pins one by one, and the dark silky mass spilled slowly down her neck and over her shoulders. The candlelight turned her few white hairs into light-ning gleams of silver.

She listened attentively, asking a question from time to time. When he finished, she sat silent for a while. Then she said, "Mr. Kestrel seems convinced that Geoffrey's secret and the murder are linked."

"He suspects they are."

"Does he think Geoffrey murdered that girl?"

"I'm sure he entertains the possibility."

"But, Robert, you and I know that can't be true!"

"My love, I'm not sure I do know that. Not long since, I would have said Geoffrey was incapable of passing secrets to the enemy in wartime. I don't trust him anymore."

"You can't think he would kill a young girl in cold blood!"

"I don't think so, no. But I can't say—as I would once have said—that it is impossible."

"My dear love, you look as if you had the weight of the world on your shoulders." She came round behind him and cradled his head against her breast. He closed his eyes. "You know, you mustn't take Mr. Kestrel's suspicions so much to heart. He's worried about his servant being in gaol, and that makes him overzealous in trying to solve the murder. I can't blame him. That lockup is a dreadful place. Robert—you know I always hesitate to interfere in magisterial business—"

He looked around at her. "What is it, my dear?"

"There seems to be so little proof against Mr. Kestrel's servant. Must you keep him in gaol any longer?"

How like her, he thought. In the midst of so many troubles nearer home, she could still spare concern for a servant and a stranger. "Tomorrow I shall either have to release him or charge him with the murder. I can't hold him for more than three days without binding him over for trial."

"What are you going to do?"

"I haven't decided. I still haven't heard from John Reeves, the special constable I sent to trace the girl's journey. If she came from London, she and Stokes could have been acquainted."

"There are a great many people in London. It doesn't seem much of a connexion."

"No. I admit there isn't much proof against him. The difficulty is, there's no proof whatsoever against anyone else."

"Mr. Kestrel vouched for him, and Mr. Kestrel seems the sort of person who would be careful whom he kept as a servant. And, Robert, for what it's worth, I saw something of Stokes before the murder—you know I make a point of observing people who come to stay in our house, even servants—and I thought he seemed a very nice young man. I can't believe he would kill anyone."

"You really think he's innocent?"

"I really do, with all my heart." Her wide, earnest eyes looked into his.

"Well, if nothing further comes out against him at the inquest, I'll order his release."

"Oh, I'm so glad!"

She put her arms around him. He gathered her against him, kissed her lips, her cheeks, her throat. After more than twenty years of marriage, it still awed him that she belonged to him—that anything so fair and bright and sweet could be all his. He thought of Geoffrey's attachment to Gabrielle Deschamps, and shuddered. Imagine being in thrall to a ruthless, manipulative woman—a woman you could not trust!

She drew back from him at last, flushed and smiling, and slipped into her seat at the dressing-table, taking up her comb again. "At least poor Mr. Kestrel needn't be burdened any longer with the investigation. He was only ever involved in it because his servant was accused."

"I think he's become interested in it for its own sake."

"He's a very clever young man, and clever young men must have their amusements. But I'm sure we can find something safer and pleasanter for him than solving a murder."

✳

Next morning, Maud caught Julian alone before breakfast. "I want to thank you for making Papa tell me about Colonel Fontclair's letters."

He shrugged. "I think he told you because he realized you had a right to know."

"I think someone made him realize it," said Maud.

He had no answer to this.

"Will the secret have to come out?" she asked.

"That depends on whether it's linked to the murder."

"Do you think it is?"

"Very likely."

"At least if the secret comes out, Papa will lose his hold over the Fontclairs. It's terrible, what he's doing! It's mortifying to both the Fontclairs and me. I've got to find some way to stop it. I wish Lady Tarleton had found the letters when she searched his room! But he says they weren't there. He says he didn't bring them to Bellegarde."

"Did he say where they are?"

"No. I asked, but he wouldn't tell me. I think they must be in the cabinet in his study at home. It's a steel cabinet he had made specially to hold important papers. The padlock was designed by the best locksmith in London. Papa wears the key on a chain around his neck, with other important keys, and he never takes it off, even at night. So you see, if the letters are in that cabinet, there's no way of getting at them. But there must be something else I can do to stop him threatening the Fontclairs. There *must* be!"

✳

The inquest lasted all morning and a good part of the afternoon. It took place at the Blue Lion, in a large back room where local clubs met and dances were held. The place was packed with people from Alderton and beyond. Julian noticed three young men, thin as whippets, their scruffy clothes flecked with city soot, their fingers stained with ink. They were alternately darting sharp glances around them and scribbling in little notebooks. Clearly, the murder had gotten the attention of the London papers.

Julian testified first, describing how he had found the girl's body in his bed. Although this story was well known by now, his public retelling of it caused quite a stir. MacGregor then gave evidence about the manner and probable time of death.

Dick Felton and Mrs. Warren were both difficult witnesses. Felton was enjoying himself and dragged out his evidence as long as he could, while Mrs. Warren was so struck with fear she could hardly speak at all. Senderby testified about what had been done to investigate the crime. There was a murmur of uneasiness among the listeners, as it became clear that there was no evidence of robbery or illegal entry at Bellegarde. People could not but realize this ruled out the most mundane explanations for the murder.

A shadow of suspicion inevitably fell on the Fontclairs. Yet, as MacGregor had predicted, the coroner did not call them as witnesses or enquire into their whereabouts at the time of the murder. He spoke of them with great deference, and expressed his profound regret that they had been dragged into this sordid business. What he clearly hoped to establish was that Mr. Kestrel's servant was the likely culprit. But there was simply no evidence linking Mr. Stokes to the crime or the victim. The jury had no choice but to bring in a verdict of willful murder by a person or persons unknown.

After the inquest, Julian lost himself in the crowd, determined to avoid the three avid Londoners with the notebooks. He kept an eye out for Dick Felton and, finding him, asked to have a word with him alone.

Felton brought him to a small deserted yard next door, behind the greengrocer's. "Have you got any work for me, sir?" he asked eagerly. "Police-type work, I mean?"

"I have a little job that needs doing, yes."

"I'm your man, sir! I'm game for anything."

"Do you know Bliss the pedlar?"

" 'Course I do! Is he the one as done it, sir—the murder?"

"I doubt it. But I want to find him. Senderby is making efforts in that direction, but he doesn't attach the importance to Bliss that I do. You said you could take some time away from your work at the Blue Lion. Will you have a try at finding Bliss for me?"

"Won't I just! I'll ask in all the villages if anyone's seen him. I'll track him like a red Indian." His face fell. "Only I couldn't stay away more nor a few days. My brother, who'd be taking my place at the Lion, is starting work on a farm at the end of the week."

"Give it a few days and see what happens. You may find Bliss by then, or at least get an idea where he's gone."

"What should I do if I find him?"

"Try if you can to persuade him to come back and answer some questions. Tell him I'll make it worth his while—I hear nothing charms him like the jingling of coins."

"He'll do anything for money, sir, no mistake."

Julian made a wry face, remembering how he had once hoped a sojourn in the country would be a relief to his pocketbook. "If you find him, or any trace of him, I'll make it worth your while as well. And I'll pay your expenses, whether you find him or not. Is that a fair bargain?"

"Yes, sir!"

"One more thing. Can you arrange to have your brother take your place without telling him or anyone else what you're doing for me?"

"Never fear, sir. I'll fob 'em all off. This is strick'ly on the quiet, then, is it?"

"Exactly."

"Then mum's the word, sir. I won't split on you. 'Split on' is thieves' talk for—but *you* probably know that, don't you, sir?" Dick said slyly.

Julian began to get an inkling of the boy's suspicions. He smiled, wondering what St. James Street would say about Julian Kestrel's being mistaken for a barbarous Bow Street Runner. To the Quality, the Runners were a plague and a nuisance—forever raiding gaming hells, breaking up duels, interfering with all a gentleman's amusements. But if the sons of peers knew how exciting it was to solve a crime, thought Julian, they would be joining Bow Street for a lark, the way they now paid to spar with professional boxers or handle the ribbons of a stagecoach.

✳

Late in the day John Reeves, the special constable, returned from tracing the murdered girl's journey, and came to report to Sir Robert at Bellegarde. Julian did not hear about his visit till afterward, and was immediately suspicious. Why had he not been sent for to hear the man's findings for himself? He sought out Sir Robert in his office.

"Mr. Kestrel," Sir Robert greeted him. "I was just going to look for you. You'll be glad to know I've given Senderby orders to release your servant. I don't believe there are sufficient grounds to charge him with the murder."

"I'm very glad to hear it. Thank you."

"You ought to thank Lady Fontclair. She was very concerned about Mr. Stokes, and spoke warmly on his behalf, and yours."

"That was very good of her," said Julian slowly. Of course he was pleased about Dipper's release, but something about the manner of it gave him a prickly sensation at the back of his neck.

"I must ask that you and your servant remain in the neighbourhood for the present, as you may be needed to give evidence or answer further questions. But there shouldn't be any difficulty about that: you are still our guest, and I hope you'll finish out your stay, in spite of this unfortunate incident."

Sir Robert sat down at his desk, as though he regarded their interview as at an end. But Julian asked, "I heard Reeves was here. What did he find out?"

"Were you meaning to remain involved in the investigation, Mr. Kestrel? Your servant is now at liberty. Surely your principal motive for concerning yourself with the murder has been removed."

Yes, thought Julian, you've very neatly removed it—at the instigation of Lady Fontclair. "Dipper may be out of gaol, but he'll remain under suspicion as long as the real murderer is unknown. For that matter, the public is more than a little dubious about *my* role in this business. If the crime isn't solved, both Dipper and I may bear the taint of it for the rest of our lives."

"Do you suppose I shall let the matter rest till the murderer is brought to justice?"

"I think you'll do all that can be expected of a man, when his every move threatens the people he most loves."

"I know you believe I can't be impartial. To be frank, I had the same fear myself. That is why I agreed to let you take part in the investigation—to act as a gadfly, spurring me on to face possibilities I would rather have blinked away. I don't need you to play that role anymore. Control of the investigation won't remain in my hands much longer."

"I don't understand."

"Reeves tells me the girl set out for Alderton from a posting house in London. She had no companion and no servant; she made all her travel arrangements herself. Beyond that, he found out nothing to the purpose. Few people saw or spoke with her. If she gave her name, no one remembers it now. I have no choice but to circulate advertisements in London, on the chance that she lived or was known there, and offer a reward for information about her."

"If an investigation is carried out publicly in London, Bow Street is bound to become involved."

"Yes. You can imagine how little I welcome that prospect. Professional policemen are certain to root out the business of Geoffrey's letters and Craddock's use of them—and, unlike you, they won't have any qualms about making public whatever they find out. But the matter is out of my hands. Enquiries must be made in Lon-

don—the girl's identity is crucial to solving this crime. It seems
there's no avoiding Bow Street now."

Julian was no more pleased than Sir Robert. If Bow Street joined
the investigation, the odds were that Dipper would be recognized,
and his criminal past exposed. That might provide Sir Robert with
just the foundation he needed to charge Dipper with the murder.
Dipper's reprieve from prison was liable to be all too short.

# * 25 *
# AN OLD FRIEND
# OF DIPPER'S

———

Dipper was distressed at the way his master's clothes had been cared for in his absence. "I wouldn't have used a goffering iron on this," he said, shaking his head over one of Julian's shirts. "Look how it's queered the collar."

Julian was not attending. Dipper watched him take several turns about the room, then asked, "Anything on your mind, sir?"

"Sir Robert told me the investigation is moving to London. That means the Bow Street Runners will almost certainly become involved."

"I thought they would in the end, sir," nodded Dipper. "If they blow upon me, I'll say you didn't know nothing about me when you took me on. I'll say I gammoned you into thinking I was on the square."

"That should do wonders for my reputation for judgement," said Julian lightly.

"You got to let me bonnet for you, sir, there's no sense both of us getting lagged—"

The dressing bell rang. Julian, ducking Dipper's protests, began to change for dinner. "You know," he said, frowning, "your name will probably crop up in the newspaper accounts of the inquest. If the London police read them, they may blow upon you, as you call it, even before they're drawn into the investigation."

"That depends, sir. They know me as Dipper, on account of that's what I was called when I was a fingersmith. They might not know the name Stokes."

"Then it's a mercy you were always referred to as 'Stokes' at the inquest." He made a rueful face. "I ought not to have gone on calling you by your old nickname. It just seemed to suit you so well."

"I always liked it better nor Stokes, sir. A name ought to say something about a cove, that's what I say."

"According to Lady Tarleton, my name suits me famously—a small and rather noisy bird of prey. Well, I could be worse off. Imagine going through life with a name like Silas Vorpe."

Dipper blinked at him. "How do you know about Mr. Vorpe, sir?"

"Do *you* know about him?"

"He's the Maggot, sir."

"I beg your pardon?"

"That's what we called him, me pals and me. If you was to see him, sir, you'd understand. He's very big and white and soft, and bald as a billiard ball."

"How do you know him?"

"Well, betwixt you and me, sir, he's an angling cove. What would you call it? A receiver."

"Of stolen goods?"

"Yes, sir. Though the pawnshop he runs is mostly on the square. Otherwise the cove as owns it would be down upon him and turn him out, and he needs the shop so as to seem respe'table. He's got a fencing crib he runs on the sly, but sometimes we used to bring him moveables at the pawnshop—small things like tickers and wipes, that we'd just nicked and had to get rid of in a hurry. He fenced 'em for us, no questions asked. Never give us anything like what they was worth, but what could we do? If we was caught with the swag, we'd go straight to boarding school."

"Did you know it was Craddock who owns that pawnshop?"

"No, sir," said Dipper, much surprised.

"He thinks Vorpe is extremely dull-witted, but honest."

"Well, he's wrong twice over, sir. Mr. Vorpe's neither of those. Flash to every move, is Mr. Vorpe. And his memory's something wonderful—all he has to do is set his oglers once on a ticker or a glimstick, or whatever kind of moveable you like, and he can call it to mind years later, like it was yesterday."

"Can he indeed? Dipper, I think it's time I told you what I discovered while you were in—boarding school. But keep this strictly between the two of us." He explained how Craddock had found Geoffrey's letters and used them to blackmail the Fontclairs. "What puzzles me," he finished, "is that Mr. Vorpe, who according to you has amazing powers of recollection, could remember nothing at all about the person who pawned the jewelry box."

"He probably thought it was pinched, sir, and he didn't want to peach on the thief. We're his livelihood, ain't we, sir? He'd have nothing to fence, if he was to get a name for splitting on his pals."

"Do you realize you always say 'we' when you talk about thieves? You still think of yourself as one of them, don't you?"

"It dies pretty hard, sir. I mean, when you're in the Family, it's like you got your own world, and everybody that's in it is your friend, and everybody else is against you. But I don't miss it, sir, and I wouldn't go back to it now. God strike me blind if I would!"

"I believe you."

"Anyways, I expect Mr. Craddock could have got Mr. Vorpe to blow the gab, if he'd pressed hard enough. But Mr. Vorpe fakes people into thinking he's soft, sir." Dipper tapped his head significantly. "Most likely Mr. Craddock thought he really didn't know nix-my-doll about the jewelry box."

"Dipper," said Julian thoughtfully, "does Vorpe know you gave over thieving?"

"I don't see how he could, sir. 'Course, he hasn't seen me for nigh to two years, but he probably thinks I'm in quod or marinated—sent over the water, I mean."

"And does he know you as Thomas Stokes, or only as Dipper?"

"Oh, only as Dipper, sir."

"So that even if he reads about the murder in the newspapers, he won't connect you with it."

"Most likely not. You got something in mind, sir?"

"Yes," said Julian, his eyes gleaming. "As a matter of fact, I do."

✳

In the drawing room before dinner, Miss Craddock asked Julian for news of the investigation.

"I haven't told Sir Robert yet," he said, "but I mean to go to London tomorrow and beat some bushes there."

"How funny. I'm going to London tomorrow, too." She began to blush, and hurried on, "I have ever so much shopping to do for the wedding, and I need to get away from Bellegarde for a few days, after everything that's happened. I've been wanting to give Miss Pritchard a little holiday, and Lady Fontclair said I might take her with me for propriety's sake, and to keep me company. Papa's not coming—I think he wants to stay here and keep an eye on the Fontclairs, and the investigation."

She ended with a little gasp for breath. Julian felt sure she had given him every possible reason for her trip except the true one.

"You must let me take you in our carriage," she added. "It's a new barouche-landau, and very comfortable. If the weather is fine, we can let down the top."

"That would be delightful. Thank you."

He thought privately that he would have travelled much more quickly alone. With two ladies, the journey would take up most of the day, what with keeping the horses to a moderate pace, and getting out at every posting house for fortifying cups of tea. All the same, he thought he had better go with her. He suspected she was playing some kind of deep game, and might need his help.

Sir Robert came in, and Julian excused himself, saying he wanted to speak to him before dinner. She watched him take Sir Robert aside; then they left the drawing room together.

✳

Hugh had been watching Miss Craddock and Kestrel. He could not keep from watching them when they had their heads together like that. He was driven partly by jealousy, and partly by a wish to understand Miss Craddock, who was an ever more tantalizing mystery. That afternoon he had invited her riding, just the two of them, but the outing left him more puzzled and unsatisfied than ever. He never seemed to get close to her. They talked a good deal, but always she kept gently, maddeningly aloof. She charmed him in a thousand little ways, but without trying—without even noticing. He yearned to read her heart and found it locked against him. And he tormented himself with wondering if Julian Kestrel had the key.

She was walking back and forth before a window now, her hands clasped under her chin. Hugh summoned his courage and went up to her. "I enjoyed our ride today."

She turned to him, with a smile that made him feel a little breathless. But almost at once she dragged down her gaze. "So did I."

"Am I intruding? Would you rather I kept away? I know it wasn't your choice to be engaged to me. I don't want to burden you with a bridegroom's attentions, if you'd rather be left alone. If I only knew your mind, I'd study to please you—but I don't, so I just go blundering about."

"Oh, no! You're very kind to me! It's like heaping coals of fire on my head, after the way my father's behaved toward your family. I wouldn't blame you if you hated me."

"I would never be so unjust! I know you're not responsible for what your father is doing. You would never countenance anything low or deceitful or dishonourable."

The colour flamed up in her face.

"Why do you look away? Please don't be embarrassed! I don't blame you, no one blames you for any of this. It's so beastly unfair that we've had to be caught up in this tangle! If we'd been allowed to get to know each other in the ordinary way—"

She looked around at him, with bright eyes and parted lips.

He caught her hand in both of his. "Miss Craddock—Maud—my mother told me you were leaving tomorrow to spend a day or two in London. Why shouldn't I come with you? We could really get to know each other, far from your father, and my family. If Miss Pritchard comes with us, and I stay at our house in town, no one could possibly think it improper."

"Oh, but I—I wouldn't want to take you away from your

family—what with the murder and—and everything. It's such a
short trip, we're going to shop the whole time, I'm sure you would
be bored—"

"I understand," he said stiffly, dropping her hand. "Pardon me
for putting you in such an awkward spot. Since you find my company
so distasteful, I won't thrust it upon you again."

He bowed and turned away—but slowly, hoping against hope
she would call him back. But her throat felt so tight she could not
get out a word. Besides, what could she say? He would never believe
it was for his own good that she dared not go with him to London.

∗

Julian told Sir Robert he was going to London to pursue a lead
from a confidential informant. "I can't tell you who he is, but if
you'll let me hunt about for a few days, I think I may uncover
something very important. And at least I can make my enquiries
discreetly, without involving the professional police."

"Mr. Kestrel, why can't you leave this matter alone, and let justice
take its course?"

"You mean, let justice stumble along when I can speed it on
its way?"

"No. No." Sir Robert went away to the window, looking out
with unseeing eyes. "I'm not so deaf to all sense of duty as to stand
in the way of any course of action that might help solve the murder.
Yes, by all means, Mr. Kestrel, you may go."

∗

At dinner, there was desultory talk about Maud's shopping trip.
Julian mentioned he had business in London and would be travelling
with her. Hugh started, and looked from Maud to Julian as if to
say, "I might have known!" The others threw Julian uneasy glances,
but if they guessed his journey had something to do with the investigation, they did not say so. The Fontclairs rarely spoke of the
murder in his presence anymore. It was one of the ways they had
quietly closed ranks against him.

Sir Robert and Lady Fontclair were called away after dinner to sit
up with Philippa, who had had trouble sleeping since the murder.

For the others, the evening in the drawing room seemed never-ending. Craddock sat in a corner and wrote letters. Geoffrey fidgeted. Catherine paced. Guy tramped about the garden, smoking. Isabelle sat quietly embroidering Maud's wedding slippers. Hugh attached himself to her and talked with forced animation about art, the estate—any topic that might make Maud feel excluded. Maud shrank into a window recess with her workbox and a large handkerchief. Julian managed to entice her out to play backgammon with him.

At last it was time to go up to bed. A footman handed candles to people as they left the drawing room. Craddock, on his way out with Maud, took Julian aside. "Just remember: If Maud marries against my wishes, I'll cut her off with a shilling. So if you're planning a hole-in-corner wedding in Scotland once you get her away with you, think again."

"Please, Papa!" Maud entreated, taking him by the arm.

For her sake, Julian swallowed his irritation, bowed, and withdrew. To avoid another confrontation, he waited till the Craddocks had gone upstairs before he went up himself.

He climbed the grand staircase, the light from his candle darting along the wall. The house, though very quiet, seemed strangely alert and aware. He could almost feel it breathing, like a living thing. From the top of the stairs, the shortest way to his room was through the great chamber. He went in.

The room looked fantastic by candlelight. The gilding on the woodwork gleamed; the birds and flowers on the plaster ceiling seemed alive. Moonlight silvered the Gothic windows and threw pale shadows on the marble floor. Julian could see why Philippa thought this room should have a ghost—

And it did. A woman's shape stood, motionless, on the other side of the room. She was small and slender, like the dead girl. Julian started violently, then got a grip on himself. "Who's there?"

"Hush!" She came forward, her skirt swishing softly along the floor.

He held his candle toward her. "Lady Fontclair."

"I have to talk to you, Mr. Kestrel. Please don't go to London tomorrow."

"I'm afraid I must. I'm sorry."

"You don't understand the harm you may do. You may find something out that, standing alone, seems to prove one of us a murderer. But you don't know us, Mr. Kestrel. How can you tell what we've done, or might do? None of us—none of my family—would kill anyone. I know them. I know them all."

"I understand how you must feel. I had the same faith in my servant when he was accused. Of course a servant isn't the same as a blood relation—except that I haven't any family but Dipper, so it was the same in my case."

"But he's free now. Isn't that enough? Why must you keep on with your investigations?"

"Is that why you brought about his release—so I'd have no excuse to go on trying to solve the murder?"

"I hoped that in common kindness you might leave us in peace, once he was no longer in danger. Can't you let Robert handle everything now? He's a magistrate. He knows what to do."

"I have information that only I can make use of. That's why I'm going to London—why I *must* go."

"Is there no way I can move you?"

She came close, laying her hands on his shoulders with a light, tender, almost seductive touch. He felt a little bewitched. The moonlight, this enchanted room, her beautiful, pale face so near, the breath of perfume clinging round her—

He took her hands from his shoulders. "I wish with all my heart I could do as you ask," he said gently, "but it isn't possible. If you'd rather I didn't stay at Bellegarde any longer, I'll understand. Sir Robert asked me to remain in the neighbourhood, but I'm sure I can find accommodation at the Blue Lion."

"No." She drew back, shaking her head. "My son invited you. You're the man he chose to be groomsman at his wedding, and the man my husband trusts to pursue the investigation on his behalf. It isn't for me to deny you admittance to Bellegarde. Besides, what good would it do? If you find out something in London that might harm—anyone here—keeping you out won't prevent the damage. The wheels of what's called justice will turn all the same."

✳

Maud brought her father a cup of chamomile tea before he went to bed. "Mrs. Cox let me make it myself," she said.

He took it, but looked at her shrewdly. "You don't fool me, my girl."

"Don't I?" she said faintly.

"You're trying to put me in a good humour so I won't guess you're up to some mischief. But I know you are. Tell me the truth: Do you mean to run off with Kestrel?"

"*No*, Papa. There's nothing like that between Mr. Kestrel and me. I didn't even know he was going to London when I decided to go. But since he's leaving on the same day, it would have been churlish of me not to offer him a seat in my carriage."

"That man means no good by you, Maud. He's after your money."

"Please don't worry. I don't believe Mr. Kestrel wants to marry me, and even if he did, I wouldn't accept him. Truly, I promise."

Craddock suddenly drew her to him and kissed her on the brow. "You're a good girl, Maud," he muttered. Then he turned away brusquely, and so did not see the grieved, guilty look on her face.

# *26*
# A LOCAL HABITATION
# AND A NAME

Next morning, Julian, Maud, and Miss Pritchard left for London in the Craddocks' sumptuous barouche. Dipper and Maud's maid, Alice, rode behind them in a more demure travelling chaise that carried most of the luggage. Alice could not decide whether Dipper's sojourn in gaol made him sinister or romantic, so she kept him in a state of confusion by flirting with him one minute and cowering from him the next. He consoled himself with memories of Molly Dale, who had welcomed him back to Bellegarde very warmly last night. She had invited him to share a flask of ale with her in a disused storeroom. "I can only stay a very little while," she said, but she stayed a good part of the night. As a result, he got very little sleep, and departed for London heavy-eyed but happy.

Julian asked after the Misses Fontclair, whom he had not seen since the murder. "Miss Joanna was dreadfully upset when she heard about it," said Miss Pritchard. "Miss Philippa took it much better—asking questions of everybody, wanting to know 'why' this and 'why' that, till I had to tell her, really, it's not a fit subject for a young lady to be so curious about."

"Isn't she better off taking too lively an interest in the murder than being afraid of it?"

"But she's afraid now, sir. Or at all events, she's brooding. She sits by herself and stares at nothing, won't eat, won't attend to her lessons—"

"Oh, poor Philippa!" said Maud. "Could I help somehow? I'd be happy to talk to her when we get back to Bellegarde."

"That's good of you, Miss Craddock. It can't do any harm, and it might help, one never knows."

Soon Miss Pritchard's head drooped, and little ladylike snores came from under the brim of her bonnet. Julian whispered to Maud, "You seem to have dispensed with my services as knight-errant."

"What makes you say that?"

"You're going to London on some ticklish errand, and you don't mean to tell me what it is, much less let me help."

"I'd like to tell you, but I can't. Only I can do what needs to be done. And I don't want anyone else to have to share the blame if anything goes wrong." She rallied him, smiling, "You haven't told me *your* business in London."

"That's entirely different. Your enquiring into my business would be merely inquisitive, while my enquiring into yours is an absolute necessity. I'm under an oath of chivalry, and bound to do any dragon-slaying that's required to be done on your behalf."

"You mustn't worry. This isn't such a very big dragon. And if I really need your help, I'll ask for it. I always have."

Travelling by easy stages, they reached London in the late afternoon. The carriages pulled up in front of Julian's flat in Clarges Street. Maud told him she was returning to Bellegarde the day after tomorrow, and would be happy to take him with her if his business in London was finished by then.

He thanked her and went indoors. He would have liked to take a stroll in Green Park to stretch his legs, but thought it best to avoid being seen in public. "I'm not at home to anyone," he told Dipper. "If I once begin receiving visitors, I'll spend all my time in London fending off questions about the murder."

He went to the window, closing the curtain to screen himself from view. "It's good to be back. I've missed the clatter and clamour of these streets. That country peace and quiet gets infernally on my nerves. No sound but the birds, and they wake up too damned early.

Another one of their daybreak symphonies, and I should have chucked the fire irons at them."

Dipper thought the birds had sounded very sweet that morning —but, then, Molly had put him in a mood to be beguiled. "I was thinking, sir: before I unpack and put the flat to rights, I'd best bring off to one of the rag-markets and get some togs for tomorrow. I can't go rigged out like this."

"No, I suppose not. I rather fancy you in a bandanna and an earring, but I suppose that would be a bit showy for an English thief."

\*

The sign of three gold balls hung outside a shop near the Strand. Inside was a long, narrow room, with pieces of furniture piled up carelessly in the centre, as though someone were planning to make a bonfire of them one of these days. Along the walls, tables displayed small objects—books, lamps, china figurines, dressing cases. Larger items, like walking sticks and fire irons, stuck out inconveniently into the aisles. Valuable objects like watches and jewelry were kept locked up in cabinets. Silas Vorpe was not a trusting man.

The light from the shop's one grimy window petered out long before it reached the counter at the opposite end. An oil lamp burned there, casting a lurid glow on Vorpe's big white face. He yawned. Business was slow this morning. The only customers just now were a young couple who walked about hand-in-hand, occasionally bumping into things. About to be married, and poor, was Vorpe's guess. They would look wistfully at one thing and another, but not spend a farthing. He was right. They moved toward the door, still holding hands. A young man just coming in tipped his cap and stepped aside to let them pass.

Vorpe peered across at the young man, and all at once a broad smile split his face. "As I live and breathe!" he exclaimed in a full, melodious voice. "Dipper!"

"Morning, Mr. Vorpe!" Dipper came forward, making his way dexterously through the clutter. "You're looking very niblike, I must say. Business good?"

"My dear boy, I barely keep my head above water. Things are the same as ever—I struggle along on the brink of ruin. But you—where have you been all these ages?" He leaned across the counter and whispered sympathetically, "Been polishing the King's iron with your eyebrows, have you?"

Dipper put on a sweetly pathetic face. "I'd as soon not chop about it, if it's all the same to you. I'm trying to put it behind me."

"Of course, my boy, of course. These little setbacks happen to the best of us from time to time. Best not to dwell on them, isn't it?" He sank his voice again. "You wouldn't happen to have any little article you care to dispose of? Because this seems an excellent opportunity, there being no other customers in the shop who might—er—distract my attention."

Dipper glanced swiftly around him, then reached into an inside pocket of his coat and produced a silver snuffbox. "Have a gun at that, Mr. Vorpe."

"Very nice, very nice. A pity there's so little demand for this kind of thing."

They haggled for a while, Dipper pleading, and Vorpe regretfully shaking his head. "I wish I could, my boy, I wish I could," he said. "But times are so hard, you understand, and silver just isn't fetching the price it used to."

They settled on an amount at last. Dipper pocketed the money and was bidding Vorpe good-bye, when all at once he appeared to recollect something. "Mr. Vorpe, there's some'ut I want to know, and I was thinking you might be able to put it down to me."

"Of course I should be delighted to oblige you any way I can. What is it?"

"Well," said Dipper softly, "there's a jewel coffer, black and gold japan, and I heard it was lumbered here. You know anything about it?"

"My word, there's a deal of interest in that box. It must be worth far more than I had any idea. I haven't got it, I'm afraid. The Owner took it for himself."

"That's no matter. It ain't the coffer I'm on the lay for. It's the person as lumbered it."

"I can understand that." Vorpe smiled slyly. "Why, if I were a boy your age, I'd be looking for her, too. She was a very dainty morsel, indeed."

Dipper hid his excitement at this, playing up to Vorpe with a conspiratorial smile. "Can you tell me aught about her, then? I been trying to find her ever since I come out of the jug."

"Well I wish you luck, my boy, but I've heard nothing about her since the other girl came asking after her, and that was weeks ago."

"If you was to start at the beginning—" Dipper suggested.

"When I first saw the two girls, you mean? That was more than a year ago now, but you know I pride myself on my memory for faces. You have me to thank, by the way, for the fact that the young lady you're seeking isn't in the hands of the law. The Owner questioned me closely about the jewelry box and how I came by it. I was very much surprised—I thought the girl was legitimate. But, of course, once the Owner started asking questions, I concluded the young lady must have—er—found the box before it was lost. After that, I promise you, my lips were sealed. I pretended to remember nothing about her. I even went so far as to—misplace—the record of the entire transaction. Such is my devotion to you and your professional colleagues."

"You're a bob cull and no mistake, Mr. Vorpe."

"Thank you, my boy. Now, let me see, it must have been in February of last year that I did business with the two young ladies, since it was this past February that the jewelry box was due to be redeemed. One of the girls was called Louisa—a towheaded creature, very sturdily built, not pretty, poor thing. The other, the young lady who brought the jewelry box to be placed in my care—but I needn't describe her to you, since you're obviously well aware of her charms already."

Dipper thought quickly. "How do I know it's the same mort?"

"Don't be silly, my boy, who else should she be? I must say, she was a lovely piece of French porcelain. I quite applaud your taste."

"French, was she?" By now Dipper felt secure enough to gamble. "A small mort, red hair, blue glims?"

"Exactly so. She spoke very little English. The other girl, Louisa, acted as her interpreter. A very disagreeable young person, Louisa —most unbecomingly insistent about the price."

Louisa had done nearly all the talking, he said. The French girl seemed very shy and skittish. He gave her a pawn ticket, and she told him her name and address: Miss Amy Fields, residing in Puddle Street, not far from Vorpe's shop.

"Amy Fields," repeated Dipper. "It don't sound French."

"No. But not many in your profession go by their real names, do they? I suppose I ought to have guessed she was one of your compatriots, but the other girl, Louisa, seemed so moral and upstanding. I couldn't imagine her mixed up in anything irregular. Obviously she was taken in by her pretty friend. Because a month or two ago, she came in and asked me if I'd seen Miss Fields. It seems her friend Amy had up and run away without a trace."

Louisa thought Amy might have come to his shop to redeem the jewelry box, he explained. He told her that he had not seen Miss Fields since February of last year, and that the jewelry box had been sold a few weeks earlier. "I thought it best not to mention the Owner had it," he explained. "Louisa seemed rather a strong-willed girl. She might have made trouble of one kind or another."

"You always was one to drop down to a person, Mr. Vorpe. You know life, that's what you do."

"My dear boy, these tributes quite overwhelm me."

"This mort Louisa—where does she doss?"

"I had the impression the two young ladies lodged together, in Puddle Street."

"Thanks, Mr. Vorpe. I knew you'd do the trick for me."

"Impatient to be off now, are you, and keep on with the search. I can't say I blame you. What a delightful thing it is to be young and in love. You must let me know if you find her. And if any more little trinkets should happen to come your way, I do hope you'll let me take them off your hands."

\*

"I knew it!" Julian paced his front parlour, like an animal on the prowl. "I knew there had to be a connexion between the murder and Colonel Fontclair's letters. How did this girl Amy Fields come by the jewelry box, I wonder? She could have been a servant or acquaintance of Gabrielle Deschamps—then again, she might have found the box, or stolen it. She doesn't seem to have known about the secret compartment containing the letters. But if she knew nothing about Colonel Fontclair or his secret, then how in the name of all that's wonderful did she end up murdered at Bellegarde?"

"It's a rum start, sir," said Dipper, shaking his head.

"The other girl, Louisa, might know something to the purpose. She lives in Puddle Street, you said?"

"Yes, sir. I went there, after I left Mr. Vorpe's, and asked after a bleached mort named Louisa. Seems she lives and works at her mother's nob-thatching crib—E. P. Howland, Milliner, it's called. I went by and had a peery at it, but it was shut up."

"I'll go there all the same, and see if I can find her, or anyone who knows where she is."

Dipper brought him his tall silk hat, gloves, and walking stick. "I almost forgot, sir. Here's the blunt I knapped for your sneezing-coffer. Mr. Vorpe didn't fork out much for it, he never does, but it put him in a cheery mood."

"Then it was well worth the sacrifice. I had no use for it, anyway. It was given to me by a marchesa I once knew, who had me confused with another Englishman who took snuff. She gave him the music stand that was meant for me. He didn't play, but it made rather a good hat tree." He drew on his gloves. "Amy Fields," he mused, as though tasting the name on his tongue. "I wonder if that was her real name. It certainly isn't French—Good Lord. Dipper, I am an idiot."

"Sir?"

"It isn't an alias—it's a translation. *Fields*, in French, is 'Deschamps.' "

✳

Puddle Street was one of London's little self-contained worlds. It had its own greengrocer and barber-surgeon, stationer and public house. Each shop thrust out a minute bow window, displaying a single item to identify the shopkeeper's trade: a workman's boot, a secondhand book, an apothecary's mortar and pestle. In the window of E. P. Howland, Milliner, was a papier-mâché head with faded black eyes and pink cheeks, wearing a calico bonnet.

Julian tried the door but found it locked. He peered in through the window. The shop was dimly lit, but he could make out two small worktables and a few plain wooden chairs. A large deal table was strewn with bolts of cloth, ribbons, and artificial flowers. Several heads like the one in the window displayed finished bonnets, while skeletal straw frames lay about waiting to be trimmed.

There was nobody inside. He knocked at the door, but no one answered. Several passersby looked at him curiously. A gentleman like him—a regular swell—was a rare sight in this neighbourhood.

He knocked again, more loudly. This time there was a sound of movement overhead. The shop might be empty, but there was someone on the floor above. He heard footsteps coming to the door. It opened, and a young woman looked out.

She was stocky and healthy-looking, though weary just now, her eyes bloodshot and smudged with shadows. Locks of hair, so pale it was almost white, strayed out from under her cap. She had a snub nose and round, clear, light blue eyes.

"We're closed—" she began. Then, seeing Julian, she broke off in surprise. "Is there anything I can do for you, sir?" Her tone suggested she could not imagine what that might be.

"I'm looking for a young lady named Louisa."

"I'm Louisa. Louisa Howland."

"How do you do, Miss Howland. My name is Julian Kestrel. I have something very important to speak to you about. May I come in?"

"Well—I suppose it's all right. My mother's sick, but she's sleeping just now. If she wakes, I'll have to go up to her."

She led him into the shop. "What is it?"

"I believe you once knew a young lady called Amy Fields."

Her eyes lit up. "Do you know something about Amy? Where is she?"

He hesitated, wanting to break the news gently.

"Oh, I see how it is!" she burst out. "You should be ashamed of yourself—*ashamed!* I wonder you can face a Christian woman, after what you've done!"

"Miss Howland—"

"Why couldn't you have left her alone? She was a good girl, and trying hard to live respectable, in spite of being taught all wrong and having a mother no better than a cat's, and how you could take advantage of anybody as weak as she was—! And now you come wanting me to put right whatever you've done to her. Well, I'll go to her, and I'll take her away from you and your kind, and she can live with Mother and me again—I don't care how bad she's been. Where is she? What've you done with her?"

"Miss Howland, I never knew Miss Fields. I never even laid eyes on her—until after she was dead."

"Amy's dead?" she said in a small voice.

"Yes. I'm sorry."

"How did she die?"

"She was murdered."

"What? Somebody *killed* her? Who'd do that? And why?"

"That is precisely what I should like to find out."

He explained his connexion with the murder—how he had found the body in his room at Bellegarde, and his valet had been accused of the crime. He said as little as possible about the Fontclairs, and nothing about Geoffrey's letters. He felt an obligation to the Fontclairs not to spread that story any further than he could help.

She fished out a handkerchief and clumsily blew her nose. "I heard there'd been a murder at a country squire's house. People've been talking their heads off about it the past few days. But I've been so taken up with nursing Mother, I haven't had time to go out much, or look at a newspaper. I never thought it could have anything to do with Amy. You hear about terrible crimes, but you never think the person it's done to could be somebody you know. You don't think she was—I mean—the killer, he didn't—"

"No. No. She wasn't molested in any way."

"I'm glad. Amy couldn't have borne that. She was shy with men. They scared her."

"But you thought at first she was having a love affair with me."

"That's because I couldn't think why else a gentleman like you would be asking after her. And when a girl as pretty as Amy runs away all of a sudden, you can't help but wonder if there's a man in it somewhere. But it didn't sound like Amy—that's what's puzzled me all along. She was never one to run after the men. She was shy with everybody, but men most of all. You know, she had a mother who was nothing but a doxy—taking up with men for what they could give her. Amy didn't want to be like that."

"Was her mother's name Gabrielle?"

"Yes, that's right. I never knew her. She died before Amy came to England—and just as well for Amy, though I know that's not a Christian thing to say. Amy never said in so many words how bad her mother had treated her, but I could tell. That's why she couldn't take care of herself. She was so used to being kept down by her mother that she couldn't stand up to people. She was like an animal that ought to have a shell but doesn't, so she was all soft and shrinking and easy to hurt."

He got up and walked a little away. He knew he needed to hear all this—but, good God, it was painful. Much easier to think of the murdered girl as a cipher, the central piece in a puzzle—something less than human.

"How did you and Miss Fields come to know each other?"

"Her name wasn't really Fields. We called her that because her French name was hard to say. She said it meant 'fields' in English. But her Christian name really was Amy, though she said it more like 'Aymay.' "

"Aimée. It means 'loved.' "

"Well, she wasn't that, except by Mother and me. Hardly anybody cared a rap about her till she came to us. She never knew her father, and her mother—well, I told you what *she* was. I think that's why Amy was so stuck on her colonel. He was the only one of her mother's fancy men who treated her decent."

He started. "What colonel?"

"She never told me his name. She was afraid of getting him into trouble. Her mother'd lured him into some wicked business in the war in Spain—spying or smuggling, or something like that. Amy was only a child, so she didn't really understand it. She talked to me about him all the time—how he used to bring her sweets, call her by pet names, tell her stories about England. Little things like that meant the world to Amy. She was starved for love. After she and her mother left Spain, she didn't see him for years, but she never forgot him. She came to England after her mother died, just to be near him. She had daydreams he'd adopt her, make her really his daughter. She was always wanting to find out where he lived and try to see him, but she didn't dare. She was afraid he might hold it against her how her mother'd used him."

She broke off. Mr. Kestrel's greenish eyes had a dangerous glint, and his face was set and hard. "I wonder," he said softly, "would the colonel recognize her after all these years?"

"She had it all worked out how she'd make herself known to him. She had a keepsake he'd given her—a silver trinket shaped like a scallop shell. She wore it around her neck all the time. If he didn't recognize her right off, she'd show that to him, and he'd know who she was."

# * 27 *
# CLUE IN
# A NEWSPAPER

So Geoffrey had known all along who the murdered girl was. Even if Aimée had changed too much in a dozen years for him to recognize her, he must have realized who she was when he saw the silver scallop shell he himself had given her. For surely he must be Aimée's colonel. There were not likely to be two English colonels, both lovers of Gabrielle, both enticed into giving information to Bonaparte's army in Spain. If any more proof were needed, Geoffrey had deliberately lied, saying Gabrielle had no relations. Why would he have concealed that she had a daughter, except to hide the fact that her daughter was the murdered girl?

The most obvious solution to the murder now was that Aimée, overcome by her longing to see Geoffrey again, had come seeking him at Bellegarde, and Geoffrey, already overwrought by Craddock's threats, had killed her in a fit of panic or rage. But why in my room? Julian asked himself for the thousandth time. And how did she meet him in the house without any of his family seeing her? Or are they all lying—closing ranks to protect one of their own?

He reined in his speculations. There was no point in trying to put the puzzle together till he had all the pieces. He said to Louisa, "Tell me how you came to know Miss Fields."

"It was in February of last year—round about St. Valentine's Day. Mother and I were working late in the shop one night, when Amy came asking for work. We felt for her—she had no warm clothes, and not enough flesh on her bones to keep a mouse warm. We asked her in and gave her something to eat. She didn't speak much English, but we got out of her that she'd just come to London from Italy, where her mother had died. We wanted to help her. It was clear that if she walked the streets much longer, she'd go to the bad. She'd have to, to keep from starving. That happens to lots of girls."

"I understand."

"We gave her some sewing to do, and it turned out she was handy with her needle, so we took her on to help in the shop. We were doing much better in those days, before Mother got so sick." She looked wistfully at the closed worktables, and the bonnets lying about untrimmed. "She wasn't much good with customers—her English was bad, she was shy with people, and she never could count change. She mostly sewed in the back room. She was good at trimming hats—very quick and deft."

Julian nodded, remembering how Mrs. Warren had praised the girl's skill at needlework. "What do you know about the black and gold jewelry box she pawned?"

"It was her mother's. It was one of the few things Amy had left of hers. Most were sold to pay her mother's debts after she died. Amy needed warm clothes, and we hadn't the money to give her an advance on her wages. The jewelry box looked like it might be worth something, and Amy didn't set any store by it, so I said why not pawn it. I went to the pawnshop with her so she wouldn't get put upon by some gripefist pawnbroker."

"Did she ever regret pawning it or want it back?"

"I don't think she cared if she never saw it again. Though after she ran away, I went back to the pawnshop, just on the chance she'd come in and tried to get it back. She hadn't. And the pawnbroker said he didn't have it anymore."

"When did she run away?"

"It was about six weeks ago, around the end of April. But I think whatever made her run away started earlier, in March. Because that was when she started acting strange."

"In what way?"

"She got skittish, absentminded. She'd fall into fits of brooding and then jump, guiltylike, when she was roused. She wouldn't let on there was anything wrong, but I'd known her for more than a year, and I knew better.

"Then one day at the end of April, she went out to deliver a bonnet—at least that's where she said she was going. She'd been making deliveries for us lately, now she knew more English and wasn't quite so shy. She tripped off with a bandbox in her hand, and that was the last we saw of her. When she didn't come back for hours, I went up to our room—she slept upstairs with me— and found a note she'd left. The hat she was supposed to deliver was lying on the bed, and some of her things were missing. She must have taken them away in the bandbox instead of the hat."

"What did the note say?"

"I'll bring it to show you."

Left alone, Julian glanced into the small back room where Aimée had worked. It was dark, and smelled musty and unused. He wondered what Louisa and her mother lived on while their shop was closed. To judge by Louisa's worn frock and tattered apron, they were in a bad way.

She came back with Aimée's note in one hand and an old, yellowing newspaper in the other. She gave the note to Julian. It was written in a careful, childish hand:

*Dere Louisa and Mrs. Howland,*

*You have ben so kind to me I am sory to leve you like this without won word of goodbie. Please do not think too badly of me. I do not want to go but I must. It is of the most importance to me that I do this. Please foregive your Amy and do not wory there is no nede. I pray to the good God to see you againe soon. I embrace you both.*

*Aimée*

*I leve behind some clothes I can not carry. Please kepe them I give them to you.*

"What did she leave behind?" he asked.

"Her best dress and hat, and an apron and shawl. She didn't take anything but the clothes on her back and a couple of handkerchiefs and caps, and a few toilet things. Oh, and her rosary. She was a Papist, though Mother and I were always trying to break her of that."

"When she was found dead, she was wearing an expensive shawl, silk slippers, and gold earrings."

Tears welled up in Louisa's eyes. "God forgive her. And curse the man, whoever he was! I never thought she'd go wrong that way. She wasn't one of your light-skirts. She was *modest*, Mr. Kestrel. She cared about being good."

"It may not have been a lover who gave her those things," he pointed out gently. "Whoever killed her may have tried to buy her off first, or given her presents to win her trust."

"Why would anybody have to buy her off? She couldn't do anybody any harm."

Oh, but she could, thought Julian. She could harm one man—one family—very much. Of course, if she was as devoted to Colonel Fontclair as Louisa said, she would not be likely to betray his secret, but he might not believe that. He might fear she would be as unscrupulous as her mother.

"I wanted you to see this, too." She held out the newspaper. It was the *Morning Post*. "I found it under Amy's pillow after she ran away. I was searching all over for anything that might give me an idea where she went. I don't know why she saved it. I read it all the way through, but I couldn't find anything in it that had aught to do with her."

Julian took off his gloves and unfolded the newspaper, glancing at the date: April 23, 1824.

"That's five days before she ran away. I don't know where she got the paper. We don't buy them, but a customer might have left it behind in the shop. Amy liked to look at newspapers, though she wasn't much of a reader. She only liked books with pictures—fashion plates and such."

"If you don't mind, I'd like to read this through."

She nodded. "That'll give me a chance to look in on Mother. Oh—can I get you anything, some tea?"

"No, thank you." He thought the Howlands must have little enough to spare.

She went upstairs, and he sat down with the newspaper. It was only four pages long, but its narrow columns were packed with print. Parliamentary debates. Foreign news. Sporting and social gossip. Advertisements for concerts, mantua-makers, medical treatments. What was there here to attract Aimée's notice—to impress or excite her so much that she slept with the newspaper under her pillow?

The answer leaped out at him when he reached the third page. Here, among the tidbits of Society news, was Mark Craddock's announcement of his daughter Maud's engagement to Hugh Fontclair.

What the devil did this mean? Had Aimée been leafing idly through the paper and caught sight of the announcement? She would surely have guessed the bridegroom was related to her beloved colonel. Did seeing the name Fontclair awaken in her such a longing to see Geoffrey again that she ran away to find him?

It seemed the most likely explanation—though in some ways it made no sense. The newspaper was dated only five days before Aimée ran away, yet, according to Louisa, she had been in a nervous state for weeks. And why did she run away at all? Geoffrey lived in London. Once she found out his address, she could simply write to him or pay him a visit—she did not have to uproot herself from her only home. But perhaps she had not meant to do anything so drastic. Perhaps, during the five days that elapsed between the newspaper announcement and her flight, she had been to see Geoffrey, and he had induced her to run away.

Yes: Geoffrey could have taken her under his wing, thinking to buy her silence about his past with gifts and affection. She was so devoted to him, she would have gone anywhere, done anything he wanted. Which raised a nasty possibility. It was common knowledge up and down St. James Street that Colonel Fontclair had a taste for very young girls. Perhaps his experience with Gabrielle had made him wary of clever, worldly women. Aimée was beautiful, and all but alone in the world. It might have been all too easy to take advantage of her love for him.

But if Aimée were Geoffrey's mistress, why had she spoken as she had to Mrs. Warren? She had declared there was nothing to be ashamed of about her love for the person who gave her the silver scallop shell. The pure, dutiful love of a daughter—that was how she described it. And—damnation!—she had said something more. She had told Mrs. Warren the scallop shell was her only remembrance of the person who gave it to her. That would make no sense, if Geoffrey had been keeping her for the past six weeks, and showering her with clothes and jewelry.

Julian looked again at the wedding announcement. Geoffrey was not mentioned, of course. The bridegroom was identified as Hugh Fontclair, son of Sir Robert Fontclair, Bart., of Bellegarde. What might have occurred to Aimée when she read those names? Could she have taken it into her head to approach Geoffrey through one of his relations? Louisa said she longed to see her colonel again, but feared he would hate her for what her mother had done. Maybe she hoped to win the sympathy of someone in his family, who might intercede for her with him.

Which of the Fontclairs might she have approached? That depended, first, on which of them were in London at the time Hugh's engagement was announced. Hugh himself, of course; it was during that period that Julian met him at the gaming hell. His parents most likely came with him—perhaps Isabelle as well. Geoffrey, Guy, and Lady Tarleton were all in London for the season. Aimée could have found out easily enough where any of them lived. And all of them would have had a motive to kill her, once they knew she had it in her power to ruin Geoffrey and disgrace the Fontclair name.

There was one other possibility: Mark Craddock's name was in the announcement, too. It was hard to see why Aimée would have sought him out. He would be of no interest to her—unless of course she knew he had the letters Geoffrey had written to her mother. But how could she have found that out? She did not know the letters were in the jewelry box, or she would not have pawned it with othem inside. And how could she have made the connexion between the pawnbroker and Craddock? Even Dipper, who knew Vorpe pretty well, had not known it was Craddock who owned the pawnshop.

But just suppose Aimée had made herself known to Craddock He would have had his own reasons for wanting her out of the way. He was obsessed with marrying his daughter to Hugh, and he could only do that by threatening to publish Geoffrey's letters. But if someone else came along and sprang the secret of Geoffrey's treason, the letters would be worth nothing to him. The ruin of the Fontclairs was not what he wanted. He wanted to bend them to his will.

Louisa returned, and Julian showed her the announcement. "Do you remember Miss Fields ever mentioning the Fontclairs or the Craddocks?"

"No. But she was killed at the Fontclairs' house, and now here's an announcement saying someone named Fontclair is going to be married. That can't be a coincidence, can it?"

"I should be astonished if it were."

"I'm beginning to wonder if those Fontclairs can be trusted."

"I've been wondering that for some time."

"I wish I could go to that place Bellegarde myself, and see that Amy's done right by. But I can't leave Mother."

"How is she?"

"She was feeling a bit more herself when I went up. So I told her about you and asked if she could think of anything else to tell you about Amy. But she couldn't."

"Please give her my regards and tell her I'm sorry I hadn't the pleasure of meeting her." He put on his hat, and casually took a bill from his pocketbook. "Here."

She looked hungrily at the money, but shook her head and put her hands behind her. "Mother and I don't take charity."

"I should think not. But you're a material witness. Naturally you have to be paid."

"I thought witnesses only got a reward if they helped catch the criminal, and he got convicted."

"My dear Miss Howland," he lied, "a witness has to be paid for the time and trouble of coming forward with evidence."

"Oh. I didn't know that." She reached out gingerly and took the money. A little breathless sound of relief escaped her. For the first time, she smiled.

"Will you do one thing for me?" he asked. "Will you keep it a secret for the present who the victim of the Bellegarde murder is? I should like a free hand to deal with the Fontclairs in my own way."

"You'll see justice done?"

"I will, upon my honour."

"You won't let those Fontclairs bully you, or buy you off, or hush up Amy's death?"

"I swear to you, I won't give up till her killer is brought to justice."

"Then I'll do as you ask, if you'll let me know how you get on, and tell me when the killer's found."

"I will."

"Because if he's not found, I'll hunt him down myself, if I have to seek him all over the country."

Julian believed her.

✳

Maud, Miss Pritchard, and Julian had agreed to return to Bellegarde early next morning. The barouche-landau called at Julian's flat, with its attendant travelling chaise in tow. The weather was fair and warm, so Maud had let down the folding roof of the carriage. As Julian got in, his eyes fell on a large, ungainly book in her lap.

She blushed and clasped her arms more tightly around it. "This is my mother's Bible. It's been in her family for generations. All their history is in it—marriages, births, and deaths. It used to be passed from one eldest son to another, but since Mama hadn't any brothers, and neither have I, it came to me."

"It doesn't look as if it would travel very well." He glanced at the worn leather covers and broken spine

"I told her that, too, sir," said Miss Pritchard. "At the very least, Miss Craddock, you ought to have packed it away in one of the trunks. I'm afraid you won't get it all the way to Bellegarde without losing some of the pages."

"I'll take very good care of it. I was afraid to pack it—I've heard so much about trunks being stolen on the road. It's very precious to me."

Then why bring it to Bellegarde at all? Julian thought. He cocked an eyebrow at her, and she blushed again. It's no good asking, said her eyes. I'd like to confide in you, but I can't.

# *28*
# THE DANGER
# OF PRAYER

Julian arrived at Bellegarde late that afternoon and asked to see Sir Robert. But he had gone to meet with some local authorities about road repairs, and was not expected back till after dinner. Julian did not choose to confront Geoffrey in his absence. That would only forewarn Geoffrey of his danger, giving him a chance to think of new lies or excuses.

He decided to call on Dr. MacGregor instead. They had not talked since he found out about Geoffrey's letters and Craddock's blackmail. He had missed MacGregor's shrewd mind and unabashed frankness, and was curious to know what he would make of all his discoveries. There could be no objection to his confiding in MacGregor now about Geoffrey's secret. Sir Robert had agreed it would have to come out, if it proved to be linked to the murder.

He called for his horse to be saddled and brought round to the front of the house. When he came downstairs, he found Isabelle standing at one of the tall, mullioned windows in the great hall. She was wearing a gown of the same light grey as her eyes, with a high waist and long sleeves gathered into puffs. In that dress, with her pure, clear profile framed by the window, she looked like a painting by Ghirlandaio or Botticelli. He stood lost in admiration.

"Good afternoon, Mr. Kestrel. I hope you enjoyed yourself in London."

He came forward. "It was the same as always," he shrugged. "Too many people, and not enough fresh air to go around. I can never quite make out why I wouldn't dream of living anywhere else. Do you go very often?"

"No, hardly ever. Uncle Robert and Aunt Cecily don't like town."

"I suppose they had no choice but to go this past April, when Hugh got engaged to Miss Craddock."

"Yes." She looked at him with lifted brows.

"Did you go with them?" he asked, as casually as he could.

"Yes."

So Isabelle had been in London when Aimée ran away from the Howlands. Suppose Aimée, after seeing the announcement of Hugh's marriage, had gone to the Fontclairs' London house and seen Isabelle there? If she had it in mind to approach Geoffrey through someone in his family, she might well have chosen a girl of about her own age to be her confidante. What would Isabelle have done, if she discovered that this French girl knew a humiliating secret about Geoffrey—one that could destroy him and dishonour all the Fontclairs? She might well go to drastic lengths to protect her family. And she was intelligent enough to plot a complex murder, and cool-headed enough to carry it out.

She looked around at him, sunlight slanting across her face. His thoughts veered wildly off course. He imagined drawing her toward him—feeling her slender body in his arms, her breasts soft against his chest. He looked at her lips, so serenely closed, and thought of them opening under his—

"Why are you staring at me?" she asked.

"Was I staring? I didn't mean to."

"I thought perhaps you were searching my face for signs of guilt."

"You're mistaken, Miss Fontclair. I was looking at you, as I often do, for entirely personal reasons."

"I wonder if you flirt with me merely to amuse yourself, or because you think you might get information out of me that way."

"All I've ever accomplished by flirting with you is to prove I have the Englishman's penchant for doing battle against impossible odds."

"I've told you, I don't think of myself as a citadel for men to storm. I only wish them to leave me alone."

"Is there no man you've ever wanted to marry?"

"No." Her head moved back a little, warily.

"Not even your cousin?"

She stared. Her breath seemed to stick in her throat. "You presume, Mr. Kestrel! If you must ask offensive personal questions, I beg you will confine them to the subject of the murder!"

She went quickly away. He stood looking after her for a long time. I hope to God that doesn't mean what I think it does, he thought.

❋

"It's nothing to me if you want to go gallivanting in London," MacGregor snorted, "with the murder unsolved and everything here at sixes and sevens. What happened—Lady Somebody-or-Other gave a ball you just couldn't miss?"

"I went to London to make enquiries about the murder. I thought you knew that."

"How would I know it? It's not as though you breathed a word to me about what you were up to. Never occurred to you I'd be the least bit curious."

"My dear fellow, I was pining to tell you everything I'd found out. But I'd learned it in confidence, which I couldn't breach at that time. If you'll let me explain, you'll see why I had to play a lone hand."

He told MacGregor all about Geoffrey's secret, Vorpe's revelation of the murdered girl's identity, and his own visit to Louisa Howland. When he finished, MacGregor shook his head, stunned. "This is a terrible thing. I didn't want to believe any of the Fontclairs could have committed the murder. I knew the evidence pointed that way, but I couldn't accept it. I couldn't see any motive. But now—God help them, one of them's a killer. There's no getting away from it."

"I'm sorry."

"It's not your fault. You're just a bearer of bad tidings. And you've done the right thing, getting all this out in the open." He frowned. "There's one thing I don't understand. How did you get that fellow Vorpe to tell you the girl's name and address, when he wouldn't tell Craddock?"

"Will you let me claim the magician's privilege of not telling how that trick was done?"

"Have it your own way."

"Now, don't fly up in the boughs again. The fact is, it was my valet who got the information from Vorpe, but I should rather not have to explain to Sir Robert how he did it."

"I always knew there was something rum about that servant of yours. He was worse than a beggar before he came to work for you, wasn't he?"

"He was a thief. Not a ruffian, you understand, but an artist—a person of talent and ingenuity—in short, a pickpocket."

"What in the Lord's name possessed you to hire a pickpocket as your servant?"

Julian saw he would have to tell the whole story. "One night about two years ago, soon after I came back from Italy, I was out walking with a friend near Covent Garden, and this unkempt young fellow reeled against me and staggered off again. He reeked of spirits, and of course I assumed he was foxed, but all the same I ran my hands over my pockets, and I found my watch was gone. My friend wanted to call a watchman, but you know on any given night in London half the watchmen are asleep in their boxes, and the rest are at least eighty, and lame into the bargain. My blood was up, and I tore off after the thief myself.

"He caught sight of me. He'd only been pretending to be drunk—thieves call it 'gammoning lushy'—and he ran like a hare. He dodged around corners and zigzagged up and down narrow streets. I almost lost him a score of times, but I clung on, and finally brought him to a stop by flinging my walking stick at his head. I pulled him down, and we started grappling in a heap of filth and rotting vegetables. I'd just managed to pin him down when my friend came panting up to us with a watchman. We got back my watch, which was all I really wanted—well, that and the chance to throttle the thief, but I'd had that as well. I would have been glad to part company with him at that point, but the watchman said we had to take him before a magistrate, so we dragged him off to Bow Street. He was very gracious about it, didn't curse or ask for mercy—being caught was just one of the hazards of practising his trade. I liked him for that. There's nothing I admire more than grace under fire.

"Even then, I wasn't planning to let him off. But the magistrate heaped praise on me for catching him, and it made me wince. I don't mind people going about unobtrusively being good, but I can't stomach moral indignation. By the time he finished declaring what a sterling example I was to the British public, I felt thoroughly depressed, and was hard put not to go off and drown myself directly. The end of it was, I refused to press charges. The magistrate was disgusted, but there was nothing he could do.

"I was about to go home and contemplate the ruin of a very good set of evening clothes, when the thief came up to me and thanked me very civilly for letting him off. He didn't apologize for stealing my watch, which I thought showed a certain integrity. Stealing was his profession—it would have been absurd to say it was all a mistake and he was sorry. But he couldn't resist asking why I'd suddenly come over to his side, and we talked for a bit, and, just as in love affairs, one thing led to another. He's been in my employ ever since."

"How did you know he wouldn't steal from you?"

"I didn't." Julian shrugged. "Who can say why one trusts a person, in spite of all manner of reasons not to?"

MacGregor nodded, thinking how he himself had come to trust Kestrel, whom he thought of at first as a coxcomb, if not worse. "So now you think it was Colonel Fontclair who killed the girl?"

"He's certainly become the favourite in this race. But any of the Fontclairs would have had a motive to kill her, to stop her revealing his treason."

"Do you think she tried to blackmail them?"

"I doubt it. Miss Howland says she was devoted to Colonel Fontclair, and not at all the venal, unscrupulous woman her mother was. But the Fontclairs didn't know her and might not have understood that. They were already in thrall to Craddock, and whoever killed Aimée may have decided that one outsider knowing their secret was enough."

"It's a wonder the murderer hasn't tried to kill Craddock, too. Why stop with the girl?"

"It isn't necessary to kill Craddock to ensure his silence. He can be bought. And once his daughter marries Hugh, he'll protect the Fontclair name for her sake. Besides, he has the letters, and killing him won't get them back. In fact, an investigation into his death would all too probably bring them to light. Aimée, on the other hand, had no proof of Colonel Fontclair's treason—only her own knowledge, which could be wiped away by taking her life."

He discussed with MacGregor the possibility that Aimée contacted one of the Fontclairs in London after seeing the wedding announcement in the *Morning Post*. "Consider the temptation toward murder she presented! She knew a deadly secret about Colonel Fontclair. She was longing to see him again, and would probably have trusted blindly anyone who promised to reunite her with him. And she was all but alone in the world. She could have been made to disappear with impunity."

"But she wasn't made to disappear. She was killed brutally, and her body was left where somebody was bound to find it directly."

"In some ways, it certainly looks as though the murder were on the spur of the moment. It's possible the murderer planned to kill her, but not at that time, in that way. She may have said or done something to force his hand."

"But his tucking her into bed afterward looks like a piece of deliberate mockery," MacGregor pointed out. "That argues a person in full possession of his wits."

"Or a person who'd completely lost them. Anyone acting rationally would have washed off the blood from his hands and run away at once. The time he spent tucking his victim into bed was time in which he could have been discovered. But this crime is full of contradictions. It makes me wonder if more than one person was involved."

"What do you mean?"

"Let me give you an example. Suppose Aimée found out somehow that Craddock was blackmailing Colonel Fontclair with the letters. She goes to see Craddock in London, to plead or remonstrate with him on the Fontclairs' behalf. He tries to buy her off—that accounts for the rise in her fortunes during the six weeks between her disappearance from Puddle Street and her arrival here. He succeeds for a time, or thinks he's succeeded. But she goes to Bellegarde secretly, hoping to foil his plans. The colonel comes face to face with her unexpectedly, panics, and kills her."

"If it was Craddock who was buying her off, it could have been Craddock who killed her."

"If he did, he could only have done it within a very limited time. He was outdoors until about twenty minutes past five, and when he came in he went up to his room, where we now know he quarrelled for a long time with Lady Tarleton. Still, he might have run into Aimée outside his room, bundled her away to my room, and killed her. But, either way, there's still the question of how she got into the house."

"Now, don't start all that business about entrances and exits again! We've been through it a score of times, and there's no making head or tail of it." MacGregor paced up and down in front of his desk— a well-worn track, to judge by the condition of the carpet. "You know, until now I thought that if any of the Fontclairs committed the murder, it was most likely to be Guy. But in light of what you've told me, that won't wash. You said the colonel's made a point of keeping this business of his letters a secret from his son. If Guy didn't know about it, he'd have no motive to kill the girl."

"It's true that Colonel Fontclair begged Sir Robert not to tell Guy, and Guy's been kicking up a dust about being kept in the dark. But how do we know that isn't all a hum? The colonel may have told Guy the whole story, and Guy may be elaborately pretending not to know it."

"You're the most suspicious fellow I've ever met."

"I've been lied to at every turn. How can I help but be suspicious? Guy has the strongest motive, after Colonel Fontclair, to keep the Gabrielle affair a secret. In the first place, I think he has a real affection for his father, but even if he didn't—remember, a convicted traitor's property is forfeit to the king. You've said yourself, Guy is always in want of money. He wouldn't fancy having his inheritance swept away at one blow."

"I don't see any way out of this thicket, Kestrel. Any of them could have done the murder. There's no knowing which."

"I may get something out of Colonel Fontclair by springing it on him that I know who the murdered girl is." He looked at his watch. "I'd better go. I'll let you know what happens."

✳

Julian returned to Bellegarde and went upstairs to dress for dinner. As he turned down the corridor that led to his room, he heard a strange noise: the muffled, choking sound of someone weeping, but trying not to be heard. It was coming from the great chamber, at the other end of the hallway, opposite his old room. He went in to see what was the matter.

Philippa was sitting huddled on the floor in a corner, hands pressed to her mouth to stifle her sobs. She looked small and forlorn in that vast, ornate room. When she saw Julian, she hiccupped, swallowed, and stared at him with big, dark eyes.

He was dismayed. What the devil did one do with a weeping eleven-year-old girl? "Shall I send for your mother?"

"Oh, do you have to? I'm not supposed to be in this part of the house. Josie and I are supposed to stay in our own wing and not bother the guests."

"Then why are you here?"

She began to cry again.

Good Lord! he thought. He glanced down the hallway, but there was no help in sight. He would just have to do the best he could.

He went over to Philippa and dropped down beside her, holding out his handkerchief. "Blow your nose," he advised.

She did.

"Now then, what's stirred up this tempest?"

"I know who's responsible for the murder."

"Who?" he said, startled.

"*I* am!"

"Forgive me, but that's a bit hard to credit."

"I don't mean I'm the one who killed her."

"No, I eliminated you as a suspect fairly early."

"You're laughing at me, but you don't understand. I heard the servants talking. They said the murdered girl's ghost is haunting the house. I think it must be all my fault! I told you I wished

Bellegarde had a ghost. Remember, the first night you were here, I showed you this room and said it ought to be haunted. Now perhaps it is! People say the danger of prayer is that you might get what you pray for."

"You must think the angels are extraordinarily muddle-headed, misinterpreting your wishes like that."

"I didn't think of it that way." She cocked her head, considering. "All the same, they must have thought I was wicked to wish for someone not to go to Heaven and be at peace."

"I don't doubt they understood you weren't wishing that fate on anybody. You only meant that if there were anyone already a ghost who hadn't anything better to do, you hoped he would pay a visit to Bellegarde."

"Yes, that's just what I meant! You don't think there was anything wicked about that, do you?"

He pretended to think it over carefully. "No," he said at last, "I don't think there was."

"I feel much better. I shan't ever wish for a ghost again—not Olivier Fontclair or anyone else. You remember, I told you about him—he was our ancestor who was supposed to have taken part in the Babington Plot. I hope he went to Heaven, even if he did plot against his Queen. After all, the Babington Plot never came to anything, really. It was nipped in the bud before it could do any harm."

"I don't remember much about it. Wasn't it some sort of conspiracy to put Mary Queen of Scots on the throne—"

He stopped. Then he said slowly, "Why would Olivier Fontclair have supported Mary Queen of Scots?"

"Because she was a Catholic. Our family was, too, in those days. Didn't you know?"

"No," he said softly, a gleam coming into his eyes. "I didn't."

"Of course we kept it a secret. You had to, or Queen Elizabeth would have thought you were a traitor. We converted in the reign of Charles I, but no one quite knows how that happened, because so many of the family papers got burned up in the civil war. I'm glad we're not Papists anymore. I wouldn't like to go to school in a convent, the way young ladies do in France."

He did not answer. A theory was taking shape in his mind. It was certainly a leap in the dark; if it were a horse, he was not sure he would bet on it. All the same, he resolved to put it to the proof. He wished he had the cooperation of one of the Fontclairs, but there was no one among them he could trust.

Philippa got up, shaking the creases out of her skirt. "I have to go back to the schoolroom before Pritchie comes looking for me. Thank you for being so sensible. You're practically the only grownup I know who doesn't talk to me like a child."

"That's because I don't know how to talk to children."

"Yes, you do. It's the same as talking to grown-ups, only there are more things you have to explain."

He waited till she was out of sight, then went across to his old room and tried the door. No use. Sir Robert was keeping it locked, to ensure that no one disturbed the scene of the murder.

✳

"I shall be late to dinner again," Julian remarked, as he put the finishing touches to his cravat. "That should please Lady Tarleton —she's always glad of an excuse to look daggers at me."

"She's a tartar, and no mistake, sir. I've been hearing tales of her in the servants' hall. She can't keep a lady's maid more nor a month, on account of the way she knocks 'em about. She fetched one of 'em such a conker she tapped her claret, and one of her ivories come loose."

"A very violent woman."

"Violent enough to croak that mort, do you think, sir?"

"Possibly," Julian mused.

"Something got you down in the chops, sir?"

"I'd give a monkey to have an hour alone in my old room. But Sir Robert is keeping it locked, and I can't ask him for the key without having to tell him why I want it, which I'd rather not do just yet."

"It ain't Sir Robert as has the key, it's Mr. Rawlinson, Michael says."

"Dipper, I mislike that angelic expression on your face. What are you thinking?"

"Well, sir, Michael says Mr. Rawlinson carries the key around in his fob-pocket. And I was thinking, if you wanted it bad enough—" His voice trailed off suggestively.

"Do you realize the trouble we could both get into if you were caught?"

"I'd have to look sharp and not get caught, then, wouldn't I, sir?"

"I might have known you'd find an excuse to steal something sooner or later. I think you've been itching to ply your old trade ever since I sent you to see Vorpe."

"It ain't that I want to go back on the game, sir—Newgate seize me if I do! But the fact is, I was a bowman prig, sir. I mean, I had a gift." He flexed his fingers wistfully. "And when you got a gift, even if it was the Devil give it to you, you get a hankering to use it now and again."

Julian looked at him, much struck. It's like keeping a wild animal, he thought. I can tame him, teach him to live in my world, but I can't change his nature. He may be the gentlest soul on earth, but he was born and bred a predator. And I suppose, if you're going to keep that sort of animal about you, you have to let it hunt once in a while.

He said, "What if Rawlinson misses the key after you've stolen it?"

"I could pinch it, sir, nip up and unlock the door, and then plant it back in his pocket, and him none the wiser."

"You could put it back without his knowing?"

"Same skill as taking it out, sir, only there ain't so much call for t'one as t'other."

"No, I suppose not. All right, I'll let you do it, but for God's sake, be careful. I didn't go to all that trouble to keep your old line of work a secret, only to have Sir Robert find you out now."

# * 29 *
# DIVIDED
# LOYALTIES

————————

Julian went down to dinner, but instead of going directly to the drawing room, he went through the screens passage to the servants' hall, and so to the back stairs. The servants looked after him curiously, and Molly Dale followed him a little way on tiptoe, to see what he was about. He went up to Mr. Rawlinson's office for a few minutes, then came down again and disappeared into the waiting room. Perhaps he meant to go out the back door for a smoke in the garden before dinner, Molly thought. But when he came in a short while later, there was no smell of tobacco about him. He's a deep one, she told herself, as she watched him go tranquilly off to dinner.

Sir Robert was not home yet. Colonel Fontclair sat at the head of the table in his absence. He did not look well. His usually florid face was grey, and his eyes were bloodshot and heavy. Lady Fontclair, too, seemed under a strain. She was resolutely gracious to everyone, but her charm and gaiety were wearing thin, and her anxiety showed through. Catherine was peevish, and Craddock grim. Isabelle seemed very much her graceful, inscrutable self.

Guy was drinking heavily. He had stayed surprisingly sober since the murder, but tonight his self-control gave way. Wine made him talkative and reckless—was that why he had been keeping away from it?—and he questioned Julian persistently about what he had been doing in London. Julian parried his questions with light remarks about fashions and entertainments, racehorses and bankruptcies.

After dinner, Guy started getting rowdy over his claret, but the colonel took him in hand, and bore him off to join the ladies in the drawing room. The other gentlemen followed. Lady Tarleton dragooned the colonel and Lady Fontclair into a game of whist. She grudgingly accepted Craddock as the fourth player, but declared she would on no account be partnered with him. Lady Fontclair hastened to claim Craddock as her partner, and a very unhappy game began.

The young people drifted into the music room. Julian asked Isabelle to play, but she said she needed to work on Maud's wedding slippers. "I have to devote all my leisure to them, if they're to be finished in time for the wedding."

"Please don't go to so much trouble," Maud begged. "There's plenty of time."

Isabelle looked at her as though she were an unfamiliar sort of animal—odd, not terribly interesting, certainly not dangerous. "I told you I'd have them finished by the end of your stay here, Miss Craddock. I mean to be as good as my word." She sat down, opened her workbox, and looked up at Julian. "I've heard you're a very fine musician, Mr. Kestrel. Perhaps you would be good enough to play for us?"

He complied. From behind the piano he watched the others, while seeming absorbed in his music. Hugh was hanging about Miss Craddock, trying to get up courage to speak to her, when all at once Guy planted a chair beside her and started talking animatedly, his voice low and intimate, his face close to hers. This was certainly a change of heart for Guy, who not long ago described Maud as "dull as ditchwater." But that was before Julian made friends with her, and before Hugh began seeing her with new eyes. Julian never ceased to marvel at how easily led people are—how they form their tastes and aversions by watching what others do and slavishly following suit.

Maud was repelled, though she tried not to show it. Guy's breath smelled of spirits, and he looked at her as she imagined a cat might look at a succulent mouse. Julian thought about rescuing her, then decided that was really Hugh's business. But Hugh only hovered at a distance, darting outraged glances at Guy. Do something, for God's sake, Julian thought. If I'm going to fight all her battles, I might as well marry her myself.

Just then he heard Sir Robert's voice in the drawing room next door. He shut up the piano, unnoticed, and went in to speak to him.

"Mr. Kestrel," said Sir Robert. "I've just been asking after you. I knew you were expected back today, and finished my business as quickly as possible so that I could come home and hear your report. Shall we go into my study?"

"I think it might be best if Colonel Fontclair came with us."

Geoffrey lifted frightened eyes. For a moment Sir Robert's eyes mirrored his dread. Then he banished all expression from his face. "If you would be so good, Geoffrey."

The colonel struggled to his feet. Julian noticed, not for the first time, how his lameness got worse when he was upset.

"What's happening?" Lady Tarleton demanded.

"Mr. Kestrel is going to report to me about his investigations in London."

"I knew it!" she cried. "I knew he went to London to spy out information to use against us!"

"He went to London under my aegis, and with my blessing. Now, if you'll excuse us, Catherine."

He went out, followed by Julian and Geoffrey. Lady Tarleton flung away to a window. Craddock sat hunched forward, his large hands spread out on his knees, frowning.

Lady Fontclair slipped out of the room. Softly, at a discreet distance, she followed Sir Robert, Geoffrey, and Julian to the study.

✳

It was cold in the study. The window was open, and there was no fire in the grate. A breeze blew in, ruffling the curtains and bending back the candleflames. Colonel Fontclair shivered a little and moved restlessly in his chair.

Sir Robert sat opposite his brother. Julian stood between them.

"I wanted you to be here," he said to Geoffrey, "so that I could ask you, in Sir Robert's presence, what you know about Aimée Deschamps."

Geoffrey closed his eyes and dropped his head in his hands.

"Who is Aimée Deschamps?" asked Sir Robert.

"Aimée Deschamps is the young lady I found dead in my room."

"You've found out who she is? But—but Deschamps is the name of the woman who—" He broke off, staring at Geoffrey's hunched, silent figure. "You knew all along who she was!"

"I knew she was Gabrielle's daughter. I don't know how she got here, Robert, or how she died."

Lady Fontclair came in quietly. Sir Robert was too shocked to pay her any heed. "You told us Gabrielle had no relations."

"I know. I was afraid to tell you about Aimée."

"You admit she was Gabrielle's daughter? And you expect us to believe you had nothing to do with her death?"

"It's the truth, Robert, I swear! I never set eyes on Aimée from the time the French were routed from Spain till you had us all come in and look at her lying dead on that sofa. Of course I knew by then it must be Aimée. I recognized that little trinket I gave her—the silver scallop shell. It's a symbol of the patron saint of Spain. I bought it off a gipsy in a marketplace. It was a trumpery thing, but I knew if I gave Aimée anything that was any good, Gabrielle would take it for herself. She seemed to like it—Aimée did. She was very religious."

"Why didn't you tell us at once who she was?" Sir Robert broke in impatiently.

"I couldn't! I'd have been the only one here who knew her! You'd think—just what you're thinking now! That I must be the one who killed her, that I had the most to gain by putting her out of the way! But I didn't kill her, I was fond of her once, I wouldn't have hurt her for anything. I was shocked when I realized it was she who'd been killed! I couldn't imagine how she got here, or what she was doing in Kestrel's room. Cecily will tell you!" He turned eagerly to Lady Fontclair. "I *was* shocked, wasn't I? I could hardly believe it was Aimée."

The colour drained out of Sir Robert's face. He came slowly to his feet, staring across at his wife. "You knew who the murdered girl was? And you didn't tell me?"

"Robert, don't look at me like that!" She went to him and laid her hand on his arm. "Geoffrey told me the day after the murder that the girl was Gabrielle's daughter. He had to talk to someone. He needed advice. I wanted more than anything to go to you and lay it all at your feet, but I didn't want to inflict another burden on you. I knew you'd feel obliged to investigate Geoffrey's guilt, and the whole story of Gabrielle and the letters might have to come out. And what was the point, when I knew—I *knew* Geoffrey wasn't guilty?"

"In five-and-twenty years of marriage, I've hidden nothing from you. I trusted you absolutely—you can't know! How could you conspire with Geoffrey to deceive me?"

"It wasn't like that. Geoffrey confided in me, I couldn't betray him. And I know your sense of justice. I was afraid you'd put him through the utmost rigours of the law, rather than seem to show any partiality toward him. I had to protect him. I couldn't let him be suspected of a murder I was sure he didn't commit."

"I understand. You had to choose between your loyalty to Geoffrey and me, and you chose him. Perhaps you regret in your heart of hearts that you didn't choose him years ago, when we both wanted to marry you."

"No, no! You don't understand. Geoffrey was in danger—he needed me, you didn't. You're so strong and steady and brave. Geoffrey isn't like that." She looked at Colonel Fontclair, with the love of a mother for a dear though wayward child.

"Unlike you," Sir Robert said coldly, "I can't take it on faith that Geoffrey had nothing to do with the murder. He has committed treason, and now perjury. I won't stand between him and justice any longer."

"What are you going to do?" Geoffrey stammered.

"What I ought to have done from the beginning. I shall write to another magistrate and ask him to take over the investigation. And when he does, I shall lay all the truth before him—Gabrielle Deschamps, her daughter, the letters—everything." He looked grimly at his brother. "My last act as magistrate is to order you not to leave this parish. You are now the principal suspect in the murder. Be thankful I don't have you locked up as I did Mr. Kestrel's servant, with far less cause."

He turned to Julian, controlling his voice with an effort. "Mr. Kestrel, thank you for making the girl's identity known. You've enabled me to give her a proper funeral under her own name, which is the very least I owe her." He turned and went to the door.

Lady Fontclair gave a little cry, ran after him, and caught his arm. He freed it. "I had rather you wouldn't hang on me. I wish to be alone."

✳

Julian tactfully left the study after Sir Robert, without making his presence felt by even a brief good night. He decided it was late enough now to go up to his old room and try the door. Dipper had had several hours to work his magic with the key.

As he started up the grand staircase, he heard footsteps behind him. He turned. Guy was coming toward him across the great hall, weaving a little, his face flushed and merry. "I always said it! Hugh wouldn't believe me, but I knew Isabelle would prove me right in the end. Even she can't rein in her feelings forever."

"What are you talking about?"

"Isabelle lost her temper right royally this evening. It's a pity you missed it—it may not happen again these twenty years. We were all in the music room after you left, and Isabelle was sewing away at those confounded wedding slippers, when all of a sudden she pricked her finger. She dropped one of the slippers, and up jumps Miss Craddock to pick it up for her. But Isabelle snatches it up, and, I swear, I thought she was going to hit Miss Craddock with it. 'Give me that!' she shouts. 'Leave me alone!' Miss Craddock ran like a rabbit. So much for Hugh's idea that Isabelle only wants to be a sister to him! She hates Miss Craddock for cutting her out with him. I always told him so."

Julian did not answer at once. When he did, he said merely, "I hope Miss Fontclair is feeling better now."

"Damned if I know. She slunk upstairs to her room, and I haven't seen her since. Miss Craddock had a fit of the dismals and went up soon after. You know, she's a taking little thing. I didn't think so at first, but now I do. And she listens to a fellow very nicely, without wanting to talk all the time herself." He yawned. "Well, I'm for bed. I might actually sleep tonight."

"Haven't you been sleeping?"

"No, I haven't. You can write that down in your catalogue of clues, if you think it's important. But I'll wager none of us has slept any too well since the murder. We're all as nervous as cats. Except you, of course." He smiled unpleasantly. "Nothing rattles you. Anybody would think you'd been finding corpses in your bed all your life."

Julian said nothing, only looked at him with lifted brows. I really have become a policeman first and a gentleman second, he thought—trying to lure a fellow into talking rashly while he's in his cups.

"And maybe you have," Guy went on. "Who knows what you got up to before you turned up in London a few years ago? You could have had ten wives, killed them all, and stuffed them in a sea chest." He leaned so close that Julian could smell the liquor on his breath. "Maybe all this hunting the murderer is a hum. Maybe you did it yourself, and you're having a good laugh on us all."

"Do you think the murderer is laughing? I think he's more likely racking his brains for ways to cover his guilt. He might even be going about accusing other people, to throw them off the scent."

"Kestrel, I'm not— I didn't—"

Julian waited. "Talk to me," he urged. "I'll help you any way I can."

"I don't have anything to tell you! Except that I'm done-up, and I'm going to bed."

He hurried away, his walk remarkably steady all of a sudden. Fear could certainly do wonders to clear a man's head.

Julian went upstairs. His heart beat quickly as he turned the corner into his own hallway. He glanced around to make sure he was quite alone, then went to his old room.

Now for it. He tried the door. It was unlocked. "Dipper—

*bravissimo!*" he said softly. He went inside and shut the door behind him.

✳

Julian got up next morning without a single groan at the earliness of the hour. He felt filled to his fingertips with energy and purpose. He understood far more about the murder than he had a day ago. The only question was how best to use his newfound knowledge.

He was mulling this over as he coaxed his neckcloth into the severe style known as *trône d'amour.* Dipper, who was cleaning his shaving gear, yawned for the fourth time. "I hope I don't keep you awake," said Julian solicitously.

"I'm sorry, sir."

"The devil you are. You look confoundedly pleased with yourself."

"I dunno what you mean, sir."

"Don't you?" said Julian, eyes dancing. "I'll wager Molly Dale does. Shall I ask her?"

Dipper was spared having to answer this. Michael, the footman, came to tell them Dick Felton was at the back door and would like to have a word with Mr. Kestrel before breakfast. "Good Lord," said Julian, "I'd all but forgotten Felton. Tell him to wait for me in the silver lime courtyard. I'll be down directly."

Felton was sitting on the edge of a fountain, swinging his legs and whistling. The sound helped Julian find him amid the thick growth of trees. When he saw Julian, he jumped to his feet. "Thanks for coming out so prompt, sir. I'm due back at the Lion in time for the mails, or I wouldn't have come so early."

"Did you find Bliss?"

"No, sir, I didn't. I'm sorry. I followed him a good way. He was headed north—I knew, because I met up with people who'd seen him. I was gaining on him, but I had to turn back before I'd run him to earth. My brother couldn't take my place at the Lion for more nor a few days."

"I understand. At least we know he left Alderton alive. I was half afraid we'd find him facedown in the mill stream, or at the bottom of the village well."

"Oh, he's safe and sound, sir. I've got proof of that." He picked up a bulky parcel wrapped in brown paper, and handed it to Julian.

"What's this?"

"It's his sack, sir—the pedlar's sack he carried, that's made of bits of cloth in all different colours. I bought it off the grocer's wife in Little Finchley. That's a village near Peterborough, that Bliss passed through a day or two before me. Seems she saw the sack and took a fancy to it, so he sold it to her. I had a time getting her to give it up. I had to pay her 'most all the money you give me, and make sheep's eyes at her into the bargain. But I thought you might like to have it, so, anyways, here it is. Funny to think of him without it. It seemed as much a part of him as his head."

"That may be why he sold it—because it made him too easy to identify. And perhaps he'd decided to give up the peddling trade."

"But, how would he get his living— Oh, I see, sir! You think somebody paid him to light out of Alderton."

"Very possibly. Have you told anyone about my sending you to look for Bliss?"

"Not a soul, sir. I let on I was going north to see a friend that was took sick."

"Good. Keep to that story for the time being. You know, you really would do well to offer your talents to Bow Street one of these days."

"Would you put in a good word for me, sir?"

"I think I should tell you, in all honesty, I'm not a Bow Street officer."

"Oh, no, sir!" Felton winked broadly. "Not you!"

Julian gave it up. "We'd better settle our accounts," he said, taking out his pocketbook.

Felton lingered for some time, embarrassing Julian with vows of eternal loyalty and offers to have his brains blown out in Julian's service at a moment's notice. But at last he scampered off, and Julian went inside, concealing the brown-paper parcel as best he could under his arm.

Back in his room, he unwrapped the parcel and took out the gaudy patchwork sack. It was empty, and none too clean. "You want to keep that away from your togs, sir," warned Dipper. "The moths've got at it."

"Moths or no moths, it could well be worth more than anything my tailor ever turned out." He explained whose sack it was and how he came by it. "The fact is, I'm holding several good cards I didn't have yesterday."

"What are you going to do now, sir?"

"I'm not prepared to lay my whole hand on the table. So the only thing for it is to bluff."

# *30*
# BLUFFING

Toward midday, Julian rode to Alderton and managed to catch Dr. MacGregor between patients. He told him about his confrontation with Geoffrey last night, his clandestine visit to his old room, and his recovery of Bliss's sack.

"By thunder," said MacGregor, "you *have* been discovering things at a great rate!" He shook his head. "I can't get over Lady Fontclair's keeping a secret like that from her husband. I wouldn't have believed it of her. So now you say he's going to turn this business over to another magistrate?"

"Yes—a fellow named Ayres. He wrote to him late last night. This morning Mr. Ayres wrote back agreeing to take over the investigation, but saying he couldn't come to Bellegarde to hear the particulars till tomorrow. That gives me just the respite I need. I have a plan."

"Lord help us!"

"I don't know why you should put on that Cassandra-like face. I think my plans have been turning out rather well lately."

"Well, don't get too cocksure of yourself. Remember how that theory you had about Lady Tarleton being the murdered girl's mother exploded in your face."

"That theory was a bit wide of the mark," Julian admitted. "But it served a useful purpose. It provoked Lady Tarleton into telling me the truth about Colonel Fontclair's letters."

"I don't think insulting a respectable female is anything to congratulate yourself about!"

"It isn't, and I don't. If it's any consolation to you, my conduct toward her hasn't gone unpunished. She never misses a chance to abuse my manners, morals, and origins to anyone who'll listen."

"Well, a woman as proud as Lady Tarleton is bound to get her hackles up, when you come right out and accuse her of bearing a child wrongside of the blanket."

"That's true. Why do I feel it's not enough of an explanation? Why do I think there's something more behind her hatred of me?"

"What more could there be?"

"That she wasn't indifferent to Craddock when he made advances to her twenty years ago. That she's guilty in thought of what I accused her of, even if she never committed the deed, and she can't forgive me for putting my finger on the greatest shame of her life. That, for some reason I don't understand, she's afraid of me."

MacGregor shook his head. "All that's beyond me. Tell me about this plan of yours."

Julian told him.

"Does Sir Robert know what you mean to do?" MacGregor asked.

"No. I thought it best not to tell anyone at Bellegarde. All the same, I need an ally. That's why I came to you."

"Me? What can I do?"

"I understand you're coming to dinner tonight."

"That's right. I always dine at Bellegarde on Fridays."

"Dinner is the only time today I can count on finding all the Fontclairs and Craddocks together. I want to be the last person in the drawing room, so I won't come down till just before seven. I should like you to do what you can to detain anyone who's disposed to leave the drawing room before that time. And if anyone does leave, or doesn't appear at all, send me word in my room, and I'll put off my experiment till later in the evening."

"I'll do it. A week ago, I wouldn't have dreamed I'd be conspiring to lay a trap for the Fontclairs. But, Heaven help us, if Lady Fontclair can humbug Sir Robert like that, there's no trusting any of them!"

"They've all lied about one thing or another. It's curious, isn't it, what base acts people will commit to protect their honour? It's like taking money out of principal to pay one's debts. One keeps off creditors from attacking the core property—but the property itself becomes damaged and diminished, till it's hardly worth protecting anymore."

✳

All day, Bellegarde kept up a semblance of normality. Julian thought Lady Fontclair was mainly responsible for this. Estranged from Sir Robert, faced with imminent exposure of Geoffrey's secret, still she went on gamely making lighthearted conversation and ministering to everyone's needs. It helped that most of the family apparently did not realize how close to catastrophe they were. As best Julian could tell, no one but Lady Fontclair, the colonel, and himself knew of Sir Robert's resolve to hand over the investigation—and the family secrets—to another magistrate.

The hours hung heavy on Julian's hands. Toward the end of the day, he went to the music room in search of the one remedy he could count on to soothe and distract his mind. He had not been at the pianoforte more than a few minutes when Miss Craddock came in. "Please don't stop," she said. "I like to listen."

"I think you'd like even more to talk." He closed the piano and came over to her.

"Something's going to happen, isn't it? I can feel it."

"I think we may be very close to solving the murder. I can't say any more."

"I understand. I only hope whatever happens won't be too painful for the Fontclairs." She sighed. "I suppose it won't be long now before they're free of Papa and me."

"It does seem likely Colonel Fontclair's secret will come out one way or another. If that happens, your father will lose his power over the Fontclairs, and if you wish to release Hugh from his engagement, you may."

"You know I don't wish to. But I have no choice—it's the only right thing to do. But, oh, it's hard! Never to see him again, to know he'll marry someone else! Do you think it will be Isabelle? I know his family wanted him to marry her—Lady Tarleton made sure to let me know that, the very first day I was here. And Isabelle hates me for coming between them. I didn't realize it till last night, when she snapped at me like that. She practically bared her teeth at me! It was terrible. I felt as though I'd ruined her life."

"The way I heard it," said Julian, carefully neutral, "Hugh's marrying Miss Fontclair was just a dynastic notion of Lady Tarleton's. There wasn't any engagement between them."

His reasoning could not reach her. She was fast sliding into despondency. "Isabelle would make him such a good wife! She can talk to him about art and music, and she knows everything there is to know about Bellegarde, and being a country gentleman's wife. And she's so graceful and elegant! Her feet don't seem to touch the ground when she walks. I feel ordinary next to her, like calico next to silk. She's—she's the kind of young lady men write poetry about. Nobody would write a poem about someone like me."

Julian recited, as though to no one in particular:

> "I saw her upon nearer view,
> A Spirit, yet a Woman too!
> Her household motions light and free,
> And steps of virgin-liberty;
> A countenance in which did meet
> Sweet records, promises as sweet;
> The reason firm, the temperate will,
> Endurance, foresight, strength and skill;
> And yet a Spirit still, and bright
> With something of angelic light."

Maud's eyes filled with tears. She reached out to him blindly, and buried her face in his shoulder. He put his arm around her waist.

Hugh came in suddenly. "What is this?" he sputtered.

Maud's head came up. Her face was flushed, her hair a bit dishevelled. "Oh! Mr. Fontclair."

"I hope I'm not interrupting!" Hugh said savagely.

Julian came to his feet as composedly as he could. He knew he was in an awkward spot, yet he could not help feeling amused.

"Miss Craddock was very much moved by a poem we were discussing."

"Oh, really," cried Hugh, "you'll have to do better than that!"

"Perhaps we should talk about this somewhere else," Julian recommended, seeing that Maud was growing alarmed.

"When and where you like!" said Hugh. He wondered if he was about to fight his very first duel, and pictured himself returning in grim triumph with a smoking pistol, or expiring gracefully on the field of honour with words of forgiveness on his lips.

"You can't mean to quarrel?" Maud faltered. "Why should you? I don't understand!"

"This doesn't concern you, Miss Craddock. I think Mr. Kestrel understands my meaning very well."

"I don't, really," Julian confessed. "If I weren't a guest in your house, I'd think you meant to call me out, but I can't conceive you intended such a breach of the code of honour."

Hugh was chagrined. It was true that a host ought not to challenge a guest, whatever the provocation—though it was rather shabby of Kestrel to hide behind such a technicality.

Julian was not ashamed of ducking the quarrel. He liked Hugh, in spite of his silliness, and would rather not have to shoot him. Fortunately Hugh changed tactics. "Mr. Kestrel, I should like to speak to Miss Craddock alone. Please have the goodness to leave us."

Julian looked at Maud questioningly. She mustered her courage and nodded to him to go. He inclined his head and went out.

Hugh drew himself up. Maud had never seen him look so like his father. "Miss Craddock, rather than draw inferences from your conduct that—in short, I think it only fair to allow you to explain yourself."

"What?"

"I mean that if you have anything to say that might excuse your behaviour, I am willing to hear it."

"What are you talking about?"

"Oh, for God's sake!" cried Hugh, stamping his foot, "you know what I mean! You're making me ridiculous, and I demand an explanation!"

"Excuse me, Mr. Fontclair, but I—I think the only person making you ridiculous is you!"

Hugh opened his mouth, but at first he could get out only a few infuriated gasps. "Miss Craddock, I know this engagement wasn't of your seeking, any more than it was of mine, but I think in common decency you might make it a little less obvious you wish Kestrel were in my place! You've been glued to his side ever since he first came to Bellegarde, you couldn't spend two days in London without taking him with you, and now I find you practically swooning away in his arms!"

"How *can* you? Mr. Kestrel is my friend! He's never sought to be anything more, and I never wanted him to be."

"Forgive me, but, really, that's doing it a bit too brown! If this is the way you conduct yourself with your friends, then I take leave to tell you, you're a deal too *friendly* for common propriety, let alone honour!"

"Honour! Honour! Papa is right—that *is* all you and your family ever think about!"

"You wouldn't understand, naturally. You weren't brought up to set a value on anything that can't be reckoned up in pounds, shillings, and pence."

"I might have known sooner or later you'd sneer at me for being a tradesman's daughter."

"I'm not sneering at you. I just think we need to understand the differences between us. Perhaps among people of your sort it's acceptable to fling yourself at one gentleman's head while you're engaged to another. Here, it's not at all the thing."

"Well, you needn't worry that I might be an embarrassment to you! Because I wouldn't marry you now for anything!"

"What a relief for you, Miss Craddock! What would you have done if I hadn't given you an excuse to break this mockery of an engagement? Married me, and become even better *friends* with Kestrel afterward?"

"Oh!" She pressed her knuckles to her mouth and ran out of the room.

Hugh stared after her, aghast. How could he have said those

things? He must have been mad. He felt he knew now what it was to be possessed by devils.

He had to tell her he did not mean any of it—had not known what he was saying. He rushed to her room and knocked. Her maid, Alice, opened the door and gaped at him. Her young lady's bedchamber! Everyone knew the Quality were rather free in their ways, but an engaged bridegroom is not the same as a husband, and Mr. Fontclair ought to know it! "Miss Craddock is dressing for dinner, sir, and can't see anyone!" she said, and shut the door in his face.

He paced frantically up and down the hall, imagining Miss Craddock weeping and humiliated and miserable—and more in love than ever with Kestrel, who would never have spoken to her like a brute and a villain. And, Lord!—what would Craddock do when he found out the engagement was broken? Would he carry out his threat to publish Uncle Geoffrey's letters? Hugh felt that coals of fire were being heaped on his head.

Only one thing was clear. Even if Maud would never again consider marrying him—which was no more than he deserved—he must get down on his knees and beg her pardon for the monstrous things he had said. After that, it did not matter what became of him. And he went away to dress for dinner, with the air of young Werther on his way to his suicide chamber.

✳

Hugh came down to the drawing room early, hoping to catch Miss Craddock alone before dinner. But she did not appear until nearly seven, and by then the whole company was assembled—all except Kestrel, for whom Hugh was always on the lookout when Miss Craddock was about. Hugh got entangled in a conversation with his father and Dr. MacGregor, from which he had some trouble escaping. He was making his way toward Miss Craddock at last, when Aunt Catherine stepped into his path. "Is Mr. Kestrel going to be late to dinner *again?*"

"I don't know, Aunt," Hugh said distractedly, his eyes on Maud.

"I suppose he's off grubbing for clues again, like the low, foul-minded Bow Street Runner he is at heart."

"I'm sorry you think so badly of the Runners," said Kestrel's voice. "I'm beginning to have a great deal of respect for what they do."

He was standing in the doorway of the drawing room, so that only the right side of his body could be seen. He remained there till everyone's eyes turned toward him in puzzled expectancy. Then he came all the way inside, so that they could see the gaudy patchwork sack draped over his left arm.

Guy jumped out of his chair. "Where did you get that?"

Julian's gaze had been sweeping the room, but now it fastened on Guy. "It belongs to Bliss, the pedlar."

"But how did you—" Guy checked himself, looking around at the surprised faces turned to his. He sat down again, groping behind him for his chair as though in a daze. "I thought he'd left town. I thought he couldn't be found."

"I sent Dick Felton to look for him."

"You told me nothing of this, Mr. Kestrel," Sir Robert protested.

"I'm telling you now." Julian spoke to Sir Robert, but his eyes remained fixed on Guy. "I'm going to make a clean breast of everything I've learned in the past four-and-twenty hours."

Guy was shaking a little. "Why are you staring at me like that? You could drive a fellow distracted, coming after him with those eyes!" He started up out of his chair again. "Look here, if you know something, say it! Just say it! I—I can answer it. Tell me, for God's sake! If Bliss is spreading lies about me, I'd just as soon know what they are."

Instead of answering, Julian reached into a pocket of his waistcoat and took out a small scrap of yellow cloth. He held it out to Guy.

"What's that?" Guy started back.

"I believe it's the bit that was torn off the bottom of the murdered girl's dress. I found it clinging to a jagged stone on the stairway."

"What stairway?" Sir Robert asked.

"The secret stairway that leads from my old room, where the body was found, to the back door in the servants' wing."

A murmur of astonishment ran through the room. Guy staggered back as though from a blow. "Bliss can't have told you about the passage! I never told *him!*—did I? I can't remember—"

"Guy!" cried Geoffrey. "What's all this about a stairway, a passage?"

"But I know of no secret passage or stairway at Bellegarde," Sir Robert said, bewildered.

"But *you* do, don't you?" said Julian to Guy. "I make no doubt you could tell us all about it. That room was yours when you were a boy. You found the passage, but it seems you never told anyone about it. And a week ago today, you brought the girl known as Amy Fields through it to my room."

Guy stared at him. Then, out of his throat came a choking noise that turned out, horribly, to be laughter. Once he started laughing, he could not stop. He fell back in his chair, gasping, "You devil, Kestrel! You devil!"

Geoffrey dropped his walking stick with a clatter, and covered his face. Lady Tarleton's mouth fell open, but for once she had nothing to say. Hugh edged toward Maud and stood by her chair protectively. Isabelle bowed her head and turned her face away. Mark Craddock's lip curled, and he looked at Guy with unutterable contempt.

Sir Robert closed his eyes. His face was ashen. Lady Fontclair went to him and put her arms around his shoulders. He reached out blindly and covered her hand with his.

"So," said Guy, his eyes wild but his laughter abating, "I suppose Bliss told you everything."

"I haven't spoken to Bliss," said Julian. "Felton couldn't find him. All he found was this." He indicated the patchwork sack.

"You mean—that's all you have?" Guy gaped at the sack. Laughter convulsed him again. "You mean, if I'd only held my tongue— No, really, this is funny! It's an absolute screamer, don't you see? On the strength of a worm-eaten pedlar's sack, I've put a rope around my neck! I don't care. I'm glad it's come out. You don't know what hell I've been living through—keeping up appearances, wanting to know what the devil'd been found out about Amy, but afraid to seem too curious. What happens now—trial and execution? Oh, God." He stopped laughing. A fit of trembling seized him. He shrank back in his chair and looked around him with terrified eyes.

Sir Robert said grimly, "As I'm still the magistrate in charge of the investigation, I'll hear your confession and have Rawlinson take it down."

"I want to be there, Robert," said Geoffrey. "You've got to let me be there with him."

"Very well. I should like Mr. Kestrel to be there as well, as I have questions to put to him. And you, Doctor: I hope you will attend as an impartial witness."

"But, Uncle—" Guy began.

Sir Robert rounded on him. "I'll hear nothing from you! You may speak on your own behalf—if there is anything you can say in extenuation of this—this atrocity—when you make your confession. I hope you mean to confess. I can't compel it, but I appeal to you, if you have any last, lingering regard for your name and family, to admit your guilt and spare us the humiliation of a trial."

"Listen to me, Uncle, for God's sake—all of you!" Guy leaned forward, clutching the arms of his chair. "It's true I brought Amy into the house. It's true I left her in Kestrel's room. But I won't confess to murder. I won't, because, before God, you've got to believe me—*I didn't kill her!*"

# *31*
# A NEST OF
# SECRETS

Guy told his story in Julian's old room. Sir Robert chose to question him there so that Guy could explain exactly what had happened on the afternoon of the murder, and Julian could show where the secret passage was and how it worked.

The room looked enchanting in the early evening. The ebbing sunshine cast a soft glow on it, like a sprinkling of gold dust. But now its vibrant beauty was linked forever to ugly memories. There was the bed where Aimée had lain—where someone had tucked her carefully under the covers like a sleeping child. There was the washstand, where the murderer—Guy?—had washed off the blood from his hands, and perhaps from the weapon as well. The shieldback chair where Guy was sitting now was the chair on which Aimée had left her shawl and bonnet. Along the back of that chair was a scratch, corresponding to a scratch on the wall behind it. And on that same wall, above Guy's head, were the five faint smears of blood that seemed to have been made by a person's fingers.

Geoffrey pulled up a chair beside his son's. Sir Robert sat opposite. Julian stood before them, keeping all their faces in view. MacGregor paced back and forth, his head lowered like a charging bull's. Julian noticed he kept close to the door; perhaps he was afraid Guy would try to bolt. Rawlinson, unobtrusive as ever, took notes at the desk in the window recess.

"You've got to know it all from the beginning," said Guy, "or you'll never understand. Even then, you may not believe me. But, I swear, this is exactly how it was.

"I met Amy this past March. I saw her walking up Fleet Street with a bandbox on her arm. She was creeping along close to the wall with her head down, but I could see enough of her face to know I wanted a better look. I went up and tried to talk to her, but she took fright and hurried on. She wouldn't stop or so much as look at me—till I told her my name. That brought her up short. She was so much struck, I asked her if she knew anybody in the family. She said she didn't, but she'd heard we were an old county family, great guns among the Quality, that kind of thing. She asked all about us—what our names were, and where we all lived. When I found she was so dazzled by the name Fontclair, I played that card for all it was worth. Because once I got talking to her, I was pretty well floored. You don't know what she was like—I mean, you never saw her alive. She had this way of opening her eyes very wide and peeping up through her lashes. It drove me distracted. I had to have her. I don't know when I've wanted a girl so badly."

"Did she show a particular interest in your father?" asked Julian.

"I don't think so." Guy frowned. "Well, maybe she did. I thought it was because he was a war hero. Amy was French, but she didn't seem to hold any grudge about the war. Maybe her people were royalists—I don't know, she never said much about them. She'd given herself an English name: Amy Fields. I don't know what her real name was. I never asked her.

"I met her pretty often after that. She'd find excuses to get out of the shop where she worked, and we'd talk in streets and public houses and even churches. I was always trying to get her into a carriage or a certain kind of house—you know the game—but she wasn't having any. She'd walk and talk with me, but she'd hardly let me lay a finger on her. She said she didn't want to go wrong and ruin her chances of getting respectably married. She said she'd never had anything to do with a man up to now. That might have been true. Hang it, it *was* true."

He shifted in his chair, wetting his dry lips. MacGregor, stony-faced, poured him a glass of water. Guy, who had clearly been hoping for something stronger, drank it off resignedly.

"I dangled after her for about a month, and I was beginning to think the game wasn't worth the candle, when something happened that changed everything. Amy saw the announcement of Hugh's engagement to Miss Craddock in the *Morning Post*. She asked me about it. I said there wasn't much to tell—only that Hugh'd got himself engaged to the daughter of a rich cit who used to work in our stables, and the family was pretty cut up about it. I didn't mean to put ideas in her head, but I did. I could read her like an open book. She was thinking: If Hugh could marry so far beneath him, why couldn't I?

"So then I knew how to come round her. I let on I might marry her—not straightaway, but later, when the family'd had a chance to get over the shock of Hugh's marriage. All right, of course I didn't mean it. She ought to have known I didn't! How could I throw myself away on a little French ladybird—no money, no connexions? But she believed it, and that's how I got her to come away with me."

Louisa's words about Aimée and her colonel came back to Julian, with a new and tragic force: *She used to daydream he'd adopt her, make her really his daughter.* How could she resist the chance to become his daughter, by marrying his son?

Guy went on, "I got her to leave her trumpery hatshop and let me find her a place to live. But she got this maggot in her head that we had to keep our affair a secret. She was terrified my family would find out she was my mistress, and they'd never accept her as my wife. She wouldn't be seen in public with me, she'd have nothing to do with my friends or their women, she was dead set on living like a hermit till we were wed.

"I set her up in a house owned by a woman I know named Daphne Bane. She runs a couple of—young ladies' academies—but she also has a little house near Hampstead, where she holes up when things get too hot for her in town. I talked her into letting Amy stay there. It was a retired kind of place, so Amy didn't have to worry about people seeing me visit her.

"At first, her being so secretive was pretty convenient. She never went anywhere or saw anyone but Daphne, so she couldn't get in the way of anything I wanted to do, or have jealous fits about other women. And she was never after me for money or expensive presents. I bought her some clothes and trinkets all the same—though I don't think she liked anything I gave her as well as that scallop shell she wore around her neck. She never took that off. I tried to make her once. I said if it came from another man, she'd no business to wear it now. But she said it was a symbol of some saint, that she wore for luck.

"I'd kept her for about a month, maybe six weeks, when I was asked on this visit to Bellegarde to meet the Craddocks. I thought about taking her with me—finding her lodgings in the neighbourhood, where I could visit her on the sly. But when I told her, she went into a blind panic. You'd have thought I was trying to drag her into the blackest pit in Hell. She wouldn't on any account go anywhere near Bellegarde or my family."

"She was probably afraid your father would see her and recognize her," said Julian. "She must have known your family would do all they could to stop you marrying her, once they knew who she was—and who her mother was."

"Why, who was her mother?" Guy looked at him blankly, then turned to Geoffrey. "What do you know about Amy?"

"I knew her and her mother once, a long time ago."

"How did you— Oh, my God, Amy wasn't my sister, was she?"

"No, no!"

"Thank God! I'm in trouble enough without that!"

"Never mind for the moment how your father knew Miss Fields," said Sir Robert. "Go on."

"Amy and I had the devil of a row. I said I'd had enough of her secrecy, and if she was so afraid of being seen with me, I'd take myself off for good, and be damned to her. She wept—she was a great one for tears, God knows where all that water came from, she never ran dry—and said she'd go anywhere with me but Bellegarde. And it all ended with my storming out and saying I was finished with her. I wasn't—not by half—but I wanted to give her a fright, make her come to heel. She did, with a vengeance! She was in such a funk, she came all the way here from London to make it up with me.

"The problem was, she couldn't think how to get word to me she was here without my family knowing. She was still bent on keeping things between us a secret. The morning after she arrived, she went out early and met Bliss on the road. They got talking, and when she found he knew the neighbourhood, she got the idea of sending him to me with a message. He told her I'd likely go to the horse fair, so he'd look for me there first. I expect the old devil just wanted to go there himself; he never misses a chance to cadge at places like that.

"When he first saw me at the horse fair, he couldn't deliver Amy's message, because I was with Hugh and Kestrel, and Amy'd told him to catch me alone if he could. He kept an eye on me, and came sidling up as soon as I went off by myself. He told me Amy was here and had sent him to fetch me. He'd put her in the old mill for safekeeping, meantime. I was glad she'd come to heel, but she was still being hell-fired secretive, and I was sick of that. And I wasn't too keen on being summoned like a lackey, with Bliss laughing up his sleeve at me the whole while. So I told him I wasn't ready to leave the horse fair, and if Amy wanted to see me so badly, she could damned well wait till I had time for her. I gave him money and sent him back to tell her to stay at the mill till I came." He turned to Julian. "You know, I almost told you and Hugh all about it on the way home from the horse fair. I wish I had now—then you'd know it all happened just the way I've said."

"Why didn't you?"

"I got an idea. I wish to God my brains had rotted before I ever thought of it, but at the time I thought I was monstrous clever. I remembered that after luncheon Hugh was taking you round the estate, and I thought it would be a lark to bring Amy up to your room through the secret passage."

"It's time we talked about that," said Sir Robert. "How long have you known there was a secret stairway to this room?"

"Since I was a boy. I found it by blind chance, and when I realized

I must be the only one who knew about it, I decided to keep it that way. I was always looking for ways to get out of the house at night on the sly. I can't stand being cooped up—I never could."

He halted and grew pale. They knew what he was thinking: that he might well be facing a worse confinement than any he had ever known. Julian had little sympathy for him. Wherever he might be imprisoned pending trial, it would be far superior to that foul lockup where, thanks to Guy's concealment, Dipper had spent three long days.

"I can't imagine how there could be a stairway in the house that we know nothing about," said Sir Robert.

"I have an idea about that," said Julian. "Ever since the murder, I've been racking my brains to think how the girl could have got into the house, and up to my room, without being seen. It never occurred to me there could be a secret passage, because devices like that never are a secret nowadays. They're a source of entertainment, shown off proudly on tours of country houses. When Miss Philippa told me your family were Catholics in Elizabethan days, I began to wonder if the house might have a priest-hole—a room or passage where a visiting priest could hide from the authorities. But I couldn't imagine how a priest-hole could be known to the murderer, yet unknown to anyone else.

"Then I remembered something else Miss Philippa told me. She said she was writing a family history, but she found it hard, because most of the family papers were destroyed in a fire in the civil war. I thought, what if no architectural plans of the house had survived? The sketches you showed me, Sir Robert, are only about half a century old, and you said this part of the house had hardly been altered since Queen Elizabeth's time. There might just be a means of access to this room that none of you knew about, because in all the upheavals of the civil war, the secret was lost."

He went over to the wall abutting the servants' wing. The others gathered around him. "I reasoned that, if there were a secret way into this room, the entrance was likely to be in this wall. Your office, Rawlinson, is just the other side of it, and below your office is the waiting room where the back door is. I remember thinking your office looked surprisingly large on the floor plans of the house

Sir Robert showed me. I know why now: whoever drew up those plans didn't know about the secret stairway between your office and this room.

"This part of the wall interested me most." He went over to the place where the wall met the window recess at right angles. Here, barely visible on the oak panelling, were the five small smears of blood. "The bloodstains are here, and so is the chair where the girl left her shawl and bonnet. I looked along the panelling for some way the wall might open, but there wasn't any crevice where a spring could be hidden. So I looked here instead."

He indicated the carved wood panels in the window recess. "These carvings are all emblems of saints. I noticed that the first night I was here, but I didn't make anything of it. Now I think this room must have been given to priests in Queen Elizabeth's reign. They would have come to the house masquerading as ordinary guests, but these sacred emblems were an acknowledgment of their true identity. I probed, and at last I found the key to the mystery—appropriately, here."

He pointed out a carving in the left-hand panel: two crossed keys, the emblem of St. Peter. Where the keys crossed, there was a little hollow in the wood. He pressed it firmly.

A long, low creak, like a wail of protest, sounded from the adjacent wall. The next moment, the panel at right angles to the window— the panel where the bloodstains were—swung slowly outward. Cold air, and a smell of damp and dirt, flowed in from the darkness beyond.

The men peered inside. As their eyes adjusted, they made out a stone cavity some ten feet square. A rough-cut stairway spiralled down, its depths lost in shadow. Julian remembered how he had felt his way down those steep, uneven stairs last night. He had kept the secret door propped open with a chair; it made his skin crawl to think of it swinging to and trapping him in that cold, dank place. Who knew for certain there was any way out at the bottom?

But there was. He explained how he had found a door at the foot of the stairs, leading into the waiting room in the servants' wing. "From there, of course, an escaping priest could go out the back door and escape through the kitchen garden—or, better still, the silver lime grove. The trees there would give capital cover to anyone fleeing from the house."

They were all eager to examine the secret door, and to work the spring that opened it. To Julian's relief, they did not think to ask how he had gotten into the room last night to look for the passage. He would just as soon not have to explain how he came by the key.

"How did *you* find the passage?" the colonel asked Guy.

"One night when I was climbing in the window, I happened to grasp the panel right where the hidden spring was. The next thing I knew, the wall nearby gave a groan and swung out at me. That knocked me a regular cock, I can tell you! I went down the stairway and found where it led. I knew then I'd never have to climb out the window again—I could sneak in and out of the house any time I liked. And on top of all that, I knew something about the house that nobody else did, which I thought was a pretty good joke. So I kept it to myself. I didn't use it much when I got older, because I didn't have this room anymore: Aunt Cecily'd made it into a guest room and moved all the family into the new wing.

"Anyway, I got the idea of sneaking Amy in through the passage. With Kestrel gone, I might just be able to get her in and out while the servants were at dinner. The more I thought about it, the funnier it seemed—to bring a bit of muslin under the ancestral roof, with no one the wiser.

"The col— my father nearly dished the whole thing at the last minute. I was in the library, keeping watch out of the window for Hugh and Kestrel to leave. At about half past three I saw their horses being brought round, and I was just going to rush off and collect Amy, when in comes my father and says, What about a rubber of piquet? I didn't have time, but he was looking blue-devilled, so I didn't have the heart to turn him down flat. So I said I was fagged out, and thought I'd go up to my room and have a nap. I went partway upstairs and hung about on the landing till there was no one in sight. Then I slipped out the front door and made a beeline for the old mill. But my father didn't know that!" he added fiercely. "When he told you I went up to my room for a nap, he thought he was telling the truth."

"Never mind, my boy," said Geoffrey.

"I do mind," insisted Guy.

"What happened then?" said Sir Robert.

"I got to the mill about four o'clock. Amy was there; so was Bliss. He'd stuck to her like glue ever since I sent him back to her. I suppose he thought there was more money to be made from us than from hawking corncob pipes at the horse fair. Lord, it turned out he was right about that!

"Amy was worried to death I was never coming. She flung herself at me and begged me to forgive her for refusing to come to the country with me. I asked her if she was willing to prove she was sorry, and she said she was. So I told her my plan to sneak her into Bellegarde, and of course she bucked, but I said if she was going to fight me again she could turn around and go straight back to London. She started spouting tears and wailing and calling on the Virgin Mary, but in the end she agreed.

"I took her through the Chase, because it was the most direct route to Bellegarde. She was glad to keep away from prying eyes, but it was rough going for her. She wasn't dressed for it. The place was such a tangle, oftentimes I had to cut our way through. By the time we got to Bellegarde, she was as nervous as a cat. I whisked her through the silver lime courtyard—Kestrel is right, those trees make deuced good cover—and we nipped in through the back door without anybody seeing us. I let us into the secret passage—you know, you can get in from that end, too, through a hidden door in the waiting room. I figured out how to do it years ago, after I found out how the mechanism worked up here. We didn't have a candle, so we had to feel our way up the stairs. It's dark as pitch there, even in the daytime. I let us into Kestrel's room—"

"Hitting that chair with the door," guessed Julian, pointing to the shieldback chair by the wall.

"I did, now I come to think of it. How did you know?"

Julian pointed out the twin scratches on the wall and the back of the chair. "We thought at first the chair had been knocked against the wall in a struggle. But since nothing is ever what it seems in this business, it turns out to be the wall that hit the chair."

Guy dropped into an armchair by the hearth. He looked like a man in the grip of an illness—white and exhausted, but unable to rest. The others drew close, impatient for the climax.

"We came in here. Amy made us scrape the dirt off our feet before we stepped on the carpet. The things women worry about! At first everything went all right. She was so taken up with looking at the room, she forgot to worry someone might come in and find us. But soon she started in on me to take her away. I didn't want to leave so soon. I wanted—I mean—there was a bed— I'm pretty ashamed of myself about this."

"Go on," said Sir Robert grimly.

"She put up the deuce of a fight! She said if my family caught us together like that, she'd die. She said she couldn't stand any more. All right, I know what you're thinking, but you're wrong! I was angry, I admit it. But I didn't kill her. I had another idea. I thought I'd lock her in Kestrel's room and leave her here. I knew she wouldn't be able to get out by the secret passage—she didn't know how to get into it from this end. That would teach her to fret herself and me to death about secrecy. And I thought it would be a good joke on Kestrel. I wondered what he'd do when he came back and found a hysterical female in his room. Because she was pretty well off her head by then, weeping and wailing. I told her there wasn't much point in trying to keep her presence a secret, if she was going to cry fit to bring the house down.

"Anyway, I left her here. I locked her in and left the key on the hall table, and went off. I could hear her crying all the way down the hall. It was a pretty shabby way to treat her, I know. But the devil got into me, and—I did it. That's all."

MacGregor stared. "You mean, that's the last you saw of her?"

"As God's my witness, that's the last I saw of her, alive."

# *32*
# JUSTICE

Guy's listeners exchanged bewildered glances. All the while he talked, they had felt a bleak sense of relief, thinking that, one way or another, the crime would be solved at last. But if Guy was telling the truth, the mystery remained to plague them. The murderer eluded them still.

Julian asked the question he thought most likely to narrow the field of suspects. "What time was it when you left her here?"

"Quarter past five. I remember, I looked at my watch."

"What did you do next?" asked MacGregor.

"Pretty much what I told Uncle Robert when he questioned us after the murder. I went to my room, rang for my man, and dressed. When I came down to the drawing room, I was surprised nobody seemed to have found Amy yet. Then I heard dinner was delayed because Uncle Robert had some kind of business with Kestrel. So I thought, well, they've found her at last. But nobody asked me about her. Nobody paid any heed to me at all. I began to think she must be braving it out, pretending she didn't know me and had got into the house by herself somehow. I decided to hold my tongue and see what happened. The truth is, I didn't think my joke was so funny anymore, and I knew Uncle Robert would cut up savage if he found I'd brought a ladybird into Bellegarde on the sly. So I just waited. I played patience to keep my hands occupied, so I wouldn't look as nervous as I felt. I wondered what was happening to Amy, and thought—" His throat closed. "I thought I'd make it up to her—once I got her away from Bellegarde—

"Look, it's not as though I didn't feel anything for her! When I heard she was dead, I couldn't take it in. I thought at first she'd killed herself, and I knew if she had, I was to blame. Then when I found she'd been murdered—my God, I didn't know what to think. I couldn't imagine who'd done it. I still can't. But I knew one thing. If I let on I'd brought her into the house, I'd be pegged as her killer straightaway. So I pretended I didn't know anything about her. That wasn't always easy. When I saw her lying dead on that sofa—well, you can see why I felt sick and had to bolt.

"I realized how lucky I was she'd been so secretive about our love affair. There was just a chance nobody would ever find out I'd had anything to do with her. Of course I'd have to square Daphne, and that would be expensive. But if I could fork out more than she'd get as a reward for laying information against me, she'd hold her tongue. There was no love lost between her and Bow Street; she'd as soon not have anything to do with them if she could help it.

"The most important thing was to get rid of Bliss. I knew where he was: he'd told me if I had any more errands for him, I could find him at the old mill. So when the household finally settled to sleep, I went out in that cursed rainstorm to see him. I found him asleep—and for half a minute, I understood why people commit murders. I thought, all I'd have to do is fetch him a good, stiff plug on the brainpan, and he'd never be able to open his mouth to do me any harm. But, I don't know, I wasn't bad enough, or brave enough, to take that route. I woke him up and gave him all the money I could scrape together in exchange for his promise to cut and run, and not breathe a word about Amy and me. Of course when I saw Kestrel had that infernal sack, I thought he'd been found and had talked, and I lost my head.

"I've told you the whole truth now, I swear it. I expect it's a crime to hide evidence, but that's the worst thing I've done."

There was a silence. Julian broke it. "When you cut a way for you and Amy through the Chase, what did you use?"

Alarm flashed into Guy's eyes. "I didn't have a knife, if that's what you mean! When I said I cut our way, all I meant was I broke off branches and kicked away undergrowth."

"Have you told us everything Miss Fields said when you and she quarrelled here?" asked Sir Robert. "Did she demand that you marry her? Did she threaten you in any way?"

"Threaten me? How do you mean?"

"Are you telling us you know nothing of the connexion between Miss Fields—or, rather, Mademoiselle Deschamps—and your father?"

"You all keep hinting about something between Amy and my father, but I'm blistered if I know what you mean." He appealed to the colonel. "What's all this about?"

"I hoped you'd never have to know," Geoffrey said quietly. "But I'll tell you. I'll tell you everything."

Sir Robert rose and looked coldly at Guy. "In my judgement, the evidence against you is more than sufficient for an arrest. But I leave that decision to the magistrate who is taking over the investigation tomorrow. In the meantime, I shall treat you exactly as I did Mr. Kestrel's servant when he was accused. Rawlinson, be good enough to take him to your office and lock him in there for the present. Then go to my office and write up a statement he can sign."

"Do you have to lock him up?" pleaded Geoffrey.

"Do you suppose I can take his word—as a gentleman!—that he won't try to escape?"

Guy flinched and looked away.

"May I go with him?" Geoffrey asked.

"Very well. But I warn you, if he makes any attempt at flight, I shall have him caught and dragged back, if I have to raise a hue and cry all over the county."

Guy went out, flanked by Geoffrey and Rawlinson. At once MacGregor burst out. "I'm sorry, Sir Robert, I know he's your nephew—but how can we believe any of that rigmarole he told?"

"I believe him," said Julian.

"You do, do you?" MacGregor's eyes narrowed.

"I think it sounds exactly like him—leaving the girl locked in here as a punishment for her and a joke on me. And it explains the locked door. If she were dead when he left her, why would he bother to lock her in?"

"To confuse us," declared MacGregor. "And it worked, because you've been puzzling over that locked door from the beginning."

"He would have had to keep a very cool head, to be able to think of conundrums for us to solve, with the girl lying dead before him. And we know he was anything but coolheaded—in fact, he must have lost his head completely. Otherwise, why didn't he hide her body in the secret passage?"

Sir Robert and MacGregor looked at each other uncertainly.

"Of course he'd have had to dispose of the bloodstained bedding, too," Julian mused, "but a missing sheet and coverlet would have caused a good deal less commotion than a corpse. The fact that the girl's body was left in the bed for anyone to find is the single best argument for Guy's innocence. Only he knew about the passage. He could easily have hidden the body there and got rid of it later, on one of his nightly forays."

"Perhaps he couldn't get the passage open," said Sir Robert.

"It opened very easily for me once I learned the knack of it, and Guy had opened it many times. But, you know, that brings up an interesting point—"

He stopped. The solution caught up with him—stared him in the face.

"What point?" said MacGregor impatiently. Then, in an altered tone, "Kestrel, are you all right?"

"Yes, doctor." Julian drew a long breath. There could be no turning squeamish now. He had to finish what he had begun. "How do you suppose those smears of blood got on the panel where the secret door is?"

"Maybe Guy tried to open the secret door after he killed her, and couldn't!" MacGregor said eagerly. "But he pressed against the panel, and blood from his fingers got on the wall!"

"You can't move the panel by pressing against it," Julian pointed out quietly. "The spring that opens it is in the window recess. And Guy knew that."

"Well, how do you think the smears got there?"

"I think the girl was killed by someone who knew there was a passage, but didn't know how to get into it. The smears were made by that person's vain attempt to push open the door."

"How would the murderer have known there was a passage at all?" Sir Robert objected.

"From the girl. Suppose someone came in and found her here after Guy left. One of the first things that person would ask would probably be, how did you get here? And the girl might have said, I came through an opening in the wall—just there."

"But, great Heaven," cried MacGregor, "we're back where we started! Anybody who got talking to her might have found out she was the daughter of that Frenchwoman, and killed her to stop her revealing Colonel Fontclair's treason."

"No." Julian shook his head. "Not just anybody, Doctor. It's true we could still spin all manner of complex theories. Anyone could be lying, any two people could be giving each other an alibi. But if we assume all the suspects told the truth, just short of an actual confession, we know who the murderer is. The murderer can only be one person."

Sir Robert and MacGregor stared at him, afraid to ask, afraid to speculate.

"Of course," said Julian quietly, "it would be difficult to prove. But I don't think we'll be put to the trouble of proving it. I think, now that Guy stands accused of the murder, the real murderer will confess."

※

"Thank you for agreeing to meet me here, Mr. Kestrel. I had to give this to someone for safekeeping, and since you've played the principal role in the investigation, you seemed the right person. I also thought you would be the easiest person for me to face. Here. This is my confession. I wrote it while Guy was being questioned. You'll find in it everything you or the authorities might wish to know about the murder."

Julian hardly glanced at the sheaf of papers put into his hand. "I'm sorry."

"You don't seem very surprised."

"I felt fairly sure in the end it must be you. I hoped I was wrong."

Isabelle smiled ever so slightly. "Sometimes you've hinted you had a *tendre* for me. I hope that isn't so. Because, strange to say, I have nothing against you, and I should be sorry to see you suffer. I *wanted* to be found out—to have the luxury of confessing and being punished. But I had to think of my family—the disgrace I would have brought on them. Of course, once Guy was accused, I couldn't keep silent any longer. Even if it had been someone other than Guy, I would have spoken. Even for my family's sake, I couldn't let an innocent person be blamed for my crime. You must believe me, I'm not so base as that."

"I believe you."

She walked a little away from him. Even now his eyes lingered, with aching appreciation, on the slender, graceful curves of her body, the shimmering fall of her hair. Her fingers trailed absently along the top of a long table. She and Julian were in the library, where she had sent for him to meet her after the interrogation of Guy.

She asked musingly, "Would Guy have been found guilty, do you think, if I hadn't spoken?"

"I don't know. I didn't believe he was, once I'd heard his whole story."

"I knew you were clever. I knew from the beginning that if anyone were to find me out, it would be you. How did you find me out in the end?"

"It was mostly a matter of timing. Guy told us he locked the girl in my room at a quarter past five, which meant she must have been killed between that time and twenty minutes to six. That eliminated Colonel Fontclair completely, since he was out riding from five o'clock until after six, and there was no way he could have got back into the house without being seen. Unless, of course, he used the secret passage, but he claimed not to know about it, and I believed him, since anyone who knew how to get into the passage would surely have hidden the body there. Sir Robert, Lady Fontclair, Lady Tarleton, and Craddock were all in the house between a quarter past five and six, but not in the right place at the right time. Because, since no one but Guy knew the girl was at Bellegarde, no one could have purposely sought her out, either to kill her or for any other reason. Someone must simply have happened on her between a quarter past five and six, and no one was so likely to have done that as you."

He halted. The sheer, unearthly strangeness of this conversation overcame him. Here he was calmly expounding his reasoning to Isabelle as she stood on the brink of disaster, all her ties to civilisation breaking, all her hopes of happiness draining away. But she looked at him expectantly, interested in his explanation. He realized she had long since parted company with happiness and civilisation. If she had ever been afraid to take the consequences of her crime, she was not afraid anymore.

He went on, "Lady Fontclair says she never left the conservatory between four o'clock and six. Sir Robert went to get a book from the library at one point, but that wouldn't have taken him upstairs, or anywhere near my room. Craddock came in through the front door at twenty minutes past five, and he did go upstairs. But when he reached the top of the grand staircase, he would have gone toward his room at the front of the main house, not toward my room at the back. He remained in his room from then on, quarrelling with Lady Tarleton. And, of course, Lady Tarleton went nowhere near my room. She was searching Mark Craddock's."

"Aunt Catherine was searching Mr. Craddock's room? Why?"

"You still know nothing about the letters Craddock has?"

"Letters that hurt my family, I suppose. I knew he must have some power over us, or Uncle Robert wouldn't have agreed to the marriage between Miss Craddock and Hugh. But, no, I don't know anything about any letters. How should I?"

"No reason. I used to think the letters had something to do with the murder, but I can see now that isn't so."

"Of course, once you'd eliminated all the others, you were left with me."

"Yes. And I knew you had passed close to my room shortly before half past five, on your way to Miss Craddock's to show her your design. Guy said he left Aimée crying hysterically in my room. I think you heard her crying as you passed by, and went in to investigate."

"Yes. I felt odd about going into a gentleman's room, but I

thought I ought to see what was wrong. Of course I was surprised to find the door locked, but the key was right there on the hall table, so I unlocked the door and went in. I would give anything to have that moment back, and to be anywhere but in front of that door, with the key ready to hand. But I was there—I went in—I talked with her—and I killed her, with the knife from my sketching box. Do you know why I killed her, Mr. Kestrel?"

"I think so. You don't have to talk about it, if you'd rather not."

"How did you know? I don't think anyone in my family did, and they had far longer to guess the truth than you."

"But I was watching you very closely, trying to guess what went on in your mind, behind your eyes. Your family probably saw you less clearly, simply because they saw you every day. They took it for granted they knew you. They wouldn't have dreamed you had anything to hide."

"You suspected me from the beginning, then?"

"I didn't suspect you of the murder. Though I did think you were holding something back, perhaps shielding one of your family. That gave me a reason to watch you—I suppose I should say, it gave me an excuse. You know I've been drawn to you from the moment we met."

"And you know I warned you to stay away. I didn't know then what disaster I'd bring on any man who cared for me, but I knew I could never feel anything for you. I hope you aren't in love with me."

"I could have been, all too easily. If you'd ever softened toward me even a fraction, God knows what would have become of me! They say Pygmalion loved a statue, but I don't believe that's possible. There has to be at least a hint of a living, breathing woman underneath. You never gave me so much as a glimpse of that woman in you. All I knew about what you felt, and what you must be suffering, I figured out from linking stray facts together, like so many beads on a string."

"What facts?"

"Do you remember when you let me look through your sketch book? I was surprised to find you'd drawn everyone in your family except Guy Even on the page where you drew contrasting portraits of all their faces, showing how the family features varied from one to another, he wasn't there."

"I do draw him, though. At night when I can't sleep I sit up and sketch him over and over. I don't need any light to draw that face. Afterward I put the sketches under my pillow, and in the morning I look at them, and then I burn them. I always feared that if anyone saw a sketch I made of him, it would give me away. They all seem to show my feelings so clearly, the paper burns my fingers. But my sketchbook alone couldn't have made you so certain."

"I wasn't certain. I didn't know what to think. When I asked you yesterday if you'd ever wanted to marry your cousin, I hardly knew myself which cousin I meant. But then I heard how you'd lashed out at Miss Craddock last night  Guy thought you were overcome by resentment of her because she was going to marry Hugh. That wasn't the conclusion I drew."

"I never wanted to marry Hugh. People thought I did, and I let them think so. Anything was better than their knowing it was Guy— it was always Guy I—" She swallowed hard. "I had nothing against Miss Craddock, before last night."

"When Guy suddenly took it into his head to dance attendance on her."

"Yes. You'd think I would be past caring. You'd think, after what I did to that girl, I would be too chastened and remorseful to be jealous on his account, ever again. But it's no good. There is no cure. I think when I'm dead and lie under the earth, my heart will still feel this same tearing pain, to think somewhere he's giving his smiles, and his lips, and his— his body— to other women.

"Don't think I admire him, Mr. Kestrel. Don't think for a moment I even like him. I know he's vain, selfish, irresponsible, willful. Do you know what it is to love someone unworthy? When you can't respect the person you love, you can't respect yourself. My only comfort was that at least he would never know. Now I've lost even that—now everything will have to come out. And that's only right  Who am I to have any modesty or dignity, ever again? But there was a time when I clung to the consolation that he had no idea how I felt. If he knew, he might try to take advantage of my weakness  Or worse, he might not think it worth his while—he might not feel anything but amusement and triumph to know I was in thrall to him, like so many others. You don't know—you don't know what it's like for me to hear about his conquests! People don't talk to me about them, it wouldn't be seemly, but I hear things, and I know what he is. I know he's had mistresses—so many!—and I hate them all! I hate them! Whores!"

She covered her face with her hands. Tears splashed through her fingers. "But I'm worse than any of them. Because I called myself a gentlewoman, I made a show of virtue. And all the time I would have sold my soul to be with him, just once, as the least of those women has been!"

"Isabelle—" He tried to hold her, comfort her—anything to stop this hemorrhage of pain.

She shook him off and moved away. Even now, she must shut him out, shut everyone out. She would never change.

She stood leaning her arm against a pillar, and her forehead against her bent arm He followed her, and silently offered his handkerchief. She took it, wiped her eyes, and blew her nose "Thank you," she said, turning toward him with the ghost of her usual cool, direct gaze.

"Is there nothing I can do for you?" he asked

"There is something. I need a little time to compose myself before I face Uncle Robert. I'm going to my room. Would you wait here for a quarter of an hour, and then deliver my confession to him?"

He started to say, of course he would. Then enlightenment broke over him He shook his head bleakly "I can't. I'm sorry "

"It seems a small thing. And you asked if you might help me somehow "

"I can't help you like that It isn't a small thing I know what you're asking me to do "

"Then you must know it's the only right course Uncle Robert won't suspect you of contriving with me You can't know for certain what's in my mind You can tell him afterward, with perfect truth, that you didn't know what I intended "

"I'm not concerned with what Sir Robert might think This is between you and me, and I tell you, I cannot do it Miss

Fontclair—Isabelle, you may well be acquitted. Juries are often lenient to women, even women who've killed in cold blood."

"And what would become of me afterward? I should be a millstone round my family's neck—an outcast—a prisoner counting the days till my release! I won't live that way, Mr. Kestrel. I won't wait for release when I can fly to meet it. Besides, it's justice. The law might be lenient with me, but the law is weak and partial. I'm a murderess, Mr. Kestrel, and there are times when the fever comes over me again, and I'm glad—I'm glad I killed her! I deserve to die."

"You think so now. But it's been only a week. You're in shock —you have no perspective—"

"I'm not in shock. This isn't a decision I've made suddenly. I always knew what I would do if I were found out. If I were a man, you would stand aside and let me do the honourable thing. You would even applaud me for it."

"But you're not a man, and I am, and it's not in me to let you take your life. Let me go with you to Sir Robert, let me help you through whatever happens—"

She was shaking her head. She bent toward him, soft with entreaty, and clasped his hand between both of hers. "Please! I've never begged for anything before. Please, I beg of you! Have pity on me!"

"Oh, God! I wish I could. I'm sorry."

She let go of his hand. Her face closed up. It looked grey in the candlelight, and very still. "Then do what you must. Ring for a servant, and send for Uncle Robert. I'll see him here."

She turned away. He went to the door and pulled the bellrope that hung there. Across the room, he saw her bow her head, pluck at the sash of her gown. Suddenly she raised her arms. There was a flash of candlelight on steel.

He cried out, ran toward her, reached her in time to catch her as she fell. The pearl-handled knife that had belonged to her father— the knife that had killed Aimée Deschamps—was buried in her breast.

He cradled her in his arms. Whether she saw or felt him, he could not tell. She did not speak any last words. Her eyes glazed over, and she died.

# *33*
# MAUD'S
# FAMILY BIBLE

---

The servant who answered the library bell took one look at Isabelle lying lifeless in Julian's arms, and raced off to fetch Sir Robert and Dr. MacGregor. When they rushed in, stunned and out of breath, Julian told them what had happened and turned over Isabelle's confession to Sir Robert.

Official wheels began to turn. MacGregor examined Isabelle's body and pronounced her dead. Sir Robert forced himself to read her confession, then summoned Senderby from Alderton to let him know the investigation was at an end. Rawlinson released Guy and Geoffrey from his office, and set about drawing up a formal statement for Julian to sign regarding Isabelle's death. Meanwhile, Lady Fontclair gathered the family together and broke the news, patiently explaining to those who were too shocked to take it in, and comforting those who progressed more quickly from incredulity to grief.

For Julian, reaction set in with a vengeance. When all the questions and explanations were over, and he was no longer needed, he went back to the deserted library, from which Isabelle's body had been removed. He put out the candles and sat for a long time, hiding his white face and shaking hands in darkness and solitude.

MacGregor hauled him out again and bore him off to the dining room. He sat him down at the table and thrust a glass of brandy under his nose, waving away his protests that he was really all right. "Bosh! Nobody who's been through what you've been through could possibly be all right. You can't bamboozle me; I'm a medical man. Now, drink that down, before I have you strapped to the chair and administer it through a funnel."

Julian smiled in spite of himself. "You're a very violent man, Doctor. I had no idea."

"I can be if I'm crossed. Are you going to drink that or not?"

Julian drained the glass. The brandy burned through him, leaving behind a soothing, steadying warmth. He sat back and closed his eyes. Suddenly he wanted more than anything to go to bed and sleep for a long, long time. But he knew that, though his body was exhausted, his mind would not rest till he had cleared away the last shreds of mystery clinging to the murder. He had not read Isabelle's confession, and was not sure he wanted to. But MacGregor had read it, and Julian asked him to fill in the details lacking from his picture of the crime. MacGregor nodded, realizing that the young man needed to understand before he could forget.

Isabelle had followed the sound of violent weeping into Julian's room, thinking one of the maids must be having hysterics. Aimée, distraught and disheveled, flung herself at her, clinging to her gown and babbling wildly in French and broken English. It was not her fault. She had not wanted to sneak into the house through that hidden door in the wall. Guy made her do it, and she had been afraid to refuse. She did not want to lose him. He had promised to marry her.

Isabelle, her heart bursting, demanded to know if Aimée was Guy's mistress. Aimée shrank away in shame, then burst into tears again and flung herself facedown on the bed. Isabelle stood over her, the sketching box under her hand. She reached inside. Her fingers closed round the knife—drew it out—plunged it into Aimée's back. Just one swift blow—but it landed, by blind chance, where it was bound to be fatal.

"It's hard to believe, even now," said MacGregor. "I never really thought I knew or understood Isabelle—but to do this!"

"I can believe it, after talking to her tonight She was half mad with jealousy and frustration. That banked-down passion ate away at her like a poison. She was like an animal that kills in a frenzy of pain or hunger or fear."

"It's a dangerous thing to go through life playing a role like that, suppressing natural feelings. Too much self-control is as bad as too little."

"Are you suggesting there's a lesson for *me* there?"

"Just a word to the wise," said MacGregor, smiling.

He explained that, after Isabelle struck Aimée, she dropped the knife on the bed and turned Aimée over on her back. Finding she was dead, she was horrified to think what she had done, and how she had dishonoured her family. She racked her brain for some way to hide her crime. Aimée had said there was a secret door in the wall, and Isabelle tried desperately to push the panel open, hoping to hide the body there. But the panel would not budge, and she dared not try too long. Time was slipping away; Guy might come back at any moment, or Julian might come home. She would just have to leave the body where it was.

She washed her hands and the knife at the washstand. There was no point in cleaning the blood off anything else. With a dead body lying there, what was the use of scrubbing the washbasin or the wall? But as she was about to flee, her eyes fell on Aimée lying across the bed. Hatred welled up in her again. Why should the girl be found like that, a victim to be pitied and avenged? She ought to be discovered tucked into a man's bed, like the harlot she was. That was why Isabelle closed her eyes and slipped her under the covers.

She went away, leaving the door locked behind her and the key on the hall table. It seemed best to leave everything as nearly the way she had found it as possible. When she got to her room, she closely examined her clothes and sketching things, but the girl's wound had bled so little, there were no telltale stains. She rang for her maid, dressed for dinner, and went downstairs.

"Imagine what it cost her to brave it out in the drawing room, waiting for the murder to be discovered!" MacGregor marvelled. "Wondering all the while if she'd left any clue behind to give her away! But she kept her head till the very end. She told the truth whenever she could, admitted she went to that part of the house between half past four and six—even admitted she had her sketching box with her, with the knife in it. Her idea was, since she couldn't be sure what was known about her movements and what wasn't, she'd better own up to everything short of confessing to the murder."

"She was an extraordinary woman."

"She had courage, I'll give her that."

"How is the family getting on?"

"The last I saw of them, Miss Craddock had drawn her father off, to give the Fontclairs some privacy. They're in a pretty bad way. Who can blame them? Lady Tarleton was hit hardest. It was too much for her, finding out that a Fontclair had committed murder, and suicide on top of that. She fainted dead away when she heard the news. I had her put to bed. Lady Fontclair is sitting with her."

He got up. "Time I went home." In reality, he thought it was time Kestrel got some sleep. "I'll look in on you all again tomorrow."

"Tomorrow," Julian repeated. He could not quite imagine there being any tomorrow. The end of the mystery seemed to bring the curtain down on Bellegarde and everyone in it, including himself. "But it isn't over," he said slowly. "I feel somehow there's something left unfinished—some piece of the puzzle still missing."

"You've been wrestling with the murder so long, you can't take it in that it's over and done with."

Julian was in no fit state to argue. He rose, feeling very light headed, and took up a candle. "You know, the murder's been solved without Colonel Fontclair's secret coming out."

"Well, that's something the Fontclairs can be thankful for, Dutch comfort though it is."

"But it means Craddock still has his hold over them. If they want to salvage what's left of their family honour, they'll have to go through with the marriage."

✳

Craddock said as much next day, in the drawing room after break fast. All the Fontclairs and their guests were gathered there except Lady Tarleton, who was still too shattered to leave her room. The others divided into small groups. Guy stuck close to his father, looking ready to bare his teeth at Craddock or anyone else who might threaten to harm him. Lady Fontclair sat beside Sir Robert, her hand in his. The wave of disaster that had broken over them had drawn them together, in spite of her betrayal of his trust. He had loved and depended on her for too long to thrust her from him at a time like this.

Hugh stood close by his parents, but his eyes were on Maud. He wanted more than ever to catch her alone, not so much to apologize for the things he said yesterday—that seemed like a hundred years ago now—as to make sure she was not too distressed after last night's tragedy. But he had had no opportunity, what with his own grief for Isabelle, and the need to help his family through this crisis. He only hoped it was not too late to mend the rift between them.

All the Fontclairs were dressed in mourning. Maud, doing her best with the clothes she had at Bellegarde, wore a sober dark green gown and a black ribbon in her hair. She had in her lap the withered old family Bible she had brought from London. She clasped it tightly, her eyes resolute, her breath coming quickly. Julian thought she looked like a diver about to plunge into a cold sea.

"The wedding will have to be postponed for a decent interval," Craddock was saying. "I understand that The question is, how long?"

"This is no time to speak of weddings," said Sir Robert

"We might as well set a new date and be done with it, so the plans and invitations can be changed."

"Papa," said Maud, "there isn't going to be any wedding."

"Don't try my patience, girl. There was going to be a weddmg before all this happened, and there's going to be one now. Nothing's changed. I still have Colonel Fontclair's letters."

"No, you don't, Papa. *I* have them, and I'm giving them back to Colonel Fontclair, because they belong by rights to him."

She opened the family Bible. From inside a tear in the worn leather binding, she pulled out some half-dozen sheets of yellowed parchment. She ran to Colonel Fontclair and put them in his lap.

Craddock sprang toward the colonel to seize them back. Guy and Hugh jumped up with one accord and barred his way  They mounted guard in front of Geoffrey, daring Craddock to come any closer. Craddock stood balked, fists clenched at his sides, breathing hard through his nostrils. His eyes slewed round to Maud. "How did you get those letters?"

"I— I took them from the cabinet in your study at home."

Craddock began tearing at his neckcloth. From inside his collar, he pulled out an iron chain with three keys hanging from it. He thrust them at Maud, brandished them in her face. "I have all my keys! How could you have got the cabinet open?"

"One of them isn't your key, Papa. It's the key to my jewelry case. I hoped you wouldn't notice. All the keys in our house look so much alike. I hoped that, as long as you had three keys on your chain, you wouldn't think to look at any of them closely."

"You planned this whole business! You stole my key, broke into my cabinet—!"

"I *had* to. I hated doing it—I felt so guilty and deceitful, you can't know. That chamomile tea I brought you, the night before I went to London—I put laudanum in it. I remembered the time you had the toothache—how you took laudanum, and it made you sleep so soundly we could hardly wake you in the morning. After you drank the tea and went to bed, I came back to your room and—and exchanged the keys.

"When Miss Pritchard and I got to London, she went to bed early, and I went to your study and took the letters from the steel cabinet. I wasn't sure what to do with them. I was afraid my maid would find them if I hid them among my clothes. Finally I decided to hide them in Mama's Bible. I felt she would have understood what I was doing—that it was for your good as much as anyone's."

"For *my* good! That's rich!"

"Yes, Papa! I know you had your heart set on this marriage, but it wouldn't have made you happy. All your life, you'd know the Fontclairs made you stoop to doing something wrong and unjust. And when you do a wrong to people, you're bound to them forever. You'd never have got free."

"Since you think so highly of freedom," Craddock snarled, "I'll give it to you! And it'll be the last thing I give you. Hear me,

Maud: From this day on, never come near me, never knock at my door, never send me word if you live or die! These people are your friends—well and good. Look to them to keep you!"

He strode to the door, then turned and shot one last look around at the Fontclairs. "I'm leaving for London as soon as my man can pack for me. What becomes of this one"—he jerked his head at Maud—"is your business now." He went out, slamming the door.

Maud's legs buckled under her. The Fontclairs, like statues come to life, flocked around her, easing her into a chair and holding hartshorn under her nose. Lady Fontclair tucked a pillow behind her. Geoffrey stammered out his thanks. Guy wrung her hand almost too vigorously. Sir Robert made a sort of speech.

Hugh knelt down and put a footstool before her. It was all he could do not to pour out his feelings. But she must not think he was declaring himself in a momentary burst of gratitude. And she looked so wan and exhausted, it would be cruel to put her through any more shocks or upheavals, of any kind.

Julian slipped out unnoticed. Soon after, MacGregor found him in the garden, absently plucking dead leaves and crumbling them to powder. "I just heard the news about Miss Craddock giving the colonel back his letters. That's a very plucky young lady. If Hugh Fontclair's got any sense, he'll go through with the marriage, blackmail or no blackmail."

"I don't think he'll need any persuading."

"And the girl—she'll have him, I suppose?"

"I don't doubt it."

MacGregor looked at him more closely, taking in his subdued manner and pale, averted face. "What are you going to do, now all this is over?"

"It's not quite over. There has to be an inquest into Miss Fontclair's death, and as the last person to see her alive, I shall have to testify. That's the only reason I'm still here—if I had the choice, I'd take myself off at once. The Fontclairs must be longing to see the last of me, though they're all being frightfully decent, and keep urging me to stay. I suppose it's only fair I shouldn't be allowed to decamp in the night, but should have to stay and see the consequences of what I've done."

"You're not sorry you did it?"

"I don't know Isabelle is dead, the Fontclairs are reeling with grief and shame Would it have been so terrible if the crime had never been solved? Isabelle would have punished herself, all her life, as bitterly as the law could have punished her, and the innocent needn't have suffered."

"Listen to me." MacGregor laid a hand on his shoulder "You feel this way because you're here with the people mourning for Isabelle and feeling the consequences of her crime. To them, the price of truth comes very high. They're certainly not going to have any love for whoever brought it to light. Remember what Milton said about truth? He said it's like a bastard child: nobody wants it, and nobody has anything good to say about whoever gave it birth But there are people like me, who think truth is always worth finding out for its own sake, and to those people, you're a hero, Kestrel "

"Don't be absurd!" said Julian sharply

"Can't take a compliment, can you?" MacGregor chuckled "Not about anything important, anyway. If I said I admired the shine on your boots, you'd preen like a peacock, but let me suggest you're a fine man, as well as a fine gentleman, and you can't fend me off fast enough "

"I'm sorry I didn't mean to be ungracious Somehow it was too much, to hear it just now "

"Never mind I've got an idea Why don't you come and stay with me till the inquest is over? Longer, if you like, though I shouldn't think a smart young fellow like you would want to be stuck at a country doctor's, with the London season at its height."

"The London season be hanged. I should like nothing better than to stay with you. Thank you "

"Hmph—well—that's settled, then Don't expect any luxuries mind I live simply, and I'm not changing my ways on your account I don't drink, smoke, play cards, or entertain company I have my dinner at two o'clock, same as I did before it got to be the fashion to dine at night, and I'm up every morning by six I don't suppose you'd get up at that hour if the house were on fire '

Julian rallied "I like that hour very well I often stay up all night so as not to miss it

"Dicing and drinking and God knows what else, I'll be bound. How you can fritter away your time, waste the brains God gave you lounging in clubs or prinking in front of a looking glass—"

Still scolding, MacGregor started back toward the house. Julian went with him. He found he rather liked being lectured. His friends who complained of tyrannical fathers and nattering old aunts little knew how dreary it was to go through life with no one to disapprove of you, and nothing but your own weary sense of self-discipline to stop you from doing exactly as you liked.

✳

Maud and Julian met in the music room before Julian left Bellegarde.

"Miss Craddock, you are magnificent." He kissed her fingertips.

"No, how silly," she said, blushing.

"I'm serious. I thought some of my own stratagems were clever, but you've knocked spots off me. I cede the palm to a master."

She smiled. "You see now why I couldn't tell you what I was going to do in London. I was afraid of bringing down Papa's anger on anyone who seemed to be helping me. Papa was already— I mean, he had silly ideas about— about you and me. I'm sorry if he said anything to offend you."

"I shouldn't call being accused of winning your heart an offence. I should call it a crown of laurels."

He smiled into her eyes. Her heart fluttered. For the first time, she asked herself if she had been honest with Hugh and her father when she said she cared for Mr. Kestrel only as a friend. If she had not met Hugh first—

She stopped herself. She must not think along those lines. To divide her heart was to destroy it; she could not bear ambiguity in love. Anyway, she did not think Mr. Kestrel was in love with her, or likely to be. She was too simple—too peaceful. He needed the kind of woman who would baffle and bedevil him.

She felt herself blushing and looked away. "Papa's gone, you know. He left for London about an hour ago. The Fontclairs have been wonderfully kind to me. They've invited me to stay on at Bellegarde as long as I like  I mustn't outstay my welcome, though.

It would be different if I were—if Mr. Fontclair and I were still engaged. But that's all over now. Do you think I might find work as a governess? I know I'm awfully young, but I can't think of any other way to earn a living. Perhaps Miss Pritchard could advise me."

"Miss Craddock, I think you'd make an enchanting governess. But somehow, I don't think it's on the cards."

\*

"I'm sorry you're leaving," said Philippa. "I haven't half finished telling you things."

"It might be just as well to save something for the next time we meet," Julian pointed out.

"But that won't be for a long time, will it? Mama and Papa won't want to go to town, after everything that's happened, and I don't suppose you'll come to visit us here again."

"That might be awkward," he admitted. "At least for the time being."

"I hoped you'd come often, till you were quite one of the family. And then, when I was old enough, you might like to marry me. I shall have money, you know, and I *am* a Fontclair."

"If I were you, I should wait for a husband who cared for something besides my pocketbook and my pedigree."

"I don't think anybody would marry me for myself. I'm *eccentric*, and I always say the wrong thing, and I'm not pretty, like Josie. I have a horse face. I heard Cook say so."

"The other day I found three peas in the raspberry trifle, which suggests to me that Cook is remarkably nearsighted."

"Do you think there's any chance I might be going to be pretty?"

"Being pretty is no great matter. Any young lady with bright eyes and passable teeth can claim that much. Better to be clever, quick, and intrepid—to charm with your mind and enchant with your wit—in short, to be the one radiant Circe in a season of dreary Helens."

"Could I do that?"

"I have no doubt of it." He lifted his brows. "I hope you don't presume to question my judgement on a matter of taste?"

"No," she said slowly. "You *are* supposed to know about those things." She pondered. "I shall be eighteen in seven years. I suppose you'll have forgot all about me by then."

"It's you who'll have forgot about me," he said lightly.

"Oh, no." Philippa shook her head. "I have a very long memory."

# *34*
# THE LAST PIECE
# OF THE PUZZLE

Julian adjusted to life at MacGregor's better than MacGregor had predicted. To rise at six in the morning was beyond him, but he usually managed to be up and about by nine. He found plenty to occupy him while MacGregor was seeing patients. He perused anatomy books, looked at bits of hair and bone under a microscope, and listened to his heart through a stethoscope—a wooden cylinder held to his ear, with the other end against his chest.

In the evenings, he played the harpsichord. He had been surprised to find such a dainty instrument at MacGregor's. With its slender frame and delicately painted panels, it could only have belonged to a woman. "It was my wife's," MacGregor explained. "I ought to have sold it long since—it's no earthly use now—but I never could make up my mind to part with it." He added, "She loved music."

"I didn't know you'd been married."

"No reason you should. She died more than twenty years ago. A fever took her off, and our son, too."

They said no more on the subject. But every evening Julian played the harpsichord for an hour or two, and MacGregor left open the door of whatever room he was in, to hear the music.

*

The verdict at the inquest was that Isabelle took her life while the balance of her mind was disturbed. The coroner's jury needed only a few minutes to reach their decision. It was hard enough on Isabelle's family that she had confessed to murder. No one wanted to heighten her guilt, and their shame, with a finding of deliberate suicide.

The Fontclairs passed the rest of that day very quietly. Maud, listening to the muted conversations around her, thought how sad it was that no one had been close to Isabelle. They were not mourning her loss so much as the fact that they had not really known her, or had the smallest inkling of the anguish that was eating her away.

Next morning, Maud went for a walk in the park of Bellegarde with one of the dogs, a lively red and white setter. It had rained earlier, but now rays of sunlight were finding their way through the clouds. A playful wind tugged at the brim of her bonnet and tangled her skirt around her legs.

"It's blustery, isn't it?" said Hugh.

Maud spun around. "Oh— Mr. Fontclair. I didn't see you."

"Would you rather I hadn't come?"

"No." But she felt bashful and confused. She watched the dog frolic around him, rubbing happily against his legs. Things were so simple for animals.

He ruffled the dog's silky ears, trying at the same time to calm her transports of affection. "I've been wanting to talk to you——" he began. The setter flung herself against him, wagging her tail furiously. "Take a damper, Bellona!" He looked at Maud, between laughter and vexation. "Why don't we keep walking? Something's bound to come along to distract her."

They walked on, Bellona capering around them. Maud said, her eyes on the ground, "Actually, I wanted to talk to you, too."

"Did you? What about?"

"I was wondering—your mother doesn't seem to know we aren't engaged anymore. The other day she took me all around the house, as though she thought it might be mine some day. I didn't know what to say to her  Haven't you told her that I— I've released you from your obligations?"

"I told both her and my father that I was appallingly rude to you, and you'd very rightly broken things off between us. I also told them I was going to ask you to reconsider."

Maud stopped walking. "To— to reconsider?"

"Yes. I don't know if you can forgive me for the way I acted the other day. I also don't know if you can bring yourself to marry into a family with a murderess in it, and a traitor."

"My father tried to blackmail you and your family. That's very nearly as bad."

"Maud, couldn't we forget it all and start fresh? You don't have to say you'll marry me—it would be enough if you thought you might come to like me a little."

"I think I might." Her lips quivered into a smile.

"Oh, Maud!" He caught her hands and kissed first one and then the other. "I've been wanting to tell you how I felt for so long— but I thought you were in love with Kestrel."

"Poor Mr. Kestrel! I mostly talked his head off about *you.*"

"Maud, are you saying— can it be that you— oh, my dear love!" He kissed her hands again.

Bellona, who had been eyeing them uneasily, jumped between them and tried to leap up on Hugh. "Oh, the deuce!" He picked up a stick and flung it as far as he could. Bellona went bounding after it. Hugh put two fingertips under Maud's chin, coaxed up her face, and kissed her on the lips.

Bellona scampered back and dropped the stick at his feet. If it had been a lighted torch, he would not have noticed. "Maud, can I tell my parents we're engaged again?"

"If you want to," she whispered.

Later, when they were walking back to the house arm in arm, he said, "I thought, when you didn't want me to go to London with you—"

"I did want you to go, very much. But I was afraid Papa might find out I was trying to steal the letters from him, and if you were going to London with me, he might think you were involved and do something to hurt you."

"I wouldn't have cared about that."

"*I* cared."

Hugh had to stop and take her in his arms again. Bellona flicked her tail in disgust and ran off.

Much later, Hugh asked, "Do you miss him very much? Your father, I mean."

"Sometimes. I'd be miserable if I really thought I'd never see him again. But you see, I think he'll forgive me one day. He doesn't have anyone else."

Hugh smiled and drew her arm through his. "Perhaps when he's got a grandchild."

✳

With the inquest over, there was nothing to keep Julian in Alderton. He had no intention of losing touch with MacGregor, but for now he needed to get away from the neighbourhood of Bellegarde He heard (from Dipper, who must still be contriving to see Molly Dale) that Maud and Hugh were reconciled, but the idea of his being groomsman at the wedding was allowed to drop His only direct contact with Bellegarde was when Sir Robert sent him the hundred pounds' reward that had been posted for solving the murder To Julian, it seemed more like thirty pieces of silver. He sent half the money anonymously to Louisa Howland and gave the other half to the parish fund for poor relief

On his last night in Alderton, he went for a walk. It was nearly nine o'clock, but the days being at their longest, it was not yet dark The sky was violet, translucent as mother-of-pearl. The moon was rising, and the brightest stars were twinkling into life Julian strolled aimlessly at first, then began to walk more briskly For a long time he tried to pretend to himself that he did not know where he was going.

No one tried to stop him entering the park of Bellegarde Undoubtedly there were gamekeepers on patrol, but if such a large estate could be effectively guarded, poaching would not be the lucrative trade that it was He went round to the far end of the garden, where the flowering trees grew wild and the ordered paths snaked into meandering trails. Passing through a wicket gate, he spotted the rose arbour, its lacy fretwork etched against a slightly paler sky.

Some ten days ago, he had seen the arbour bathed in sunshine, the pink and red roses in full bloom, and a lovely woman seated among them. Now the roses were closed, the moonlight had drained them of colour, and the woman would never sit there again—

He stopped in his tracks. There *was* a woman sitting there, silhouetted against the twilight. She was tall and slender and straight, the image of Isabelle. For an instant his mind reeled. He did not believe in ghosts. And yet, there she was.

She must have heard him. She turned, and he recognized Lady Tarleton. His heart sank. She was the very last person on earth he wanted to see tonight. But it was too late for retreat: she was gazing toward him, willing him to go to her. He went. She was entitled to have her say, he supposed. And in a way, it would be a relief to be reproached and upbraided by one of the Fontclairs. The others had been so excruciatingly just and forbearing toward him about Isabelle's death. At least he could count on Lady Tarleton to show him no such mercy.

She sat enthroned among the roses, her proud head tilted back to meet his eyes. Even by moonlight, she looked years older. The white had all but driven the red from her hair. Her face was thin and pinched. But her eyes were the same—full of glitter and venom, burning with the fevered radiance some fires have before they die

"What are you doing here?" she hissed.

"I once talked with Miss Fontclair here. I came here to think about her."

"Were you in love with her? I hope you were! I hope you're suffering all the torments of hell, knowing it was you who destroyed her!"

"Miss Fontclair was more generous toward me than you are prepared to be"

"Are you asking for mercy, Mr. Kestrel? When did you show us any? Oh, it's ironic—bitterly ironic!—that though I hate you for what you've done, though I shall hate you all the days of my life, you are the only person in all the wide world I can talk to I am utterly alone! I've never been so alone before. Even an enemy is better company than no one at all!"

"I don't understand."

"You've never understood. You tried, of course! How clever you thought you were, making out that that miserable little French doxy was my natural daughter! Do you imagine any child of mine would live and die so contemptibly? My daughter died like a Roman— like a Roman, Mr. Kestrel!"

"What— what are you saying?"

"You were so close to the truth—so close, and you never lit on it! I made sure you wouldn't. I threw you a bone—I told you about Geoffrey's letters. I knew it was the one thing that would draw you off prying into why I went to France all those years ago. Oh, yes, it was in order to hide my shame! And I succeeded. My family never knew. And *he* never knew—Mark Craddock. He might gloat over the fact that I yielded to him, that one mad, terrible day. But he never knew there was a child. I would have died before I gave him that satisfaction!

"I meant to give the baby away. I was planning to leave her to be raised by some French family. But after she was born, I couldn't do it. She was mine, and she was a Fontclair! There was nothing of that man in her, nothing! But how to keep her near me, how to give her my name, and acquaint her with her heritage? It seemed hopeless.

"Then one day my old governess, who was with me in France, ran into my cousin Simon in the street. He and his wife had just come back from Barbados, where they'd been involved in some plantation venture, and of course had made a hash of it, as they always did of everything. They were keeping out of England because they owed so much money there. Well, I saw at once how to make use of them—they seemed sent to me by God! No one knew anything about their life in Barbados. It wouldn't be a nine days' wonder if they'd had a daughter without anybody hearing of it. So from that time forward, Isabelle was theirs. They brought her back to England and raised her as their own. I'd done it, Mr. Kestrel! I'd given her my name, made her a true-born, legitimate Fontclair!

"Of course it cost me dear. I had to settle Simon's debts, and pay him and his wife a very pretty income besides. Once I married Sir Bertrand, I had his fortune to draw on, but he made a nuisance of himself, always wanting to know where the money was going. And even with all I gave to Simon, the fool couldn't live within his means. He and his wife died penniless, when Isabelle was three. By that time, Sir Bertrand and I were living apart, and I wanted desperately to adopt her, now she was supposedly an orphan. But I didn't dare! Everything I'd done, I'd done to protect her from the pain and humiliation of knowing the truth about her birth. I couldn't risk undoing all my good work by showing too marked a partiality toward her. So I stepped aside and let Robert and Cecily have her.

"I spent as much time at Bellegarde as I could. What matter if no one wanted me—if they thought I was intruding, that I'd outstayed my welcome a hundred times over? I was near *her*—that was all I cared about. She didn't have to know I was there for her sake. She never would know what she meant to me.

"One thing, above all, I was resolved to do for her. I never lost an opportunity of urging on Robert and Cecily what a good match she would make for Hugh. Because then she'd be truly secure! Even if the secret of her birth came to light, no one could take the name Fontclair away from her.

"And *he* ruined everything! Coming to Bellegarde with his threats against Geoffrey, forcing a marriage between Hugh and that common little daughter of his! Can you wonder I hated him so much? Can you wonder I searched his room, trying to find those letters and put an end to his scheme? When he found me there, I went so far as to threaten to tell Robert what he had done to me twenty years ago. That's what your eavesdropper overheard us talking about. Of course, I never could have brought myself to carry out my threat, but *he* couldn't know that for sure. He was frightened enough to lie for me, to hide the fact that I'd been in his room that afternoon. He knew Robert would never let Hugh marry the daughter of a man who'd dishonoured me—no matter what the consequences to Geoffrey

"At least I made him suffer a little in return for all the agony he put me through. All the while he was at Bellegarde, I was terrified every moment that he might find out about Isabelle. The night I saw her sketching his portrait, I thought I would run mad. She mustn't look at him, mustn't think about him—they must have nothing to do with each other! They might sense some link between them, and I couldn't have that! She was mine, I tell you, mine! There was nothing of him in her!

"I was right not to tell her the truth about her birth. I was right, can't you see that? It would have broken her heart. Better for her to think her father was a Fontclair, even a dolt like Simon, than to know he was a servant, a tradesman, a nobody! I shall never understand it, never forgive myself! How could I have fallen into the arms of a creature like that? A thing out of the stables! A groom!"

Julian looked at her, but it was Isabelle's voice he heard: *Do you know what it is to love someone unworthy? When you can't respect the person you love, you can't respect yourself.*

"I was right," she kept muttering. "I was right How could I have known any harm would come of her thinking Simon was her father? The first time I saw her using his knife to sharpen her pencils, I said, don't be a fool, you'll cut yourself, sharpening pencils with a blade like that. But she said she liked that knife, she had so little to remember her father by. If— if she'd used a penknife— she could never— But how was I to know? It wasn't my fault! You destroyed her! You, not I!"

"She destroyed herself." And for the first time, he realized it was true. He felt a great weight lifted from his conscience. "Isabelle knew she was no one's victim That was what she tried to make me see, the last time we spoke She didn't blame me, and she wouldn't have blamed you, for the tragedy that overtook her."

"You may forgive yourself, Mr Kestrel, but I shall never forgive you!"

He wanted to urge her to forgive, not him but herself—for Isabelle's birth as well as her death. But he knew he would only be flinging his words to the winds.

"Is there anything I can do for you?" he asked helplessly

"There's only one thing I ask of you to forget everything I've said! I didn t want to confide in you. My grief drove me to it. I had to talk to someone. Now it's finished. Promise me you will never speak of it again. Not to my brothers, not to Mark Craddock, not even to me. Promise me!"

"I promise," he said

# FOR THE BEST IN PAPERBACKS, LOOK FOR THE 🐧

In every corner of the world, on every subject under the sun, Penguin represents quality and variety—the very best in publishing today.

For complete information about books available from Penguin—including Puffins, Penguin Classics, and Arkana—and how to order them, write to us at the appropriate address below. Please note that for copyright reasons the selection of books varies from country to country.

**In the United Kingdom:** Please write to *Dept. EP, Penguin Books Ltd, Bath Road, Harmondsworth, West Drayton, Middlesex UB7 0DA.*

**In the United States:** Please write to *Penguin Putnam Inc., P.O. Box 12289 Dept. B, Newark, New Jersey 07101-5289* or call 1-800-788-6262.

**In Canada:** Please write to *Penguin Books Canada Ltd, 10 Alcorn Avenue, Suite 300, Toronto, Ontario M4V 3B2.*

**In Australia:** Please write to *Penguin Books Australia Ltd, P.O. Box 257, Ringwood, Victoria 3134.*

**In New Zealand:** Please write to *Penguin Books (NZ) Ltd, Private Bag 102902, North Shore Mail Centre, Auckland 10.*

**In India:** Please write to *Penguin Books India Pvt Ltd, 11 Panchsheel Shopping Centre, Panchsheel Park, New Delhi 110 017.*

**In the Netherlands:** Please write to *Penguin Books Netherlands bv, Postbus 3507, NL-1001 AH Amsterdam.*

**In Germany:** Please write to *Penguin Books Deutschland GmbH, Metzlerstrasse 26, 60594 Frankfurt am Main.*

**In Spain:** Please write to *Penguin Books S. A., Bravo Murillo 19, 1° B, 28015 Madrid.*

**In Italy:** Please write to *Penguin Italia s.r.l., Via Benedetto Croce 2, 20094 Corsico, Milano.*

**In France:** Please write to *Penguin France, Le Carré Wilson, 62 rue Benjamin Baillaud, 31500 Toulouse.*

**In Japan:** Please write to *Penguin Books Japan Ltd, Kaneko Building, 2-3-25 Koraku, Bunkyo-Ku, Tokyo 112.*

**In South Africa:** Please write to *Penguin Books South Africa (Pty) Ltd, Private Bag X14, Parkview, 2122 Johannesburg.*